S0-AAK-653

THE
Thirteenth
DISCIPLE

BY Bette M. Ross:

Song of Deborah
Gennie: The Huguenot Woman
The Thirteenth Disciple

THE
Thirteenth
DISCIPLE

Bette M. Ross

Fleming H. Revell Company
Old Tappan, New Jersey

Scripture quotations are from the Revised Standard Version of the Bible, copyrighted 1946, 1952, © 1971, 1973.

Quotations from THE COMPLETE GREEK TRAGEDIES, Vol 1: Aeschylus, D. Grene and R. Lattimore, eds., © 1942–60, published by permission of the University of Chicago Press.

Library of Congress Cataloging in Publication Data

Ross, Bette M.
    The thirteenth disciple.

    1. Priscilla, Saint, 1st cent.—Fiction. 2. Church history—Primitive and early church, ca. 30–600—Fiction.
I. Title.
PS3568.0842T5 1984   813'.54   83–23032
ISBN 0-8007-1394-X

Copyright © 1984 by Bette M. Ross
Published by Fleming H. Revell Company
All rights reserved
Printed in the United States of America

For Laurie and all her sisters

Acknowledgments

I wish to thank Dr. Norbert A. Moke, pastor of
Covina Presbyterian Church, for uncounted hours
of thoughtful guidance.

". . . Who is my mother, and who are my brothers?"

Matthew 12:48

And the point is, to live everything.
Live the questions now. Perhaps you will
then gradually, without knowing it,
live along some distant day into the answer.

Rainer Maria Rilke
A.D. 1875–1926

THE
Thirteenth
DISCIPLE

Chapter 1

The high priestess of Artemis advanced to the eastern edge of the temple platform and faced the coming dawn. Her bare feet yielded to the cold edges of the chiseled limestone. In one hand she clasped the branch of the asherah. The other would soon clasp the snake.

Five young women, wearing thin, sage green gowns, knelt behind the high priestess of Artemis. At the center of the five, the maiden Prisca tried to concentrate on the rough stone surface that bruised her knees and the chill breeze that prickled her skin. She was acutely conscious of her position as elder among the young priestesses. But her eyes kept returning to a basket placed in front of her as she imagined its deadly contents. She hated this moment. Each month it came. Each month she dreaded it more. Masking her dread for the sake of the others, she made herself stare at the back of her superior.

Unmindful of Prisca's troubled thoughts, the high priestess, Thyatira, advanced to the eastern edge of the temple platform and faced the coming dawn. Her feet were bare to the cold, chiseled limestone. In one hand she clasped the branch of the asherah; the other would soon clasp the snake, now coiled in Prisca's basket. Her strong face betrayed no passion.

The platform upon which the priestess watched for the dawn was dominated by a thirty-foot statue of the goddess, Artemis, carved of pale gray Corinthian marble. From the south edge, twelve steps led down into a rose garden. Along the west edge of the platform, five black basalt columns formed a colonnade that threw bars of shadow across a cypress grove below.

"I, Thyatira, weep for Tammuz." The priestess's voice rang out with strength and resonance, yet with heartrending reverence.

The chorus of young priestesses repeated, "We weep for Tammuz."

Prisca rose with a grace that was effortlessly beautiful. Her gray green eyes were stilled to obedience to the sacred moment. Her chestnut hair caught the reddish tones of the sunrise, which imbued her skin with the perfection of warm, polished ivory. Advancing toward the high priestess, Prisca knelt a little behind her, so that when Thyatira turned, she would be ready at once to receive the sacred branch from the high priestess and

9

to proffer the deadly contents of the palm basket.

As she waited, the ache that Prisca had experienced low in her back upon arising that morning returned. She welcomed the pain.

Thyatira turned. Her eyes met Prisca's. The older woman smiled into the girl's eyes. Love, trust, and confidence mingled in their glance, as if Thyatira were reminding the young priestess, *See now, how Artemis keeps us safe!* The asherah bough lay across Thyatira's outstretched palms. Prisca took it and placed it next to the basket.

Resisting a shudder, she uncovered the green snake coiled in the bottom of the basket. It did not move. Within a year she would be expected to receive the gift of vision herself. As much as she loved and revered Thyatira, this moment repelled her. But faith demanded it. She picked up the basket. Her hands were steady as she offered it up to Thyatira.

With easy familiarity Thyatira dipped into the basket and cradled the venomous green snake. It writhed sluggishly. Turning, she offered it to the sun. She bared her left arm to the shoulder and allowed the snake to coil about its chilled warmth.

The dawn struck gold in Prisca's eyes, betraying none of her inner turmoil as she gazed steadily up at her mother. Still kneeling, she folded her hands, the rose-tipped fingers of one hand laid across the others, thumbs interlocking, and listened with apparent tranquility to her priestess:

"I am Nature, the universal Mother, mistress of all elements, primordial child of time, sovereign of all things spiritual, queen of the dead, queen also of the immortals, the single manifestation of all gods and goddesses that are. My nod governs the shining heights of Heaven, the wholesome sea breezes, the lamentable silences of the world below."

Thyatira's arms stretched forth in supplication, toward the sun, which now crested the hills, drenching the slopes with rose gold. The snake barely moved on the column of her arm. She tipped her head back, and the cloak fell from her raven hair as she flung out the ancient words:

"Though I am worshiped in many aspects, known by countless names, and propitiated with all manner of different rites, yet the whole round earth venerates me. The primeval Phyrgians call me Pessinuntica, Mother of the gods; the Athenians sprung from their own soil, call me Cecropian Artemis; for the islanders of Cyprus I am Paphian Aphrodite, for the Eleusinians their ancient Mother of Corn. Some know me as Juno, others as Hecate, or Diana, but both races of Ethiopians, whose lands the morning sun first shines upon, and the Egyptians, who excel in ancient learning and worship me with ceremonies proper to my godhead, call me by my true name—Queen Isis!"

With a swift motion she brought her right palm to her left shoulder. In that instant the snake struck. Thyatira flinched, and so did Prisca. Slowly two rubies of blood bloomed on Thyatira's inner elbow. She turned, looked beyond Prisca to the others.

With an effort she said, "Rise, my children. Stand watch, stand steadfast in the faith, act like true daughters of Artemis, be strong." She lowered her arms and closed her eyes. The snake slipped from her arm into Prisca's waiting basket. A glaze of perspiration suffused Thyatira's face as the other four priestesses broke forward and ushered her away.

Prisca watched without emotion as her sisters led Thyatira toward the chamber of visions beneath the marble feet of Artemis. Thyatira had won release from her body. She would perceive the meanings of happenings of the past month. She would visit the future. From now until she awakened, perhaps tomorrow, perhaps in a day and a half, Thyatira's body would be lovingly tended.

Prisca checked the cover on the snake basket to assure herself it was firmly seated, then gave it to the elder servant, Maya, who would return the snake to its cage and feed it a rodent; meanwhile, the asherah must be burned. Prisca had risen to this responsibility. She would burn the asherah at the foot of Artemis, who blessed their land and protected their sanctuary. The fragrant smoke would rise and by its substance reveal to her the direction of Thyatira's visions.

This was the first month they wept for the god, Tammuz, the dying consort, the son and lover of the Mother Goddess. Each year when the blaze of summer died into autumn, Artemis, through her faithful priestesses, wept for Tammuz. Each spring brought forth his rebirth.

Prisca breathed a sigh of relief that the monthly ritual was over. She allowed her gaze to wander over her city, eagerly seeking signs of life this fine autumn morning. Tyre had been an impregnable island fortress until besieged three hundred years ago by Alexander the Macedonian. He had demolished the city on the mainland, then built a causeway two hundred feet wide to harness the walled island to the ruined mainland. Centuries of shifting sand and tides had widened the causeway to an easily traveled peninsula, bringing caravans and lone travelers to their very gates.

Artemis's temple and its grounds were a haven of stillness amid the bustling city. The haven of the lucky, Thyatira said. Still . . . again Prisca felt that undefinable sense of longing wash over her. Below the altar were hidden many small subterranean chambers that contained the elements of worship and afforded solitude for private meditations and sacrificial unions. The temple lay within a cool garden sanctuary that contained living quarters for the high priestess and her minions.

To further beautify Artemis's home (a modest one, compared to her dwelling places in other cities), generations of slaves directed by priestesses had planted groves of cypress and aloes before the temple and within the walled sanctuary behind. From the fragrant aloes the slaves extracted resins from which were refined the precious oils the priestesses used in their rites. From distant oases men on caravans had brought them bundles of grapevines and clumps of palms that, when planted, spread and multiplied into cool, green canopies along the tended paths. An aqueduct had been constructed to bring water to the island from the mountains south of Tyre. Using the same principles, they designed splashing fountains and cool, trickling pools, now surrounded by lush ferns.

Prisca loved the beauty of her home. She had dim memories of another place, of coming here with Thyatira when she was very small. But Thyatira never spoke of it, and Prisca, though sometimes seized with that strange restlessness, for some reason feared to ask.

Her mind on these things, Prisca stripped the leaves from the asherah and bent the bared green branches until they broke. Carefully she made a nest of them in the brazier at the feet of Artemis and dropped the leaves over them. She thrust a flayed twig into a small pot of charcoal embers beside the brazier and with it coaxed the asherah into flame. A thin spiral of fragrant white smoke drifted up.

Prisca's tender lips drew into a rueful line. Would she ever be able to discern meanings from such signs? She thought of a recent argument she had had with Thyatira, one that in spite of herself was cropping up more frequently. Why did they worship the goddess? Who had dedicated her to the goddess? But enmeshed with her desire to know was her unwillingness to know finally where she had come from, and she always dropped it before Thyatira reached the edge of her self-control and might have told her.

Suddenly a movement at the edge of her line of vision distracted her. A young man was staring boldly at her from the border of the grove of trees beyond the rose garden. She rose swiftly. Citizens were not forbidden to observe the sacred rites, providing they had purified themselves first.

Apparently realizing that he had been noticed, the man ambled amiably toward her, ignoring the carefully laid out paths among the rose bushes. Prisca's impulse was to turn and flee into the sanctuary. But her first duty was to read the smoke. With a cry of dismay she saw that it had gone out. An evil omen!

The man reached the stone steps and paused with one foot on the bottom step. He grinned nonchalantly up at her.

She saw that he was young. Was he also an idiot, that he did not respect holy ritual? He was not garbed like a Tyrian merchant. His cloak was of the rough weave of a poor traveler, perhaps an itinerant peddler, with broad stripes of natural brown, russet, and gray goat hair. She knew without asking that he had not been purified.

" 'Morning. If you'll be warming milk, I'll have a cup."

"How dare you? Now the fire has gone out. Artemis will be displeased!"

"Sorry." He shrugged his slender shoulders and glanced around as if to see if anyone else had observed his indiscretion. "Go ahead, I'll wait."

Prisca gasped. He spoke the Aramaic of unlettered village people, with an accent unfamiliar to her. His hair was the color of wet bark, his eyes a pale blue wash. She watched as he found a bench in the rose garden a few feet from the platform and made himself at home on it.

Prisca had never met with such boorishness. Who was he, and where on earth had he come from?

"There is a fountain in the aloe grove." She pointed. "And a cup hanging there." Determinedly she put him out of her mind and turned back to the sacrificial branch. *O Artemis,* she thought, *please forgive this fool! Thou knowest how stupid mortals be!* Patiently she rekindled the green leaves and bits of bark and waited. The chill wind of early dawn had disappeared. Earth was cloaked in stillness. Usually she could feel the trembling of a single leaf. She felt—nothing. Anxiously she glanced at the sky, hoping a storm was coming to account for this strange uneasiness, this pall over her feelings. Prisca shivered.

She fixed her gaze on the strangled wisp of smoke rising from the green wood. No! It mustn't go out again! Anxiously she lit another corner from the glowing charcoals, coaxing, praying, willing it not to go out. After an eternity, during which the smoke wavered neither left nor right, the branch was consumed to ash, and Prisca felt as wilted as a fig leaf plucked and forgotten in the sun.

When at last she arose, she saw the young man was back again. Their pottery drinking cup rested on the bench beside him. His quick eyes beaded on her. They reminded her of a ferret's eyes. He had removed his cloak and was sitting with his back to the sun. His undergarment was of no better repute than his cloak, she decided.

"Who are you?" she asked in Greek, refusing to speak the heathen dialect.

"Limaeus of Galilee."

"Are you lost?"

13

Limaeus smiled his crooked grin, his eyes boldly flirting. "No."

She felt awkward, standing before him as he sprawled on the bench. Her brow knitted in distress. "Very well, then. You are welcome to rest in Artemis's garden. If you lack money for food, we will feed you before you leave."

Evidently realizing she was dismissing him, Limaeus bounded to his feet. "Who are you?" He also spoke Greek now.

"I am called Prisca. I am a servant of Artemis."

"Priestess, heh? That mean you just stay here all the time?"

"We are here to serve the needs of her people."

A speculative gleam entered his eyes. "Come with me to the city."

"*I?*"

"What is the matter? Doesn't your goddess let you out of her sight?"

She did not care for his mocking tone. "My goddess. Whom do you serve?"

"The One True God."

"I should have known. Your accent. A Jew." Prisca took pains to conceal the contempt she felt for him in his ignorance. She had been well trained. But then, in an inexplicable rush of pity, she sat beside him on the cold stone. He was so near she could smell the dust and sweat in his clothes. To cover her confusion she studiously attended the task of composing the folds of her thin robes to conceal the soft contours of her body. Last, she folded her hands in her lap and straightened her spine. She smiled at him impersonally. "Not many of you come to Tyre. Are you here alone?"

The intensity of his stare unnerved her. "You smell like a garden," he said. "And you are so beautiful. Sure you aren't a goddess yourself?" Suddenly the arrogance dissolved into a boyish appeal. "Please come to the city with me. I—I didn't mean to scare you this morning. I got ahead of our company, and this place looked interesting. I saw your leader with the snake. And then, when I saw you, I just couldn't leave until I got a chance to speak to you." He had slipped back into Aramaic.

Suddenly Prisca smiled. "Our mother does not like us to be seen in the city. We go when necessary." She gazed at him curiously. "Shall you be here long?"

He shook his head. "I am traveling with a teacher and his friends. I'm an advancer," he added with a note of pride.

"A what?"

"I am good at getting food and finding places to sleep where we are out of the way of brigands. 'Course I got to say this for our Roman masters, the roads are safe, mostly. I thought this was only a grove, a pleasant place for our teacher to rest." He gazed up at the statue of Artemis. His eyes traveled over the strong, helmeted head, the quiver of arrows secured by a slender cord strung between her proud breasts, the bow balanced against her thigh. He broke out in a grin that Prisca was quick to identify. She had seen it on the faces of many males. "But I see now that it would not do."

"Artemis would allow it," she said, but guessing that his teacher also served the god who refuses to share his altar. She arose. Her robe fell in graceful folds to her small, sandaled feet. "I wish you well and hope you find your master a good resting place."

"Oh, he's not my master, I just, well, I make myself useful because I like to be near him. I like to listen to him. His stories are the best you will ever hear. Come to town," he repeated. "If not today, then tomorrow. I'll make certain that he is here then, by the well near the main marketplace, when the heat of the day is over."

Prisca lifted her eyebrows. This young man was certainly full of his own importance. Still . . . it was hard to resist a good storyteller. "Where is your teacher from?"

"He is a Nazarene."

"Oh." Prisca loved to hear the storytellers from Corinth and from Macedonia and Damascus. In truth, she and the other priestesses sometimes invented excuses to venture into Tyre when word arrived of a new storyteller in town. She thought of Daphne, of the cloudy black hair and large, dark blue eyes and ingenuous expression. At sixteen, two years younger than herself, Daphne had come to them late, an orphan, and not yet used to the strict ways imposed upon the priestesses. She would probably leap at the chance for an excursion to town.

Limaeus was still there. He was standing beside her, too closely. "Promise me that you will come."

"No."

"I'll look for you."

"Good-bye."

"Come." He threw her a cocky grin. "Oh. Here." Without warning he tossed the pottery drinking cup at her and turned on his heel.

Prisca caught it deftly and choked back an exclamation of outrage.

But as she turned back to Artemis, her mind was already busily planning what dire need she might invent that would take her into Tyre.

Chapter 2

"How is our mother?"

"Restless. Her visions must be dreadful, Prisca."

Prisca noted the worried expression in Daphne's deep blue eyes as the two of them, followed by a pair of elder female servants, emerged from the cypress grove onto a street of Tyre. "Not necessarily," she said with a reassuring smile. "I'll look in on her when we return."

Daphne caught her underlip between her teeth. "What will she do when she learns we came into the city?"

Prisca took a deep breath. "I don't care!"

"Prisca!"

Prisca laughed joyously. "A new storyteller is in town! Doesn't that warrant just a tiny disobedience? I've a few shekels with me, too, Daphne. We may just find a Syrian peddler with silks. Even Thyatira loves new silks," she added slyly.

"You keep looking at the passersby," Daphne accused. "I think you are hoping to see that young man who was at the temple yesterday."

Prisca sighed. Perhaps they had been a little too strict with Daphne. The girl seemed afraid that any act that was not specifically ordered would bring the wrath of Artemis upon them. Prisca squeezed her hand. "I am not looking for him. I am seeking the storyteller."

They were approaching the main market area of Tyre, which lay inside massive cedar gates at the head of the causeway. Peddlers who were not locals held forth from temporary tents and lean-tos set up against the high walls. Some strutted about with heaping baskets of goods on their shoulders, crying their wares. Others balanced halters of exotic birds from Ethiopia or strings of metal utensils that clanked together as they dogged the dusty streets. The shopkeepers of Tyre did their best to attract customers away from the haggling itinerants.

Prisca attended to none of them, turning her head neither left nor right as she walked. Her proud carriage drew admiring glances from passersby, whose gazes then lingered on her startling beauty, on the gray green eyes that picked up color from her sage robe. By the distinctive color of their robes, the two were recognized as priestesses and accorded respect. Prisca behaved as if she were unaware of the attention, but Daphne picked up the edge of her silk veil and drew it across her face until only her blue eyes were exposed.

Prisca's attention was drawn to a knot of bystanders just ahead of them, five or six men clustered about a man with shoulder-length brown locks the color of rich river silt. She slowed uncertainly. Whatever he said must have been uproarious, for his listeners suddenly burst into hearty laughter. The face of the speaker beamed with conviviality. The priestess and the novitiate were about to pass when the man spoke again. His voice arrested Prisca where she stood. She knew without doubt that this was the storyteller Limaeus had praised.

Prisca seized Daphne's arm and pulled her into the shade of a rug merchant's stall. The shopkeeper glanced at them once, then he, too, turned his attention back to the foreign storyteller.

The stranger was ruggedly handsome. His eyes held a quality that was utterly fascinating. Were they hazel? Blue, like the waters of the Great Sea? Impossible to tell. One of his listeners was asking a question, and the stranger raised a strong, tanned hand to stroke his beard. Prisca noticed his long, sensitive fingers. The nails were clean and square. When he spoke, Prisca felt herself drowning in his voice.

"What is he talking about?" asked Daphne in a low voice.

Prisca shook her head sharply, willing her companion to silence. She could not make sense of the words. They might have been gibberish for all she knew, though he was speaking Greek, a tongue readily understood by the Tyrians. His voice was strong and assured, with a resonance that made it immediately compelling, despite the raucity of the marketplace. Who was this man? Certainly no ordinary storyteller. Why had they not heard of him before? She felt Daphne tugging her arm.

"Come, Prisca. You promised we might peek into the shops."

"Don't you want to listen? Don't you want to?"

Daphne sighed, disappointed. "May I go on, then?"

"Yes, take Maya with you. I'll not be long." Prisca scarcely noticed as Daphne and the servants moved off.

The storyteller had plunged into another tale. Prisca glanced curiously at those pressing in on him. Their faces glowed. Such expressions she had never seen upon the faces of street folk. Exactly like family, like Thyatira and her priestesses when they broke the fast together in the morning; too trusting, open looks, making of them a community in the midst of commotion. She strained to listen.

"No more do you put new wine into old wineskins; if you do, the skins burst, and then the wine runs out and the skins are spoiled. No, you put new wine into fresh skins; then both are preserved."

There were grunts of agreement from the circle.

His tale is about preserving wine? thought Prisca.

The storyteller was smiling. Suddenly his eyes met hers. Prisca gasped, nearly overwhelmed by the force of his personality. Her eyes filled with tears, and she was forced to look aside.

She heard another's voice, questioning the storyteller. She found that she was leaning forward, to miss no part of the answer. Somehow the teller knew she was listening, for he, too, turned and moved nearer. His community moved also, as if knit by an invisible field, into the radius of the storyteller.

His voice seemed meant for her alone. "And no one sews a patch of unshrunk cloth onto an old coat; for then the patch tears away from the coat and leaves a bigger hole."

But everyone knew that! Why did it sound new when the storyteller said it?

"He told the very same story in Capernaum," someone said.

The high, masculine voice sounded familiar. Prisca turned. There stood Limaeus, grinning with a proprietary air.

"It must be important."

"Would you like to meet the teacher?"

"Me? He would not want to—"

Limaeus pressed a forefinger to his temple with mock astonishment. "Oh, come now, Prisca! Where is my haughty priestess? I think it might all be rather interesting."

His tone jarred her. It did not match the mood she felt surrounding the storyteller. More, surely, than a storyteller! Limaeus took her arm. He guided her to the stranger.

"This is Jesus, the storyteller I told you about. Her name is Prisca, teacher. She is a priestess at the temple of Artemis."

Prisca felt the angry intakes of breath, the hisses of outrage. Oh, this was madness! All of them must be worshipers of the God of the Jews! But then the man called Jesus was talking to her, and she felt as if she'd known him all her life.

His followers shrank away in tight knots, though remaining within hearing, Prisca knew. She sensed they wanted their storyteller to feel their displeasure. The teacher ignored them. Gently he questioned her. She stumbled over answers and found herself telling him about her life at the temple.

At length Jesus said, "As I told another, a Samaritan woman in the city of Sychar, so shall I say to you: You worship what you do not know."

"I—"

"Prisca!" Daphne pushed her way through the throng and tugged at her arm. "Amrylla is here. Thyatira is calling for you. We must go back!"

Against her will, Prisca allowed herself to be pulled away from the teacher. She looked back. He was smiling at her! She did not know why, but it filled her with such joy that she could hardly bear to leave. A radiant smile captured her face. She knew he understood. Nothing would keep her from coming back to hear him again.

"Prisca, what is the matter with you?"

Ordinarily Prisca would have at once squelched a scolding by a novice sister. Instead she hugged her impulsively.

"Prisca!" As they hurried home, Daphne told her what had happened. Immediately after they left the temple, a visitor arrived all the way from Rome. He must have been someone of importance, for Thyatira, who had passed from the trancelike state of her vision into ordinary sleep, had immediately been awakened. Rather than being angry, Thyatira had called for a strong drink to clear her head and had received him.

"Who is he?"

"Amrylla refused to say."

Why would Thyatira request her presence? Prisca felt a sense of foreboding. She recalled Daphne saying that when she attended Thyatira, their high priestess's dreams had been troubled. She recalled with a sense of guilt that, yesterday, when interrupted by Limaeus, she had allowed the asherah flame to die before the branch had been consumed. And then, when it did finish burning, she had not been able to read the smoke! Surely Artemis was displeased with her. Trembling, Prisca hurried through the cypresses with Daphne, the two servants and the messenger Amrylla at her heels.

Silken drapery and tapestried cushions softened the sunken living quarters of the high priestess of Artemis. Wall hangings depicted scenes of the goddess in her various forms: as huntress, with a dying hind slung over her strong shoulders; as mother to the world, with a hundred breasts to nourish her children; as Corn Goddess, her hair composed of a thousand intricately worked ears of tasseled, golden corn. In a dozen niches rested exquisite statues of Artemis, as tall as a woman's arm, sculpted of all the colors of marble in the world: mottled blue and gray, rust brown, moss green, pale yellows, ivories, and pristine white, including all the colors of all the skins of women and men Artemis protected.

19

Prisca paused between two narrow, round columns, overwhelmed, as always, by this room. Her fingertips trailed lightly on either column as if for reassurance, before lifting the veil from her hair and letting it fall to her shoulders. A breeze waffled the silk curtains and her hair. She captured the stray wisps, smoothed them back and stepped down into Thyatira's presence. And into the chilling presence of a Roman tribune.

The soldier stood with the easy grace of an athlete, his hands loosely coiled at his sides. He turned and scrutinized her with shrewd eyes, as if she were a prize horse. Prisca flushed and lifted her chin with tart displeasure.

"So this is Prisca." His deep voice ended on a tremulous note.

She flashed a glance at Thyatira. A strange expression of pride lighted the features of the high priestess.

"Yes, my lord."

A smile played about his face as Thyatira presented her to him. His head was of noble proportion, square, and clean-shaven like that of the emperor, Tiberius Caesar, which graced Tyrian coins. His short hair was sunburned blond, and his skin gleamed like fine, oiled leather. He was called Marcus Sistus.

The name meant nothing to her. Prisca's sense of alarm increased. Was this to be the day that her body was used to plead a cause before the goddess? Prisca knew that sisters far younger than she had already been chosen. She should be proud. And a Roman tribune! Surely it was an honor. An honor. . . . Her rebellious thoughts carried her back to the marketplace, listening to the storyteller again.

"Is she well schooled, Thyatira?"

Thyatira! What loose form of address was this? Who was this man?

"Tell me, Prisca, have you studied your Latin and Greek?"

She glanced at Thyatira. Thyatira would not help her. Very well, then. She gazed fearlessly at him. "Yes, my lord. And mathematics and astronomy and the healing arts, too." She kept her voice impersonal.

"Shall we sit?" said Thyatira. "Prisca—," she indicated a cushion at her side and motioned Amrylla to bring refreshment.

Tribune Sistus reclined with muscular grace in a wooden chair having arms and back carved in the shape of an eagle's wings and feet formed as eagle claws. He thrust a foot out before him and returned Prisca's gaze. "And is your body healthy?"

She flushed and looked away. Was she expected to tell him that her flow was upon her? "I am healthy," she replied coolly. She studied him beneath her thick, black lashes. He did not appear to be a cruel man. He and

Thyatira seemed quite at ease with each other.

Sistus nodded as if satisfied with her answers and glanced at Thyatira.

Thyatira took up the questioning. "Why were you in Tyre today, my daughter?"

"I heard there was a new storyteller," Prisca confessed. "Oh, my mother, you should have seen him. A beautiful man!"

Thyatira's shapely brows arched, as if to say, *And when did I give permission?* "Indeed. And his tales, were they good?"

Prisca laughed. "I confess I was so taken with his manner and his voice that I scarce remember his words." She bit her rouged fingertip. "But I do remember something strange he said to me, just before Amrylla summoned us. He said, 'You worship what you do not know.'"

Thyatira started. "Were you in attendance upon me?"

"No, my mother. Our younger sisters cared for your body while you were apart."

Thyatira's fingers drummed against the silver goblet held in her other hand. She turned to the tribune. "Forgive me, my lord, for subjecting you to trivial matters, but I must question Prisca about this." He nodded and signaled her to continue. "Did he say anything about us?"

"Us?"

"Priestesses of Artemis, foolish girl!"

Her tone stung Prisca more than the words. She was being reprimanded like a child before this stranger. "No, mother, he said nothing about us!"

"Prisca, you are not to hear him again. Leave us. You must go directly to the goddess and offer prayers. Do you hear me?"

"Yes, mother, I—"

"Go, now!"

Humiliated, not daring a last glance at the Roman, Prisca fled from her mother's presence.

Chapter 3

Moments later, Prisca slowly ascended the twelve steps to the temple platform. She tilted her head back and gazed squarely at the helmeted features of Artemis, as if seeing them for the first time. One side of her profile was bathed in the red orange aura of the sun setting over the Great Sea. Cut in sharp relief by the low angle of the sun, her other half seemed veiled in mystery.

"O Artemis," Prisca said softly, extending cupped palms in supplication, "Thou who art good and all-knowing, why do I disobey our mother Thyatira? Why do I shrink from offering my body to obtain blessings from thee? Surely my fruit shall be blessed also. If the tribune has come with a petition, I shall submit to him with good grace, trusting in thee. . . ."

Brave words. Restlessly Prisca dropped her outstretched hands. Thoughtfully she paced before the goddess. The muted voices of her sisters beginning their evening meal drifted to her ears. Then she heard the grate of a sandal on stone and turned as Tribune Sistus ascended the top step. He remained at the edge of the platform.

"I wanted to see you again before I left."

Prisca's face flamed with embarrassment. He must have heard her words. She could not see his features clearly. They blurred and blended in the soft maroon twilight.

"Then you are leaving?" she asked with unfeigned relief.

He laughed softly, as if amused at some private joke.

"Who are you?"

"A soldier."

"Did you truly come all the way from Rome just to visit our Thyatira? Do you live in Rome all the time?"

"I live where I am ordered. Wherever Caesar needs my men."

"Always?" She could not fathom such a life. "Have you no real home?"

"I have lived in Macedonia. Babylon. Alexandria in my younger days."

"You are not very old now."

His laughter was couched in velvet. "It seems not only because you are so young. Do you like where you live, Prisca?" His words contained a caress.

"It is my home." She hesitated. "But sometimes, I wish. . . ." Suddenly she longed to confide, to cry her unnameable fears, this aching emptiness that Artemis knew nothing of.

"What do you wish?"

Shaking off her melancholy, she replied, "To have adventures!"

He laughed, then said soberly, "Perhaps someday you shall. But not yet. This is a dangerous world we live in. Be warned, Prisca."

"Warned?"

"Against girlish . . . infatuations."

Prisca snorted scornfully. "No one would dare to touch a priestess!"

His voice lost its softness. "Heed your mother," he commanded. "Continue to study. Curb your impetuousness."

"*Why?*" the word broke out in a wrenching cry. "What is my future?"

"That remains to be seen. May all the gods bless you, Prisca of Artemis."

"Wait!"

He raised a hand that at once cut off her response and bade farewell.

"Tribune Sistus!" Prisca swept up her robe and followed the sound of his footsteps down toward the rose garden. She heard a soft laugh.

Limaeus stepped out of the shadows and ambled toward her.

"You! What are you doing here?"

"Like the tribune—I wanted to see you again."

The shadows had deepened, and she felt uneasy in his presence. "Please go away."

"No."

"I shall call our guards."

"Don't you want to know about the storyteller?" he wheedled.

"The high priestess has forbidden me to go again."

"And—?"

Prisca sighed impatiently. "What about him?"

"He is leaving Tyre soon. May not be back this way for months."

"You are impossible! I am calling the guards!"

"Not necessary. I came to see your chief priestess."

"Truly?"

"Truly," he imitated her voice and bowed mockingly.

"What makes you think she will see you?"

"She will. Go ask."

Thyatira agreed, and a few minutes later Prisca ushered him into her presence. She herself remained in the background, hoping not to be sent away.

Thyatira appraised him in one swift glance. Prisca could see that Limaeus's unkempt appearance, the scruffy sandals and torn cloak, did little to enhance his trustworthiness with her. She did not bid him sit. She sat where Tribune Marcus Sistus had sat, running her long fingers possessively out the carved eagle feathers of the arms. She caught Prisca's eye and did not forbid her presence.

"Are you a worshiper of Artemis?" she said.

Limaeus smiled his lopsided grin. "Well, not exactly, lady, but I need her on this one."

"You have a petition for her?"

"That's it." Limaeus withdrew a bulging pouch from the front of his clothing and tossed it gently up and down. "Now I know petitions cost money. This is all yours. This temple doesn't look any too prosperous—not to be criticizing—so I'm going to give it all to you."

Thyatira sized up the contents of the bag with a practiced eye. "What is it you desire?"

Limaeus wheeled until he faced Prisca. "My petition will only be satisfied when I lie a night with her."

Prisca gasped. Her eyes flew to Thyatira's and read the priestess's cold dislike for the man standing between them. Prisca held herself rigidly under control, fearful, yet certain that Thyatira would not honor this—this foreigner's petition.

"What has brought you to Tyre?" Thyatira asked.

"Passing through with my friends."

"And your friends are—"

"A Nazarene storyteller and his men. Well, he's a rabbi."

Thyatira said nothing. She studied him closely, then looked at Prisca. She stroked the length of her long, fine nose with the tip of her forefinger. A frown knit her brow. At length, she said, "Do you also worship the Jewish God?"

Limaeus shrugged.

Thyatira rose and strolled a few paces, Limaeus and Prisca watching her. "Artemis is a tolerant, loving goddess," she said over her shoulder. "She would not refuse a petitioner from another god, providing he went through the purification rites." Her calculating blue eyes flicked to Prisca and back to Limaeus. "Return at this time tomorrow, and you shall have your answer."

Prisca heard the ocean pounding in her ears. She stared at the spume-colored marble wall across from her. She had an impression of Limaeus sneaking her a look of triumph as he took leave. The antechamber echoed her silence.

"Well, Prisca?"

"My flow is upon me."

Thyatira laughed. Prisca was shocked by its unpleasant ring. "You are such a child in many ways."

"I do as I am bid!" she cried furiously.

"But . . . ," the high priestess prodded.

"*Why*, Thyatira? Why him? I was prepared to help the tribune make his sacrifice, but this—this—he is not even of our faith!"

Thyatira fixed her with an unreadable glance. Prisca caught the unmistakable impression that it had something to do with Tribune Marcus Sistus.

Then Thyatira said abruptly, "Come into my rooms, Prisca. Let us talk."

Bewildered, Prisca followed her from the antechamber. The many forms of Artemis smiled upon them from their torch-lighted niches as she dropped to a cushion at the foot of Thyatira's stool.

"There is no greater honor for a priestess than to make of her body a vessel for Artemis. You understand that."

"Yes, my mother."

"I have sensed in your dedication a reluctance. Therefore each time someone has asked for you, I have refused him. I have been unwilling to jeopardize even the smallest petition by offering a man a priestess who does not believe wholeheartedly in the efficacy of her sacrifice."

Prisca caught her lower lip between her even, small teeth. She knew that Thyatira spoke truly.

Thyatira placed an affectionate palm on her head. "Do not be overtroubled. Girls your age frequently doubt the goddess of their ancestors—I did once. But now I would die for Artemis!" she added with quiet passion.

Prisca lowered her head. The words Thyatira wanted from her would not come. Her stubbornness surprised even herself. She heard a low, sad moan from the one she loved best in all the world, and yet could not repent.

"Foolish girl! In Artemis lies our safety! Is it the same quarrel, Prisca? What shall you do? Where will you go if you leave her service? Look at me! Have you family? Have you honor anywhere but before Artemis?"

"I—I've not thought about it. It is just that sometimes. . . . I suppose that I pray Artemis will send a perfect lover for me, who will then desire me for his wife." Thyatira's hand stilled upon her head, then lifted.

"Will you be directed by me in this?"

"Yes." Artemis be blessed! Thyatira knew a way out for her! She gazed up with a worshipful look upon her face.

"Then lie with Limaeus. Not tomorrow, but after your flow. To attract the perfect lover you must be skilled. You can gain skill even with a man like Limaeus, who does not confess his faith in Artemis. And since he does not believe, if the petition bought with your body is denied, who would blame us?"

Dread filled her body, as if she had swallowed a basket of stones. Blinking back tears, she forced herself to meet Thyatira's triumphant look. "I will obey."

Thyatira smiled at her with the old affection. She reached down and insinuated a lock of Prisca's dark hair around her pale finger. "And we will save Limaeus's purse for your dowry."

Pleased that Prisca did not oppose her, Thyatira generously invited her to remain for supper after their talk. Wine mellowed their tongues and shored up Prisca's resolve. When she had finished eating, she watched Amrylla refill their goblets and brush into a salver the remains of a round of goat cheese, the ruby seeds of pomegranate and stems of grape and bread crumbs from the low table set between their couches.

"My mother," she began timidly.

"You may speak."

"Will you come with me tomorrow, into Tyre? Will you hear the storyteller with me? Thyatira, there is something so wonderful about him!"

"What?"

Prisca gave a half laugh, her eyes now brilliant emerald with reflection. "I do not know. He makes me feel different. Important."

"A mere storyteller makes a priestess of Artemis feel important? Have you not got the leaf before the bud?"

"Come. Please?" she wheedled.

Thyatira scowled. "Brush my hair, will you? It helps me to think."

Prisca got up and crossed to Thyatira's dressing table. Fetching a silver brush inlaid with topazes, she unbound the glistening, raven locks of the high priestess and began stroking.

"Sometimes prophets or teachers come along. . . . They attract a following—good men and women—but somewhere along the way their words become twisted, like the vine around the stake. Alas. The dead seldom correct the living. . . . Which way did the smoke rise when you burned the asherah?"

Prisca stopped brushing. "First it went out," she confessed. "When I rekindled it, it refused to burn properly. Then it rose straight in a thin line. I could not read it."

A cold stillness seemed to drop over Thyatira.

"What is it? What is the matter, are you ill?"

Thyatira shook her head. "Do not stop." Prisca continued the rhythmic strokes, and Thyatira mused as if to herself, "I felt it as I dreamed. We are entering a dangerous time, Prisca. It is a time to cling closely to Artemis, lest we imperil our souls. I shall not go to hear your storyteller. I do not think he has anything for me. But I think that to save you for Artemis, I must not forbid you to hear him. Pray about it tonight. If you go, therefore, listen well. Listen with your mind as well as your heart."

Prisca's heart leaped. She would see him again before he left! Suppressing her excitement, she replied carelessly, "Yes, I shall. He is no ordinary teller of tales."

"No, he is not. Tribune Sistus warned me about him. All these obscure prophets coming and going, and Rome never interferes. . . . Perhaps they should."

Thyatira sucked in her cheek as if recalling a private joke. "I did hear something about him, a long time ago, if he is the one they call Jesus."

"He is! What did you hear?"

"One of the servants heard it from a pot mender who travels frequently by caravan, coming through the village of Capernaum, by the Sea of Galilee. He and his wife and many others were listening to Jesus tell stories. That is his native country, around Galilee—"

"Thyatira, please!"

She shrugged indifferently. "His mother was there and wanted Jesus to come to her. He mocked her."

"He did what?"

"Truly, he did. He said—to everyone!—'Who are my mother and my brothers?' "

"They must have heard wrong! What did the lady, his mother, do?"

"Since I was not there, I do not know." Thyatira gazed out beyond the drapery, at the star-filled night. "The pot mender said that he was puzzled, too. I guess the people were outraged. As properly they should be. After all, she was his mother, and he had humiliated her by denying her in their own city. But he heard aright. Your Jesus—strange man—went on to say

that all the people listening to him were his mother and brothers. He said
—let me see if I can recall—'Whoever does the will of God is my brother,
and sister, and mother.' "

Thyatira fixed her eyes on Prisca. "Strange man," she repeated. She
rose, shaking off Prisca's ministrations with a toss of her head. "Go now,
I am tired." But as she prepared to leave, Thyatira stopped her. "Did you
remember to thank the goddess for your flow?"

Prisca smiled ruefully. "I did, but my heart was not in it. Why must
the flow bring pain?"

"That is not for us to ask. Thank her for the pain. Nothing is bought
without pain. The blood of new beginnings flows from her through you.
New! All is new!"

Prisca pondered her superior's words as she wrestled with sleep. *All is
new. Yes. New beginnings. New wine. New cloth.*

She slept.

Chapter 4

Prisca hurried through her morning prayers. Her heart was brimming with love for Artemis this morning. Life seemed so good! There was no better! As she arose from her knees at the altar, the wind riffled her robe and teased her nostrils with the scent of the aloes with which she had anointed herself this morning. Her saffron veil pelted playfully against her smooth cheeks. Today she would see the storyteller again.

Smiling, she gazed southward, toward distant Egypt. Slowly her smile faded. The strange longings that had tormented her soul during the tribune's visit yesterday surfaced again. Egypt . . . where the mother goddess was Isis, so terrible and splendid that her priestesses sometimes killed themselves when they displeased her. Perhaps she should make a pilgrimage to Isis, to discover the root of the contradictory feelings within her. She considered the power of the gods and goddesses over their lives. Just a few months ago one of the sisters had sinned and the next day had been run over by a chariot. She could not even remember what it was Althea had done.

Determinedly Prisca shook off her disquieting thoughts. She admired the delicate pink tinging the sails of the fishing boats leaving the open curve of the southern harbor. Turning on her sandaled foot, she faced the other way, in the direction of Sidon, some twenty miles distant. Tyre's northern harbor was the main seaport. A breakwater extended from the island to meet the natural curve of the mainland, like the pincers of a crab protecting its dinner. A host of boats lay at anchor within the curve, among them merchant vessels from Ephesus and Roman galleys from Lycia and Macedonia. Should they ever carry her to any of those places?

Her ruminations were broken by Maya, painfully climbing the high steps to the altar platform. "Our mother says I must go with you," she said grumpily. Though still of childbearing years, Maya was considered old. Her joints were knobby and sometimes painful, a fact she was willing to share. It was her opinion that, after all she did for Artemis, the least the goddess might have done for her servant was to keep her free from the aches and ugliness of infirmity. Many of the sisters avoided her, not

29

wishing to hear the litany of ills that Maya stocked like a day's catch in a fishmonger's stall.

Prisca picked up her sage wool cloak. "I shall enjoy your company," she replied courteously. "Let me help you." Truth be told, she'd far rather have gone alone. Sometimes one wished to think thoughts and experience the sights and fragrances of life in solitude.

Gently but firmly she grasped the servant's elbow. In the other hand Maya clutched her staff. "Shall I ask our mother to allow someone who is rested to accompany me? Yesterday's trip was too much for you." She almost said "someone who is younger," before remembering that Maya was still vain about her age and her supposed vanished beauty.

"No. I feel better with you," Maya declared. "You understand me."

As she helped Maya down the steps and they made their way through the rose garden and the cypress grove, Prisca knew what she meant, though they had never discussed it. She had experienced this clinging with others, priestesses and servants alike, though usually when they were older than Maya. The closer to the grave, the more they feared its black depths. Why did they fear? There were no horrors beyond the grave. Did not Artemis teach them that life ended all personal being? As a leaf withered and fell and took on the mottled sponginess of decay, so old life returned to the seamless soul of the universe.

But she supposed she herself would feel as Maya did if crippled with infirmities. So she comforted her without rancor.

When they reached town, her heart quickened. Now she chafed under the leisurely pace, sensing a certain sadistic intent from Thyatira in sending the least agile member of the community, with her. Her rebelliousness dissolved as she spied a man who seemed familiar. He was a lumber hauler of a man, striding toward them with steps that swallowed huge gulps of street at each stride.

Prisca reached out. "Excuse me!"

The man stopped abruptly, his gaze sweeping over her. "What is it? I am in a hurry." His fingers were already probing in a pouch she saw poking out from the folds of his girdled robe.

"We are not beggars, sir. I wish directions to where the storyteller is speaking today."

"Storyteller!" the man expostulated. His heavy dark brows beetled together.

She flinched. "Y-yes. The one from Galilee. Were you not with him yesterday?"

"Jesus? Of course. That is where I am going now. I am late. I overslept."

30

A tentative grin split the full beard, and she caught a flash of strong, white teeth.

Prisca smiled. The man seemed suddenly less fearsome. "May we walk with you?"

He looked at Maya.

Prisca said quickly, "Please, do not mind us. Just tell me how I may find Jesus again."

"Of such are the kingdom," he muttered.

"I beg your pardon?"

"My master would tell me that I am right where he intended me to be. Let us go. My name is Peter."

"And I am Prisca, priestess of Artemis, and our servant Maya."

Peter stopped for the second time. *"Priestess of Artemis!* You're the one!" He seemed to struggle with himself, finally heaving a sigh. Coming round to Maya's other side, he took her elbow. "Take your time, mother, our master will wait." To Prisca he said, "Our men were talking about you last night. We were sorting over the day's events. I had not realized who you were." His eyes traveled knowingly over her. "They say—well, never mind. They were all for chasing you away. Jesus stopped it."

Prisca felt giddy with pleasure. "He did?"

"He said we were to welcome you when you came again, and that is good enough for me. Though I confess half the time I cannot follow his reasoning," he mumbled, with a sidelong glance at her.

To Prisca's relief, Peter seemed to forget his haste as they sauntered through Tyre. It was not only for Maya's sake, but because she wanted to question him. "Is Limaeus one of you?"

"Oh, him. He's another one."

"Another one what?"

"Jesus picks up the strangest characters." Peter stared straight ahead.

Prisca smiled to herself. Did he realize he was including them in that description? "You seemed angry when I called him storyteller."

"Sorry."

"But why?"

Peter stopped again and bent his earnest brown eyes and furrowed brow upon her, as if he could not explain and walk at the same time. "Because he's not a storyteller! Well he is, but not just a storyteller. He is the Christ."

"The what?"

"I told him he should stick to Jews," he muttered. "We better go. He will be wondering where I have gotten to this time." He flashed her a boyish, guilty grin, so completely out of context with his gigantic frame that Prisca laughed with sheer joy.

The women followed Peter through the town and over the causeway. When he saw that Maya was growing short of breath, he stopped a cart driver and bartered with him to carry her in his cart. By this time the crowds were increasing. Prisca had never seen so many Tyrians on the road. They were a true shore community. No one went by foot where boat would take them in more comfort. In truth, her own feet were blistering by the time they had crossed the causeway, passed under the aqueduct, and begun climbing the low hills. Her sandals, of fine, tooled leather, were not meant for lengthy treks.

Now she could see that they were part of a multitude, those from Tyre joined by men and women with children from Sidon and the southern villages as well. The way was rocky. She could feel the sharp stones through her sandals. Tall, brittle weeds grazed her calves and snagged in her dress. She glanced reassuringly up at Maya, to find her having a marvelous time, perched head and shoulders above the others, her knobby hands clutching the side of the cart, her seemingly frail body swaying contentedly.

Peter was muttering again.

"What is it?" Prisca asked.

"I don't know what we are going to do with all these people."

"You don't mean they are all going to hear the storyteller?"

His resigned glance said, *Of course, what did you think?*

Prisca remained near Jesus all that day. She put everything else out of her mind: Thyatira's demands, Maya's health, Daphne, even her beloved Artemis. For once Maya did not grumble about being uncomfortable. When noontime passed and still the crowds showed no inclination to leave, the disciples gathered around their teacher. Then Peter came and told them to gather into groups of fifty, and they would be fed.

"I have some money, if some are going to buy food."

"Keep your money."

Prisca was never able to explain to others, after that day, exactly how she and Maya, like the thousands around them, were fed. She remembered that none went hungry, and there was food left over. As the sun dipped behind the masts of the boats in the Tyrian harbors, some families and other groups climbed to their feet, beat the dust off cloaks and robes, and prepared to leave.

Gradually the hillside grew quiet and took on a deserted look. Prisca remained where she was, her cloak tucked around her drawn-up knees, her arms clasped about them. She rested her cheek on one knee. Her veil had slid off, and her hair, burnished to a rich nut brown by the sun's rays, streamed about her shoulders. She glanced over at Maya. Curled on her robe, Maya had fallen asleep. For the last hour, Prisca's eyes had seldom left the face of the teacher they called Jesus.

His face fascinated her. It was strong, yet not severe. At times it filled with sadness, yet a few moments later he would be throwing back his head in shared laughter. Now he was in relaxed conversation with a few who still clustered about him with questions, and his face appeared tired. Prisca raised her head and looked about her. Some families were starting cooking fires there on the hills, those like her reluctant to leave Jesus' presence; she wondered if others were as filled with new thoughts as she, with more questions than answers.

Suddenly she realized Peter was standing beside her. She scrambled to her feet and lifted her veil over her hair.

"People are leaving now. I asked the cart man to take you back. He is already paid."

"That is thoughtful of you, Peter." She glanced at Maya. "Maya is ready to go home. . . . Will the Mas—will Jesus spare me a word with him?"

Peter stiffened. A look of disapproval escaped from his face before he could suppress it. "The Master is tired."

"Yes, I can see that," she replied.

Peter sighed and stepped aside.

Jesus was seated on a rock, his big, sandaled feet spread firmly on the ground before him. He was drinking a cup of water. He balanced the cup on one knee and smiled as she approached.

"Hello, Prisca. I have seen you here all day."

"Every time I thought to leave, your words kept me. I know you are weary. . . ."

He flashed an affectionate smile at those sitting or sprawling near him. "Are not we all?" A rumble of masculine laughter acknowledged his words.

"Master," said Prisca, unaware of the term which had escaped her lips, "May I ask you a question?"

Jesus nodded.

"I heard that once you did deny your mother."

Peter grew red in the face, his lips compressed as if he might explode. Jesus laid a hand on his friend's sleeve.

"When you heard this, did the teller know all the story?"

"She had heard it said that you had told everyone they could be your mother and your brothers only by doing the will of God."

Jesus thought for a moment, then nodded. He smiled at her. "That is good. I have wondered, sometimes, whether those who listen remember as well."

"Then you did say that?"

"Yes."

She frowned, her mind struggling with foreign thoughts. "I am a priestess who serves the goddess Artemis. All those who serve with me are my sisters. The high priestess, Thyatira, is our mother, she through whom the goddess instructs us." She felt a palpable hostility in the air around her.

Jesus seemed not to notice it.

"Jesus, I think we had better go," Peter interrupted them. "The wind is coming up. We do not want to be caught up here tonight. And besides, we have plans to make."

"It will wait," said Jesus. He turned his steady gaze back to Prisca.

Though she knew by now that he was an emissary of the Jewish God, Jehovah, she felt neither recrimination nor condemnation in his eyes, only that he was inviting her to say what she wished. So she asked, "Is she your mother as Thyatira is my mother?"

"Now that is too much, Master!" someone hissed.

"As I told you yesterday, Prisca of Tyre, you worship what you do not know. Mary of Capernaum is my mother. But her glory is not in being my mother, but in doing the will of my Father. In that she is also my sister and my daughter."

"Oh, that I could be your sister!" Prisca blurted.

Two of the men with Jesus sprang to their feet. "Lord, this woman is evil! By her own lips is she condemned. She's not even Jewish!"

"A menstruant from the cradle!"

"Get hence, harlot!"

Prisca's fingers flew to her lips. Her other hand clutched her robe to her breast.

Peter went from one foot to the other, looking miserable, but held his tongue.

"Behold!" said Jesus angrily. "Did you not beg me to explain to you the parable of the sower and his seeds? Have not I continually taught you that all who hear my words and take them to heart shall bear fruit? Take heed what you hear. The measure you give shall be the measure you get!"

His men flinched at the rebuke.

Jesus ignored them. He took Prisca's hand away from her lips and held it. "What is it you wish?"

"To learn. My—mother—says Artemis is wisest of goddesses, for she willingly shares her throne with other gods. You say your God does not, nay, that he is the only God. Does not this anger the other gods? My servant, like many, is fearful of death, though Artemis promises only the sweet oblivion of herself, no pain. Your God promises life, not oblivion. How life without pain? And how can a single God be so powerful that he can afford to anger the others that inhabit the heavens? How can even a God promise that which is impossible?"

"My father, who is in heaven, desires only steadfast love and not sacrifice, Prisca. Knowledge of God, rather than burnt offerings. You ask for knowledge of God. Are you willing to give steadfast love?"

Prisca heard a low chuckle nearby. Half turning, she spied Limaeus, standing on the fringes of the gathering with his arms folded, wearing a crooked, amused smile. The pact between Limaeus and Thyatira rushed into her mind. She threw Jesus a despairing look, able to repeat only, "I —I wish to learn."

Jesus held her hand for another moment in his big, strong, brown ones, while he gazed at her. She felt a current from his gaze and his hands, filling her body with strength and her eyes with unexplained tears.

"I shall be teaching nearby for a few more days. Then we are going up to Sidon. You may come and listen while I am here."

Prisca could not speak. Swallowing hard, she nodded and turned away.

Chapter 5

But you have taught us to question! To be unafraid of examining our thoughts." Prisca set aside her hoe and examined the dirt ingrained in her fingers, as if seeking the answer there.

"I want to know why you have set Artemis's temple in an uproar," Thyatira said quietly. She tucked her fingers into the opposite sleeves of her robe and moved back a pace, out of the path of Prisca's vigorous hoeing around the new grapevines. "Now, if you are over your foolishness, I wish you to leave this job to the slaves and come with me."

Not waiting for an answer, Thyatira walked away, holding her robes carefully away from the snagging grasp of the vineyard.

Prisca realized that slaves and sisters alike had been listening to Thyatira's words. In the cool of evening, many of them worked in the vineyard by choice, pruning or tying back vines, or in the fruit orchard or among the aloes, reverencing through work the closeness of she whom they served. But Prisca's labors this week were not to attain closeness to Artemis. Thyatira had grudgingly granted her the right to travel each day into Tyre, to listen to the man she had called the storyteller. Each evening she had returned to the temple with spirits elated and thoughts in turmoil. Unable to bear the gentle questioning of her sisters, helpless even to formulate words that expressed what she was feeling, she had avoided them, Thyatira above all, to wrestle with her own spirit in the ungiving soil of the vineyard.

"Mother, you are not asking me anything I have not asked myself a thousand times," Prisca said miserably as they attained the aloe grove and some measure of privacy.

Thyatira turned aside into a little niche created in the grove to provide a leafy bower, with a small statue of Artemis gracing a clear, miniature pool lined with rounded stones. Here she sat on a bench and looked up. Her face had a peculiar set that Prisca recognized. Thyatira was prepared to do battle.

Prisca dropped to her knees beside the pool, thankful for the coolness of the bower after the vigorous glow she had worked up hoeing around the vines. How tired her body felt! But it was a good tiredness. "Mother, when we were little, you used to tell us—well you still do, the new sisters —you used to tell us about Artemis, how she came to earth in the form of a great meteor and all the people loved her and looked up to her to govern the seasons and grant good harvests. . . ."

Thyatira smiled. Her handsome features relaxed. "Yes, I remember. You know you have frightened some of the novitiates by your actions, Prisca. Daphne especially. When I prayed to Artemis, it seemed her will that you should be allowed to listen to this Jesus. I felt comforted, knowing that after a few days you would come to your senses."

"I have not lost my senses. I am the same person I have always—"

Thyatira shot to her feet in a flare of renewed anger. "I am sick to death of hearing about the miracles he works. Food out of nowhere! A woman's hemorrhagic flow stopped. A boy's seizures."

"I didn't—"

"No, you didn't. Maya told me. It is all they speak of in the city." She stared down at her priestess. Her voice grew soft, persuasive. "Miracle workers are nothing new. Who does he claim to be? Not a priest, you say. A teacher. Maya says they call him a prophet, too. Prisca, you are an intelligent girl. How can you listen to a man who refuses to recognize his earthly mother, but who would call any piece of rabble brother! One who claims that your goddess is not who she says she is and not only that but is powerless! When we know what she has done for us!" Suddenly her voice spun out of control and ended in a high wail. "You tell me, Prisca, where this will end!"

Prisca picked at a torn fingernail. "He is gone from Tyre," she said. "I do not know when he will be back." *If he will be back,* she mourned. She had so many questions. . . .

"And—"

Prisca threw her head back to challenge Thyatira eye to eye. "I do not know, mother. When he comes back, I do not know what I will do."

Their eyes locked for a long minute. "The first man who asks for you shall have you." Thyatira stalked out of the bower.

Prisca stared after her. She would think of something before Thyatira could make good her threat. She leaned over and washed her hands in the pool. "Jesus' God does not require such sacrifices," she whispered softly to her reflection.

The coolness of the water brought him to mind. All through the heat of his last morning near Tyre Jesus had preached. He had spoken of a new kingdom, with greater urgency than ever before. He spoke to them of men and women leaving their old lives and following him.

"But where is this new kingdom?" Prisca had asked. "Is it beyond Egypt? Farther than Babylon?"

Her question drew snickers from some, but Prisca noticed that they crowded in as eagerly as she for his response.

Jesus had smiled and drawn a deep breath of the clear, warm air. "Have you never made bread, Prisca? In my mother's house the air is fragrant with yeast. A woman takes yeast and mixes it with her flour. Then she must wait until it is all leavened."

"Yes, I have done just that. Until the dough rises, it is useless to bake it, if the bread is to be any good."

Jesus nodded. "Just so the kingdom grows."

Others were clamoring for attention, and Prisca allowed herself to be pushed aside. Was she so ignorant, that his words made no sense to her? Some of his disciples had nodded sagely at his words and cast superior looks in her direction. Well, she would wait until he was free to converse again. Perhaps by then her questions would resolve themselves.

At last bidding farewell to the crowds, Jesus and the disciples headed for a small cove on the shore of the Great Sea, a little north of Tyre, to rest before beginning the trek to their next destination. Prisca and the other women went along.

As they walked along the shore, conversation flowed idly among the followers. As usual, Prisca remained silent. Though she had been among them for several days, men and women alike regarded her with distrust. None save Jesus showed her the friendly concern they exhibited with each other. But for his influence, she was certain they would have cast her out.

Thus she was pleasantly surprised when Jesus' friend Andrew dropped back to walk with her.

"I am surprised you stayed with us the whole week." Andrew's sandy eyebrows and pale blue eyes reflected the whiteness of the sand and sky.

She laughed. "I, too. But each day I learn so much from the teacher that come I must, if only to seek answers to the questions he raises in my breast. I knew nothing of the Jews. At the temple we study the Romans and of course our own Greek history."

"You are a Greek citizen?"

"Greek by birth, but also a Roman citizen, I am told."

Jesus was now far ahead of them, a solitary, striding figure in natural linen dress and shoulder-length brown locks, visible clearly against the stark shore.

Peter, Limaeus, and several others had drifted close enough to hear the exchange between Andrew and Prisca. "When did you become a priestess?" asked Sapphira, a small, dark woman with elongated eyes.

"I do not remember. Our high priestess brought me to Tyre when I was about eight years old." Prisca smiled at her, warming to her friendly tone. She was one who had been most hostile the past days.

"And how many animals have you lain with?"

"*What?*"

"Sapphira!" said Andrew.

Prisca heard a high giggle from Limaeus, palpable silence from the others, as if they were waiting for what she would say.

"Well, it isn't as if we don't know what goes on in those temples!" retorted Sapphira.

"Not in our temple, Sapphira. Perhaps where you were brought up," said Prisca sweetly, controlling her astonishment that one who followed Jesus could behave so cruelly.

"I was brought up in a good Jewish home in Tyre! My father is a Pharisee."

"Oh. Then that is where you learned such bad manners."

"That is where I learned the evil of false gods, Prisca of Artemis! What are you doing around Jesus, anyway? Our rabbis are our own."

"Jesus is only for you?"

"Yes!"

"Perhaps not, Sapphira," said Andrew. "If you go among the crowds, you know that many of those who come to hear him are not of our faith. Watch the Master. I confess that watching what he does teaches me more than his words sometimes. Have you ever seen him send anyone away?"

Prisca flashed Andrew a grateful smile. Sapphira scowled.

"Look at Limaeus," Andrew went on. "Only his mother is Jewish, yet he comes with us."

"Of course he has a lot of growing to do, don't you, Limaeus?" Peter cuffed him playfully.

Limaeus came only to the big fisherman's shoulder. Lowering his head, he punched away at Peter like a small dog attacking a ram. His comic cavorting drew a laugh from the others.

When they reached the cove and moved apart, Limaeus sidled up to Prisca. "Well spoken, Prisca. That woman is a thorn in anybody's side. She's jealous, you know."

Prisca studied Limaeus's face. It had certain feral qualities that made him an unlikely disciple for Jesus. One cannot change one's features, she realized, but strange how faces come to mirror their owners' souls. Sapphira might begrudge Prisca her beauty, but she doubted it. It was more likely that Limaeus himself was jealous that Prisca, who was a woman and a devotee of another religion, had won acceptance by the teacher. Limaeus scurried off to place himself near Peter. Even a cuffing signals some sort of recognition.

As the company rested, she found a place next to the master, a position seldom vacated, so eager were the disciples to be counted first. She smelled the dried sweat of his skin, the sweet-salt warmth radiating from his overheated body. She felt an urge to wipe the dust-caked sweat from the creases in his brow, but felt suddenly self-conscious.

Though they had never spoken of it since she had first said she wanted to be his sister, she felt that Jesus accepted her as such. As she had grown up in the company of women, having known neither father nor brother, she did not know the right way to treat a man who was a brother. Her impulse was to tend him, to be sensitive to his wants as the sisters at the temple were sensitive to each other. At the same time, aware that only Jesus fully accepted her, she did not want to jeopardize that trust. So she did nothing, unwilling even to use these precious moments to prod him for answers. Contentedly, she allowed the closeness and the trust that she experienced every time she drew near him to wash over her like warm winds.

Then Jesus spoke to her. "It is hot enough for a swim, isn't it?"

"Yes, rabbi," she answered. She used the Hebrew word without thinking.

Peter overheard him and jumped to his feet. "I'll swim with you, Jesus!" Two or three others arose and began casting aside their outer garments.

Jesus arose. "Are you coming with me?"

The sounds of the waves of the Great Sea, gentled by offshore reefs, lapped invitingly at their ears. She saw that several of the women were already standing gingerly in the foam of waves, holding their robes above their ankles. Their voices tinkled pleasantly over their shoulders. None of them invited her, by look or gesture, to join them.

She wanted to be one of them so badly she ached to toss caution to the winds. She cast a yearning glance at Jesus. His flashing grin and compelling eyes seemed to be laughing at her, saying, *Why are you so timid, little Prisca?*

Oh, Jesus! Shall I risk offending those who have followed you for nearly three years? Prisca looked away, murmuring, "I saw some nice vegetables just a short walk back. While you swim, I shall buy some for our meal." She fled from his presence before he could dissuade her.

As she walked back toward town, she realized how many times their teacher taught them by asking questions. Probing their hurts, he drew from them their fears and turned them inside out, illuminating them with the goodness of his own nature, forcing their owners to confront them in manageable size.

Several times she had tried to get up courage to confide in Jesus, to ask his advice about the pact between Thyatira and Limaeus. Each day she was with Jesus, she grew more convinced that Limaeus's request was based on falsehood. If he were a true follower of the Master, why would he seek out a priestess of Artemis? When they were with the teacher, Limaeus's watchful eyes missed no interchange between Jesus and his followers and Prisca. Among the brethren, he treated Prisca with careful diffidence.

How could Limaeus justify what, as far as she knew, he still planned to do? Yet she feared to lay the matter before Jesus. None of the others had ever asked such a question. How they would scorn her! Would Jesus, too? She could not bear the thought of being cast away from him.

Prisca looked up as Maya came hobbling along the path. It had grown dark while she had been lost in thought at the pool in the aloe grove.

"Yes, Maya? Are you seeking me?"

"Mistress sent me to find you. You must come and prepare to honor Artemis with your sacrifice."

Honor Artemis! A supplicant wanted her? Now? Then Thyatira would have her vengeance. If Peter and the others knew this, how they would scorn her. Numb with fright, her stomach curdling with horror, Prisca climbed to her feet to obey the summons.

Chapter 6

Maya's words stunned Prisca like a blow to the head. The cool steadiness of her voice surprised her as she said, "Thank you, Maya."

In a daze she followed Maya along the twisted path to the temple, each step crushing a link of kinship with Jesus and the new life that had beckoned. Dreamlike, she took into herself the tales that her sisters had told of this time in their own lives. She herself had helped prepare many of her sisters.

Now it was she who was met at the foot of the temple, who was led into the baths for ritual bathing and application of aromatic oils to her virgin parts, who was ushered to privacy at the small, tapestried altar in the catacombs to purify her thoughts before meeting the supplicant.

Run away! said a struggling voice inside her as she stood immobilized before Artemis, palms cupped outward, head tilted back, damp hair flowing like a dark river past her waist. She was garbed in the finest pale blue silk, girded with a twisted belt of silver, symbols of the sea and the air.

She would not run away. This was her destiny. She willed the tales of the teacher into mist, fables spun by a beguiling young Galilean who promised something that was impossible. This was possible, not that other life. And by giving herself now she would be helping a supplicant to realize a prayer.

Prisca lowered her arms and gazed resolutely at the doorway. Beyond the thick tapestry waited a man who had bought her intercession with Artemis. She parted the curtains.

"You!"

Limaeus grinned. "Couldn't leave without completing my 'sacrifice.'" His glance slid from her to a plump couch. It was draped in heavy silk plush, of the deep blue for which Tyre was famous, inset with red and gold tapestried squares depicting the goddess in her various forms. Candles in a lampstand in the corner guttered over Limaeus's features, revealing a nervous smile.

Fumbling with the fastening on his cloak, he finally unhooked it and waited for her to lift it from his shoulders. He had obtained new garments from somewhere. Prisca wondered where he had come upon the money for tonight and to purchase his clothing. Whenever food had needed to be purchased for the brethren, Limaeus was noticeably absent.

Prisca carried the cloak to a carved chest near the lampstand. He was watching her. Coolly, as if she had done this a thousand times, she laid it on the chest with as much care as if it belonged to a potentate.

"Now what?" Words tumbled out of him. "Do we burn a little incense or something?"

She followed his glance to the shallow bronze dish set over a small brazier beneath the niche where a statue of Artemis watched over them.

"I will light the brazier now if you wish."

Limaeus hooked his thumbs in his girdle. "I wish."

How his manner had ever seemed attractively boyish to her that first day escaped her. Now it was brazenly sacrilegious. He seemed determined to mock every one of her beliefs. She knew herself betrayed by Thyatira. Thyatira could read any man. She knew about men like Limaeus! Why had she accepted his petition?

"This is just a game to you," she burst out.

Limaeus's smug grin vanished. "Well, if you mean do I expect that statue to climb down off the wall and do magic, I don't. If you mean do I expect to get what I paid for, I do."

Prisca turned her back on him and knelt before the form of the goddess, conscious of Limaeus's eyes burning into her back. She felt as if she had been stripped. She struggled to empty her mind of all but Artemis as she took a pair of tongs and drew forth a burning coal from a ready metal box. She dropped the coal in the gleaming dish. From another box she took a pale, dried powder and was about to sprinkle it over the glowing coal when Limaeus seized her wrist.

"What is that stuff?"

"Sandalwood." Waiting, her gray green eyes smoked in shadow, Prisca met his gaze.

"Oh." Limaeus dropped his eyes and stepped back. As she prepared the incense she could hear him removing his girdle and sitting on the couch. "Come and remove my sandals and wash my feet."

Prisca's eyes lifted to the blank stone gaze of the goddess. *Artemis, help me,* she prayed. *Help me get through this night.* She knew intuitively that whatever she did to please Limaeus, he would ask more of her until she refused. And then what? It was comforting to know that her sisters were near.

She did as he asked, then returned to her ritual preparations. As she went through the motions before Artemis, Limaeus vented his impatience

43

by calling out from time to time, "Are you not finished yet?"

Prisca bit her lower lip. No supplicant with a true petition would hurry a priestess. Knowing how false were his beliefs gave her small comfort. At last, reluctantly, she rose in a graceful motion and turned to face him, her palms flat, her fingers crossed at right angles, held loosely below her waist.

Limaeus sat up. She had not realized he had disrobed. She averted her eyes. Sitting cross-legged on the couch, he contemplated her. "Go ahead and look at me. By Mithra you've never been with a man before, have you? Well, have you?"

Prisca's chin lifted. Her eyes flashed as she returned his gaze.

"Come on. What is there to be afraid of? I am just the little man who is the butt of cuffs and jokes!"

Because you see yourself that way. She kept silent. If he knew her thoughts, they would only enrage him. She could not bring herself to speak the words she knew would soothe his vanity.

"Come over here." Limaeus slid off the couch.

Prisca obeyed, willing her heart to cease its frightened thumping. An icy smile settled on her chiseled features. When his hand touched her shoulder, a ripple passed over her skin like a shock of cold water.

Limaeus undid the shoulder clasp of her gown. The silk slipped to the floor with a sound like a sigh. He stepped back and echoed the sigh.

"By Mithra, Prisca, you are the most beautiful woman I have ever seen! Don't be afraid, I won't hurt you. I promise not to hurt you."

O Artemis, Prisca cried out in silent anguish, *what has this to do with reverencing you? Why must the seed of men be cast before you will honor their desires?* As Limaeus explored her with sight and touch, bringing a flood of shame to her face, Prisca kept her eyes on the figure of Artemis. Now she seemed such a cruel mistress. Those sightless eyes, too removed from lives of mere mortals! No god demeaned himself by caring about earthly creatures. Playthings for the gods. She knew that was all she was.

There was neither grace nor beauty nor reverence in the way that he took her. She bit her bottom lip until she swallowed her own blood, yet refused to cry out her betrayal, her pain and shame, her anger at Thyatira and—yes, Artemis, too, for demanding this of her. Those cold, stone, staring, sightless eyes! Suddenly Prisca understood: Artemis saw all she would ever see.

The realization plunged her into profound sadness, pain so deep, so terrible, that the pain of her body was as nothing next to it. She was trembling now, and cold, grieving that she had neither true mother nor father, nor any living kin, and knowing that what she worshiped was nothing but beautiful stone.

Limaeus rolled off the couch and looked down at her. His face was flushed. He wore a triumphant grin. "You'll learn, my girl," he promised.

She turned her face away. This was what Thyatira had promised, too. That she would learn how to please a man and so attract a worthy husband.

He padded across the stone floor and poured them some wine.

Prisca accepted the silver goblet and drank deeply, her hands trembling.

Limaeus returned their goblets to the salver and fetched a fur robe, which he spread over both of them. "Prisca, my adored girl." She did not resist as he gathered her in his arms. "We have the whole night ahead of us. Now I truly do bless your Artemis."

Thyatira left Prisca alone after that night. Jesus and his men were gone. Limaeus had left also, presumably with them.

Spring warmed the lands, causing a riot of wild flowers to carpet the slopes of the mountains on the mainland. Prisca worked at a furious pace, seizing upon the most menial tasks, at which she was unlikely to encounter any of her sisters or Thyatira.

One day Daphne cornered her, working on her knees in the vegetable garden. Her skirts were hiked up about her smooth, muscular calves and tucked in her waistband.

"Prisca?"

"Yes?"

"I have brought you a drink, my sister." Daphne handed her a large goblet.

"Thank you." Prisca tasted the cool barley water flavored with mint. It was refreshing, and she awarded Daphne an appreciative smile.

"We haven't had much chance to talk lately."

"What is it you wish to talk about?" Prisca shaded her eyes against the sun, pulling her veil in a canopy over her brow.

Daphne plumped down on a grassy spot next to the garden and hugged her knees. Her deep blue eyes were large and serious. "Well, we all know how angry Thyatira is with you. I feel as though I am partly responsible."

Thyatira angry at me! You've read it backward, my girl! Prisca sat back on her heels. She smiled at the earnest young face. "That is gossip, Daphne. Evil spirits feed on such talk."

"That is what I wanted to talk about."

"Evil spirits?" She began to work again.

Daphne laughed, pulling off her veil and riffling her fingers through her hair, then becoming serious. "No. . . . Though our sisters do say that something has bewitched you. They say you have forsaken Artemis."

Prisca's fingers stilled in the soil. "Do they?"

For a while, neither said anything. Prisca heard a lark singing sweetly in the aloe grove.

Daphne lay back in the grass and cushioned her head on her hands. "Prisca . . . remember the storyteller?"

Prisca's eyes shot with tears. She averted her face. "Who?"

"The man who was in Tyre last month. The Galilean."

"What about him?"

"Nothing . . . I was just thinking about him. If I hadn't gone with you to hear him that day, maybe all this would not have happened, and things could be like they used to. Only . . . ," Daphne sat up. "Prisca, tell me another of his stories. Tell me again about the farmer."

"About letting the tares grow up with the wheat, so that none of the good seed is lost before the harvest?"

"No, the one about the son who ran away from home and squandered all his inheritance and then the father—oh, you tell it." Daphne selected a long-stemmed weed to suck on and settled herself back to listen.

Prisca smiled, her heart warming as always to this sweet child. "Once upon a time. . . ."

When the tale was finished, Prisca was in a pensive mood. She began weeding again, scarcely aware when Daphne thanked her with a kiss and wandered off.

She supposed Thyatira *was* angry at her.

After Limaeus had left that morning, Prisca had stalked into Thyatira's quarters.

"Give me the purse Limaeus left with you," she demanded.

Thyatira was not ready for the day. Her hair was in disarray. Black smudges of kohl around her eyes suggested that she had gone to her couch after too much wine and spent a restless night. She was clearly not happy to be interrupted in this state by Prisca.

"Was Limaeus satisfied that you did all in your power to convey his prayer to Artemis?"

"Artemis—Artemis!" said Prisca. Her fine brows pulled into a straight line, like the wings of a swooping bird. "You knew what sort of man he was! He has no more belief in Artemis than—than I do!"

Thyatira paled and clutched her robe to her breast. "Prisca, don't. They'll hear you!"

"Who?"

"The gods—the evil ones—who knows? Just don't!"

"I want that money."

"Why?"

"It's mine. I earned it."

"You've changed."

"Isn't that what you intended?"

Suddenly Prisca saw Thyatira in a different light. This was not the high priestess, the surrogate goddess for Artemis. She was a woman like herself, not immortal; no, the gods knew that none were immortal save themselves, and they would go on destroying human lives for all eternity.

She let the anger go out of herself. "May I sit?"

Thyatira nodded.

"You have always said I should be proud that I am a Roman citizen. Who are my parents?"

Thyatira looked shocked.

"I remember coming here when I was young. Where did I come from, Thyatira? Did I come with you as I remember?"

Thyatira's eyes misted with tears. The black kohl gleamed like a blackened eye. She shook her head. "What would you do if I could tell you?"

To keep from crying, Prisca snapped out the words, "Then I am the child of a temple union. I have no family?"

"You have me, Prisca." Thyatira took a step toward her, opening her arms.

Prisca whirled out of the chair. "Is this all I have?"

"This is what you are!"

"I still want the money."

"Then take it!" Thyatira cried. "I have loved you as well as I could. I have seen to your education, your manners. How many other women can converse in six languages? Or even write their own names? Would you rather be herding goats or be one of several wives to a man who beats you when he feels like it?"

"Stop it!"

"In the temple we have freedom, Prisca! Never forget that!"

Thyatira stumbled over a stool in her rush to a large chest. With a curse she threw back the heavy lid. "Here, take it! May it bring you happiness! What else does a woman have beside her body?"

Love! She can have love, Prisca later remembered thinking as she left.

47

She glanced at the sky. Heavy clouds had moved sluggishly in from the Great Sea, pressing her down to insignificance. The shadows of the vegetables had disappeared from the earth. Her pile of weeds looked lifeless already. After her session with Thyatira, Prisca had half expected to be blasted out of existence for her apostasy. When nothing happened, she began to reexamine her position more cautiously.

Thyatira had been right about one thing: It does not do to tempt the gods. She could deny the power of Artemis in her own life, but something made the earth. Something caused the frost to melt, the ground to grow warm and receiving, like a fecund woman. Easy to deny a stone figure. Impossible to deny the order and beauty of the world.

Suddenly the words of Jesus came to her as clearly as if he stood beside her, words spoken on the day he had fed the thousands on the hill. Jesus had said, to all the disciples, that these were gifts such as any loving parents would give their children. If your earthly parent can give such gifts as these, think how much more your Heavenly Father can give you.

"But which heavenly father?" she had asked.

"Blasphemy!" muttered Peter. "There is only one Heavenly Father."

"That proves this woman has no business with us, Lord!" one of the others had said.

How clearly the anger and hostility in their voices came back to her. But how firmly Jesus had always risen to her defense. Jesus. Would she ever see him again? Ever be able to ask him how he was able to feed the people? This feat, as much as his miracles of healing, had thrown her mind in turmoil. True, any person of skill and devotion had healing powers. Many ill people brought to the temple had been healed by Thyatira and the sisters and by herself. But never had she seen anyone command demons to come out of those possessed as he had done for the daughter of the Syro-phenician woman. Or the blind made to see! How could anyone do such astonishing things unless he was sent by a god or was a god himself?

But. . . . No. She must put him out of her mind. When he came back, he would teach her again.

Having won some measure of contentment, Prisca rose to her feet and brushed at the dirt on her hands. She examined the nails. She had ruined a perfectly good manicure, digging weeds. But worth it. Working in the soil always released her mind to roam.

"Prisca!" rasped a high, reedy voice. "I have been seeking you everywhere! You have got to hide me!"

"Limaeus!"

Chapter 7

"**H**ide me! Hide me!"

"Limaeus! What are you doing here?"

"Oh, they are after me, Prisca!" Limaeus seized her hand. His recently new clothes were stained and travel worn. "Haven't you heard what happened? Now they are after all of us, even ones like me, who only listened because he told such good stories. Remember? You liked his stories, too. Everyone knows I was the one who took you. Everyone knows Artemis is my protectress. How could they be after me?" His eyes darted fearfully behind him.

Automatically Prisca glanced about, too. Men were forbidden in this part of the compound. How had he found his way back here? She realized that she would get no coherent account of what was happening until he felt safe.

"Come." She led him back to a small storehouse in the catacombs. "Sit." She pointed him at some sacks of barley stacked against a wall. "Stay here while I fetch some wine." She was back in minutes.

Limaeus drained the goblet and held it out for refilling, wiping his mouth on his sleeve. His face was etched with dust. His reddened eyes betrayed either weeping or nights without sleep. Finally he expelled a long, shuddering sigh.

"Have you heard from any of Jesus' men?"

"No. I have not left the temple for weeks." Her heart soared with hope. "Is he back?"

"They killed him."

"*Killed him?*"

"Jesus."

A cry broke from her lips. "Killed Jesus? He's been killed? His own men?"

"Prisca, don't act stupid! The Jerusalemites, the Romans—what does it matter?"

Prisca fell into a chair. "Killed him! Oh, no!" She broke into sobs.

Limaeus sighed with noisy impatience. "Do you want to know what happened, or don't you?"

Prisca clamped a hand over her mouth and nodded. Fresh tears sheeted down her cheeks.

"Everywhere we went, they knew he was coming, and the mobs came out in force. Every time he healed a sick person, ten more showed up. Even though he begged those he healed to keep quiet! Oh, he knew what would happen. He knew it! I told him he shouldn't heal anyone else, he was scaring people. You could see it in their eyes, Prisca! They'd been around sorcerers before, but Jesus was doing things that were impossible!"

Limaeus rolled his eyes. "And then we went back to Jerusalem. Peter and the others began calling him the Christ, the Son of God, the Jewish Deliverer, the one who had been promised for ages in their sacred writings. By this time, some of the most powerful rabbis in the Temple of Jerusalem were sniffing around—Oh, they did not like it at all, I can tell you!" Limaeus seemed caught in the horror of his recollection and stopped abruptly.

"Please, Limaeus, you must go on!"

"He got arrested. Then they crucified him, like he was nothing but a thief. They were rounding up everyone who followed him." Limaeus kneaded his hands together. "It was always so exciting being around him! He was the center of attention everywhere we went. It was like—like, well, I never was the center of attention before—"

"Limaeus, please!"

A confidential smile twitched at the corner of his mouth. "It was lucky I got out of town."

Prisca stared at him in disbelief. *He left the brethren, when they were in trouble?* "How could you! How could you leave them?" Her mind was numb. Jesus, her friend, her brother. More alive than any person she had ever met.

"I should get killed to show my loyalty?" The sneer on his face told her he considered her dull witted or worse.

"What are you going to do now?" she said automatically.

"Why, stay here with you. The Jews from the temple—Sadducees mostly, but some of the Pharisees, too—they are on a rampage. In every city where he taught they are trying to root out the ones he left behind. Oh, Prisca," Limaeus seized her and tried to cover her with kisses. "I really hope the others got away."

She pushed him away with a cry of revulsion.

"Yes, yes, it's not the time." Rubbing his hands together, he paced with increasing agitation. He halted before a small icon of Artemis and stared up at it. His nervous glance slid to Prisca. "You'll tell them I've been here all the time, won't you? I mean, after all, just because a man's mother is a Jewess and he happens to hear a rabbi, that is, a storyteller, and the man is exposed as a criminal—"

"Limaeus, stop this! You may not stay here. Why should anyone want to kill you, or Peter, or any of the others?"

"Because," his voice spiraled into a high wheedle, "don't you see? Remember the kingdom he was always talking about? Overthrow of the government!"

"But that is not true!" Her heart filled with the poignant memory of how Jesus had explained the kingdom to her. "He said it was like a grain of mustard seed, that when it grew into a tree, the birds made nests in its branches. What could be farther from revolution than that?"

Limaeus didn't answer.

She stared at him thoughtfully. "Is it true that they called him the Jewish Deliverer? Their prophesied One?"

"That is what the brethren said."

Prisca's brow knit in confusion. "But other men killed him, believing he meant to cause a revolt. . . . If he truly did mean to start a revolt among the Jews, then all those who are Jewish who believed in him are in danger."

"That is what I have been telling you, you stupid girl! But not me, I was never one of them. I want you to remember that. I sacrificed to Artemis. I'm not one of them! How was I to know he was a criminal? They can't persecute a man for that, can they? Where are you going?"

"To ask our mother to grant sanctuary."

"Oh, Prisca!" he seized her hand and would have kissed it, but she pulled it away impatiently.

"Not for you. You say you are in no danger. Well, I believe it. The others. Think you they are coming to Tyre?"

"I don't—"

"No matter. I will ask protection for them."

Limaeus sat heavily. His head drooped. "I am more weary than I thought. If I may rest—"

"You may not stay here! I shall not permit it!"

Limaeus looked up at her through his bloodshot eyes. "Just for an hour or two? Then I shall be on my way."

Prisca looked at him coldly. He hunched like a beaten animal. And only a few months ago he'd used the pretense of worshiping Artemis to steal her virginity. She longed to be rid of him, to be alone to grieve for her brother, Jesus. Yet she could not turn away even a cornered animal. "Very well, Limaeus. I will even ask the servants to prepare some food for your journey. On one condition."

Limaeus looked up in surprise. "Condition?"

"That I never have to see you again. Do not seek me even to bid good-bye." She waited for his assent. When he nodded, she said, "Where will you go?"

"So you can tell the others?" A crafty gleam entered his pale blue eyes. "I don't think I'll tell you. Only remember this: I did make an expensive sacrifice to your—to Artemis. I am not one of them. No!"

Suddenly she could stand the sight of him no longer. That men like Limaeus had found Jesus as attractive as she did repelled her. And Jesus had welcomed him!

These confusing thoughts exploded in her head as she ran lightly down the corridor, through the nearly black passage that linked the catacombs with Thyatira's chambers.

Thyatira crowed triumphantly when Prisca burst in to pour out her story. "There, you see, Prisca! Where is your Galilean now? How many people can he heal from Hades? See what happens to someone who challenges the goddess. Oh, I knew it would come to this! Go to her. Down on your knees, Prisca! Beg her forgiveness!"

Prisca fled outside into the lowering afternoon. It was impossible to ask for sanctuary for the brethren. As she could not confront Limaeus again, neither could she face the knowing looks of her sisters. She gave instructions to the servants to provide for Limaeus, then wearily climbed the steps to the altar of Artemis.

Flanked by the stately basalt columns, the inscrutable presence of the goddess towered above her. Slashes of tarnished copper danced across the heavens, in seeming celebration of Artemis's victory.

Was Jesus' death proof of her mighty power? The long shadow of Artemis fell across Prisca, engulfing her own. Had Artemis revenged herself on a man who had challenged her place in heaven?

Her limbs feeling as heavy as clay, Prisca thought of the love Jesus had taught. Not revenge, not hate, not deceit, not adultery. Love, for God, for each other, for oneself. Not fear, not placation through sacrifice, not intimidation. Surely if there was a god, he or she would not be one of a host of beings whose petty jealousies and pranks caused the world to suffer. No. It would be a mighty Being who loved the world, who made it beautiful for its children, who found ways to teach them how to grow toward godliness, who created trees for nesting birds.

Suddenly Prisca began to weep. She threw herself on the rough stone platform and yielded to wrenching sobs that she had repressed before Limaeus and Thyatira. Oblivious to encroaching night, she ached with remembrance of the brief week of glory she had known in the company of Jesus. Desolate. Alone, so alone.

Suddenly Prisca felt a presence near her. She rolled over and sat up. "Thyatira?"

"You did not choose me, but I chose you."

"Jesus!" She scrambled to her feet, scraping the tops of her toes in her eagerness. "Oh, Jesus! I heard you were dead! Where are you?"

"You cannot turn back now, Prisca. I have shown you a new way."

She fell to her knees and wept for joy. "Oh, Jesus. My heart was torn from my body. What shall I do?"

"You came to follow me."

"Yes, yes! Where are you? I cannot see you!"

"Follow me still, gentle Prisca."

"But I have served Artemis. I have—"

"In my Father's house are many mansions. Follow me."

"I will. Oh, I will! I will find the disciples. I will ask them to teach me so that I will be a worthy servant of your God. I—I will follow Artemis no more. . . ."

Prisca passed into a deep sleep. Overhead the stars in the bowl of heaven moved slowly in their ancient paths. She dreamed that twin columns of gossamer pearl radiated from heaven into her breast and back again, transporting her with such love as she had never known.

When Prisca awakened, the wide altar was blazing with sunlight. She was not cold. From where she lay on the warming limestone, her eyes traveled upward to the sweep of the goddess's marble skirts. To the shapely, muscled arm, to the waves of hair that swept and furled behind the noble brow to meet the helmet. To hollow eyes gazing at hollow spaces.

She got to her feet. She crossed to the foot of the pedestal and lay soft, exploring fingers on the sandaled toes of the goddess. Had Artemis ever moved? Had she ever interceded for any of them? Not for poor Althea, certainly. Not for herself, in the base agony forced upon her by Limaeus.

She knelt.

"My blood shall be no more for Artemis," she said softly. "It shall be for Jesus, who somehow lives, who has done such things in the name of his God as have never been done. If it be within the power of Artemis to deny this, let her. I shall worship in her court no more."

"Prisca!"

53

Prisca heard Thyatira hurrying up the steps behind her.

"I never dreamed you would still be here. Daphne told me you did not come to bed last night. I am sorry, my daughter, for my hasty words. I know the storyteller was your friend."

A stillness seized Prisca. She rose to face her.

Thyatira's sleek hair was coiled in a neat bun, her frame girdled in green, over a fresh gown of natural linen. Thyatira looked at her and gasped. "Prisca, your face! What has happened? Are you feverish?"

Prisca laughed. She felt so giddy, so carefree. "It really is true. . . . It really is true!" She felt excitement pounding, bursting within her.

"What is true?"

"Jesus is not dead! Limaeus said they killed him, but he was wrong. He was here last night!"

"Oh, to be young!" Relieved, Thyatira smiled indulgently. "Cares sit upon us for a night and then are gone. Of course he died. Even our slaves know that; they heard it in Tyre. But look at yourself—your robes are wrinkled, your hair is all atangle. Prisca, my daughter," her voice becoming serious, Thyatira tucked her arms in the opposite sleeves of her work dress and paced a few steps away. "Last night I had a dream of evil portent. There is a force abroad that hates the serpent of wisdom. It is connected with the young man who died."

"He did not die," Prisca repeated softly.

"It is an evil force—"

"Then it is no part of Jesus, Thyatira." Her voice sounded euphoric in her ears.

Thyatira looked the length of her aristocratic nose at her rebellious priestess. "Beware, Prisca! Why else would he suck you from the bosom of your Mother in heaven, if he did not serve the one who hates the serpent?"

The girl smiled. Thyatira, who was so wise about so many things, had no notion of the forces that had driven her lately. She had tried to share what Jesus meant to her. Devotion to Artemis paled into insignificance beside the possibilities of life that she beheld when Jesus spoke to her. But Thyatira had listened only with a parent's indulgent ear.

"I am leaving here, Thyatira."

"Oh, Prisca," the older woman caressed her arm lovingly, "can you not serve our goddess here as elsewhere?"

She wanted to sing! She wanted to fling her words in the face of Thyatira. But old bonds of love restrained her. "No, my mother. I am leaving Artemis to you. Oh, come with me! Jesus has shown the way to a new life. He isn't dead, mother! He came to me last night—it wasn't a dream, I swear it wasn't. I have sworn to follow him. I must leave this day. I must find the disciples and tell them that Jesus escaped!"

Thyatira backed up until she stood at the foot of Artemis. She gaped at her in disbelief. "You would really leave? You would deny her now, Prisca? If it is because of that other young man, the dirty one—"

Prisca shook her head, eager to be done with this. "No, no. He no longer matters."

Thyatira compressed her lips. Her face took on a crafty look. She nodded. "Then the least you can do is grant Artemis the dignity of leaving her presence by permission. Will you submit?" What did Thyatira mean, *submit?*

For the first time, Prisca mentally asked Jesus what she should do. She recalled the day he told them how important it was to acknowledge who they believed in. What better way to announce her belief in the God of Jesus than to publicly renounce the goddess of Thyatira? Her breathing grew shallow with fear.

"Yes," she said faintly.

"Very well, Prisca. Let us do it immediately. I would not have you serve Artemis for one moment beyond your desire."

The other priestesses were hastily summoned. Maya and the others who had served long enough to gain some autonomy crowded into the rose garden below. Silently they gaped up at her.

Prisca bit her lip and steeled herself to hear Thyatira intone the ancient chants. As Prisca stood with her back to the towering figure of the goddess, a change came over her. Her fears vanished. She watched the faces of Daphne and the other priestesses and began to pity them.

One by one, at Thyatira's direction, her garments were stripped from her and her hair unbound. These, together with a lock of her hair, were placed in a brass salver. Thyatira doused them with oil of pine. Her lips drew back, exposing her teeth, as she touched it with fire.

A gasp went up in the silence as tongues of flame licked at Prisca's hair and her clothing. The silence grew while everything that had bound Prisca to Artemis crackled and smoked and transformed into ash.

"And so you die," Thyatira said. Without a glance at Prisca, she left the platform. Prisca shuddered for an instant. A curtain of unseen demons hovered just over the finges of her consciousness. But almost immediately she felt warmed by her courage. She straightened her bare shoulders.

One by one the priestesses and servants left, till only Maya and Daphne remained. Over her arms Maya held a cloak. Her eyes were filled with angry tears. Painfully she mounted the steps and threw the cloak around Prisca's naked body.

"Why, Prisca? Who will care about poor old Maya, now that you are leaving?" Tears streamed down her cheeks. Maya turned on her heel and hobbled away.

A brisk wind had risen, flattening the cloak against the proud contours of her young body, causing her unbound hair to stream out from her face. She drew in a welcome draught of pure, fresh air. She glanced at Daphne, who remained uncertainly near the edge of the platform.

"May I come to your chamber?" Daphne asked hesitantly.

"It's yours, too."

"I thought you might want to leave without any good-byes."

"Oh, Daphne!" The two girls embraced and walked arm in arm down the steps. When they reached their living quarters, she saw that Daphne had laid out a cloak and a gown that she had been wearing when she came to the temple last year.

"I'm afraid they are not very good—"

"Yes, they are. They are perfect!" The shift was a pale, virginal blue, with a matching veil embroidered with tiny silver sea gulls. The cloak was nearly new, a dark blue wool that matched Daphne's eyes. Garments that had been purchased for a beloved daughter. Prisca's eyes misted with tears. She said, "When I know where I will be, I will send you a message. I will always want to know that you are all right, and Thyatira, too."

Daphne nodded and swallowed. "Thyatira said to give you this." She withdrew a small parchment scroll from her sleeve. It was tightly rolled and secured with a thong.

"What is it?" She unrolled it. "My citizenship!" Eagerly she scanned the handsomely embellished document. It was signed and dated in Rome. She did not recognize any of the signatures. Disappointed, she retied it and thrust it in the pouch containing her silver shekels. She smiled at Daphne. "Thank her for me."

Daphne nodded, blinking back tears as she watched Prisca tie the drawstrings of the pouch firmly around her waist, next to her skin, then don the garments and tuck her other belongings into a pack.

The two young women embraced again. "Oh, Prisca, I shall miss you! You looked so different this morning. As if you were a different person! I would—I would almost like to go with you, but I am afraid! Tell me where you are going."

"I do not know. I must find Peter and Andrew. If they are not in Galilee, then I shall go to Jerusalem."

"Jerusalem! They do not worship Artemis there. Their God is Jehovah. I have heard terrible things about him." Tears collected on Daphne's lashes.

Prisca smiled. Daphne's heavy lashed eyes swam in tears. She seemed so young! Prisca caressed the curve of her soft cheek. "You have met Jesus. Did he terrify you?"

"Oh, no, Prisca. But he was—"

"No. Not was." A joyous smile radiated on her face. "Jesus is alive!" *And I am finally free to go to him!*

"Alive!" Daphne shrank back, her eyes widening to pools of terror.

"Yes, yes! I tried to tell Thyatira, but she did not understand. It is just as well. That is why I must go to find the disciples. Oh, it is a wonderful beginning!"

At last Prisca raced down the hill. Her limbs weighed no more than the hollow stems of a bird. She felt like singing, laughing, teasing. She could hardly wait to join the disciples. She was a disciple now. Probably one of hundreds of men and women Jesus had called! She laughed. Before, Jesus had only twelve. How would he ask her to serve? To wash the feet of other disciples, as he had done? To garner food from houses of the villages they carried the good news to? Might he let her in due time preach the good news of the kingdom herself? She would do all of this for him—and more!

Chapter 8

Well, well, so you did leave after all."

Prisca whirled. Leaning against a tree not three lengths from the gate she had just passed through was Limaeus, his arms folded across his chest, an insinuating smile on his feral face.

She quickened her pace and passed him without speaking. When Prisca left the temple grounds, she had been thinking that she must engage a suitable servant, or possibly a married couple, strong and adventurous enough to accompany her on her journey.

Limaeus caught up to her and fell in beside her. "You are separating yourself from the protection of Artemis. You have family somewhere?"

Prisca kept her eyes cast down and continued her purposeful stride.

"Hm. You *are* going to join your family! Or is it that you think you can join the disciples?"

"I want to serve where I am needed."

"You are not a servant."

"I will serve the God of Jesus Christ."

"As a priestess or a whore?"

She stopped. "How dare you? I will serve as a—a servant. Like the others who go with him. And—and tell people about Jesus."

"*You?* A woman? And who will listen to you? The goats? The sheep? Or perhaps you will go into Samaria and preach to the swine."

Prisca faced him with a passionate glance. "I *will* join the brethren. I *will* be one of them!"

Limaeus smiled contemptuously. "They will not have you." He turned and walked away.

Prisca compressed her lips in a stubborn line, wanting to curse him for making her aware how vulnerable she was without the cloak of Artemis. She stood in the dusty street and felt clogged with indecision. How tempting to go back to people who loved her. She willed herself to go on. *Find your servants,* she told herself. *It will be better then. People will not take you for a woman alone.*

"Prisca?" called a soft quavery voice.

Glancing around, she spied a small, veiled form tucked in an archway.

"Maya!" she burst out gladly. "What are you doing here?"

Maya smiled tremulously at her from the shadows. A small bundle, neatly tied in a length of coarse linen, rested at her feet.

"I decided to come with you," she announced, retrieving her bundle and marching into the street. "Artemis knows, you need someone to take care of you!" Her bullying tone failed her. Anxiety glimmered in her eyes. "I want to come, Prisca. All my life I've served the goddess. Yet my life seems so empty. Please take me with you."

Prisca gave an exasperated laugh. "Maya—I don't know what to say. I do not even know where I am going! I know for a certainty that the way will be hard."

Maya nodded vigorously. "I'll be a help to you. I will not hold you back. And I've a little money—gifts from the priestesses on feast days. It is all yours, Prisca. . . . You're the only family I have. . . ."

Prisca could see that she was close to tears. *Jesus, what do I do?* she thought. And she thought of Peter's bemused voice saying, "The master says, 'Forbid them not.' " It was Prisca's turn to shrug helplessly and open her arms.

"Oh, thank you!" Maya embraced her with bony ferocity. "I told Daphne you'd take me. I told her I'd not be back!"

Together the women walked the rest of the way into town. First Prisca inquired when a caravan would be traveling through Galilee. Assured that a band of travelers large enough to discourage brigands would be leaving that very afternoon, Prisca purchased provisions, sleeping rugs, and an ass to carry them. Finally they set out.

Several days later word ran through the caravan that they were nearing Cana. Prisca recalled hearing about a wedding in Cana, where Jesus and his mother had been guests. When the celebrants had run out of wine, Jesus had mysteriously provided more from six jars of well water. Eagerly she watched for the village, counting each miniature white block that gleamed in the distance. Herds of goats scattered out of the way as they approached, while they were ignored by flocks of sheep munching fixedly on the tufted slopes. As they neared the village cultivated green fields took on identities of grains and vegetables.

At last they entered the gates and were met by a confusion of squawking fowl, barking dogs, and the rambunctious chatter of children at play. Some women were sitting along a low, whitewashed wall near the well, under the drifting shade of olive trees. The leisurely cadence of their voices blended with the harsher sounds of the marketplace.

They would know more about the goings and comings of the town than anyone, Prisca reasoned and directed her steps to them.

"Good day, women of Cana," she greeted them in Greek. "May I have water for my servant and my ass?" The women looked at her, but no one answered, so she repeated the question in halting Aramaic.

"Why isn't your servant fetching water for you?" a young woman said sharply.

"Esther!" an older woman reproached her gently, her hapless gaze telling Prisca Esther was like that. "Take all you need," she said.

"Thank you." Prisca smiled at her benefactress, noting the fine quality of her dress and the cultured tones of her voice.

Maya dropped the rope of the ass and came to the well. "The lady is right, mistress. You go sit in the shade. I will fetch the water."

"You have had a long day, Maya. I'll get it."

"Please, Prisca," Maya whispered. She seemed so determined to be a good servant before these strangers that Prisca acquiesced.

Prisca waited for the women to invite her to join them. Instead they watched her movements with suspicion. By her accent they knew she was not Jewish. From the minute scrutiny awarded her dress, she guessed they assumed the worst. Ah, well, she was used to that reaction. It was no different from that she had received from the women of Jesus' band.

Yet the hospitality of the Jewish people to strangers was widely known, so she smiled peaceably at the line of women perched on the wall and waited beside the ass for Maya to fetch her water.

Finally the older woman addressed her again, this time in Greek. "Have you come far, lady?"

"From Tyre," she responded.

"I have been to Tyre. My husband, may God rest his soul, was a merchant, and I traveled with him on occasion. It is a beautiful city when the weather is mild, with the harbor filled with ships. You must tell me what it is like these days."

"Gladly. I miss it already. This is my first trip away."

"And are you traveling alone?" The woman switched to Aramaic. The other women were now listening intently.

"Yes," Prisca nodded. She marveled at the subtle way in which the lady, evidently a leader in the community, brought them into the conversation.

"My name is Joanna. I miss those days of travel." Glancing at her friends, she continued, "Cana is not on a frequently traveled route. The few travelers who come are always just passing through."

"I am Prisca, and this is my servant, Maya. I am seeking the people who followed a man named Jesus. He and his mother were once guests at a wedding in these parts."

The women exchanged knowing glances. Prisca wondered if perhaps Jesus was hidden here. She dare not reveal too much.

"Why do you seek them?"

Prisca hesitated. Finally she said, "It is a family matter."

"You know what happened to Mary's boy?"

"I know what they say," she said cautiously. She studied them. Only sadness lingered in their attitudes, no hidden secrets, no exciting news their husbands had forbidden them to tell.

No one spoke for a while. A tiny breeze sprang up and tossed the strands of hair that escaped Prisca's embroidered blue veil. "Does she live in Cana? Can you tell me where she is?"

"She was staying with relatives. Jesus took her with them the last time they were here. But that was long ago."

"That was a dreadful thing to do!" muttered Esther.

"To take her with them? So who else should take care of her?" demanded another.

"Not that. Trouble followed that young man. He should not have put Mary to it."

Prisca noticed Esther's hands. They were oddly gnarled. How painful they looked. One part of her mind automatically wondered why she had not asked Jesus to heal them.

"Yes," agreed one of the others. "Even here there were threats against him. He ought to have known better than to drag his poor mother to Jerusalem."

"He was just a troublemaker," Esther repeated.

Prisca eyed her curiously. "He is a healer. Did no one need healing while he was here?"

"You think I'd let Mary's boy try anything so silly?" retorted the woman.

"He changed water into wine."

"Perhaps he did. I did not see it."

"I have seen him heal," Prisca said gently. When no one responded, she made a conciliatory gesture. "Has anyone heard from—from Mary since?"

The women looked at each other.

"Have any travelers come from Jerusalem with new reports?"

"About Mary?"

"About Jesus." With her heart in her throat she added, "That he escaped."

"Oh, no. He was executed. Came to a bad end, he did. With his poor mother right there watching."

"But he—but he somehow lives," Prisca insisted. She felt their recoil. "Do not be afraid," she implored them.

"*Lives?*" They looked at each other, ill at ease. "There have been stories—"

"Yes, the children. The shepherds grazing the sheep near the caravan route. There have been stories."

"They are true!" Prisca burst out, unable to contain the good news any longer. "That is why I must find his people. But surely they know!" She saw the shock on their friendly faces. Clearly, they did not believe her. Perhaps they even considered her mad. She saw one steal a glance at Maya, with her eyes closed, resting against the bole of a nearby tree. Prisca suppressed a smile. Did she think the servant was her keeper?

"Mary is a good woman," one of them said cautiously. "She's had enough trouble. I hope that she will be all right now."

Of course Mary would be all right. Didn't these women know about Jesus' new kingdom? How much joy was in store for all of them! How did one go about explaining it? Oh, she needed to talk to the disciples. So much needed to be done! She asked, "Is there an inn where we may rest tonight?"

The women glanced at each other uncomfortably. "Those who are not of our faith do not usually ask us for shelter," said Joanna. "But you are traveling alone, and I would like to know more about how you came to know Jesus," she said with a smile that included the other women. "Since I have no husband to consult, I will consult myself and offer you hospitality. Providing you do not bring any foreign food under my roof."

"Oh," Prisca said humbly, "I gladly accept your offer, Joanna, for myself and my servant, and pledge to carry no food of my own under your roof."

"Then—welcome!"

One of the women offered to send over dates and pomegranates for their supper, and Esther surprised Prisca with an offer of fresh goat's milk and cheese and bread.

In the evening, after a plenteous meal shared with the widow, they were joined by several others, all drawn by the delicious aura of mystery surrounding this young, beautiful woman obviously on pilgrimage. By ones and twos they trooped up to the flat rooftop, to catch any particle of breeze from the airless night. Prisca noticed with a smile that Maya stubbornly refused help climbing the steep steps that ran along an outside wall.

"Where did you meet Jesus?" Esther wanted to know when they had all found cushions.

A friend, Prisca started to say, before realizing that was untrue. Limaeus was no friend. But he had done something for her that had changed her life. She would have to think more about that later. "I've always loved to listen to storytellers," she said with a smile.

The women settled in more comfortably, prepared to be entertained. Oh, yes, everyone loves storytellers! Prisca grinned. "The first thing he said was, 'You cannot put new wine in old wineskins—' "

"Yes, he told that at the wedding," said her hostess.

"One day a woman came while he was teaching at Tyre. She was a Syro-phenician, a Greek by birth. The disciples wanted him to send her away," Prisca said. "But she had a daughter who was sick, so she nagged after him like many a woman must do. . . ."

A chorus of knowing chuckles came out of the night from her listeners.

"I've never understood Jesus' answer."

"What did he say?"

"Let the children be satisfied first, it is not right to take the children's bread and throw it to the dogs."

"Hah, that's a good one." Esther stamped her foot. "That proves you are no Jewess."

Joanna patted Prisca's arm. "If you were Jewish, you would have understood Jesus' answer, Prisca of Tyre."

"What does it mean?"

Joanna seemed a little embarrassed. "All Syro-phenicians are dogs. He meant that his teaching was meant for Jews, that is all. I am curious. What did the woman do?"

"She refused to be put aside. Her daughter was ill, and she wasn't leaving until he had done something about it. So she said, 'Sir, even the dogs under the table eat the children's scraps."

"Oh, ho! And what did she get for her saucy words?"

"Jesus laughed, as if he admired her spirit. He said to her, 'For saying that, you may go home content; the unclean spirit has gone out of your daughter.' And it had. She was back the next day to thank him."

A murmur of sympathy arose from her listeners. Yes, when your child is sick, nothing else matters but getting her well again.

"A woman after my own heart," said Joanna.

"He healed her without even seeing the child?" asked one of the women thoughtfully.

"I was there," said Prisca.

"What do you care about Jesus?" said Esther. "He was a Jewish rabbi."

"I promised to follow him," she said simply.

As she did not say more, the women filled the silence with stories of their own, heard from the lips of Jesus when he was a guest at his relatives' wedding. Slowly the realization took root that Jesus could not have been an ordinary man.

Then they were filled with questions. How did he learn so much? Where had he been, to store up such a treasure house of stories?

Something happened during the swift passage of the hot night hours. The women became linked in a strange new way they did not understand. Prisca was tempted to tell them how Jesus had visited her at the altar of Artemis, but was afraid to reveal it. First she must ask the disciples to explain to her how he had come to be there when no one knew he had escaped from Jerusalem. Even to her own ears it seemed a myth of the ancient ones.

When she departed in the morning, Prisca embraced her hostess and then, at the well, each of the other women. In one night she had become closer to them than to some of her sisters at the temple.

Esther grasped her hands in her gnarled clasp. "If only I'd known when he was here—"

"Yes. Surely he would have healed you." She smiled warmly at Esther. Impulsively she kissed the crippled fingers, surprising a wellspring of tears in the other's eyes.

Well refreshed and hopeful, Prisca led Maya in the wake of the caravan through the gates of the city.

Chapter 9

As they neared Jerusalem, several days later, the roads grew thick with travelers. Commercial caravans jostled for preeminence with shepherds guiding flocks numbering in the thousands; lone or small bands of travelers gave way before both; and all stepped aside for the legions of Roman soldiers, which marched with formidable precision wherever they chose to go.

Prisca pulled the ass off the road as they reached the fringes of a knoll covered with olive trees. She glanced around to be sure Maya was following. To her credit, Maya had voiced none of her usual complaints since leaving Tyre. But now she was puffing and red of face, walking gingerly as if her feet were sore. Several other travelers had also sought the shade of the olive grove. As Prisca tethered the ass within reach of a bit of grass, Maya trudged up to untie their waterskin, which was nearly empty.

"Maya, you must rest. I will fetch water." Prisca found a pleasant place among other peasants and unrolled their small rug over a bed of twigs and dry leaves. Straightening, she felt a fragrant breeze brush her cheek and a sense of peace filling her. She smiled contentedly. Then, noticing that other travelers had taken their waterskins and headed down a small decline, she followed them and discovered a much used well.

A heavily bearded man knelt beside her as she refilled the waterskin. She felt his eyes upon her, but kept modestly intent upon her task. Suddenly the slippery, wet, leather bag squirted from her grasp.

"Oh!" She grabbed for it too late and sent it into the well. A moment later she heard the splash as the skin landed in the water. "I shall never get it out of there!" she cried. "How could I be so careless?"

"Allow me to help, mistress," said the man at her side. At the snap of his fingers, a small boy appeared. A rapid command in Arabic and the lad dashed away, to reappear moments later with a fresh waterskin, larger and better made than her own. A further command and the lad filled it and presented it to his master, dripping and glistening.

The man took the skin and dismissed the boy with a curt gesture, as if he were no more than a dog. With a broad, attention-demanding gesture, he offered it to Prisca. "I am Eleazar, lady. How is it that you are drawing your own water?" His heavy jowls folded in a smile, but his thrust-out lower lip imparted a petulant look.

Prisca accepted the water with a gracious smile. "I am Prisca of Tyre. My servant is tired."

Eleazar shifted his bulk and hooked his thumbs in his girdle. "From Tyre with only one servant?" When she nodded, he asked, "How does it come to pass that someone with your beauty and youth is alone? The gods have protected you."

Prisca thanked him distantly, not wishing to encourage his patronage, and picked up her skirts. Carefully she made her way up the incline.

"I can see you are not used to dealing with servants." Eleazar fell in behind her. "They always say they are tired. How much farther are you traveling?"

"Only into Jerusalem."

"Have you been here before?"

She shook her head.

"Come over here." Without waiting for a response, Eleazar put a hand under her elbow and guided her toward a spot where the trees thinned. "Look."

Prisca was so stunned by the familiarity of his gesture that she allowed herself to be drawn. Following his gaze across the valley, she caught her breath. Spires and temples of the city of Jerusalem gleamed whitely in the sun. One huge structure dominated the landscape, a sprawling square with many columns, which seemed to encompass many buildings.

"The fortress of Antonia. Home of the Roman garrison." His voice was carefully noncommital.

"I have noticed a lot of soldiers."

"Aye, lady. Jerusalem is a bit unruly for any governor. Or for lone travelers, for that matter."

She turned to him. "Thank you, but we are not alone; we are meeting friends." She turned away deliberately and retraced her steps to where Maya waited.

"What kept you?" said Maya, relief sharpening her voice.

Prisca merely smiled and sank beside her. Maya produced her little cup. While she filled it, Prisca reflected that whatever else women had to do, it seemed there were always people under their care. She had thought to be alone, with servants who cared no more for her than the extent of their wages. Instead she had Maya, whose care was loyal, personal, and dependent. But she had discovered one also depends upon those one must care for.

"What are you smiling about?"

"I am thinking how glad I am that you are with me. You were right; I do need you."

Maya beamed. "Of course," she said.

What would Jesus think of that? she wondered, and wished he were here so that she might ask him. The disciples would know. Eagerly now, her tiredness forgotten, she rose. "Come, Maya, we are almost there!"

Everywhere, the sounds and colors and excitement filling the air proclaimed a great city. Prisca had never dreamed the existence of any place so sprawling, so immense. She felt her insignificance as they passed the towering columns of the fortress of Antonia, with the golden eagle of imperial Rome emblazoned over each entrance.

A quarter of an hour later they passed a white, marble temple devoid of statues of the Roman and Greek gods and goddesses, a shining, stately, colonnaded edifice that made her poor temple at Tyre seem paltry by comparison. Her eye caught a hand-lettered placard posted high on the side of one of the temple buildings. The Latin words began: JESUS, THE KING WHO NEVER REIGNED, WAS HERE CRUCIFIED FOR PROPHESYING THE DESTRUCTION OF THE TEMPLE.

Prisca gasped. "Maya, halt a moment. I must read this." The proclamation was long. It recorded that the veil in the Jewish Holy of Holies had rent in twain when Jesus died.

"What does it say, mistress?"

Prisca told her, though it meant nothing to either of them. "And it calls Jesus the crucified miracle worker!" How had he managed to fool everyone so completely? Miracle worker he was indeed!

Overwhelmed by the bigness of its buildings and the purposeful hurrying of its citizens, Prisca turned a corner into a narrow street of stark brightness and shadows. A thin slice of sun illumined the shops and vendors on one side of the cobbled street. She slowed to an uncertain halt.

"What shall we do now, mistress?"

"I do not know. I do not know how to find Jesus' disciples."

Suddenly a strong voice rang out with authority, "Make way! Make way for the Egyptian!"

Prisca and Maya pressed against the wall as a gang of cutthroats, surging six abreast, consumed the entire street, striding like limbs of the same menacing animal.

Maya clutched Prisca's arm. "Who are they?"

A peasant guarding his vegetable cart beside them answered, "Assassins. The Egyptian's brigands. He has sworn he has the power to bring down the walls of Jerusalem. If many more join him, maybe he will," he muttered under his breath. "Ruffians, every one." The man wiped his sweating face.

Silently they watched a magnificent chariot rumble by, drawn by a powerful team of horses. The man driving the chariot was garbed in helmet and gauntlets that gleamed like gold in the poor light. Over a short tunic he wore a wide leather collar studded with nuggets and jewels. His face was large, with gross, protuberant features, a picture of licentiousness and cruelty.

The Egyptian's eyes seemed bent on the road ahead. Suddenly the elephantine head swiveled. His heavy-lidded eyes met Prisca's. His bold glance pinioned her. Prisca covered her face with her veil and shrank back until they were swallowed in the crowd.

"Herod should've murdered him instead of Jesus," the vegetable seller hissed under his breath. "Would've made more sense."

The women stared at him in amazement. "Do you know about Jesus?" asked Prisca.

The clangor and shouting of the Egyptian and his assassins faded, and the normal street noises filled in the silence.

Suddenly the man shifted his whole attention to them. "You're not part of them, are you?"

"Part of who?" demanded Maya.

The man shifted without answering.

"We are friends of Jesus," said Prisca. "We are seeking his disciples."

"Huh! As if any true Anointed One would let himself get executed!"

"What is that?"

"Nothing. Better not look here, lady. There's a price on their heads. Two of 'em got arrested."

"Who?"

He shook his head. "Look, I got to sell my vegetables now, or my wife will have at my head with a cheese."

"Please, sir!" Prisca gave him a pleading smile. "Please. Isn't there, somewhere, someone who can help us? I must find his disciples."

The man's eyes scoured her face distrustfully, as if he had been taken in one too many times.

"He is my brother."

Reluctantly the man nodded. "I know of a man named Andrew. They say some of them still meet in his lodgings."

The vegetable seller gave them directions and put his shoulder to the handles of his cart. Maya peered after him with an anxious expression, then glanced at Prisca. "I did not want to speak out in front of him, mistress, but that other man—that Egyptian—the way he looked at you—"

"What about him?" said Prisca, her mind intent on remembering the vegetable seller's directions.

"He's been to our temple, yes, it was him, mind. I saw him. And he saw you. Thyatira wouldn't let him, well, you know—"

Prisca glanced scornfully at Maya. "Stop it at once, Maya. It must have been another. Leave the shades to their own undoing."

Ignoring Maya's *tch-tch*ing behind her, Prisca seized the ass's halter and set off. The end of an hour found them in yet another of a seemingly endless maze of narrow streets, this one with small shops facing the street and added floors above. They stopped where sunlight knifed across a flight of stairs between the plastered walls of two shops. Prisca was certain she had found the right place. She cast about for a place where Maya might rest, and where she could tether the ass with safety.

A fruit seller across the street did not appear busy. Perhaps he would—

"Do not worry about me," said Maya, as if reading her mind. "I am perfectly capable of taking care of myself."

Prisca looked at her in surprise. In truth, since leaving Tyre, Maya had grown steadily more aggressive. There was surprising assurance in her voice, now that they were actually in Jerusalem. Prisca smiled. "Very well. I shall look for you in this street when I have talked with the disciples."

Prisca turned and made her way up the stairs. She heard voices on the other side of a heavy door. Her heart leaped. Perhaps Jesus was here now! Eagerly she knocked. The voices ceased. She knocked again.

"Andrew?" she called with soft urgency. "Andrew, if you are there please answer. It is Prisca of Tyre." She heard shuffling, muffled voices. The door creaked open.

Suddenly it was flung wide. She was pulled inside and the door quickly shut. "Prisca!"

"Andrew!" she said with a glad cry. His familiar sandy beard and pale blue eyes were the most welcome sight in the world.

"What are you doing here?" he exclaimed.

Peter loomed up darkly beside Andrew, nearly a head taller and a handspan broader. A worried scowl clouded his bearded face.

Ignoring the scowl, she exclaimed, "Peter! Oh, it is so good to see you, all of you. I could no longer stay in Tyre. Jesus has changed my life. He brought me here safely to you." She gazed expectantly around the room.

No one had clasped her outstretched hands. A nervous embarrassment etched the faces, shrouding something else, something. . . . "I—I heard that some of the brethren were arrested," she faltered. It was then she identified the palpable feeling in the room. Fear. Fear! Not of her, surely! She gazed in astonishment at the ring of scared faces crowding in among the disciples. Some she recognized. Many she did not.

Peter's low voice rumbled, "John and I were detained. They have just let us go. How long we are safe no one knows. How did you find us? What are you doing in Jerusalem?"

"I told you. Jesus brought me."

"You don't belong here. Go back to Tyre," Peter said roughly.

"Now wait, Peter," said a man of about forty years with a handsome thatch of curly, gray hair. He took Prisca's hand and led her to a place along one of the long walls of the spacious loft. His touch was rough and dry, yet gentle. "I am called Barnabas, lady. Welcome in the name of Jesus."

Barnabas smiled reassuringly. He was a large man, and fit. "Will someone please fetch her a sip of wine?"

She flashed him a grateful smile. He seemed a calm, take-charge sort, rather like a father or an elder brother to the young disciples.

It was Sapphira who brought the wine. Prisca recognized her immediately, the long, lynxed-eyed watchfulness, the narrow, distrusting face. Meeting her eyes over the rim of the wine cup as Sapphira swayed toward her, she remembered how in Tyre Sapphira had seethed with hostility toward her whenever Jesus was out of earshot.

"Thank you." Prisca's hand was shaking from fatigue as she accepted the wine.

Sapphira released the goblet as if it burned her fingers and retreated, arms gripped tightly across her chest, to stand among a group of other women. There were perhaps thirty or forty men and women in the room. They appeared uneasy, casting frequent glances at the door or peering discreetly out the narrow window facing the street. Cushions and small rugs were scattered about the floor. She saw the remains of a meal piled on a large trencher in one corner. Prisca had the impression she had interrupted a vital meeting. No one had yet invited her to sit.

Barnabas leaned against a wall that was peeling and badly in need of fresh whitewash. He read her face with an open, almost eager smile. "So you know some of the brethren. Tell me, now, who you are and why you felt you had to come here to us."

"Gladly, my lord. I am Prisca of Tyre. I was a priestess of Artemis until

Jesus called me to serve him." She gazed earnestly at Barnabas. "I must find him! He—"

"A priestess of Artemis!" shrieked a high, shrill voice. The next thing Prisca knew, an enormous woman barged through the clustered women-folk and barreled straight at her. "I'll show you!" Her little button eyes shot bolts of venom ahead of her.

Prisca blanched. For all her size, the woman was too quick for Barnabas. Reaching Prisca, she seized her veil and shoved her to the floor, at the same time swatting the wine to the floorboards, where it spilled in a shower of red drops. She landed a kick on Prisca's thigh before anyone realized what was happening. "Heathen! Pagan! Get out of here! Oh, sacrilege!"

Barnabas threw himself at her. "Easy, Jedidah! Andrew! Mary!" By the time they subdued Jedidah, Prisca was struggling to her feet. She felt Barnabas's strong hands under her arms. "Did she hurt you? I'm sorry, Prisca. It has nothing to do with you. Jedidah's husband was killed in one of the riots after Jesus' death. We all feel her sorrow."

You should feel her kick! thought Prisca, resisting the temptation to rub her injured leg.

"It's sacrilege that she is here," Jedidah cried over her shoulder as Andrew and Mary led her to the open arms of one of the other women.

"I am here because Jesus wishes it!" Prisca flung after her. She could not help noticing the pleased, sarcastic smile on Sapphira's face. Prisca felt her fingers itch. She lifted her head smartly and refastened her veil with trembling fingers.

"Listen to me!" she cried to them. "I do not know why you are so fearful or why you distrust me. Don't you know that Jesus is not dead? He came to me a week after—afterward. I could not see him in the darkness, but I heard his voice, and I felt his presence. He told me to follow him. That is why I am here. He told me to follow him. . . ."

An uneasy silence filled the room.

"Didn't you hear me? He is not dead! I don't know how; I don't understand what is happening; I only know that—"

"Yes, we know, Prisca," Peter cut in. "You are right, he is not dead."

"I think you should tell her, Peter," said Barnabas. Andrew nodded.

Peter drew a great, shuddering breath. His huge hands clenched and unclenched. "Jesus did die, make no mistake. We all saw him die. They took him down. . . . I helped to pry the nails out of his hands. Yes, he was dead. . . ."

Prisca stared at them, stunned with sorrow and confusion. He actually died? Then who visited her?

"When they put him in the tomb," said a small, dark woman with sensual, almond-colored eyes, "we went to prepare ointment and spices for the body. Then it was the sabbath, and we could not return until the first day of the week. When we went back to the tomb, someone had rolled the stone away. Jesus was gone, but there were two—," the woman paused and lifted her palms expressively, "radiant beings inside. 'Why do you seek the dead among the living?' they said."

"Mary Magdalene came and told us. We did not believe her." The disciple called John, a man with fine, pale hair and fair skin, took up the account.

"We thought it was an idle women's tale," added Peter.

"I confess I was never so frightened in my life," said Mary Magdalene. "We thought at first someone had taken his body—"

"Alive!" cried Prisca. "He was dead and is alive!" She lifted her arms in the air. "O Jesus!" She found that she was laughing and crying at the same time. The enormity of it stunned her. "I cannot believe it! And yet it is true! I know it is true, because I heard his voice! Oh, praise his name! Praise his God. The only God!"

Cautious smiles began to appear on the faces of the others.

"Where is he?"

"We do not know," Peter said reluctantly. "He told Mary Magdalene that we should wait for him here. He came to us that same evening. He was the same, yet different. He said that soon he must leave us again, but that he would not leave without sending us a Counselor in the Spirit. The Twelve must stay together until the Spirit comes. That is why we are risking our lives remaining in one place. But you cannot stay here."

"I must! I want to be with you! He told me—"

Peter was shaking his head. "It is impossible," he said with finality. "You say he came to you. Well, the Master ever had a soft spot for lost souls."

"But—"

"She isn't even Jewish!" muttered the woman Jedidah.

She heard the words in shocked silence. By their compassionate expressions most of them sympathized with her. She cast an urgent glance at Peter, at Andrew, imploring them to her defense. "But Jesus said—"

"Anyone could listen to him," Andrew said reasonably, his mild blue eyes asking her to understand. "He wouldn't turn anyone away."

"You could not possibly understand what this means," Peter said vehemently. "Jesus has conquered death itself! Through the ages our prophets,

Elijah and Ezekiel, Isaiah and Moses, foretold the coming of such a man, a Messiah. *Jesus is that man!* We are the most fortunate of men! He came back to us!" Peter shook his trunklike arms in the air. "What could an outsider like you possibly understand of that?"

"Peter," said Andrew, scratching his sandy beard, "perhaps she could remain with us. We could teach her—"

"Oh, yes! Teach me how to be a disciple!"

"A woman disciple!" came a man's scandalized voice. "Who would believe a woman?"

"Have you lost your senses?" shrieked Sapphira. "She's a foreigner, a priestess of a pagan cult! She'd bed you all in no time and have you worshiping Artemis!"

"I have renounced Artemis," cried Prisca. "Jesus has called me. I must do his will!"

"Then do it somewhere else!" came Jedidah's voice, joining that of Sapphira. Again no one gainsaid her.

Prisca pressed her palms into the burning sockets of her eyes. It could not be. The disciples, Jesus' beloved, were turning her away. She cried out in anguish, "Will no one hear me?"

One by one, the disciples and the women turned away from her, suddenly busy elsewhere, until only Andrew and Barnabas remained by her side. She felt the support of Barnabas's arm against her back, moving her inexorably toward the door. A roaring sound filled her ears. What would she do? Where could she go?

A vision of Thyatira's strong, aquiline face floated before her. Thyatira would welcome her back, an errant daughter returning to the fold, an example to other young women of the folly of turning away from the goddess. She had enough money—

"Where will you go, Prisca of Tyre?" Andrew's words cut through the roar.

Mechanically her fingers clutched for her cloak. Andrew draped it about her shoulders. Tilting her chin up, she said, "Do not worry. Jesus will not abandon me."

Peter turned swiftly and gazed at her. A puzzled frown struggled over his features. "Do you have enough money to get back?"

She nodded, not trusting herself with words.

"God bless you," he said reluctantly.

"May Jesus the Christ be with us all," she replied.

The brethren stared at her in disbelief. Mary Magdalene lifted a hand as if to stop her, but said nothing. Slowly Prisca turned and forced herself to retreat through the door, away from the presence of those with whom she most wanted to be in all the world. As the door closed behind her she heard their voices: "Do you think Jesus could have—? No! A foreigner? But he could have—Impossible! Already the devils are stirring against us!"

Chapter 10

Sounds from the street rushed up at her, sharply fragmented. Each step downward brought closer the nausea of isolation in a hostile city where Jesus had been executed as a criminal. The weight of her separation from life was like a force that threatened to suffocate her. At last her sandals met the rough stones of the street.

"You should have known better than to come," said a calm, cynical voice. She looked behind her. The woman called Mary Magdalene had followed her out of the room and down to the street. She was half a head shorter than Prisca, with a straight-shouldered, fearless look about her. Her veil was black. The beautiful almond eyes gazed pitilessly at her.

"Has your love for the Christ melted so quickly?"

"What do you mean?"

"Peter asked if you had money to get back. You nodded."

A half smile curled on Prisca's lips. "I have money. That is why I nodded. I will never go back."

Mary Magdalene smiled again, but her cynicism had vanished. "We are not so different, Prisca of Tyre. But I am truly amazed that a priestess of Artemis can be so childlike."

"Childlike!"

"Of course. Did you not hear the men? Mary the mother of James and I first saw the empty tomb and the radiant messengers. Did the brethren believe us? No. They had to go and see for themselves, hear for themselves. They still do not understand that if Jesus chose to reveal himself to women he was saying that women are equal carriers of the good news."

"But if you know this, why are you still with them?"

Mary laughed freely, with a heartiness usually reserved for the opposite sex. "Oh, my. Men are all the same, Prisca, and you are too naive to know it! You are all feeling and no business sense. To leave the disciples in anger and defiance, hugging my bright memories, will not bring men and women to Jesus, will it? There are other ways—"

"If you mean to continue letting my body be used for Artemis—!"

"Oh, la, no." Mary's eyes gleamed. "Although that probably still bothers the disciples. Women can be influential behind the scenes, as they have

75

always been. It may be easiest to persuade a man in bed, when he is at his weakest, but soft answers, gentle persuasion, and good food win for us what our weaker bodies cannot." Mary placed a consoling hand on Prisca's arm. Unexpectedly her grip tightened. "Our bodies are weak, but our wills can be like the continuous drip of water that melts the stone." Their eyes locked and held.

Prisca nodded. "Thank you, Mary. I will remember. I will be strong. I will serve our Lord."

She heard footsteps pounding down the stairs behind them, then Barnabas was bending anxiously over them. Mary stepped back and pulled her veil down discreetly over her brow.

Barnabas threw Mary a worried grimace. "Thank God you stopped her. Have you anyone with you, Prisca?"

"Oh, yes," with a great effort she mustered a smile. "Thank you for your kindness, Barnabas." More than kindness. His mere presence was comforting, as if a flow of strength were passing from him to her. Her lips parted. She waited for what he would say.

Barnabas glanced around, as if ashamed he might be overheard, and said, "Prisca, there is a temple here to Artemis. Perhaps you should go there. They would take you in. It isn't safe on the streets alone. . . ."

Prisca pulled herself to her full height. Blinking rapidly, she averted her face to hide her tears. She was not surprised at the flicker of amusement in Mary's eyes. "I thought you understood," she said with dignity, not looking at Barnabas. "There is no turning back for me. I must go now. My servant is expecting me." She looked around for Maya.

Mary nodded and silently returned upstairs.

The minutes passed. Passersby jostled them. Her feet seemed bonded to the street. In the middle of the road men cursed beasts struggling under monstrous loads, urging them to move faster. Barnabas seemed unwilling to leave her, staring at her as if struggling within himself.

At length he said, "I arrived in Jerusalem after the Master was crucified. I first heard him nearly three years ago. Since then, every time I heard he was teaching where my business took me, I went to listen. When I learned he had been arrested, I came here, hoping to be of some use." He shook his head, as if at the apparent uselessness of it all.

"For three years you heard him. . . ." The pain of her loss knifed through her breast. Still Barnabas was there, standing quietly beside her, so she said, "What will you do now?"

"Go back to Cyprus. My home is there. The disciples are in a bad way,

Prisca." As if entertained by a new thought, Barnabas grinned suddenly, his weathered face creasing around the eyes as he watched the often comical battles between man and beast before them. "I think some of the Master's followers thought the kingdom that was coming would make them all rich. Oh, not now. . . . No, those men did not stay. Still, these who are left have given up everything because of the Master. They are disorganized, and frightened, and—" Suddenly their eyes met. "Why am I telling you this?"

Prisca smiled and shrugged.

"I had some small property here in Jerusalem. I sold that and gave the disciples the money." His eyes assessed her shrewdly. "You have given up everything, too, I wager. What will you live on?"

Maya's voice cut in before she could answer.

"There you are! I have found us a place to lodge tonight. I did not pay him yet, mind, but he promised to save room for us." Maya joined them with pride evident in each jaunty step.

"Where is our ass?"

"Tethered in his courtyard. The keeper promised to watch over him. It was the most amazing thing, mistress—"

"Barnabas, this is Maya, my servant and my friend."

"And also a follower of our Lord?"

Prisca looked at Maya in confusion. "No," she said quickly.

"I am not without my loyalties," said Maya with dignity.

Barnabas nodded. "Honestly spoken." He turned back to Prisca and said briskly, "Well then. By your words, you have no family. I would offer you and your servant the hospitality of my home on the island of Cyprus. My wife is dead, but one of my sisters and my children, and my nephew, Mark, abide with me."

Maya cast a frightened look at Prisca, her self-assurance suddenly eroding.

"It is a day's journey to the coast and two days or more by ship, depending on the winds," Barnabas continued.

Prisca thought quickly. She had no trade. She must not put herself on anyone's mercy. Yet where would she go? What could she do? With Barnabas perhaps she could learn more about Jesus. Who was the man Jesus? Why was it so important that her life be linked with his? What did he want of her that his disciples could not do far more easily? Or Mary Magdalene and the other women with them, for that matter? They were even Jewish! She gazed searchingly at the man before her. She sensed a certain reserve in him, a man whose will controlled his emotions. He met her scrutiny with the open gaze of a businessman with a deservedly honest reputation.

"I have no experience at such important decisions, Barnabas. How does one decide if a decision is good?"

"Ask the Lord to know, and it will be given to you. If Jesus has called you, then you must follow him, as must we all. Do not worry if you do not see your way clearly yet. He sent you to the disciples. Though I am not one of the Twelve, this may be the way he has intended."

"Where is Mary, his mother?" she asked suddenly. "I heard that she was with him when—when it happened."

"Jesus asked John to take her in his care. She is with his family now. Did you wish to see her?"

Prisca shook her head. "Only to know that she is well. It is hard to be alone."

Barnabas nodded. "She is well."

"Maya and I will rest the night in Jerusalem, and I shall pray as you have said. On the morrow I will answer you." She took his hand—how dry and clean it felt!—and would have pressed it to her lips. "If it be the will of Jesus' Father in Heaven, I will accompany you, Barnabas."

Smiling easily, Barnabas disengaged his hand. "Hold, young lady, I am not your master, only a brother in Christ."

Barnabas insisted on escorting them to the gate of the courtyard where Maya had found lodgings and promised to return the next morning.

"It was the most surprising coincidence," Maya began as a servant answered her ring and admitted them to the courtyard.

Prisca's eyes swept the courtyard. "This does not look like an inn," she said doubtfully.

"Oh, indeed not!" Maya declared. "That is what I was going to tell you. A gentleman approached me on the street and said he had met you in the olive grove. He said he would be *honored*, Prisca, if we accepted his hospitality. He seemed to know all about us! Well, of course, I was most happy to accept. You know," Maya's face grew brightly confidential, "I did not want to say this in front of your Jesus friend, but do not you feel that Artemis is watching over us? Our host worships our dear lady Artemis, too."

Prisca felt suddenly wary. "Who is our host, and how does he know about us?" Seeing her companion's guilty expression, she said, "You did not tell him that we are from the temple! Do I have to beat it into you? I have forsworn all to do with the temple!"

Maya blanched at the harsh words. "I only thought that—"

"Let us be gone at once!"

"I would not hear of it, my dear lady," rumbled a voice behind her.

Prisca turned, immediately recognizing Eleazar and the edge of threat in his voice. He was no taller than she, but she felt the menace of his bulk as he leaned toward them. His lower lip glistened moistly.

"I knew when I met you that you were not an ordinary person."

Maya had recovered her dignity and now said loftily, "I told him who you were, my lady."

"Maya, you are a fool!" she cried angrily.

Maya recoiled as if Prisca might strike her.

To Eleazar Prisca drew herself up haughtily to cover her quaking vulnerability. "You are mistaken, sir. I am no longer a priestess. I am quite ordinary. I follow the God of Jesus."

"You are not a Jewess," he said. The jovial smile did nothing to hide the cruel greediness of his eyes.

"No. We must leave now. Thank you for taking care of my woman."

Eleazar shrugged. "I am a practical man," he said smoothly. "A businessman. You are here on business, I understand. Well, you and I may have business to transact."

"You are misinformed. As you showed me in the olive grove, it is foolish to treat one's servants well. They are untrustworthy!"

Tears started in Maya's eyes, and to her own irritation, Prisca felt ashamed of herself. How to get away from this man? Their beast was nowhere in sight. No matter. All they need do was go out the gate again and leave the ass. They could survive until tomorrow, and then Barnabas would help them.

As if he had read her mind, Eleazar moved casually over and leaned against the gate, which was now closed, Prisca realized with a start. When had someone closed it? She felt trapped.

"Why don't you refresh yourselves?" Eleazar was saying. "My servants have prepared rooms for you. And then, Prisca of Tyre, you shall be my guest for supper."

"You are most gracious, but we cannot stay. You will please open the gate."

"We will talk about that at supper, shall we?"

She could hear Artemis laughing. A woman alone, indeed!

No! The God of Jesus would not abandon her. Prisca stared coolly at
Eleazar. "Your servant may show us our rooms."

A few minutes later, she and Maya found themselves alone in a large
room with a balcony. Square grilles of plaster openwork concealed occu-
pants of the balcony from the prying eyes of anyone below, while permit-
ting them a view of the courtyard and, beyond the high fitted stone wall,
a narrow length of the street. Prisca could hear a servant noisily busy right
outside their door. As if they needed a reminder that they were being
detained. She looked at Maya.

Maya started to wail and tear at her hair. "Oh, mistress! How was I to
know he was an evil man? I only thought that if I told them who you
were, he would respect us! Back home, no one would harm—"

"We are not 'back home,' as you say, and I am not a priestess." Prisca
watched her unsympathetically.

When Maya saw that Prisca was not going to prevent her from pulling
out her hair, she stopped. "Hmp," she muttered. Then she set about
rearranging her toilet. "Now we shall have to think of something."

Prisca had to smile, feeling suddenly lighthearted. "Yes, we shall." If
the God of Jesus had not abandoned them, then there must be a way out
of their predicament. They need only be quick-witted enough to find it.

"Not angry with me?"

"No. Jesus says we must forgive seven times seven."

"I need to learn more about him."

"We both do."

A discreet tap at their door caused the women to turn. Unbidden, a
servant entered, carrying their bundles from the ass's pack.

"Well, all the gall isn't in the geese!" sputtered Maya.

"Sh," said Prisca. "Good servant—"

The boy stopped near the door. "Yes, mistress?"

"Are you not the one who gave me water in the olive grove?"

"Yes, mistress." A smile split his dark, thin face.

"I had no chance to thank you. What is your name?"

"Obed, mistress."

"It was kind of you, Obed. Tell me now, at what hour does your master
utter devotions to his god?"

"At no hour, mistress."

"He does not devote himself to any god?"

"Oh, yes, mistress, to all of them! The gods serve his convenience, he
says. If there is a particular hour at which you wish devotions, I will tell

him for you," he said eagerly.

"No. Thank you. You may leave us."

"Prisca, what are you going to do?"

"See what is in that flagon, Maya. I am thirsty."

Maya poured each of them a goblet of sparkling red liquid. She tasted it. "Juice of the pomegranate," she pronounced. "Not as good as we make at—in Tyre, but not undrinkable." She brought a cup to Prisca, who had found a large sheepskin cushion and lugged it out to the balcony.

Settling upon it cross-legged, she accepted the drink and gazed thoughtfully out through the grille. "I wonder if our host is in the business of robbing people?"

"A robber?" said Maya, horrified.

"Why else might a businessman befriend two lone women?"

"Out of respect for the weaker sex."

Prisca smiled, remembering Mary Magdalene's words. "A businessman to whom all the gods are a 'convenience'?" She twisted round to look up at Maya. "He does not sound like the noble sort, Maya. I recall some of the petitioners at the temple. Some came unwilling to part with their money, unless Thyatira could guarantee that their petitions would be satisfied. This Eleazar is like that. He wants something for his money, be certain of that."

Maya knelt beside her, self-reproach in her eyes. "Oh, Prisca, do not lie with him. He may want to make a petition before Artemis, but now I do not trust him. I doubt he would let us go, even if he promised."

"Truly. I do not plan to lie with him, Maya. I am thinking of something Jesus told us. As Eleazar has done unto others, so it shall be done unto him."

"You will rob him?"

"In a manner of speaking." Prisca drew a coin from her pouch. Rising, she crossed to the door and summoned Obed. Giving him the coin, she asked, "Are you free to run an errand for me?"

"Yes, mistress."

"Find the man they call the Egyptian."

The boy's eyes widened. "Mistress?"

"He is probably to be found near the street of the Jewish temple. Tell him the high priestess sends him greetings from Tyre and that her emissary is briefly detained. Can you remember that, Obed?"

"Yes, mistress."

She had him repeat the message, then smiled and tousled his dirty hair.

"When you return, tell me what he says."

Obed clutched his coin and darted out the door. Prisca looked at Maya. "Gather your things."

"Prisca, what on earth are you doing?"

"Now, Maya, try to think like a man used to tricking people. Would you allow your servant to carry a message unless you knew what it contained?"

"By the gods, of course not!"

"And what do you suppose Eleazar will think when he believes he is interfering with friends of that dreadful person, the Egyptian?"

Before Maya had time to frame an answer, a vigorous knocking sounded upon the door. This time it was an old housewoman, badly frightened.

"My master begs me to tell you that he was suddenly called away. He is sorry that he may not offer the hospitality of his house any longer, but begs you to realize it would be immoral for him to offer protection when he himself is not here to ensure it. Please prepare to leave immediately. Your beast has been fed and watered, and a basket of food has been prepared for yourselves."

Prisca thanked her gravely and shut the door before turning gleeful eyes upon Maya.

"Mistress, we are playing with fire!"

"This time, you are right. Quickly, before Eleazar decides to use his brain!"

"How did you know he would let us go?" hissed Maya as they threw together their bundles and hastened down the steps.

The house appeared empty, but Prisca could feel eyes watching them as they crossed the courtyard with a swift stride. Was Eleazar, too, hiding somewhere? The ass was waiting, as the housemaid had said, just inside Eleazar's gate.

"Hold these." Prisca shoved her bundles at Maya. She untied the beast's halter and tugged. "Oh, hurry, you cursed son of a satyr!"

"What will we do if he finds out you've tricked him?" Maya cast anxious eyes over her shoulder as the ass clopped unhurriedly through the gates. Maya staggered behind with her load.

"Can't you think of anything better to think about?" Hadn't Jesus' God shown her how they could escape? Breathing her thanks, she vowed to burn incense for him, before recalling that Jesus had told her such sacrifices were unpleasing to him. She concentrated on trying to remember how they had entered the maze of streets and finally, after several mis-turns, saw in the distance the Jewish temple and beyond that the fortress of Antonia. "There!" she cried in relief. "By the fortress is the gate we entered. Do you think that you could find your way back again to Eleazar's?"

"Me?"

"Yes. Tomorrow. To fetch Barnabas when he comes for us. You need not go all the way, but place yourself near a shop or a peddler where you can watch his gate," adding to herself, *And where, please God, you will be safe.*

Maya looked doubtful but resigned. "Where shall I bring him, mistress?"

Prisca hugged her. "To the olive grove."

They spent the night in the olive grove, in the company of several families traveling from Hebron. While it was still dark Prisca was awakened by a throbbing pain in her hip. She climbed to her feet and hobbled around to ease the stiffness, trying not to think vile thoughts about that bad-tempered cow Jedidah, who had kicked her. Finally she pulled biscuits and fruit from their pack and awakened Maya.

When they had eaten and she had done her best to shore up Maya's courage, which seemed to have stolen away with the night, Prisca wandered over to the promontory and gazed at the gleaming limestone fortress of Antonia. She tried to pick out the corner of the temple where she had read of "Jesus, the crucified miracle worker," and to imagine the locations of the streets she and Maya had wandered after escaping from Eleazar. How much had happened in one short day!

"God of my brother Jesus," she said softly, "thank you for showing us the way out of Eleazar's house." She felt, somehow, that Jesus himself was nearby. That if she turned, she would see him waiting with her for Barnabas. Her heart filled with joy. The disciples might reject her, but Jesus had not! She waited now with renewed confidence, eager for their journey to begin.

Chapter 11

That day Prisca became part of Barnabas's caravan. Once Maya brought their benefactor safely to the olive grove, the former priestess ceased to be afraid. Down the western hills from Jerusalem to the port city of Joppa they walked, the caravan proceeding at a leisurely but steady pace. In Joppa, Barnabas sold the ass that Prisca had bought in Tyre. She tried to refuse the profits, declaring it should go for her and Maya's passage. Barnabas would have none of it. "If you will be in Jesus' service, you'll need that and more," he told her.

A Greek merchantman riding at anchor waited to carry them to Cyprus. The first thing to catch Prisca's eye was an eye painted on the prow of the ship, just below the deck—an elongate eye, with blue iris and black pupil, to help the ship see its way safely across the sea. The ship was rounded rather than sleek in design. From a centered position, slightly to the stern of midship, rose a mast that was nearly as long as the ship. It supported a yard so wide that the ends of the beam extended beyond the sides of the vessel. A rectangular sail was furled along the length of the yard.

"Looks precious small to me," whispered Maya, before Barnabas took Prisca's arm and escorted her across the plank that had been laid from dock to deck. Maya hurried after them, helped by a youthful seaman.

Prisca stepped aboard in delighted fascination. She had traveled to Tyre by ship, but remembered nothing of the journey. How many times she had gazed out to sea from the temple confines, linking her undefined incompleteness to the lure of freedom represented by the ships. Now, for the first time, she herself would be a sea traveler. Questions bubbled up in her mind, and she looked around for Barnabas, but he had gone off to oversee the loading of their possessions.

The ship apparently carried a crew of four or five. As the women watched, a progression of cargo moved from dock to deck, to disappear down a square, black hole in the center of the deck, just before the mast. Crewmen secured a wooden cover over the hold and began to distribute the remaining cargo about the edges of the forward deck, lashing it to bronze fittings set into the knee-high bulwark enclosing the deck. Prisca and Maya moved back to the stern, out of the way.

"Mistress," Maya tugged at her sleeve. "Where will they put us? Where do they sleep and eat?"

"Do not worry. Barnabas will know." And Prisca was amazed at herself. She had known Barnabas only a few days, yet already she trusted him. He seemed more like Jesus than anyone she had met.

At dusk, Maya's question answered itself. The ship headed to shore. A dinghy ferried crew and passengers to the deserted beach, where they cooked and ate and slept the night. For the women, a small tent was erected at a discreet but safe distance. A sailor's life was a carefree life, Prisca decided, watching the glow of their campfire as she settled cross-legged before her tent. Maya had already gone to sleep inside.

A form detached itself from the sailors' camp and strode over to them. "How are you faring, Prisca?"

"Loving it," she smiled. "Please join me, Barnabas."

"Shall I build you a fire? Or will you come down to the crew's?"

"I would not cause them embarrassment. I can see they are ill at ease with women aboard. And I am not cold. Well bundled. See?" She snuggled appreciatively in her cloak, demonstrating her comfort.

Barnabas grinned and stretched out in the sand beside her, propping on one elbow. "Sailors are peculiar creatures. They only *she* they trust is their ship."

Prisca gazed at the pale aura of light created by the lucent oval of moon creeping over the sand dunes. She sighed contentedly. "If only Jesus were still here, the world would be a perfect place."

"It was written."

She turned to him in curiosity. "What was written?"

"That Jesus should die."

"Barnabas!"

"It is true, Prisca. The prophets foretold not only his life, but his death. And the manner of it."

"What prophets?"

"The Jewish prophets, Nathan, Samuel, Isaiah. Micah, too. Nathan told King David, about a thousand years ago, that God promised to raise up an offspring from David's line who would establish his kingdom forever. This Son of God would endure the rod and the lash of men. But through it all God would not remove his steadfast love."

Prisca watched Barnabas as he talked, a strong, shadowy outline against the dark night. His deep voice rumbled over her soothingly, with the reminiscent tone of one who has gone through a loss and already accepted it, so that it was unnecessary to pity him or to feel sorrow in his presence.

"And you believe this son they spoke of is Jesus. . . . A thousand years ago? A *thousand?*"

Moonlight touching his cheekbones gave the impression he was smiling. "Yes. And centuries after that, Isaiah foretold the coming of one who would be called Emmanuel."

"Emmanuel."

"It means 'God with us.' We believe Jesus was 'God with us.'" Barnabas's voice went on through the darkness. "Isaiah said this son would come from Galilee beyond the Jordan, which is where Jesus started his teaching. And Micah added that he would come from Bethlehem—where Jesus was born—to be ruler in Israel."

Prisca frowned in concentration. This is what the disciples had been talking about in Jerusalem. She struggled to understand. "I still miss our Lord. Don't you?"

"Not in the way you do. And you will not, either, when your understanding increases." His rich voice comforted her.

They remained in companionable silence. The moonlight touched Barnabas's hand, lying so close to her. She had the impulse to stroke it. Suddenly Barnabas looked up at her.

"I cannot see your face," he said. "Are you smiling?"

"Happy."

"Good." The hand on the sand scooped up a handful and let it trickle away. "Prisca. . . ." The word was followed by an exasperated sigh. Barnabas climbed to his feet. "Better get some sleep, Prisca."

A journey that should have taken but a few days stretched to nearly two weeks, thanks to a capricious spring and many cargo stops. A late rain squall deviled the craft and either blew it off course or pinioned it ashore. Maya complained that she was too old for such treatment by the gods, but Prisca did not care when their journey ended. She looked forward to the leisurely hours ashore each evening with Barnabas, which after the first night became by unspoken agreement their time together.

Barnabas was in the import-export business, she learned. Between conversations in which he delicately probed her past, she answering with unsparing honesty, he entertained her with tales of the months spent each year aboard ship, overseeing his wide-flung enterprises. Personal discomfort, despite Maya's loudly voiced opinion, was nothing when balanced against the pleasure of Barnabas's intimate companionship.

When at last she heard the seaman cry, "Cyprus to larboard!" Prisca felt regret. Nevertheless, she craned eagerly against the bulwark for her first glimpse of her new home. She was disappointed at first. Under the rain-distended clouds, the island looked like a long, swollen loaf of black bread.

The little ship lumbered up the leeward side; then, rounding a headland and veering northwest, the captain sailed her across the wind toward the harbor at Salamis. As they approached, the rain lessened and stopped. A sleek Roman war galley, twice the length of the merchantman, overtook them and slipped into the harbor ahead of them. As it passed, Prisca heard a pounding beat from the warship that matched the rhythmic dipping of two banks of oars below deck. The sound chilled her. She wondered if the rowers were crewmen or slaves. Roman prisoners often served out their sentences on the galleys, she knew. She shrank back from the bulwark and looked elsewhere.

Vessels of all sizes clustered in the harbor, the larger craft moored in the bay, the smaller tucked up close to shore. The dock was a frenzy of activity. Amid hails and shouts, the crew made fast the shrouds and dropped anchor. With a broad grin, Barnabas came to stand beside her. She had not known until the voyage began that Barnabas was the owner of this ship and several others.

She greeted him with a smile. He had changed to fresh robes and headcloth, added a small ornamental dagger to his girdle, and donned sandals of tooled Turkish leather. The wind whipping against his robes outlined his broad chest and fine legs.

"Well, how do I look?" he demanded.

"Very handsome, my lord." *A man any woman would be proud to call husband,* she thought, wondering why he had not remarried after the death of his wife.

"Coming home is always the best part." Together they watched the loading of grapes and other fruits on board a ship similar to theirs. Men strained under sacks of grain so heavy they would cripple weaker men.

"The ship the men are loading now, that's the *Lotus.*"

She caught the special note of pride in his voice. "Yours?"

"Yes. And the wheat is from my lands," he told her. "The land here —in the valley, between those ranges—," he pointed in the distance, where she could see the island cleft lengthwise by two mountain ranges. "That is my home. Your home now, too, Prisca." His voice grew husky as he added, "Truly, God has been good to me." Then he grinned down at her.

"Truly." She returned his smile. His eyes were so warm. It would not be hard to love such a man. She felt her cheeks growing warm and looked quickly back at the dock.

Barnabas turned, too, toward the dock. "Maya has not enjoyed the voyage. Is she all right, do you think?"

"Yes. She is mortally afraid of water. Of many things, poor woman. Her imagination made her sicker than the storms."

Barnabas grimaced with sympathy. "Then I hope you will not consider it too unkind of me to ask you to remain aboard awhile. I must see to my affairs ashore."

Prisca glanced up at him in surprise. "Of course not. She will be fine, now that we are in port." She was unused to such consideration for her feelings. "I hope all has fared well in your absence," she called after him.

With a wave, he strode down the wide plank and headed into the melee of men and carts clustered near the *Lotus.*

Prisca watched in fascination. Eventually Barnabas accepted papers from the man he'd been talking to, clapped him on the shoulders, produced a small pouch from his girdle, and gestured expansively at the laboring crew. Then he left the wharf and was swallowed up in a maze of warehouses fronting the Salamis harbor. The air was fresh, and Prisca could scent rain again on the vigorous breeze.

"Are we there?"

She turned. Maya was moving shakily toward her, bundled deeply in a gray wool traveling cloak Barnabas had provided. Her eyes were ringed with sickness. Wisps of gray hair escaped untidily from the bun at her nape, which had not been combed out since they started the voyage.

"We're there! Home, Maya! Barnabas asked us to wait aboard until he comes for us." She offered Maya her arm and drew her close to her side, ignoring the sour odor of sickness about her.

The deck of the boat tipped and bobbed underfoot as the last load was carried off, lightening the ship. At last she spotted Barnabas returning to the wharf. He strode at the head of a small train of servants and pack animals.

Maya watched them minutely from the time Prisca pointed him out. She pursed her lips judiciously. "He be a widower, you say?"

Prisca laughed. Maya smiled up at her, enjoying the free and joyous sound of it, and took heart. She was proud to be the servant of such a beautiful young woman. No matter if her clothing was poor and worn. No matter. Maya knew wisely that favors would accrue to her in the watershed of Prisca's radiance. Why, just look at the way this perfect stranger treated her. Like a queen!

"It is easy to see the gentleman favors you, Prisca. Look at all this, mind. Wealthy he must be!"

"Truly, and willing to give you a home and security for the rest of your life, is that what you are hinting at?"

Angry at being so transparent, Maya retorted, "If you'd be looking more to your future and less to thinking about that Jesus man—"

"It is his God who brought us here safely, Maya. Are you wanting to go back to Tyre?"

"No—no, this is better."

Barnabas had nearly reached the ship when a high shout rose from the beach beyond the dock. A young man sprinted toward them, waving and calling and robes flying, as if he would take off and soar at any moment. Barnabas stopped and turned. The women heard him cry a greeting to the newcomer. He flung out his arms and waited to embrace him. Their voices, but not the sense of their talk, drifted up. Then the newcomer gestured back the way he had come, Barnabas toward the ship, and, arm in arm, the step of one a confident bounce, the other purposeful, they swung aboard.

Barnabas was beaming. "This is my sister's boy, Mark. Prisca of Tyre . . . her servant Maya."

Mark ogled Prisca with his narrow jaw agape. His hair was thin and clung to his beardless, sensitive face like a cap. His lips were full and well-defined, and his dark eyes as thickly lashed as a girl's. "Uncle, where did you find her?"

"Mind your manners!" Barnabas said sharply. "Prisca knew our Lord. She was leaving Jerusalem, and I offered our hospitality."

Mark flushed. His cheeks reddened as a squalling babe's. "I only meant, uncle. . . . Prisca, with my uncle's permission, you are as comely as a goddess. Be thou not from Mount Olympus?"

Repressing a grin, she smiled. "Only a servant of Jesus."

Barnabas bent toward Maya. "And how is it with thee, mother?"

"Fine, sir, now that solid earth is waiting for me."

"Good, then we are ready to go. Mark says the servants have prepared a meal before we begin." He led the way down the plank.

"Begin!" wailed Maya to Prisca.

Barnabas overheard and laughed. "By land, by land, mother." As they reached shore he fell into step beside Mark. The women followed.

Barnabas's servants had erected a temporary wind shelter on the beach, a little removed from the hustle and noise of the wharf. Prisca ducked out of the gusty wind with relief. The tent was enclosed on three sides. Under it, small Mesopotamian rugs had been overlapped on the sand, ringing a spotless linen cloth spread with tantalizing delicacies. Prisca found Mark at her elbow, helping her to a seat. She murmured her thanks, noting the amused lift of Barnabas's eyebrows.

Glancing covertly around and seeing no servants' table, Maya sighed and once more accepted her lot, which in the past weeks had resembled water with no shape, being constantly asked to change to fit a new vessel. She sat to the left and slightly behind Prisca, shy and embarrassed to find herself at the same table with men.

Her eyes widened at the bounty spread before them: dishes of honey cakes crusted with sesame seeds, spiced olives, thick slices of pale cheese, marinated lamb with bits of herb clinging to it, dishes of almonds and dried fruits. Her mouth watered, even though her stomach remained slightly queasy.

"Looks delicious, Mark," approved Barnabas.

"I thought it would be a good idea. I chose this place so we'd have some privacy, at least." Mark's eyes strayed to their guest. "I told Aunt Lydia you would be hungry. You always are after a business trip."

Barnabas offered a blessing, twisted off a portion of crusty bread, then inquired, "How is Lydia?" before stuffing it in his mouth.

"She is fine, but the twins! Uncle, when you are away, they are impossible! How much longer must you wait before marrying them off?"

Barnabas laughed delightedly. "Mark, you must not let your cousins get under your skin. They know just how to twist you." To Prisca he said, "My daughters, Helen and Eleanor. They are only nine. Their mother died giving them life." He brushed aside Prisca's expression of sympathy with, "God has been good to me." He resumed his account. "A year later my sister Lydia was widowed, and she consented to make a home for her roaming brother. Mark, here, is the son of my other sister, Mary. You might have met her in Jerusalem. No?" He cuffed Mark affectionately.

The rain squall blew away while they ate, leaving fluffy cumulus clouds in possession of a deep blue sky. The servants repacked the remains of their meal and the tent and rugs. Prisca saw her small possessions and Maya's even skimpier bundle disappear into a deep basket, a pair of which were slung over the back of an ass. All the animals appeared well fed and of serene temperament, tended by men who moved them along with a peaceful attitude that she found all the more remarkable, given the short, fiery tempers of most drivers she had encountered.

The procession began the trek through Salamis and into the valley that Barnabas had described for Prisca from the ship. Swooping up each side of the valley were long mountain ranges. The south range, the Olympus Mountains, was heavily wooded with pine and juniper and cedar. From the sea Cyprus had looked most forbidding. As they walked inland, its beauty unfolded.

Prisca was captivated. Streams gushing in the fullness of early summer rushed down the mountainsides into more placid streams that wound through the valley. The abundantly fertile valley bloomed with wheat fields that were thick and green. As the shadows lengthened and crept up the slopes of the Olympus Mountains, Barnabas drew Prisca aside.

"There it is," he said with quiet pride. "Home. I came here twenty years ago, with my new bride. We fell in love with this valley." They started on again. "I have always been a trader, and my father before me. We have an old saying, 'The father who fails to teach his son a trade educates him to be a thief.' " Then he added, "But ships and spices and barrels of salt fish fail to delight me."

Prisca chuckled at his unexpected turn of phrase, emerging as if from a crack in his core of reserve.

He grinned back at her, delighted to be caught out, a flash of white teeth in the bristly beard. " 'Tis true. That is why, I suspect, that what Jesus had to say was like music from the lyre. It plucks at strings of my heart that nothing else touches—not the ships, not the trading, nor the glory some of 'em get from beating a competitor."

"Aye," said Mark softly.

She turned, not realizing he had been listening, too. "Are you a trader as well?"

Mark shook his head. "Uncle has tried to teach me, but I've no head for it."

"But Mark finds us honest, loyal men," said Barnabas stoutly. "He is steward for our farms and herds. He keeps the books, pays the men fairly, and is learning to see that their families do not want."

"But I have not made us much money, uncle," said Mark. Prisca wondered why Mark's mother had sent him to live with his uncle in such a remote spot.

"In time, lad, in God's good time you will find your niche."

Prisca wondered. Something about Mark disturbed her deeply. He touched memories she would rather forget.

Chapter 12

Fields gave way to fruit and nut trees, and soon flower gardens, as they approached Barnabas's home. The caravan veered toward a cluster of low outbuildings of unhewed stone, which Prisca guessed were warehouses, servant quarters, and a cookhouse. A bunched ribbon of bushes not far behind these buildings indicated the course of a stream.

Barnabas, Mark, Prisca, and Maya continued on to a large, attractive dwelling set apart by low stone half walls and pink blooming rose bushes, which had been trained and trimmed into hedges. Part of the structure was two storied, like a townhouse; but like the home of a prosperous farmer, the remainder sprawled generously over the land. Its thick stone walls were freshly whitewashed, the roof tiles even and unbroken.

"Father!" shrieked a high, girlish voice.

"Father!" shrieked an identical voice.

In a whirl of colored robes, two dark-headed children tore out of the house and threw themselves at Barnabas.

"My little peaches!" He swooped them up in his great arms and hugged and kissed each of them. White-robed house servants crowded in the doorway, with smiles upon their faces. Bowing, they fell back as Barnabas led them all inside.

Then Prisca saw striding toward them the most striking woman she had ever seen. Lydia was as tall as Barnabas, blue eyed, with yellow gray hair the color of sheep's wool. She moved with the same assurance Barnabas possessed. Prisca wondered if the rest of their family inherited that proud grace.

Lydia and her brother embraced, then Barnabas introduced her.

"Welcome, Prisca of Tyre." Unhesitatingly Lydia embraced her, too, in a bony grip that told of hard, unsparing work. Prisca liked her immediately.

When they had rested, refreshed themselves, and eaten a light supper, Barnabas dismissed the children and the servants. He led the way to a spacious atrium in the center of the house, open to all the rooms, where comfortable, couchlike chairs awaited them. Small pomegranate trees planted around the walls lent a wispy air, their delicate, yellow green branches courting the slightest breeze.

Mark took Prisca's arm. "Look. Have you ever seen carp?"

She bent over the pool, startled first to see not the fish, but the reflection of Mark's handsome face bent so close to hers. His sensuous eyes traveled boldly over her.

Thrown off balance by his forward behavior, she concentrated on the huge, iridescent red carp swimming lazily in the tiny pools interconnected by channels of rounded stones. The splashing water created a soothing effect that invited rest.

"Lovely," she murmured.

"You're lovely. And you smell delicious," he said in an undertone.

"Thank you," she said, strolling hastily back toward Barnabas and Lydia. Mark anticipated her, arranging couches and whipping in to sit beside her.

Avoiding his intent gaze, Prisca sank appreciatively into the soft furniture. It had been months since she had been surrounded with such serene beauty. Willingly she gave herself up to it, unconsciously stroking the soft shawl Lydia had lent her.

When Lydia had realized how paltry were her guest's belongings, she insisted upon Prisca choosing a gown from among her own robes. Prisca had selected a simple linen shift. It was much too long, but she bloused the excess around her slender waist with a girdle of soft chamois skin. When she picked up her own veil to wrap around it, Lydia suggested she let the servants wash it and in the meantime wear one of hers. As if suggestion created fact, Lydia pulled her veil away and produced a beautiful silk shawl from the Orient, woven in a teal and gold pattern of peacocks, so richly iridescent that it might have sprung from the feathers themselves.

Prisca gasped at its beauty, and tried to refuse it.

"Please." Lydia grinned down at her, displaying fine, strong teeth. "What is the joy in beauty if not to share it?"

Prisca surrendered with a smile of delight. Draping the shawl over her head, she said, "You sound just like your brother. Though talk of joy and beauty sounds most odd from a man as big as he."

She looked at Lydia now, reclining next to her brother in the atrium. Together, brother and sister shared much in common. Both gray, prematurely she was sure, both tall and assured. Their features were markedly different, Lydia's fine sharp nose more becoming than her brother's thicker one, her eyes blue where Barnabas's were—what? More the color of her own, sometimes sea green, sometimes gray. Barnabas's full beard undoubtedly concealed other similarities.

Barnabas leaned forward and smiled encouragingly at her.

Prisca knew what was coming. Although she smiled outwardly, she held her breath. Fresh from the insults and hurts heaped upon her by the brethren in Jerusalem, she had tried to dissuade Barnabas when he had told her that he wanted to reveal her past to his family.

"But why must you?" she had said. "We are all new creations in Jesus."

"Human nature, my dear. Acknowledge a bitter past before your enemies, and you disarm them."

"My enemies!"

Barnabas's hearty laugh erupted. "Not my family, but others. Later. Grow used to it now."

It did not make sense to her, but trusting him, she had consented. Now she gazed swiftly at Barnabas's nephew and sister. His words, she felt certain, would not affect her welcome from Lydia at all. The thought of Mark knowing her past filled her with foreboding.

"Barnabas—"

"Prisca has given me permission to tell you how she came to know Jesus," he began.

"Please—"

He reached over and patted her hand. "It's all right, Prisca."

No, no it is not all right!

For the next few minutes he related to Mark and Lydia nearly all that she had told him, generously including a view of her she would not have given herself. She blushed when he dwelt upon the concern she had for her servant and for her steadfastness in wishing to serve the God of Jesus even after rejection by the disciples. "Together we will try to discover how she is meant to serve."

"A priestess of Artemis," Mark said in a soft, scathing tone that only she could hear. He rose abruptly and stalked to a corner of the garden where he was out of the line of vision of Lydia and Barnabas.

"Tell me . . . ," Lydia began.

As she responded to Lydia's gentle questioning Prisca heartily wished she had stopped Barnabas. The man saw only his own generous nature in others. Surely a dangerous fault! Catching her eye, Mark ceremoniously folded his arms in derision. The look on his face was smug, knowing. *Knowing only ignorance!* she seethed. Her voice faltered.

Lydia glanced around at her nephew. "Mark, do not tease her," she said. To Prisca she said, "You poor child!"

"Not a child, Lydia! Never again." Mark had not been teasing, she knew. Barnabas had misjudged that member of his family.

"No. But if Jesus called you to serve, then serve you must. The sheep know the voice of their own shepherd."

Prisca warmed to Lydia's calm, assured words.

"She can be a servant here, uncle Barnabas," said Mark sarcastically.

Barnabas rested his big-knuckled hands on his knees and threw Mark a speculative glance. "Not the kind of servant you mean."

Prisca laughed. "Before I can serve at all, I must learn how, Barnabas. You know my ignorance. I do not even know yet what your God is like."

She exchanged a tender glance with Barnabas, recalling last night, their last evening alone together. She had wanted him to take her in his arms, had risen when he got up to go back to the sailor's camp. Barnabas had taken her hands, had kissed each of them in turn.

The look that passed between them now was not lost on Mark. He strode back to the group and stood over Prisca. "No one taught you about the God of our fathers, I suppose." It was more an accusation than a question.

"Not in my old religion." She lifted her chin and returned his bold stare.

"We study the Scriptures, the teachings of our prophets. We learned how God made the world and the first man and woman and they. . . . "

"Easy, young man," laughed Barnabas. "How many years did you study?"

"A dozen, uncle."

"And shall you teach it all to Prisca in one evening?"

"Teach her?" Mark scoffed. "She is a—a woman."

"Do not Jewish women learn your Scriptures, too?"

"*Jewish* women. Only enough to make them dutiful wives," Mark replied carelessly.

Prisca burst out laughing. "Art teasing?"

"Of course not!"

"What did you learn as a child, Prisca?" asked Lydia, pulling Mark into their circle once more with a conciliatory smile.

"Why to read and write Greek and Latin, to learn our history, astronomy, mathematics, the healing arts . . . ," Prisca stopped. She realized they were attending her as if she were a fascinating species of animal. "Are not these the things all educated people learn?"

Barnabas whistled. "Heaven forbid! Who would want to marry a woman ten times more clever than he?"

"A wise man! What greater thing could a woman bring to a marriage than knowledge and skills to help her husband prosper?"

"A fertile body," said Lydia quietly. "That is what men desire, Prisca dear."

"In the new faith, is that enough?" she asked with a smile, remembering what Jesus had said about women's glory being not in motherhood, no more than men's glory lay in fatherhood, but instead in doing the will of the Father. "That is not what Jesus wanted."

"What did he want?" Lydia asked.

She told them how he had answered her the day after he said to his mother, "Who is my mother?"

An uncomfortable silence fell as each struggled to place this new way of thinking into their own habits of thought.

"But a man must have strong sons," said Barnabas.

"You have only daughters," said Lydia gently. "Do you count them of less worth?"

"I could not love them more if they were sons, but I am rearing them for another man's pleasure. When they marry, they will no longer belong to me, but to a husband's household."

"But Jesus said that a man should also leave his parents—"

"Yes," agreed Barnabas, "I remember. But that is not the way we have always thought of marriage."

"Truly," said Lydia, "but why should the young couple belong more to the husband's family than to the wife's?" Suddenly she laughed. "Barnabas, you may rue the day you invited Prisca to live with us. As for me, I am well pleased. I can see many an evening saved from loneliness! We can all learn from each other. You knew Jesus for nearly three years, my brother. You could teach her all he taught you."

Barnabas shook his head. "No mortal could do that. But I could teach her what I understand."

"Will you, Barnabas?" Prisca's eyes shone. "Truly I am grateful. And to you, Lydia. You are already like Jesus in the generosity of your love. But I have little money," she confessed. "I must find work soon."

Lydia nodded. "I was coming to that. Do you think you could cope with a pair of lively nine-year-olds?"

"Yes, but what—"

"Helen and Eleanor's formal education has been sadly neglected—and Mark's, too, truth be known, save for the Scriptures."

"What is wrong with my education?" Mark protested. "I've studied both Latin and Greek."

"Not well enough, dear," said Lydia, her mind obviously elsewhere. "And the healing arts, Prisca, you could teach us the healing arts and all else you mentioned." Lydia spoke faster, growing more excited as each new thought occurred to her. "And as you teach Mark, so may he teach you the Jewish Scriptures, and I would have a companion!" She leaned back, pleased with herself.

"A woman teacher!" Mark's eyes blazed.

"I mislike your attitude, young man," Barnabas corrected him in a deadly voice.

"I'll teach her the Scriptures! But it is the worst mistake you ever made!" He flung angrily into the house.

"Mark!" Barnabas roared to his feet. "Get back here!"

Prisca felt acutely embarrassed for Mark. For a youth at the brink of manhood to be humiliated before a stranger! She did not wish an enemy in this household. Here, for the first time, she was tasting the warmth and companionship of family life as she only dreamed it before, a feeling like that between Thyatira and her fellow priestesses, but closer, fuller. She hastened to her feet.

"May I be excused, please?" she asked Lydia. "I must see how Maya fares."

"Wait, please. I am sorry about Mark. I cannot explain why he feels as he does."

"I never would have put you through that, Prisca," Barnabas added. "I am sorry. Mark would have been better off not knowing."

"So would I," Prisca said wryly.

"But you are not angry?" asked Lydia. "Good! And you will abide with us and teach the girls?"

"With all that I can give."

"And if Mark is to teach you, you shall teach him, too," declared Barnabas. "His is the greater ignorance."

As Prisca left them she realized that this was a side of Barnabas she had never seen, the truculence of a father toward a rebellious son. Or was it more than that? If he did not press the issue, perhaps time would still bring understanding where force of will could not. Meantime, she could not help feeling it would be better for all of them if she and Mark were together as little as possible.

Lydia had readied an unused upstairs wing for Prisca and Maya, one that would afford some privacy. Maya had her own room, a small, curtained alcove off Prisca's. Large and airy, Prisca's room overlooked the long sugar-loaf mountain guarding Cyprus's southern flank.

With a bemused smile, thinking of Mark, Prisca mounted the steps. She opened the door, and an arm shot out and pulled her inside the lightless room and shut the door.

A hand cupped over her mouth. "Not—a—sound!"

Mark! She bobbed her head.

In the darkness, she could see only his outline framed in the lighter darkness of the window. "What are you doing here?" she hissed.

"I'll do the talking. You may have my uncle seeing moons and stars, priestess, but not me. I intend you shall have a clear impression exactly what I think of you."

The sharp voice crawled with venom. Prisca was so frightened she could barely stand. Her teeth chattered. "You would not dare harm me!"

Mark seized her body roughly, cruelly twisting her tender flesh. A hand clenched her jaw and cheek. She gasped with pain and outrage as his mouth came down over hers in a bruising kiss. Then he flung her away from him. "Remember, *priestess!*"

Chapter 13

"he master is due back today," said Maya slyly, brushing Prisca's chestnut hair with long, sweeping strokes. She had been at it for the better part of an hour, and Prisca's tresses gleamed vibrantly. "It's been three months."

As always, thoughts of Barnabas brought a riffle of excitement deep inside, but she looked up at Maya's reflection in the polished silver mirror and said merely, "Is he?"

Maya's face had filled out. She had lost the gray pallor that Prisca had assumed was a mark of old age. A faint pink glow suffused her face now. She moved more quickly, found less to fault, delighted in the servants' gossip, and in every way seemed younger than when they had arrived on Cyprus two years ago.

Without being asked, she had assumed the role of Prisca's personal maid and managed a status in the household somewhat above the other servants. As she was versed in arts the servants knew nothing of, and able to fascinate them with a wealth of exotic stories, some true, they tolerated her own special view of herself.

"Yes," Maya continued, "not until midafternoon, mind. Due in port at noontide."

Prisca burst out laughing. "Where do you get your information?"

"I'm always right, aren't I?" She applied the brush with righteous vigor.

"Ouch! That will do well enough, Maya. Bind it up, please."

"I'm right," Maya muttered, deftly twisting the heavy hair into a coil, sneaking a green ribbon into the twist before pinning it into a coronet. She stepped back to admire her handiwork. The emerald ribbon wound through it, the dark coronet lent a regal air to her mistress's features, the finely chiseled nose, the strong neck.

What was the man, made of stone? thought Maya. Prisca's gray green eyes met hers in the mirror. "I finished your new green gown," Maya said offhandedly. "It would look nice for the master's return."

Prisca rose and faced her. "Maya, what is all this about? Pretty ribbons and new gowns—this isn't a feast day."

"Well, I never saw such a mewling courtship in all my days! That man has got to be prodded. If Thyatira was here, she'd have bedded him long ago and had his wedding vows, too, if she was a mind to!"

"I am not Thyatira! Do not ever again compare her to me. You know nothing! Nothing!"

"I know how to make a man think he's bedded a virgin!"

Prisca shook her. "Any more and you find a new mistress! I have not to explain myself to you! Leave me! And take your dress. I will not wear it!"

Gown clutched in her arms and hurt tears darting down her cheeks, Maya fled, but not before she was sure Prisca had noticed them.

Prisca stared ruefully after her. Her own temper was not faultless. She knew that Maya's actions were prompted by love, that she had spent days laboring nearsightedly over the length of fine hunter green linen that Lydia had given her for a gown last week, together with a wide corded silk sash of the same shade.

Minutes later a tap sounded on the door. "Mistress?"

"Yes?"

"I'm sorry, mistress. May I come in?"

"Come in."

Maya came in, shoulders drooping abjectly. "I don't know what gets into me. A devil, must be. I've been trying to be more like your Jesus, like you said. I've been trying to pray to his God. But sometimes. . . . And he's such a fine man, the master. . . . Not like that nephew of his, thinking good only of himself!" Tears dripped off the end of her nose. She sniffled and used her sleeve discreetly.

Ignoring the outburst about Mark, Prisca went to her and hugged her shoulder comfortingly. "You will learn, Maya. And I am sorry for losing my temper. After all, you and I did not have the advantage of knowing a Messiah was coming to the people. What you asked of me was not wrong. But do not worry about our future. Remember what Jesus said about the lilies of the field? Hm? You were there that day." Prisca tilted Maya's chin up and kissed the flaccid cheek. "I'll always take care of you."

Maya buried her face against Prisca's shoulder. "I could not cherish you more if you were my own daughter."

"I know, Maya, I know. Now I must go downstairs; it is time for the girls' lessons. I have set them at translating a play of Euripides from Greek to Latin." She paused in the doorway, unconscious of her beauty, the dark coronet shot with green ribbon, dark-lashed sea green eyes made the more stunning in contrast to the unbleached linen shift, which fell to her sandals. "And Maya, try to get along with Mark. He is young—"

"Your age."

Prisca chuckled. "For better or worse, women mature earlier. Maya...."

"Yes, mistress?"

"Nothing." But as she descended the stairs she wondered, dismissing all thought of Mark, was she attractive to Barnabas? He knew all about her. They had grown so close during the voyage to Cyprus, yet he had not touched her since. Perhaps.... She felt a pang of sadness. Why did Jewish men set such great store by virgin wives? Surely if chastity were so pleasing to the God of Jesus, men would want it for themselves, too. People could be virgins only the first time they lay together. Did God hold them less dear after that? If so, then all His children should remain virginal. She smiled at such a silly thought. Yes, and how long would the world last that way? She wondered if anyone had ever asked Jesus about it.

Still smiling, Prisca entered the library and found Eleanor and Helen seated cross-legged before a low writing table of polished olivewood. The twins were tall, slender, energetic girls with tawny skins and almond-shaped eyes and, with budding breasts and rounding thighs, becoming increasingly conscious of their femaleness. Already neighbors with sons were paying calls upon the girls' father, hoping to beguile him with their visions of the future.

Helen greeted her with a smile and bent back over her paper. Eleanor toyed with her stylus, then dropped it and stretched her legs out across the rug to dip her toes in a patch of sunlight streaming in from the atrium. She pushed the papyrus sheet toward Prisca.

"I've already finished, Prisca," said Eleanor in a dreamlike voice. "Please tell me it's right; I'll just die if I have to do it again!"

Prisca smiled fondly. "Knowing you, it is probably letter-perfect. Let me see it." She read aloud:

> *Kiss me yet once again, the last, long kiss,*
> *Until I draw your soul within my lips*
> *And drink down all your love.*

Laughing, Prisca lowered the paper. "This was not what you were to translate!"

Eleanor grinned wickedly. "I know, but it was more fun."

"It is because she's all moony over Dan," teased Helen.

"I am not!"

"You are! He is always hanging around our gate!"

"Who is Dan?"

"Just a neighbor," Eleanor replied primly.

"Read my paper, Prisca."

With a smile, Prisca took the stiff papyrus from Helen. The girls had given her so much pleasure since she had come. She delighted in their nonsense and in the earnest conversations they sometimes shared. She cleared her throat theatrically and read:

HIPPOLYTUS:
O Mother Earth! O Sun and open sky!
What words have I heard from this accursed tongue! . . .
*   Friends you say!*
I spit the word away. None of the wicked
are friends of mine.

NURSE:
*   Then pardon, son. It's natural*
that we should sin, being human.

Prisca looked up, startled, as Mark's voice from the doorway took up Hippolytus's next speech:

Women! This coin which men find counterfeit!
Why, why, lord Zeus, did you put them in the world,
in the light of the sun?

He was leaning against the doorway of the library, wearing a knee-length white tunic with a wine red cloak flung carelessly over one shoulder. "Good morrow, girls. And Prisca." His narrow, handsome face was expressionless. His dark eyes barely touched hers as he added, "No Scripture lesson today, Prisca. I must go into Salamis and meet uncle Barnabas's ship."

"May I go this time, Mark?" begged Eleanor.

"You went last time!" said Helen. "It's my turn, cousin Mark."

"Nobody gets to go. A man could go crazy in this houseful of females." Now his eyes met hers, defiantly.

"You do Hippolytus very well," Prisca said coolly.

"Do I not?" His sensuous lips twisted in a strange smile.

I hate a clever woman—God forbid
that I should ever have a wife at home
with more than woman's wits!

102

Prisca retorted:

> *So that's enough*
> *for me? Do I have justice if you deal me*
> *my death blow and then say "I was wrong: I grant it."*

He bowed mockingly. "Well done, 'Phaedra.' " And he was gone.

"Mark's no fun any more," said Eleanor in the silence.

"Why does he act angry all the time? We haven't done anything!" said Helen. "I think he's mean."

"He isn't angry at you, dear."

"Then who is he angry at?"

Prisca did not answer. For two years she had endured his unrelenting anger. Manhood had given Mark a simmering temper as well as sinuous muscle. He was darkly handsome, charming when he wished to be, concealing his feelings about her in the company of others, invariably taciturn in her presence. He had refused to accept teaching from her. While he taught her, he was coldly formal, and she took her lead from him, remote yet attentive, answering scrupulously.

Barnabas had meant to force him to accept that which she could teach him, but in the name of peace, Prisca and Lydia had allied to change Barnabas's mind. If only she and Mark were friends, she might have gone with him now to meet Barnabas. *Barnabas.* Her heart warmed at the picture of him that formed instantly in her mind, the grizzled hair, thick lashes, and bushy brows, the weathered, kindly face. How different uncle and nephew!

"Prisca?" said Helen. "Is it all right?"

She glanced at the forgotten paper. "Yes, it is perfect, darling. Your father will be so proud of you." She smiled at Helen. "Have you finished, Eleanor? The correct assignment, that is."

"Of course! Way before Helen. Prisca, let's go on a picnic! Please?"

Helen bounced up and down from her firm little rump to her knees. "That is a perfect idea. If we go up in the peach orchard, we can see the caravan coming."

"Excuse me for interrupting, m'lady, but more beggars are pestering at the gate." One of the servants, rush broom in his hand, stood just outside the library door. "They claim they follow the Christ."

"Thank you." Prisca rose at once. To the twins she said, "You girls can wheedle the cooks better than I."

"Then we're going? Wait'll you see the goodies we get, Prisca!" The girls were on their feet and out the door in a flash.

Prisca laughed joyfully at their exuberance. "Where is Mistress Lydia?" she asked the servant, as she followed him outside.

"Down at the winepress. Shall I call her?"

"No, we can manage, you and I."

He was muttering loudly over his shoulder, obviously meaning her to hear: "I swear they use it like a password, they does. Followers of Christ indeed! Them scarce knows one day from the next. What they be knowing of the Christ? What they knows is where food is free for the askin'."

"Stop it!" she said sharply. "What would your master and mistress think, to hear one who has been given so much behave so poorly?"

An hour later, perched upon the hillside in woolen cloaks wrapped tightly against the chill gusts, Prisca and her charges waited for the caravan. Eleanor sighted it first.

"There! See? C'mon!" and she and Helen were off precipitately down the steep slope, twisting and leaping like a pair of goats around rocks and bushes. Prisca stood up with a grin and shaded her eyes. She easily picked out Barnabas's solid figure at the front and Mark's tall, lean form mid-caravan, but who was that beside Barnabas? He looked vaguely familiar . . . sturdy, flat-footed walk, sandy beard—Andrew! Prisca uttered a glad cry. Forgetting the dignity of her twenty years, she ran after the girls.

The short caravan drew to a leisurely halt as the three raced down the hillside.

"Father!" shrieked the twins.

"Prisca!" exclaimed Andrew. "When I met Barnabas at Joppa, he said you were still here." His arms folded around her in a bear hug, his dusty face and clear blue eyes alight with pleasure. Through all the happy greetings, Prisca found her eyes drawn irresistibly to Barnabas. His eyes met hers with such intensity that she felt a giddy rush of pleasure. He had missed her! He had missed her as she missed him.

Denied the unrestrained joy of the girls, Prisca swung demurely in beside Andrew. "You look fine, just fine," said Andrew.

"How are the brethren?" she asked eagerly.

They chattered the rest of the way home, and nonstop through supper and into the fair evening. Andrew had brought with him a new disciple, Matthias, who had been chosen by lot to replace Judas. He was a wiry, dark, quiet man, who left most of the talking to Andrew.

"In Jerusalem we have gotten into the habit of feeding the hungry, as Jesus did."

"Just as we do here," nodded Barnabas.

"So I have heard," said Andrew. "Your generosity is legend. I only hope your purse holds up." When he laughed, his pale blue eyes and ruddy cheeks contorted with merriment. "I could not tell you where the money comes from in Jerusalem, but sometimes a farmer gives us an extra bushel of grain to pass out, or a fisherman a portion of his catch. Word has gotten around, so that many bring us their excess, when they have it. Is it the same with you? No, eh? Well, not as many Christians here yet," Andrew said comfortably.

"It is amazing the things Jesus taught us without our realizing it. We were all prepared to preach the good news, as he told us. But when someone is ill or hungry," Andrew spread his palms expressively, "he cannot hear words! He can listen, but he cannot hear. We learned we have to fill his belly and attend his ills before he'll let us in his head!"

Lydia nodded in complete understanding. Every woman who cares for a child knows that!

"And with our Lord's help," Andrew continued, "we manage not to turn anyone away hungry."

"What about the Jews in the temple?" Barnabas wanted to know. "Do they believe you now?"

"They want nothing to do with us." Andrew's mild blue eyes narrowed, and his lips made a downward crescent. "The truth is, they are afraid of us."

"Of the followers of Jesus?" Prisca said incredulously.

"We are not just a few any more, Prisca. Before I tell you about that, let me tell you what happened to the disciples after you left. We were waiting, you remember, for what we didn't know. We waited over a month, nearly two, all of us in that room. Then something happened."

An expectant hush settled over his audience. Barnabas had already gotten the story, but Mark, Lydia, Prisca, even the twins waited with held breath. So many rumors. . . .

Andrew's voice dropped. "It was like a mighty wind, filled with hundreds, hundreds of voices, all the human tongues. We were surrounded, filled, with the presence of God. It became unbearable in that room, overwhelming! We rushed madly downstairs and into the street. We must have looked as if we were on a wild revel."

Tears filled Andrew's eyes. "Suddenly we could *understand all the dialects of the street.* We were singing and praising God, for this wonderful

Spirit that Jesus had promised that had come upon us. Those in the street hearing us praise God and tell his wonders in their own tongues, were filled with amazement. All of us—struck with awe. We could communicate with the whole world! Us! Jesus came to us, chose us, to be part of the mightiest thing that ever happened on this earth."

Prisca found herself shivering. Her soul cried out with longing and despair that she had not been part of the wonderful moment.

Something of what she was feeling must have communicated to Andrew, for he reached over and squeezed her hand comfortingly.

"Everyone who could see us or hear us, crowded in upon us. 'What shall we do? What shall we do to be saved?' they cried. Peter seemed to change before our eyes. His voice grew and grew, like the mighty roar of a lion. He jumped up on the back of a cart and spread his arms and told them to repent and be baptized in the name of Jesus Christ for the forgiveness of their sins. Then he made them an incredible promise. Everyone—everyone—baptized would receive the same gift of the Spirit that had descended upon us in the room! Since that time, God has granted us the power to do the miracles that Jesus did. Healings, gifts of faith. . . . We all worked together in Jerusalem for a while, and then Peter told us to carry the good news everywhere, and the first place I wanted to come was here, to be the one to baptize you with the Spirit." Andrew leaned back, an expectant smile on his face.

Rising to his feet, Barnabas said, "You shall baptize Lydia and the twins and Mark and all my servants and the workers in the fields and all who have heard the good news. They must be baptized in the Spirit too."

Suddenly Barnabas glanced at Prisca. Her lips were parted and her eyes shining. He remembered those in Jerusalem who had said she could not follow Christ because she was not a Jew. He glanced swiftly at Andrew. "I never heard our lord Jesus say a man must be a Jew to follow him."

Andrew said, "Peter said these words, spoken by the prophet Joel, 'I will pour out my spirit upon all flesh.' Prisca, do you wish to be baptized now and ease my conscience?"

"Yes! Oh, yes!" Prisca's heart soared with joy. Now she would be truly a disciple! Now she would escape Artemis forever.

Midmorning of the following day Prisca was hurrying through the library to retrieve some papers she'd been writing and surprised Barnabas bending over them. He looked up when she was but a pace or two away. The expression on his tanned, seamed face startled her; a mingling of pride and desire. Her lips parted.

Suddenly they were in each other's arms. He was stroking her hair. She could feel the muscles of his jaw working. She gave a little cry as his lips bent hungrily to hers. Then she forgot everything but the longing that had tormented her for two years. Their bodies, their lips clung together like a pillar fused of desire.

"Oh, Barnabas!" Prisca murmured when at last they broke apart. "I love you. I've loved you since—"

"I love you, Prisca. I cherish you. Always remember that."

A chill seized her heart. She gazed at him, fearing his next words.

Barnabas placed a gentle finger over her lips. "Not here. Not now." There was a sadness in his voice that she could not understand. He pushed her gently away and fumbled to pick up one of the sheets. His hand trembled.

"Tell me about your work. What are you doing?"

She stared at him a moment longer. He refused to meet her eyes. With an effort she mastered her own feelings and gestured at the paper with a modest shrug. "Trying to put your teaching in my own words. To understand how Mark's teaching from the prophets fits what I am learning."

He nodded. "Then it is right." Barnabas left the library.

In the days that followed, Barnabas avoided her. She kept her grief and her painful questions hidden during the day. But in the stillness, when the night birds sang, she lay awake thinking, wondering what would become of their love.

Andrew and Matthias remained among the newly baptized in Cyprus for a month. Andrew was overjoyed to discover that so much teaching had already been done, that so many of those who came to Barnabas's hospitable home were ready to receive the final blessing of the Spirit.

Two days before he and Matthias were to leave, Andrew sought out Lydia and Prisca in the herb garden, which Prisca had planted the previous spring. "If you knew what a blessing your household has been to us." The air was fragrant from the sprigs of marjoram and rosemary which they were picking.

"In what way?" asked Lydia.

Settling on his haunches and watching them, he sighed suddenly. "So many worrisome problems. As if staying alive were not enough!"

The women looked at each other. Andrew explained, "Some of the people we've preached to receive the good news and decide to wait for him from that moment on. They will not invest in new garments or furnish their houses or buy crockery or plant their fields! It has gotten so out of hand that some of the merchants are complaining no one will buy their goods! Peter certainly has his hands full."

Lydia laughed. "Oh, Andrew, we are going to miss you and your stories. Excuse me while I take these herbs to the cook."

As Lydia left, Andrew smiled at Prisca. "Feel like walking?"

She nodded. "The good news. Is that what everyone calls Jesus' teachings?"

"Yes, for so it has been, every time we bring his words to ears that hear." With a grin, Andrew added, "Although the 'good news' has some strange bedfellows. Suddenly everyone can do 'miracles.' There was one man I remember, a trader in Jerusalem called Eleazar."

Prisca started. "Eleazar? I met one of that name. He lived near your rooms, a street or two away. A heavy man, heavy jowls?"

"Yes! Er," Andrew peered at her cautiously, "was he a friend?"

"Far from it!" she said with a laugh. "I called upon God—I did not know him well then, but I trusted him because of Jesus—to deliver me and my servant from his snare."

"Truly! Well, he has met justice. He persuaded some four hundred citizens that if they carried their treasures down to the Jordan by Jericho, he would transform them, in the name of Jesus, into ten times their worth."

Prisca grinned, her eyes dancing. "And they found him out?"

"The Roman authorities, no less! Eleazar had his robber band waiting across the river to seize all the goods and slay the people who would stop them. A legion arrived, rescued the goods, and slew him. And chastised the Jews for believing in charlatans."

"And for their own greed, I should think. Shall we ever learn?"

"Some stories are even more disquieting. I worry, lest they get out of hand."

"What sort of stories?" Prisca found a rocky outcrop and sat down to rest.

"We had a fellow arrive from Jericho a while back. He knew all about the resurrection of Jesus. He'd heard that Jesus transformed himself into an enormous eagle and flew to heaven, where he stayed for three days, then flew back again and resumed his human form.

"Travelers came through before that with an even wilder tale. It seems that a plague swept through Ethiopia, and the queen prayed to Heaven, and Jesus came with a host of angels and banished the plague, and thousands of devils rose up and blackened the sky until he called forth a monstrous wind, which swirled the plague devils into a funnel-shaped cloud and cast them into the ocean."

Prisca shook her head. "They sound more like the myths of Greece."

"Aye. You'd think they could tell the difference. Of course the Greeks had a field day with the resurrection, too. They said that Jesus' death was proof he was not divine. Any god knows better than to involve himself in the lives of humans. And if he does, he certainly wouldn't get himself killed over it!"

"But the Greek gods are not gods like God is, Andrew. They are humanlike, both bad and good. They are the tales of my childhood—such as I had," she added, half to herself. She smiled at Andrew. "It is the Greek way of explaining the unexplainable. My way, too, until Jesus drew me."

Andrew brought a foot up to rest on the rock and leaned a forearm on his knee. He gazed down at her. "You have changed, Prisca. Your spirit is calmer. You are even lovelier than when I first saw you as a maiden in Tyre. Perhaps too beautiful to be a disciple."

"That, like everything, is a gift from God."

"You need a man to protect you."

"Mark told me that in the Scriptures it is decreed that every Jewish woman be subject to a man: a father, a husband—a kinsman if she has no one else."

"For her own protection, yes. No other peoples so protect their women. Did he also tell you how much a good woman is honored in her own home? As a mother and a wife? Her authority is equal to her husband's."

"That is as it should be," she agreed. *And I shall one day belong to Barnabas,* she thought.

They left the orchard and strolled without talking, until they reached a pleasant spot along the road, where the drooping branches and compact, gray green leaf clusters of small trees swayed silently in the breeze. Prisca spread her cloak under one of them. Andrew joined her.

"Jesus said that to be a wife and mother was not women's crowning glory, Andrew, but to do the will of his Father. What did he mean?"

The ruddy face looked puzzled. "I do not know. I suppose it means that until he comes back, all of us must use all our powers to spread the good news and forget about our own lives."

This, it seemed to Prisca, was just what they had been doing, and she had never been happier. The very week that she and Barnabas had arrived from Jerusalem, Barnabas had invited his neighbors in the valley, together with their wives and children, and had begun the work of bringing Jesus' teachings to their lives. Over the weeks and months, he had continued to tell them all he had seen and heard during the three years of Jesus' ministry.

Lydia, the twins, Mark, and Prisca, listened as well. Maya and the servants of Barnabas's household were also invited to hear. Occasionally he had called upon Prisca to relate some anecdote that she had heard from the Master's lips or from the women of Cana. Gradually a deep bond of friendship formed among the families, until they knew themselves to be, in some positive way, a community closer than kin.

"God is like Jesus" was a phrase Barnabas repeated so often that to Prisca and others, a gradual linking between the two began to take place. Lost in her thoughts, she was unaware when Andrew stopped talking and began observing her curiously.

"Barnabas tells me you have devoted yourself daily to studying the Scriptures."

"Yes." She threw him a quick smile. "He teaches me himself when he is here. When he is gone, it is Mark. I confess I am not the most apt pupil. It is all so different."

"Do not be so modest. Barnabas says your grasp is as good as a man's. He says you bring a fresh view to the Scriptures and that the neighbors are eager to listen to your experiences with the Master."

Prisca felt her cheeks grow warm with pleasure. Barnabas said that?

Andrew plucked a weed stem and began to chew it. "Does Mark bear you a grudge? And why is he your teacher if he does?"

She shrugged. "He is my teacher because his uncle told him he would be. As for the other, I cannot say."

Andrew rose to his feet. "We should be getting back."

"Will you and Matthias pray with us before you leave?"

"Gladly. Barnabas, too."

"*Barnabas?* He is not leaving, too, is he?"

"Yes, didn't he tell you?"

"No." *No, no, no! How could he!* She knew he loved her. How could she endure this life without him, in the constant presence of Mark's sarcasm? It was more than she could bear. Blindly she followed Andrew down the hill.

"I cannot help feeling, Prisca, that our Lord has something special in mind for you. It is the strangest feeling. It was one of the things that drove me to seek you out again. Now that we have spoken, I am convinced it is so. We shall meet again, my child." The guileless blue eyes smiled back at her. He waited for her to catch up and hugged her. "My sister."

Chapter 14

Barnabas had been back from his latest voyage for a week when he sent word to Prisca that he wished to see her. As Prisca awaited him in the atrium she pondered their relationship. They were no longer intimate friends, and she ached for the one brief moment when their passion had not been denied. Yet even as they had grown more distant, they were closer in the spirit of serving a common master.

Two more years had passed on Cyprus. The fortunes of Barnabas's house had increased and so the numbers who came weekly to receive the teachings of Jesus.

In Barnabas's prolonged absences, more of the burden had fallen upon his family. Lydia was frequently occupied with overseeing the domestic chores; Mark, the management of the farm, the orchard, and the threshing floor. To Prisca, with the help of the twins, fell the main task of feeding the hungry. She was reminded of her similar task when she had been a priestess of Artemis. For they also had never turned away the hungry traveler.

From legend, the needy and the stranger were from Zeus. He who failed to help them sinned against Zeus himself. As she waited for Barnabas, she thought how uncannily Jesus had been able to sift what was good from people's lives and use it to the glory of God. It was good to be blessed with riches. It was good to care for those less fortunate, for thereby some entertained angels unawares. To Jesus it had not mattered that others taught the same thing, only that all should realize that riches and compassion alike came from the Father.

Whether by design or accident on this warm afternoon, the rest of the family seemed to be elsewhere. She could hear the wind sounding corners of the abnormally quiet house. Perhaps Barnabas, too, had waited until they could meet alone. It was hard to sit still. She smoothed away the tendrils of hair that insisted on working loose and curling along her neck.

"Good morrow, Prisca." Barnabas came in briskly, swung a bench around in front of her chair and sat down. He smelled clean, and his white linen robe had the sweet, crisp fragrance of fresh clothing. His gray hair was curlier than usual and appeared damp. He stared into her eyes for a long moment. Her lips parted in a smile. She knew he could read her love for him. The huge fist, coiled lightly on his knee, twitched once. He cleared his throat and looked away.

"Prisca . . . ."

Outwardly Prisca maintained her composure, drawing strength from her erect carriage. "Yes, Barnabas."

"You and I have got to talk, Prisca. I knew it when I left Jerusalem. I didn't want it to be this way. I want it—"

A coil of fear shivered and took form. "What way, Barnabas? If I've done something—"

"You haven't, my dear, dear Prisca. I've got to leave you. If I don't now, I never will. Each time it is so much harder."

Prisca's lips moved, but no sound came. She reached out to him.

Barnabas imprisoned her hands in a tight grasp. "I am leaving here. I am taking Mark with me."

"But your farm—the family. . . . For how long?"

"The harvest is ready. The laborers are few."

"I do not understand, dear Barnabas. I thought you were already hiring men for the harvest—"

"No, no. Not that."

"What, then? What has happened? Usually when you come home from Jerusalem you are full of good news of the brethren."

Barnabas groaned. He looked in Prisca's eyes, and for a moment she read his love and the anguish that these words were costing him. "Dear one, if my life were my own to give. . . ." He rose and turned his back to her, head tilted back, hands on hips and feet planted apart. Dimly she was aware of two jays fighting noisily in the pomegranate tree.

Finally, his voice husky, he said, "It is better that you should know how matters stand. One of the brethren, a young man called Stephen, full of holy zeal, decided Christ meant for him to openly challenge Jewish law and custom. He caused such turmoil at the temple that the elders flew into a rage. They caused him to be hauled beyond the city gates and stoned him to death." He turned to face her, as if to be sure she did not miss the import of his words.

Prisca gasped. "They killed him for preaching that Jesus was their Messiah?"

"Well, that was the whole of it, yes, but the final straw, the thing they could not countenance, was that he accused them in public of engineering Jesus' murder. No one really bothered us when we were just a small band in Jerusalem. The Romans treated us as just another sect of the Jewish faith, in their view more fanatic than most. The Jews didn't like what we were saying, but mostly they tolerated us because we are, after all, Jews first. As long as we kept to ourselves, kept the laws, and were powerless."

"What changed it?"

Barnabas smiled grimly. "Fear for themselves. Stephen's death served to bring it out in the open. Prisca, thousands in Jerusalem now believe Jesus is the Messiah! The word is reaching citizens who are powerful and rich, men to be feared as enemies. Before, they were called community leaders. Now as followers of Christ they've bought a reputation as rabble rousers. Such men make those in established positions of power very uneasy.

"A man named Saul seems to have a special hatred of us. He has sworn to wipe every one of the followers off the face of the earth. Anyone with any kind of grudge against us now acts without fear of punishment. They have been seizing our goods unlawfully, beating our workers, and vilifying our families. In Jerusalem it is no longer safe to meet openly. Peter has given orders that all the leaders must forsake Jerusalem and carry the word to Jews in other cities.

"I am going to Jerusalem to put my goods and ships at Peter's disposal."

"Then I must help, too. Take me with you, Barnabas!"

"Dear one," he said huskily, "when I was away on business, all the months and weeks, my thoughts were filled with you. Coming home to you—"

"It is the same with me. Why cannot we—"

He shook his head vehemently. "Remember what Andrew said? Our lives are not our own. We must prepare the way for the Lord's return."

Her lips compressed. She turned her head to hide the bitter tears.

"You wanted to be a disciple," he said softly.

She nodded.

"Jesus tried to warn us the way was dangerous. But in those days, who would have believed—I know now it is not a path meant for a woman."

"It is! It is! Jesus called me as surely as you! Do I lack courage? Do I lack faith?"

"Nothing could make me take you to Jerusalem!" he said harshly. "I would worry so about you that I would be useless for the Lord's work."

"Oh, Barnabas!" She struggled to her feet, and Barnabas pulled her into his arms. She could not keep the tears from falling. She could feel the dry sobs wrenching his body. They clung together without speaking for several minutes.

"Please take me," she sobbed against his shoulder. "Please! You know I love you!"

"Stay here with Lydia," he pleaded. "You will be safe here. I am not selling the farm. I am going to keep it as long as I can. I've talked it over with Lydia, and she feels—"

"So here you are!" Mark entered the atrium from the library and came to an abrupt stop. "Well-l!"

Barnabas and Prisca sprang apart. "I thought you were out at the winepress," Barnabas said angrily.

"I was. Shall I leave again?"

"No, Mark, forgive me. What is it?"

"Uncle, six men walked in from Salamis. I have hired five of them to help harvest the wheat. A sixth says you promised him work, but him I did not hire. He looks ill and weak."

"If I promised him work, then we will hire him."

"But, uncle!"

"In a moment. Mark, you and I are returning to Jerusalem. I was just telling Prisca."

"Prisca, too?" Mark threw her a glance of contempt.

His words cut into her soul. Biting back tears, she looked away.

" 'Prisca, too' what?"

"Nothing, uncle. Prisca must remain here is what I meant."

Barnabas did not look at her. "Mark, sometimes—Never mind. Now here is what we must do. . . ."

Barnabas, look at me! Barnabas! It was as if he had forgotten her.

"Now, my boy," Barnabas was saying, "we will have a look at the new threshers." As he left the atrium Barnabas paused, his eyes drawn back to hers in a last, unreadable look.

She wanted to dash after him, beg him not to shut her out.

Mark came back to the doorway. A slow, insinuating smile edged onto his face. "Daughter of Artemis." He turned to follow Barnabas.

She gasped. The unfairness of it! She did not deserve his hatred. She had never harmed him. Never told anyone of his assault on her four years ago. Not even when Lydia had recounted Mark's past to her. Perhaps she should have. Years ago, this same ungovernable temper was the reason Mark's mother in Jerusalem had begged Barnabas to take the boy into his care. Fatherless from an early age, he had quickly learned that his mother feared his temper and afterward refused to be guided or taught by her. For all his temper, he was a hard, tenacious worker. Barnabas and Lydia had been convinced that the Lord would turn Mark's talents to his use.

Prisca was no longer certain of that. Yet Mark was going to serve afield, and she was not. Letting out her breath, she discovered she was trembling. She sat down again, aware of the long minutes passing. Gradually the peace of the atrium seeped into her being. She closed her eyes, feeling the fragrances of trees and flowers, the hum of insects, and the cooling caress of breezes.

If the brethren were being persecuted and forced to leave Jerusalem, then clearly it was time for her, too, to be about Jesus' business. If she could not go to Jerusalem, she would go elsewhere. She would not tell Barnabas yet, she decided. She would wait until there was no time to argue.

Consciously she bade farewell to a place that had nourished her, to four years with Barnabas, to unnourished passions. To think that she and Barnabas had worked and worshiped together, brought together by a love for the Christ, and yet now were to be separated by this same love. Was he truly as torn as she? Or had his love been no more than the love he poured so generously upon his family?

An ache invaded her heart and settled there. She bent her head and covered her face with her hands. "God of him who rescued me into a higher life, make me strong enough now to do thy will."

"Prisca?"

She looked up. Lydia was observing her from the doorway. "Oh. Hello, Lydia."

Lydia's gray and faded yellow hair was braided into a coronet, lending grace to the tall, spare frame in the violet robe coming toward her. She picked up the tasseled ends of the cord bound around her waist and toyed with them. "Barnabas told you." It was a statement, not a question.

"Yes, Lydia." Prisca looked up. She smiled. "Do not look so worried."

Lydia sat beside her and reached for her hand. "I had hoped, after all these years, that I would be gaining a sister-in-law, one whom I already love as dearly as my own sisters. Barnabas loves you, too, you know."

Prisca's head drooped in dumb misery.

"Sometimes I wonder if this is what the Master really intended, for men to rush off on his business and forget their own lives! Ah!" she said with a note of disgust. "Was ever a man born who wasn't ready to thumb his nose at his family responsibilities and go off to fight a war? Much more exciting than bringing in a crop of wheat. And half as hard!"

Prisca managed a smile. "Oh, Lydia. I am going to miss you so!"

"Miss me? You mean Barnabas is taking you with him? He vowed he would not."

She shook her head. "No. He thinks I am staying. But Lydia, for four years I have been studying and praying and, I hope, growing up. If it is time for Barnabas to be about Jesus' business, then it is time for me, too."

"A woman?" Lydia burst out. "Oh, of course I know you are capable of teaching about the Christ—you've done it here for years—but who will protect you? Where will you go?"

She said the first thing that popped into her head. "I'll go into Salamis and hop on the first ship."

"You'll do nothing like it!" Then Lydia gave her a long, searching glance. "You have made up your mind to go."

"Truly."

"Have you no friends or family anywhere?"

Prisca squeezed her hand. "I have you and your family, Lydia. And I count myself rich."

Lydia thought for a moment. "The *Lotus* is in port."

"One of Barnabas's ships."

"Half his. The master of the ship, a good and trusted friend from Pontus, owns the other half. He will be sailing in a few days for Achaia and Macedonia. I have been working on the accounts. We are sending shipments of grain to several ports. In nearly all we have friends with whom you might stay. I would feel better if you would consent, Prisca." Tears filled Lydia's eyes, and she compressed her lips.

Prisca rose, needing a good cry herself. "I will go. Surely the Lord will direct my steps to the proper city."

Prisca tried not to think of Lydia and Eleanor and Helen as her caravan left the farm for Salamis. Parting from them had been nearly unbearable. Barnabas had been called away to a neighboring farm that morning, and she had not been able to bid him a private farewell. Telling him of her decision had created a scene she wished to forget. His anger had flared at Lydia for complicity and at herself for adding needlessly to his worries. Why was she not content to sit and wait on Cyprus? Most women would be glad to wait! How did she know the Lord needed her elsewhere?

For that there had been no answer, only her own unshakable conviction that it was so. With ill grace and a reluctant blessing, he had commanded Mark to escort them into Salamis.

Mark had been surly with the servants on the caravan, and it was an unusually subdued, bedraggled lot that finally appeared at the dock near the *Lotus.*

"Wait here," Mark said. Leaving the women with the beast bearing their belongings, he went aboard, returning almost immediately with another man in his wake, as if he could hardly wait to relinquish his charges. Prisca caught an impression of broad, muscular shoulders, a young man with thick, black hair worn shorter than most men's. He wore a short linen tunic and sandals that laced part way up his calves.

"This is Prisca, a priestess from the temple of Artemis at Tyre," Mark said with relish.

"*Really?*" The man stared openmouthed at her before recovering his manners. "My lady. We are not used to such beautiful passengers, but we will try to see to your comfort."

"I've got to get back," Mark said. He stared at Prisca. "You have always been too quick of tongue for a woman," he added in an undertone.

Prisca drew her lips back over her teeth. "If a brother spoke as I have, you would call him well-spoken." They glared in mutual dislike. Mark looked away.

"Good day to you, Aquila." Unceremoniously he unstrapped their bundles from the ass and piled them on the ground beside them, gave a sharp command to the ass, and led it back the way they had come.

Prisca felt her cheeks turning crimson. The young man before her shifted in embarrassment.

"Mark—uh—forgot to introduce me. I am Aquila, master of the *Lotus.*" He hooked his thumbs in his girdle—big, capable hands, Prisca noticed—looked over his shoulder at the ship, and said, "We will be ready to sail in an hour. I'll find a place where you and your servant can wait in comfort."

"Thank you," she whispered.

"Junius," Aquila summoned a sweating crewman. "Take the lady's belongings to my berth. Stow my kit with the mate's."

"Right, captain." Junius touched his forelock and easily shouldered Prisca's and Maya's possessions in one load.

"Please, Captain Aquila, we do not need your berth, just a corner with privacy."

Aquila grinned. "That's what you are getting. It is the only corner with a door. Sorry we can't offer better, but we are a merchantman." He led them away from the dock, toward a sun shield flapping in the wind. Its corners were fastened to upright poles. Under it were a table and benches, evidently used to handle shipping transactions. She smiled her thanks as he left them there, her courage nearly gone.

What was she doing? Was it truly the leading of the God of Jesus that once again separated her from people and a home she had loved? Or was it the humiliation of rejection by a man she loved too deeply?

Her thoughts turned thus inward, Prisca watched the men loading the ship. The *Lotus* was longer by half than the vessel that had brought her to Cyprus. There were the eyes painted on the prow. But a higher, round stern, with a stern post ending in a carved swan swooping to twice the height of a man.

When they finally boarded the *Lotus,* Maya immediately demanded to go to their cabin.

Junius quailed before her screech, as if unsure of Maya's place in the hierarchy, and hurried them across the deck.

The cabin was a low, oblong box built astern, with entry a few steps down a narrow companionway behind the mast. Two small squares of window opening onto either side of the quarterdeck provided fair light. Maya took one look at the dim, cramped space and announced to Prisca, "If we drown in this wretched vessel, this will make a fitting burial box! And it will be 'pon your head, mistress!" Maya's face was swollen and puffy. She had worked herself up into a proper grievance after two hours of indulgently tearful good-byes with the other servants.

"You did not have to come! Lydia said you were welcome to stay," Prisca snapped, struggling with her own depression. A little comfort and confidence from Maya would not have been unwelcome. She felt the sway of the boat as it was freed of its anchors. *Come now, Prisca,* she told herself, *pull yourself together.* She sorted through her belongings, placing them in flax bags she found suspended from hooks along the walls. Resolutely ignoring Maya, she pulled her blue cloak snug around her shining hair and marched back to the deck.

As Prisca climbed out on deck a pleasant flapping sound and the muted voices of crewmen met her ears. Shading her eyes, she gazed upward. The huge, square sail was completely unfurled. Ropes running from the bottom edge of the sail to the bottom of the thick mast and those secured along the sides of the boat creaked companionably to the flap of wind in the canvas. Forward, billowing out from a tall spar angled over the prow, a smaller square of sail danced in the wind. Some cargo was lashed to the forward bulwarks, but she noted plenty of room for walks.

Prisca turned on her heel and paced around the quarter deck. Cyprus was already no more than a mid-sized island blueing in the distance. She spied the high, arched neck of the swan rising in the stern behind the cabin and went for a proper look.

Rounding the cabin, she came suddenly upon Aquila, seated on a bale bound with fishnet. He was mending canvas.

Aquila jumped to his feet. "Ow!"

"Oh!"

"Not you. I stuck the needle in my hand. See?" A tiny globe of blood oozed from the fleshy part of his palm.

"I'm sorry, captain. Does it hurt?"

"Awful." He grinned, openly engaging her eyes.

His face was very pleasant to look upon. His eyes, she noticed, were as black as ripe olives. She glanced down, suddenly shy. "Will it bother you if I sit near?"

"Glad for the company." With his needle he pointed at another bale. As she composed her cloak she felt his interested gaze.

The wind was brisk. Prisca leaned over the rail to admire the ruffled spume of the wake created as the ship cut through the water. She cast covert glances back at Aquila when he resumed sewing. His nose was aquiline, bent slightly to the right, just below the bridge, as though it had been broken. A thin, jagged line the width of a thumb rode just above his right eyebrow, contrasting whitely with his dark skin. The scar disappeared as his black brows pulled together in concentration. Though it was early afternoon, his jaw was faintly blue, delineating a heavy beard. He had an air of rugged contentment about him that made Prisca feel that he was a man who had learned to take care of himself. She also concluded he was one of the handsomest men she had ever seen.

"Where—?" They spoke in unison and both laughed.

". . . Did you meet Barnabas?" said Aquila.

"Yes, that was my question, too."

"You first," he prodded.

"In Jerusalem. He brought me to Cyprus to live with his family. I was there four years."

"Oh. I did not know there was—ah—a temple of Artemis on Cyprus."

"I follow the God of Jesus now, the one they call the Christ."

Aquila put down the sail. "You do? But you are not—why did Mark. . . ," he grimaced and changed tack. "You'll miss him, I suppose."

"Mark? No."

"Barnabas, then?"

"Tell me about you. How did you meet him?"

He flashed a grin, displaying even, healthy teeth. "Do you want the long version or the short one?"

"The long," she laughed. "I love tales. *Aquila* means 'eagle,' doesn't it?"

"Yes." Aquila cast an experienced eye over her, stuck his tongue in his cheek, and said, "After a wild and misspent youth, I was a broken man at the age of fourteen and ran away from home."

"Did you really?"

"Yes." Home was a fishing village, he told her, along the southern shore of the Black Sea, in the Roman province of Pontus, where his father was a tentmaker. His father was a strict Jew, a Talmudic scholar who insisted upon observance of every one of the dietary laws and sabbath observances.

She could understand how it might have been a stifling existence for a boy of fourteen. She wondered about the rest of his family. How could anyone with a real family bear to leave it?

In the last seven years, though, Aquila confessed, he had grown to respect his father's teachings. "At least he gave me a skill. Tentmakers can always make a living—as sail menders if nothing else."

Aquila set aside the sail and got up and stretched. "Three years ago I was living in Rome with friends. We were whooping it up, as usual—we had a few drachmae in our pouches and too much wine in our—uh—to drink. Some Roman soldiers were about to haul us in when Barnabas intervened. You see? The long tale does have an end! Barnabas seemed like such a sober citizen that they let us go in his care. He had been on his way to a meeting. I went with him after we took the others home. That was when I first heard about Jesus."

Prisca smiled wistfully. "Barnabas has a habit of rescuing lost souls."

"Barnabas and I saw a lot of each other while he took care of his business in the city. Then he offered me a job as mate on one of his ships. I went to work for him and, well, one thing led to another, and now I own half interest in the *Lotus*. Now you know everything about me. May I ask you a question?"

"Yes." Her eyes sparkled with mischief. "I claim the right not to answer it, though."

"Were you really a priestess of Artemis?"

"Yes."

His lips formed a silent whistle and his olive black eyes swept over her, none too discreetly. "The ones in Rome are beautiful." Suddenly Aquila seemed to grasp the implication of his words. His neck reddened. "I only meant, you are as beautiful as any I—Oh, by the gods, I'm only making it worse!"

Prisca tried to remain decorous, but she burst out laughing. "I am not a priestess any longer. I was brought up in the temple as a child. I knew of no other life until the day I heard Jesus speak in the marketplace in Tyre."

"There is a magnificent temple in Ephesus. Have you ever seen it?"

Neatly changing the subject away from Jesus, Prisca realized. Perhaps he did not know yet that Jesus was truly the Messiah. "I have heard about it."

"Mark did not say where you are going."

"I do not know where I am going, Aquila. Somewhere where people want to learn more about the Christ."

Aquila whistled silently. "You want to teach about the Christ? That is it? All alone?" He studied her with renewed interest, searching her face in a different manner, as if forgetting for the moment her beauty, the allure of her pagan past. "What if Jesus isn't the Christ?" he said brusquely. "It is hard to believe that just an ordinary man is our Messiah."

"You mean you do not believe it."

"Easy now. Say that he is. Even if he doesn't have any temples or any priests. Do you have people—I mean, is it safe? How will you live? Anyway, I have not made up my mind about Jesus. I know what Barnabas told me. Did you really meet Jesus?"

"Yes. Maybe when you are not busy, you would let me tell you more about him."

Aquila grinned carelessly in his former teasing manner. "I can't think of anything better. Unless it's how to get this tub to move a bit slower than usual."

"My servant, Maya, would not appreciate that at all!" Prisca laughed, her heart suddenly far lighter than at any time since her confrontation with Barnabas. Maybe Jesus had sent this strong young man to her, to strengthen her as she began this unknown direction of her discipleship.

Chapter 15

ong days followed star-filled nights as the *Lotus* dogged the Asian coast westward, putting in at strange ports, exchanging cargo for new consignments. Gradually Prisca grew accustomed to the rhythm of the sea traders. She had not realized how pastoral her life had become on Cyprus. How sheltered. Studying, teaching the girls, gathering in the evenings to share the remembered joys of Jesus' life among them and of the lessons he had left them and the promises to be fulfilled had lulled her into forgetting the vigor and energy of a life lived elsewhere, together with its problems and choices.

When they reached a port, the stern anchors were dropped and the boat waggled sluggishly as an arthritic dog until the bow anchors followed. Then Prisca would cajole Maya into a cloak and on deck. As soon as the gangplank was slid onto the jetty or dock or shore, the women would be across it, to spend the day exploring the city.

"I have seen enough to last a lifetime," complained Maya one day as they sat in the shade of a fruit seller's stall, munching apples and some cheese brought from the ship. "Where are we going, Prisca? How will you know when you have found the place your Jesus wants you to be?" Half to herself she mumbled, "The gods know I've seen not hide nor hair of this man-god. No temples, no statues—"

"Maya!"

"Yes, mistress?"

"That will do. I will know when I know."

Prisca found that Aquila of Pontus was a restless man. When he was not at the rudder, he was mending sails or fishing or rearranging cargo. Whatever tasks he ordered of the crew usually drew him in also.

Whenever she appeared on deck, she noticed that Aquila soon found reason to be nearby. When he did so, he had a habit of picking up a conversation from the point of their last parting, whether an hour or a day had passed.

"So," he called to her, coming down the rope ladder beside the mast to land in a light spring at her feet, "I have never been forced to live by my father's predictions." A roguish gleam entered his eyes.

"And what were they?" she said, entering into the spirit of his game.

"That I would dishonor the family name by begging in the streets . . . and die of some rotten disease caused by sinful living."

Disrespectful or no, it was impossible not to join in his hearty laughter.

For several days they had been in the waters of the Aegean, stopping at Cos, Troas, Thessalonica, and Athens. At each stop she had gone ashore, seeking she knew not what and returning in disappointment.

"Have you ever been to Corinth, Prisca?"

"Never. When I was little, I used to stand on the shore at Tyre and wonder if I should ever see any of the places I read about. I remember reading about Glaucus, the king of Corinth, son of Sisyphus, who lives forever in Hades, condemned to roll a marble boulder uphill for all eternity for betraying a secret of Zeus." Her green eyes sparkled. "And Pegasus—"

" 'A winged steed, unwearying of flight/Sweeping through air as swift as a gale of wind.' " Aquila supplied.

"Yes! When I was little, I was sure that if ever I should go to Corinth, I would be the one to find his stable."

"Maybe you will." Aquila's voice was thoughtful.

"Do you know Mark well?" she said suddenly.

"Only the few times he came out on the *Lotus* with Barnabas."

"He is younger than you."

"No, a year older. Why?" Aquila perched on the creaking wooden rail and thumbed his lower lip, his eyes teasing. "Aha! You are smitten with him!"

"Oh, no! Nor he with me. You just seem—older. Wiser."

"Naturally."

She laughed. "I did not mean to embarrass you."

"A lady who speaks her mind, eh? It gives me leave to say to you what is on my mind."

Smiling, she dipped her head in graceful acquiescence.

"Why have you not married?"

She moved into herself a little more, hands seeking elbows, hugging into body, her ankles tucked together below the bench. "No one has asked for me," she said without looking at him.

She heard a sound from him that might have been sympathy or surprise. "And is there one in particular who was so unbelievably stupid?"

A smile curled about her lips in spite of herself. "Perhaps there was."

"Was?"

"Was," she said, hoping her voice sounded more positive than she felt, for who could tell? Perhaps in a year or so, Barnabas would miss her the way she missed him. . . .

He grinned. "Well! That is settled." He slid off the bulwark, giving a hitch to the girdle that rode on his slim hips. He glanced to the north. "Prisca, look to windward. Tell me what you see!"

They were sailing past a small, mountainous cape of land. She sighted a towering statue standing astride a temple of gleaming white columns. "Poseidon!" she whispered. His trident outthrust in one huge fist, Poseidon reared over his temple with outward gaze, lord of all who sailed his seas.

"Do you know why he's out there?" asked Aquila.

Prisca shook her head.

"He was banished. See, Poseidon falls in love with Athens and decides to be its patron god. So to impress the king, he goes up to the Acropolis and smites it a mighty blow with his trident. The hill splits open, and sea water gushes out and forms this pool. The king is mightily impressed. He's all ready to make Poseidon god of Athens."

Prisca was enchanted as much by the teller as the tale. "Then what happens?"

Aquila's black eyes danced as he shifted to the next role. He folded his hands and assumed a stately pose. "Well, you know how women are. Athena looks down from Olympus and sees old Poseidon as happy as a kid with a new toy. She's not about to be outdone by any sea god, so she decides she wants Athens. She gets the king's attention and conjures up a full-grown olive tree," Aquila's hands soared up in a full circle, "bearing fruit, right beside Poseidon's pool. Well, naturally, the olive being the most prized tree in Greece, the king awarded Athens to the goddess. This really puts old Poseidon out of sorts. He vows he'll flood the city."

Aquila dove into a pocket and pulled out an unfinished lanyard and began braiding the strands of hemp.

"Well does he? That isn't the end!"

Aquila flashed a teasing smile at Prisca. "So the king, good politician that he is, says the citizens should vote on which one should be their patron god. The men vote for Poseidon. The women outnumber the men, and you can guess who they vote for. The king awards the city to Athena, Poseidon keeps his word and devastates the city with a flood, and the men take the vote away from the women."

"But Athena kept her city!"

"Aha, you do know the story!"

Prisca responded with a guilty grin. "Everyone knows some version of it," she said lamely.

"Yes, she kept her city. And Poseidon was banished to the cape and has been there ever since. Well, back to work, lovely Prisca."

Nimbly Aquila went up the rope ladder and began working on the lashings that secured the yard to the mast. He hung there as though it were the most natural thing in the world to be fiddling so far above ground. Soon he was climbing down again.

She admired his muscular agility, averting her eyes as he neared the deck, but retaining the memory of the corded thighs and calves below his short tunic. He had the fine body of an athlete. She would miss him, she realized, once she found her new home.

In good weather, Prisca remained on deck all day, protecting her hair and face from the unsparing sun and wind with a heavy linen shawl pulled well over her brow. She did her best to keep out of the crew's way, loving the exhilarating sense of freedom on board ship, the clarity and ever-changing palette of colors of the shore waters of the Great Sea, the silver flash of fish just below the surface.

One morning Aquila came in search of her. "Here's something you shouldn't miss. Even the gods can't top it." He led her to the prow. "Watch," he commanded.

They were coming into port again. To her amazement, the ship did not lose speed as it neared the harbor, but seemed to cut a path right through the moored fishing boats and head straight for the village on a channel of sand, like some leviathan bent on beaching itself.

Chains clanked and heavy wet ropes were hauled and coiled on deck with thuds and grunts. She leaned over the side. Unbelievably, they were over land! Then Aquila was at her side, escorting her through the busy crew to the gangplank. She had forgotten completely about Maya. Now standing on solid ground, she looked up to see her being led shakily down the gangplank and deposited on a nearby bale.

"We'll walk from here," Aquila told them.

"Walk where?" she asked, glancing about the small village.

Aquila grinned. "Into Corinth. We're at Cenchrea."

The cargo remained aboard. The crew, laughing and talking and relieved of their jobs, left the ship and started walking, while hundreds of slaves converged on the beached craft. As she watched, the ship was pulled onto a train of rollers, which led toward a sharp cleft between two mountains, as deep and straight as if Artemis had split it with an arrow. Expertly the husky slaves began to haul the ship along the towpath.

"Corinth is only four miles from here," Aquila told her. "But by ship it means navigating Cape Malea. Sailors will tell you the man who rounds Cape Malea might as well forget he has a home. So small ships get hauled overland." He glanced back uncertainly at Maya. "Can she walk that far? She's still on her sea legs."

"If she can't, she'll have to stay here," said Prisca.

Aquila raised his eyebrows but said nothing. Maya, overhearing Prisca's words, glowered at her young mistress and got to her feet. Prisca smiled to herself and turned with Aquila to follow the crew trooping toward the pass. She'd learned long ago that to suggest an ailment to Maya was to confirm it. It did not help man nor woman to be accounted weak in this life.

As they walked Aquila entertained them with tales of Corinth. He had been there many times. Nearly two hundred years ago, he said, Corinth had been sacked by Rome. A hundred years later, Julius Caesar refounded it. As a Roman colony it became the capital of Achaia and was resettled by Roman veterans of many wars and descendants of freedmen. It was the playground of Athens, to which businessmen escaped for a week's pleasure with old wine and young mistresses. It was an open port to sailors, a haven for drunkenness and debauchery. It was a center of learning to scholars and of great devotion to the arts. At Corinth money talked. One could buy anything.

Emerging from the pass, Prisca caught her breath. Corinth lay gleaming before them in a bath of mellow gold studded with charcoal shadows. Full-grown trees lined the wide avenues, setting off buildings constructed with ordered grace. Everywhere, people: on foot, on horseback, traveling in caravans, by chariot. Corinth teemed with life. She fell immediately in love with it.

Aquila took her arm, pointing off to the right, to the gulf curving around the city like a scimitar. At its tip was the harbor, destination of the *Lotus* and other small ships hauled across the isthmus from Cenchrea.

In the opposite direction, looming nineteen hundred feet above Corinth to the southwest, was Acro-Corinthus, citadel of the Corinthian gods. The peak of the mountain was dedicated to war, but also boasted a temple devoted to Astarte, Aphrodite, and Venus, all images of the same Mother Goddess Prisca had once served.

Prisca stopped and gazed up the mountain in awe. "I feel so small," she whispered.

"One thousand priests and priestesses serve in that temple," said Aquila. "They say the lights never go out, and the music never stops."

His words cast a chill over her. *And once one has lost faith, the horror never ceases.* Bodies . . . over and over being ritually coupled in the frantic pretense that the whim of a goddess can instruct the seasons. Images of Limaeus unwillingly despoiled her thoughts. With an effort, she shook them off and concentrated on Aquila's discourse.

The temple *was* magnificent. It represented the best that men could build, the ultimate offering from a city to the gods its people created. Yet how much more difficult to worship the unseen God than to build this paean of beauty to one's beliefs and worship at its feet!

Corinth's lure was inescapable, yet she felt strangely apart.

Maya suddenly came to life. "Oh, mistress, this is a beautiful place. More lovely than Tyre and Cyprus together! Is this where your Jesus wants us to abide?" She clutched Prisca's arm tightly and tugged her forward, her head swiveling from right to left at the sights.

Sounds of timbrels, drums, and horns rose to their ears. As they followed the road into the city the crowds increased. Eagerly Prisca drank in the faces. Never had she seen a more comely people. The Greeks of Corinth were easily distinguishable from the multitude of other races. Many of the women went unveiled and wore short haircuts, and even the men's hair was curled. Their brows were wide and smooth, their noses in fine proportion. People looked so healthy and young. Few beggars accosted them, nor did she see any maimed or sickly. Smiles of passersby were coupled with the honey of geniality and salt of excitement.

"Is it always like this?" Prisca asked.

"Not that I remember." Aquila stopped a modestly robed man and questioned him.

"The games start tomorrow at the amphitheater, friend. In honor of Apollo! You got here at the right time." The man, who spoke a fluid though lazy Greek, appeared to be of the merchant class. Throwing a speculative glance at Prisca, he tugged at Aquila's sleeve, pulling him aside.

Prisca could not hear the exchange of words, but Aquila's face darkened in a scowl. She had not considered him an especially tall man, but now, leaning over the merchant, he seemed to grow before her eyes. The merchant left hurriedly.

"What did he want?"

"Nothing," Aquila snapped. "Prisca, there won't be a spare bed in all Corinth. You are coming back to the ship with me."

"But—"

They stood in the middle of the cobbled street, traffic streaming around them. "Look, Prisca, I've got to stay with the ship until she's moored and the cargo released. I do not want you wandering the streets. Barnabas would never forgive me if anything happened to you. Return to the ship with me." A note of pleading entered his voice. "We will be here a day or two, and I will escort you wherever you wish to go."

Prisca was chastened by the concern in his voice. "Very well," she said.

They continued on through the city. A band of strolling players romped by, accompanied by the instruments they had heard earlier. Maya seemed to have forgotten her grievances and chattered continually about the wonderful sights.

"Oh! Oh!" she clasped her hands. "Look!"

Beyond the marketplace, next to a magnificent fountain, rose an exquisite temple that was a joy to behold. Surrounded by fluted columns that supported a roof open to the heavens was a marble stage, in its center a lifesize statue of Apollo, strumming a lyre. His brow was crowned with fresh, green laurel leaves, in honor, no doubt, of the coming games. The sun god was the most beautiful of Greeks, son of Zeus, master musician, healer, link between god and human.

Prisca approached the shrine with reverence for the maker's genius, Aquila at her shoulder.

"Wonderful, isn't it?" he said, reading her thoughts.

She nodded, turning to him with a half smile. "It is easy to honor a god who is so beautiful."

"Yes. Or one who is powerful."

She looked at him with interest as they started walking again, through the marketplace and toward the harbor.

"I was thinking of Poseidon," he said. "There isn't a seaman alive who does not offer a prayer or two to Poseidon. It does not do to offend the gods," he said seriously.

"Aquila! And you a Jew."

"Also a sailor, lady. My father was never on the Great Sea in a small boat fighting for his life. I was. Then you pray to all the gods." His tone grew belligerent as he added, "And when we reached shore, we made sacrifice to him, too, so he would not think we were ungrateful and sink us next time."

Prisca nodded. "Fear makes people do strange things. Jesus said his Father does not require sacrifice to watch over us."

"You believe that?"

She was silent. "Yes. He has guided my steps. He has kept me safe."

"He has?"

She smiled, teasingly. "He sent you to do it for him."

Aquila laughed uneasily.

Suddenly Prisca heard her name called. She saw a hand raised, and a slight figure in scruffy gray and wine cloak and loose sandals was loping across the square toward them. An oversized fishnet bag slapped and clanked against his legs as he ran.

"Limaeus!" She shrank back against Aquila.

"Prisca! Oh, finding you in Corinth! The gods are good to me today!" His eyes shifted to her companions. "And Maya. Great times at the temple back in Tyre, eh?"

He grinned, his gaze sliding over Aquila, his demeanor insinuating a camaraderie that had never existed. Prisca felt the blood draining from her cheeks.

"You promised never to seek me out!"

"But, dear lady, I didn't!" Limaeus protested, assessing Aquila with his watery blue eyes. "Could I know you would follow me to Corinth after nearly five years? By your dress, you've just arrived." He added slyly, "And is this your servant, too, or is he another conquest from the temple?"

Prisca felt sick to her stomach, as if someone had punched her.

Aquila stepped slightly in front of Prisca. "That's enough. Who are you?"

"Prisca and I are old friends."

"Never! We were never friends. Aquila, let us go at once. Please!"

Aquila took her arm, a scowl on his face, and led her away from Limaeus. Maya hurried not to be left behind.

Limaeus sprinted after them. "Maybe we can all be friends, dear Prisca. I live here now. I sell votive offerings for the gods."

Prisca walked faster. Limaeus clung to the pace like a leech, digging into his bag. "Maya, here, let me give you a gift. Your mistress is not feeling especially gracious tonight—though it's easy to see she's come around, has she not? That Jewish rabbi was poison. We were all lucky to get out. Here." He thrust a tiny silver amulet into Maya's hand.

With a beseeching gaze Maya clutched at Prisca's sleeve.

A deep, shuddering cry tore out of Prisca's throat. She seized the amulet from Maya and ground it under her sandal. "If you ever bother us again, I will have you killed!"

Aquila stopped. His hand closed over her arm like an iron cuff. He pulled her behind him. "For the last time, on your way, peasant."

"Ooh," said Limaeus. "I'm so frightened. I live here now. This is my city." He danced away from Aquila like a yipping dog. "The gods are on my side now, Prisca," he shouted, beginning to draw a crowd. Seeing himself the center of attention, he renewed his attack. "I'm not good enough for you, eh? Not tall and handsome enough, eh? You liked me well enough that night!"

With a cry of outrage Aquila sprang after him.

Limaeus dashed away like a man gone berserk, waving his arms and shrieking, "I'll wager Acro-Corinthus could find a place for you, though you are no longer young, though you are no longer a—"

Aquila seized Limaeus by the cloak and found his throat. He lifted him off his feet. Limaeus's sandals churned in air. His sack fell to the street as he struggled with both hands to pry Aquila's fingers from his throat.

Prisca clenched her fists. *Kill him.*

His eyes bulged. A rasping noise issued from his mouth. Slowly his face metamorphosed into a red, wet mask. The men surrounding them erupted into action. Several caught Aquila's arms, fighting him to release Limaeus. Others shielded the women. Aquila was red faced, grunting, his teeth exposed for the kill.

Prisca realized with a shock that Limaeus was dying. She rushed toward Aquila and seized his arm with both hands. "No!" she screamed. "No, don't kill him!"

A babble of languages drenched their ears. An outrage, she understood them saying. Men who fought belonged in the games!

With a choking cry, Aquila threw Limaeus away from him like guts of a butchered animal. He stared at Prisca, gulping air. His burning eyes drilled into her.

"Come on," he ordered.

Chapter 16

risca leaned against the rail of the *Lotus*. Her blue cloak had blown back against her shoulders. She closed her eyes to the wind streaming through her hair and released her tense body to the sway of the deck. She heard Aquila's step, opened her eyes, but did not look at him.

His broad hand settled next to hers on the rail. His fingers, she noticed, were long and tapered, rather than blunt.

"It has been a week," he said, as if that should mean something.

A week, yes, since Aquila nearly killed Limaeus in her defense. Ruthlessly, deliberately, had nearly murdered a man. She had refused to leave the ship since.

"Prisca? Don't turn away!"

In the coolness of her present anger, she saw that Limaeus had been like a spiteful child with a dirty mouth, perhaps not even in full possession of his wits. Had not strangers intervened, Aquila would now be facing either death or life as a galley slave. And it would have been her fault, which she had been avoiding all week. Her own guilt. Memories seared into her flesh during the humiliating night with Limaeus, memories mercifully buried during the years on Cyprus. Now she saw they had never disappeared. Instead they had sunk into a cesspool of hatred that threatened to decay her very soul. Disciple indeed. . . .

Prisca drew in a deep breath and turned to Aquila. She fixed her eyes on the pattern of earth-colored geometric blocks trimming the sleeve of his linen tunic, only inches from her face.

"You have not spoken to anyone for a week. I want you to forget that gutter rat. I wish I had killed him. He doesn't deserve to live." Aquila kneaded the rail with white-knuckled hands. He looked down at her. "How in Hades did you get mixed up with someone like that?"

Unwillingly she met his gaze. She felt so helpless. Her remorse was useless to him.

He tore his eyes away and looked out to sea. "I do not know what is wrong with me. I have no claim on you. I don't even know what you are talking about half the time. And yet I've got this—this gnawing inside,

131

that if I ever let you get away—," he turned and pulled her loosely into his arms.

"Oh, Aquila! You should hate me for what I have done!"

"Hate you!"

"I wanted you to kill that man. I who am supposed to serve the God of Jesus," she said in self-reproach. "To spread the good news that Jesus loved all of us enough to die for us. To show others that doing the will of the Father is the most important thing we can do with our lives." Her mouth seemed full of tears. She swallowed and looked out to sea. "I wanted you to kill that man with all my heart. I was so full of my own hate, I did not even think of you. You would have killed him to protect me and lost your own life doing it."

She began to cry. Tenderly Aquila gathered her closer, as if comforting a child.

"I have been living in a myth," she sobbed. "I should thank Limaeus for driving away the clouds."

"Now what are you talking about?"

Her lips trembled. "I will never be able to escape what I am. I am unable to endure even the pitiful humiliation of a weak man. He was right. I should have gone to Acro-Corinthus and rejoined the priesthood!"

Aquila shook her gently. "Prisca, you are too hard on yourself. Did you want to go back to your goddess? Were you afraid you would? Is that why you would not leave the ship again while we were at Corinth?"

"The truth is, I thought I had changed. I have not. I thought I was different because Jesus chose me. I am not." Her words echoed the sadness in her heart. Still lying against his chest, she said quietly, "Limaeus is right. I did lie with him."

She held her breath, waiting for Aquila's reaction, feeling his heartbeat against her ear. She experienced the oddest feeling that he was so intensely involved with her feelings that he was a part of her, her anguish his. She went on. "It is so hard to accept. He did not speak falsely, but in half truths. I hated Limaeus the night he took me. That was five years ago, in Tyre. It was not my choice. It was forced upon me—my duty as a priestess. Then I hated him, but I did not wish him dead. But last week, when confronted by his jeering face, I ached for him to be dead! Only when you were choking him, when I saw his hideous grimace, did I see the ugliness of my own hatred. At that moment I realized you would have to pay for his worthless life! . . . It isn't over. Still I hate him. I have never forgiven him! He has ruined my—"

"Belay that, Prisca," Aquila said with a kind of rough tenderness. "You are the only one who can ruin your life."

"But Aquila, I feel ruined."

Prisca sank to a bale and covered her face with her hands. "Is it not true that among the Jews a maiden is nothing if she is not a virgin? Mark taught me that. Over and over he recited those passages and insisted I memorize them. It was as though he gloated over a past about which I could do nothing. I am not a harlot, but I am no virgin." Her hands fell to her lap. She leaned back and closed her eyes.

"It seems so long ago that Jesus came to me at Tyre." Her voice sounded exhausted to her ears. "He knew me for what I was and still he loved me. I am sister to the woman who had many husbands and yet wed none, to whom he said, 'Sin no more.' I obeyed and thought I was changed."

Aquila dropped to his haunches. His big hands shook as he pried her tense hands away from her lap. "Look at me," he commanded. "I cannot say if you have changed, for I did not know you then. You told me you were once a temple priestess. I know what that means. I do not care what you were. I only know what you are now, and you are different from any woman I have ever met. These weeks—months—that you have been on my ship have been the best of my life. Prisca, I want to marry you. Let me take care of you." A tender, crooked smile lighted Aquila's rugged face, just inches from her own.

Her lower lip trembled. "I cannot. I have forfeited all else, but I cannot."

Aquila reared to his feet and stamped around the deck in exasperation. "I wish to heaven you would not speak in riddles! What have you forfeited, and why can you not marry me?"

Her green eyes, smoky with pain, followed his progress. "Jesus promised life, not death. Love not hate. In one moment of vicious anger I chose hate for myself and death for Limaeus. I have forfeited any right to Jesus' love." Prisca hugged her knees to her chest with both arms, as if to kill the emptiness she felt. Her head throbbed.

Aquila's eyes blazed at her, willing her to make him understand.

"I really did want to dwell in Corinth, to serve Jesus there. I felt I belonged in that city. It seemed so *right* to share the good news among all that beauty. . . . I know the emptiness of lives that serve the whim of gods in the temples. But Limaeus—I could not remain where he abides!" She was silent for a moment. Thoughtfully she pulled her robe closer about her shoulders and said softly, "Did you know that the God of Jesus uses even pagans to his purpose? Perhaps Limaeus, too, was doing his will, by driving me onward."

Aquila snorted. "This is the worst mess of reasoning I have ever suffered through!" Suddenly, as though he had a flash of insight, he pulled at his bent nose. "All right, Prisca, you said once in jest that perhaps God sent me to care for you. What if this is true, too? Yes. I think that God means for us to do his work together."

"Aquila you cannot twist the God of Jesus to your own purpose! I've told you, marriage is out of the question!"

"*Why?*"

She was near the end of her resources. If she did not get away from Aquila, she would never be able to withstand him. To let herself rest in his strength was so tempting. Finally she said, "Will you listen?"

"What have I *been* doing?" Aquila folded his arms and leaned against the bulwark.

"You and I shall grow old like a garment. Like a mantle Jesus will roll us up and we will be changed, but he will never change. My life, if he will still use me, is as unimportant as a—a stone, except as I can serve him. To follow Jesus I gave up the love of my sisters and the comfort of knowing how each day would end.

"I traveled to Jerusalem. There his men were leaving their families, believing that the only way to put Jesus first was to have no other concerns. As I never had a family, I did not take this to heart; it did not affect me. Then Barnabas took me to Cyprus. I learned the seasons of a loving home and how much the men gave up.

"But now Barnabas, too, has left his family. He, too, refuses to allow a love that is not directed toward the God of Jesus. It was Jerusalem all over again!" She gazed directly at him, unsparing, unsmiling. "Doesn't that tell you that to serve him best I must also forfeit any other love?"

Aquila let out a shriek of disgust and stalked away from her.

For several days the ship was like a tinderbox. Even the crew spoke with subdued voices. Aquila was in a towering temper, the least mishap filling him with unreasonable rage. At last he summoned Prisca on deck.

"What does he want, Junius?"

"The gods only know, my lady," said Junius, leaning down to peer through the hatch of the cabin. "We be walking on tippy-toe around here lately." He hesitated, waiting for her answer. "Don't do his fever no good to keep the master waiting."

Aquila stood in the bow, one leg braced against a crate of cargo, leaning into the wind. She could sense a difference in the wind, a chill, a change of direction. She made no noise coming up behind him, yet when he spoke, his words were meant for her.

"So your days have to be full of Jesus, eh? Is this like the 'fulness of days' my father was always talking about? He never could use just every-day words and say the time's come." He turned to her, wearing a guarded expression, leaned back against the rail, and folded his arms.

"Why I—yes." Chastened again. "Barnabas said there is no time for personal lives to go on as before. We must work to spread the word before Jesus returns to bring God's kingdom to earth. That is why Barnabas left Cyprus. That is why—" She lowered her eyes.

"You and Barnabas had something going, did you?"

"How dare you?"

"I am in love with you, that is how I dare! By the gods, Prisca, do you not know the effect you have on men? How do you think it will be when you find your perfect port?" He turned his back on her. "To impress you, they will pretend to be convinced by your words."

"And be not truly convinced?"

"By a woman?" he scoffed.

"Why not by a woman? Has your father taught you nothing else? Or is it that men may believe Jesus was the Promised One, but will not believe his words about women? You are not so different from Limaeus, Aquila. He asked me whether I would serve as a priestess or a—a whore. As if there were nothing else for women to be!"

Aquila raised his hands helplessly. "I did not mean to anger you, Prisca. Why do we always fight?"

"Why are you so stubborn?"

"*Me?*"

Suddenly they both burst out laughing. Aquila opened his arms, and Prisca went into them as naturally as long-lost friends. She surrendered herself to him for a moment, nestling in the warmth of his embrace. As if Aquila sensed it, he hugged her with surpassing gentleness.

He let her go. "You've not changed your mind."

"No, dear Aquila. I may not know anything else, but this I know: Unworthy though I am, I must serve Jesus above all else."

His wide mouth hardened briefly into a grimace; then he said, "In two days we will be putting in at Pescara."

"I've never heard of it!"

He smiled. "You are a long way from home. Pescara is on the coast of Italy."

"Near Rome?"

"Rome is a hundred leagues west. Pescara is on an overland trade route to Rome. It is as far as the *Lotus* goes."

Fear mushroomed in her stomach. The end of the voyage. She could not go back. Therefore Aquila must abandon her here, and she would be alone once more. Rome. Perhaps she herself came from Rome. The citizenship papers Thyatira had given her were signed there. Suddenly a wave of homesickness threatened to make her ill in fact. Though separated by a chasm wider than the journey from Tyre, her love crossed it still, and for a moment she longed for the security of Thyatira's presence.

"So be it." Her voice trembled. "I will join a caravan in Pescara and travel to Rome."

Aquila's gaze was inscrutable. Finally he said, "Then I am coming with you. At least I know the city."

"But, Aquila! The ship!"

"I have already spoken to the mate. He is a good lad. The crew will follow him. He will carry a letter to Barnabas, instructing him to sell my half of the ship. I will take part of my profits from cargo in Pescara, for us to live on until I find work."

Aquila drew her to him once more. "I am not convinced that Jesus, even if he is the Son of God, meant for his followers to neglect their own lives. You can spend the rest of your life trying to convince me, and I will spend my life convincing you."

"Oh, Aquila," she said tenderly, curling her arms behind his neck, not caring if the crew was watching. "I could love you so easily."

"You mean you don't already?"

She buried her face against his shoulder. "I know one thing."

"Good. What?"

"I thought I was in love with Barnabas, but I was not." Aquila grunted in satisfaction. "But he is the one who refused me, not the other way around." She lifted her face to his. His lips brushed hers, gently, then his arm tightened around her back, and his kiss burned on her lips. His fingers glided along her neck, to twine in her hair. She felt the hard muscles of his shoulders flex under her hands. The banked fires of her passion suddenly broke free, and she returned his kiss with searching abandon. Then, shocked by her own vulnerability, she broke away.

Aquila grinned like a mischievous god. "I'll wager I convince you before you convince me."

She laughed at his outrageousness, then said breathlessly, "But you must allow me to teach you more about Jesus."

"You'll need someone to practice on."

She stared at him, piqued by his condescending tone, such as Barnabas might have used with the twins. To him this was no more than an adventure. He did not understand yet the power of Jesus. So be it. The cub does not know it is being tamed when first it eats out of hand.

Aquila, Prisca, and Maya entered Rome from the east, a small caravan swelled by Aquila's possessions to the extent that four asses were required to carry everything. The road was a broad highway of hewn, fitted stone, marked by milestones, and as they drew within a few leagues of the city, by a marker twice as high as a man, proclaiming to whom belonged credit for construction of this road. They began to pass monuments sited in lonely splendor along the highway, some simple colonnaded rotundas, others as elaborate as small palaces.

"Tombs," Aquila explained. "The law forbids burying the dead in the more inhabited parts of the city."

From a distance it seemed that gleaming white buildings topped the peaks of every hill in sight. They passed into the city through a gate near the temple of Minerva and soon found themselves engulfed by a stream of pedestrians wearing the poorest of dress. Children with runny noses and scabbed elbows played tag among the throngs, and beggars with clouded eyes thrust bowls under their noses.

As they neared the center of this most powerful city in the world, Prisca felt dwarfed by the massive proportions of the buildings, softened though they were by civic parks and gardens. Where Corinth had been jewellike in its loveliness, Rome demanded awe. Aquila pointed out temples to Zeus, Vesta, and Mars. They skirted a massive circular structure under construction, swarming with thousands of workers clad in rags. Aquila eyed it with interest. "That is begun since I was here."

Touched by the miserable appearance of the slaves, Prisca scarcely heard Aquila's comment.

"We're coming to the Forum, Prisca. It's the center of business and commerce, and the law, too. Someday I'll show you the emperor's palace."

"Where are we going now?"

"To the Field of Mars, just past the Forum. I want to look up a friend."

The crowds were large and rowdy. Prisca glanced over her shoulder at Maya, who was clinging to the harness of one of the donkeys, and smiled encouragement at her. Within a few minutes, they entered a broad field with several fenced-off areas.

Prisca was relieved to leave the crowds behind, but soon discovered the noise and confusion replaced by milling, whinnying horses, racing back and forth inside fenced enclosures, raising clouds of dust. Prisca had never seen so many horses. The size of the brutes frightened her.

"Who are we looking for?" she shouted.

"Man named Fabianus! Wait here!" Aquila disappeared in the direction of a low, barracks-style building. Minutes later he came back wearing a broad grin and climbed two rungs of a head-high rail fence not a dozen paces from them. Prisca saw that several men were putting horses through different exercises on the far side of the enclosure.

Aquila cupped his hands around his mouth. "Fabianus! Fabianus!"

Eventually one of the riders cut away from the others and galloped straight across the field. He brought the horse up sharply only inches from the rail. His long hair was tied carelessly at the nape with a thong. His tunic was leather and much sweat stained and scarred. On his sleeve was stamped an emblem of the imperial eagle. Below his skirt, his muscular legs were bound in protective leather sheaths, laced up the outside.

"Aquila, as I live and breathe!" Fabianus's face was gritty with sweat. He tossed Aquila the reins and vaulted over the fence while Aquila looped the reins over a middle rung. The men clasped each other in a hard, shoulder-pounding grip.

"By the gods, man!" Aquila held Fabianus at arm's length and hugged him once again.

"Whatever happened to you?" demanded Fabianus. "I remember we got passing drunk; I spent a night in jail; and when I rousted our friends the next day, no Aquila." Suddenly he took a second look at Prisca and eyed Aquila with new respect. "I'd say your fortunes have changed."

Aquila glanced at her with pride. "This is Prisca of Tyre, soon to be my wife, I hope, and her servant."

"Congratulations. Tyre! Is that where you have been?" Fabianus said eagerly, before remembering his manners. He inclined his head toward Prisca. "My lady." He straightened. "Where are you staying?"

"We just arrived. I am seeking a place to open a shop."

"Out on the Appian Way?"

"Is it still the best place?"

"You'll never be shy of customers. Lookers, anyway. Myself, I'll always be a horse trainer and lucky to be that." He patted the silky nose of the beast poking curiously through the fence. "This fellow's one of a batch of three-year-olds we are breaking to the saddle." Fabianus screwed up his face and glanced at the sun.

"The procession has started. Want to see it? Leave your animals here, they will be all right."

"What is going on?" asked Aquila as Fabianus steered them back into the eddying crowd.

Suddenly a gang of happy, shouting youths surged forward, and Prisca was shoved off balance. Aquila seized her as she stumbled.

"Watch it!" roared Fabianus with authority.

The offenders shrank back. Those following gave them berth.

Fabianus bent over her, "Are you all right, my lady?"

"Yes, where are all these people going? They look so poor."

Fabianus fell into step beside her, "To the Circus."

"The circus?"

"Circus Maximus. Sports field. It will hold a third of the population of Rome. And now there's nearly that many who are poor," Fabianus added soberly. "Caligula has declared today a holiday in honor of one of the tribunes. Back from a year's duty in Macedonia. Brought another thousand slaves with him." Fabianus glanced around and lowered his voice. "As if we needed more slaves. Half the farmers and workers are out of jobs as it is."

"Are these slaves being punished?" asked Prisca.

"You mean is that why they are slaves? Not at all. The emperor decided that slaves are a better commodity than gold. He imports them from the provinces and sells them to his wealthy friends. The rich are buying out small farmers and joining their holdings into plantations. With slave labor, they have no need to pay honest peasants or see that they live decently.

"Caligula is shrewd. He keeps the peasants from revolting by declaring a holiday now and then. His lieutenants invite them to the Circus, pass out free bread, and put on free shows. The poor devils forget for a time they've no money for their families and no prospects for making any, save an occasional bribe or some scurvy job that's against the law."

Suddenly he looked ahead and spread his arms to stop their progress. "Well," he said, "Looks like you'll be privileged to honor the tribune yourselves." He herded them off the street and up a few steps of a building, where they could see over the heads of the crowd.

Prisca's first glimpse was of purple and gold banners flying at the tips of lances. Then, at drumbeat cadence, a close-order formation of soldiers marched by, twelve abreast and twelve deep, the imperial eagle emblazoned on every shield, bronze helmets gleaming richly above bronzed faces.

Behind them, drawn on a flat, wooden wagon, by sixteen horses harnessed four abreast, was a life-size bronze of a Corinthian horse, prize spoil of the campaign. Nostrils flared, tulip ears delicately formed, mane swirling, the horse seemed to need only the touch of a god's fingertip to rear into life. The crowd exclaimed appreciatively as it rolled slowly by. Then came the golden chariot of the tribune, pulled by a unicorn of matched bays with plumes of ostrich feathers affixed to their forelocks.

Prisca stared at the noble figure of the tribune and gasped. Marcus Sistus!

Tribune Sistus braced proudly behind his gauntleted driver, looking neither left nor right.

She clutched Aquila's arm. "Aquila!" He paid no attention. She was sure it was he! Then perhaps Thyatira was here, too! A rush of gladness surged through her. Her eyes scanned the throng. She glanced back at the man at her side. He was lost to the excitement of the moment. Perhaps it would be better to say nothing. Who was the tribune? Was he even a good man? What would Aquila think, when he knew that she had met him in the temple of Artemis?

The chariot passed. The tribune was bareheaded, his golden hair bleached as pale as good wine. His handsome, stern profile seemed unchanged.

Behind the tribune's chariot swarmed a crowd of men and women, old and young, chanting repeatedly, "Look behind you and remember you will die!"

Prisca heard the words with horror. She glanced at Fabianus.

He laughed. "Keeps the man from getting too puffed up. One triumph is not a life."

But the words clung, echoing down the vast marble canyons of Rome, and the peasants danced on.

Chapter 17

With part of Aquila's profit from cargo and some of Prisca's original stake from Tyre, they purchased a shop that Fabianus located for them, facing the Appian Way, the main north-south highway into Rome. The shop had been vacated recently and was in good repair. The rear of the shop led into an atrium, smaller than Barnabas's walled garden on Cyprus. It was enclosed on the other three sides by a snug house with a modest gathering room and private sleeping quarters. A rear dining area overlooked a separate vegetable and herb garden. Screened by hedges were supply sheds and kitchen area, a well, baking ovens, and a fire pit.

Maya was delighted to be on land again, ecstatic that Aquila had not abandoned them, and quickly established her role as household manager. She cooked and marketed and gossiped with women engaged in similar tasks. Her joy was complete, she told Prisca one day, because she had never again expected to be part of such a household. When her husband had died, she had gone to the temple to find work, having no one to care for her. There she had expected to die.

"You'll be old soon enough yourself," she scolded Prisca. "Like that tribune, look behind you! And you'll be a fool if you do not get Aquila to marry you before he finds another or another finds him. Men like him do not grow on trees." That seemed to be her final word, no matter what subject the women discussed these days, Prisca realized with a sigh. She had not answered her.

They had been in Rome a month. As Aquila had predicted, good tentmakers were always in demand. They found themselves in the midst of an energetic cluster of craftspeople who lived and worked along the Appian Way. Most of the tentmakers worked in leather, for Romans as well as Greeks were partial to waterproof tents, and Aquila had few competitors for the trade in woolen tents.

Aquila had begun attending synagogue again, a practice he had given up in rebellious youth as a hypocrisy fostered by fathers who had no other way to control their children.

"I met a most interesting fellow today," he told Prisca one morning upon his return as together they opened the shop for the day's business.

"You would delight in his company." A settled life seemed to agree with Aquila. His black eyes glowed with a benign expression as he pulled a heavy piece of wool goods off a shelf and assembled his tools and threads.

"Tell me about him," said Prisca, wandering about, picking up first one thing and then another. In contrast to Aquila's contentment, she was beset with restlessness. Religions abounded. Glorious statues of all the Roman gods and emperors of the past offered showcases for anyone desiring to worship in public. No one seemed interested in hearing about an obscure Jewish rabbi who, it seemed, had risen from the dead. The most natural place to talk about Jesus would have been the synagogue, but alas, she was not even Jewish.

She had tried, once or twice, to broach the subject to Aquila's customers. "Take away the sins of the world?" Blank stares. "What sins?" Sympathetic glances at handsome young Aquila, saddled with a lovely idiot.

"Tell me about the man you met in synagogue today," Prisca repeated.

"Um. Hand me an awl, will you, please? The smallest one."

Impatiently she fingered through a shelf of tools. Bringing him the awl, she discovered Aquila's eyes upon her. "What?" she said shortly.

"You are frowning."

She sighed.

"I can show you how to make a seam that the wind cannot find," he coaxed.

She watched his long, sensuous fingers caress the wool. She wished. . . .

"Or learn to work with leather, along with me." In spare moments, Aquila was trading craft techniques with a neighboring leatherworker, to increase his expertise.

Something like a snort was her answer.

"Not happy, are you, Prisca?"

She did not answer.

"If you worked with me, instead of sulking in the background, perhaps people would be readier to listen. A good craftsperson is always respected."

"I am a Greek and a teacher."

Aquila's lips formed an O. "Too good to work with your hands?"

"Teachers do not work with their hands! Nor do—," she stopped, horrified. *Nor do priestesses,* she had started to say. Not priestesses of Artemis. But priestesses of the Christ?

Seated comfortably on the floor, with his knees crossed, Aquila studied her, his sympathy laced with a quiet smile. "Then let us marry, Prisca. Babies will cure your restlessness."

She sat next to him on the rug and hugged her knees to her chest. Her eyes roved his handsome profile as he bent over his work. The strong nose. Couldn't see the sideways-bent bridge in profile. But she loved it. It made him unique. The wide, mobile lips, now compressed in concentration. Sometimes her mind drifted into dreaming how it would be to belong to Aquila. Unbidden, the feel of his lips on hers would spring to mind and set her body stirring with desire. She wanted him. She—oh, Prisca, such disastrous thoughts! She looked away from him. *Jesus! Show me the way to teach!*

"Tell me about the man at the synagogue."

"His name is Josephus. He seems to have been everywhere and done everything, and he has a library that rivals that of the temple in Jerusalem. I invited him to pay us a visit."

"Oh, Aquila! Do you think he will come?"

"He was going to be out of the city for a few weeks, but he will come."

She longed to lean against his shoulder, to feel the warmth of his wool robe next to her cheek. Her eyes fastened on his strong, capable hands. Had not Jesus honored all work? Had he not even said that the Son of Man came not to be served but to serve?

"Aquila. . . . Will you let me teach you, while you work? So that you will know who Jesus is."

"Fire away."

She straightened. "Jesus was sent to us from God, as much above the angels as a son is above the servants. . . ."

As the weeks flew by Aquila listened willingly, his hands still at times while he questioned her. Occasionally he added insights from his father's teaching. Prisca grew confident that Aquila was growing closer to acknowledging her Lord, yet she feared to ask him.

Another month slipped away in pleasant companionship. One morning, after a troubled night, Prisca awoke with the cold realization that she was no closer to reaching others than she had been when they arrived. Perhaps coming to Rome had been a mistake. She would talk to Aquila. Perhaps his contentment was less than she imagined. After breakfast, she crossed the atrium with determined strides and entered the shop.

"Good morning," she said.

Aquila was on hands and knees on the floor, over a large piece of pale rust wool. He looked up. "Inventing a swinging bed for a babe who cries a lot," he said as if continuing a conversation already in progress. His tone was listless.

"Truly?" She knelt beside him. His eyes seemed watery and his skin flushed. "Are you well? Maya said you had no breakfast this morning."

"Of course. Just busy."

She brushed the wool with her fingertips, then picked up a corner and examined it. "You can hardly see the warp."

"Cilicium. Best goats' wool there is. Comes from Pontus and Cilicia." He smiled, a crooked, whimsical smile. "I'm using it for the baby's bed. It's tough enough for seven babies."

When the parents had brought her to the shop, Aquila told Prisca, the infant's belly protruded so that it caused a man to wince. " 'Tis only gas, poor thing, but no less painful," the mother had said apologetically. She thought perhaps a swinging bed might ease the babe until she outgrew the pains.

"Have you ever suffered through a night with a squalling babe?" the father had asked rhetorically. "God has no greater curse upon this earth!"

Prisca *tch*ed in sympathy, when Aquila finished. "Won't this wool be too rough?"

"It will be lined with linen as soft as her little behind. Want to help?"

"Me?" She caught the corner of her lip between her teeth. Aquila really did not look well. If she helped, perhaps he would have time to rest. "Yes."

"Good. First thing you can do is fetch me a draught of cool water." He wiped his brow with his sleeve.

When she returned, Aquila had a visitor, a tall young man in dark robes, with the pallor of a scholar and the dignity of an elder.

"You must be Prisca," said the man, in impeccable, imperturbable Greek.

"I am Prisca." She gave Aquila the water.

"Flavius Josephus, my lady." He bestowed a courtly bow, almost comical in one so young. "I had the honor to meet Aquila at the synagogue some weeks ago. He invited me to pay a call upon him. He mentioned the opportunity to encounter an educated lady from Tyre who was the most beautiful creature God ever made."

She glanced at Aquila and laughed. "You have the tongue of a serpent, my lord."

He smiled. "Alas. Not so wise."

Josephus had chosen this opportunity to call, he told them, because as he was about an errand his girdle had parted company at the seams. Fortuitously he had found himself in their vicinity.

Aquila had laid aside the baby bed to mend their visitor's girdle, and

Flavius Josephus accepted his invitation to settle down comfortably and wait.

Eagerly Prisca summoned Maya to serve refreshment and sat near Josephus to listen.

He had been born Joseph ben Matthias, an honorable Jewish name, he told them, but he had renamed himself (though it displeased several members of his family who were not sure that having risen so high in royal Roman esteem justified disowning his Jewish heritage) and was now Flavius Josephus. "You see, most people change their names to avoid disgrace. To them, I had already disgraced myself. Perhaps if I do so truly, I will change it back again." He raised his eyebrows, inviting them to share what he considered a good joke.

"Actually, it made wonderful sense, since now I work for Emperor Caligula."

Aquila started. He shot Prisca a warning glance, but she ignored it.

"You do?" she cried, ready to be entertained. "What do you do?"

"I am a historian. At the moment I am writing a history of my own people. I find the scrolls leave out so much of the world around them that it is hard to get a true picture of the Jews and our place in history. Studying only the Septuagint, one would think no other peoples existed. Except barbarians, of course."

"You have scrolls that tell this in your library?"

"The history of the Jews, the Romans, and the Egyptians, all written in Greek. As well as tales of these and lesser peoples, in their own tongues."

"Might I visit your library?" she asked suddenly.

Josephus's eyebrows shot up. He glanced at Aquila.

"Prisca knows several languages. Libraries are not easy to come by."

"Not to mention that reading makes women infertile and addle-brained," Josephus murmured.

"What?" laughed Prisca.

"Teasing, dear lady. It is only a witches' tale, I am sure. Of course you may avail yourself of my library. Forgive my shock at finding a literate peasant. That is to say, a goodwife who—"

"Quit while you are ahead," suggested Aquila. "There. Your girdle is mended well enough to last a while longer."

"Indeed it is," said Josephus, peering closely at the firm stitching. He withdrew a drachma from his purse.

"That is too much," protested Aquila.

"Indeed not. It was a pleasure to converse with you both." He bowed elegantly, and Prisca escorted him to the street. "I shall look forward to showing you my library. Come with me now, if you are free."

She glanced over her shoulder at Aquila. "No, but soon," she promised regretfully as he departed. She stepped back into the shop. "Oh, Aquila, imagine!" Her eyes looked at their little shop with fresh awareness. Somehow it seemed less than it had been. Secretly she was sorry she had promised Aquila to help him with the baby bed. How much more exciting it would have been to accept Flavius Josephus's invitation to visit his library!

Aquila was watching her. "Rather go along with him, wouldn't you?"

"It will wait." She laughed guiltily. "How is it that you can read me so well?"

He smiled, pleased, and took up the wool for the bed.

The hours fled like zephyrs as Prisca labored under his eye, working twice as hard because she'd rather be elsewhere. By dusk, the bed was finished. She felt inordinately proud of her minor contribution and could hardly wait for the parents to arrive.

"Now what are you doing?" asked Aquila when she followed him back from the house after supper with a handful of oil lamps. He sat heavily on the floor, propping himself against a pile of woven goods. His face was shiny with perspiration.

"I want them to appreciate the bed when they see it," she said as she distributed and lighted half a dozen lamps about the shop. It glowed with a warm intimacy, the corners disappearing in shadow. "There, isn't that better?"

"Wasteful," he growled.

"Beast!" she laughed and scampered in to tug at a handful of his hair. Aquila snatched her and pulled her down into his lap.

"Hello?" a hesitant voice said from the street entrance.

Prisca scrambled to her feet. Aquila followed more slowly. A small, swarthy-skinned couple waited at the open door.

"Come in," Aquila laughed with embarrassment. "Your bed is ready. Prisca, this is Philip and his wife, Adah. And the wee one is Zoe." They were Alexandrian Jews and had lived in Rome for years. Philip had been the first to welcome Aquila at synagogue. From him, Aquila had learned of Zoe's sickness. Neither Philip nor his wife were as tall as Prisca.

Adah waited behind her husband like a diminutive shadow. A dark veil was pulled down over her forehead and brows, nearly to her luminous eyes, and covered the bundle in her arms, from whence issued thin cries of distress.

"Zoe is our first baby," said Philip, as if apologies were necessary. "Adah thinks it is her fault that Zoe yells all the time." Philip motioned to his wife.

Adah laid back the cover and exposed the baby. Prisca felt overcome with pity. The baby's face was pinched and red. It was not crying, but merely whimpering. Despite its gross belly, its limbs were scrawny. To Prisca, it seemed that it would surely die.

"When I was in the temple," she remembered suddenly, "we fed babies an herb drink for just such ailments. I wonder if there are any of the right herbs in the garden here."

"Did it help?" Adah asked shyly.

"Many times it did."

"What sort of temple?" said Philip, suddenly suspicious.

Aquila grinned. *How are you going to get out of this one?* he seemed to be asking.

"Before I learned about the God of Jesus, who is called the Christ, I was a priestess of Artemis, in her temple in Tyre."

Adah's eyes widened in alarm. Her arms curled more tightly around her baby. "What did Artemis do with the babies?"

Prisca answered without rancor, "Artemis is but stone. But we who lived in the temple adored the babies. We held a blessing ceremony each spring for all the babies born that year in Tyre. Some of them had been born to my sisters. When they were weaned, they were sent to the homes of their fathers, many of them merchant princes. How eagerly we waited to see them again!"

Philip cleared his throat and positioned hands on hips, as if gearing up to ask a question, when Zoe began to fuss again.

"Of course," said Prisca, her eyes on the babe, "the true blessing was that the fathers' families received them. Love is a blessing, no matter where it comes from."

Suddenly she held out her arms. "May I hold her, Adah?"

Their eyes met, Adah's frightened, Prisca's inviting confidence. Philip shifted as if ready to protest, glanced at Aquila, and said, "Let her." Prisca took Zoe in her arms.

With a great rush of warmth, she cuddled the tiny bundle. What fond memories it recalled! Aquila was beaming at her, his eyes shining foolishly. Prisca, reading his intent, smiled with unexpected shyness. "May I offer a blessing for her?" she asked.

"From Artemis?"

"From the living God, in the name of the Son, Jesus."

The parents looked at each other. "What son, Aquila?" asked Philip. "Who is this?"

Prisca held her breath, waiting for Aquila's answer.

"Prisca says he is the Promised One of the Jews."

She felt a twinge of disappointment in his answer.

"Promised, yes, but you mean such a one has come?" Philip asked.

"Yes," said Prisca. "One who cares about little Zoe."

A bewildered expression crossed Philip's dark face. "I suppose it is all right. . . ."

Prisca reached for Aquila's hand. It was hot and clammy to her touch. She glanced at him with alarm. Aquila laid his other hand on the baby. Together they prayed, Prisca intent upon the relief of the parents' as well as the baby's suffering.

Adah smiled hesitantly as she took the baby back. "I do not know why, but I feel already that Zoe will get better."

"I believe so, too," said Prisca.

"By the gods, I hope so!" swore Philip. "A man needs his sleep."

"Let us go into the atrium and have some fruit and wine," said Aquila. *Not tonight,* her eyes implored. *You are ill!*

Aquila resolutely looked anywhere but at Prisca. "We can hang the bed and put little Zoe in it for a trial run."

"Do you think we might make Zoe some tea, if you have the proper herbs?" Adah ventured.

"Of course." While the men buckled the straps of the bed over the limb of a dwarf oak, Prisca roused Maya. By torchlight they found the herbs, and she set Maya to building a fire to brew the potion while she washed and sorted leaves. From the atrium, she heard the rise and fall of voices as Aquila talked to their new friends about Jesus.

Her heart bloomed with new joy to hear him. Perhaps he was, after all, a believer! She gathered her courage. She would ask him as soon as their guests left.

While Maya tended the simmering tea, Prisca served a tangy pomegranate wine she and Maya had made, together with sticky date and honey cakes and wedges of cheese and fruit.

At last the tea was ready and cooled, and Adah dripped it carefully down the baby's throat. The tiny face screwed up in protest against the bitter drink, but she was too weak to refuse. Her father took her out of Adah's arms and laid her in her new bed and gave it a gentle shove. The four watched. Soon Zoe's eyes closed, and her flailing fists relaxed and uncurled like delicate flowers against her cheeks.

The women chortled their delight in exaggerated whispers. "First one that wakes her up has to walk her!" hissed Philip, his face wreathed in smiles.

Philip and Adah left an hour later, the bed slung between them like a basket of laundry. Zoe had slept peacefully the whole time.

Aquila and Prisca saw them off down the street. "I think we've made our first new friends," Prisca said, linking arms with Aquila.

"Let me know if the bed helps," Aquila called softly after them.

"You'll be sure to know if it doesn't!" The father's laughter drifted behind him in the night.

Prisca could feel Aquila trembling. She reached over and felt his forehead. "You are burning with fever!" she cried. "You ought to be in bed!"

Aquila protested, but did not resist when Prisca propelled him through the shop and toward his own room. While Aquila undressed and fell into bed, Prisca and Maya readied cool, wet linens to bathe his face and limbs. Returning to his room, they found him already deep in a fevered sleep.

"What is it, Maya?" Prisca whispered.

Maya shook her head. "We will have to wait and see."

Chapter 18

A quila's fever worsened throughout the night, alternating with violent chills. On the following days he refused food, but gulped water like a man dying of thirst. The women brewed a variety of herb teas and forced them through his cracked lips, but nothing seemed to alter the deadly course of the fever.

Prisca prayed for his recovery by the hour, her lips moving silently as she went about her other chores. Work mounted in the shop, work that Prisca was helpless to do, even as she watched their resources dwindle. Alone and afraid, she kept watch beside Aquila's bed.

One sabbath morning, a week after he was stricken, she roused Maya at dawn. "Get up quickly! You must find a physician. Aquila has been out of his head all night. This morning he is so weak I am frightened. Go to the synagogue. When the men leave the temple, ask them to take you to the rabbi. Bid him come with a physician who knows how to treat Roman fevers."

Maya's hands trembled as she changed out of her nightclothes. "Mistress, our master won't die, will he?"

"Oh, sweet Jesus, do not say that!"

She hustled Maya into her cloak. "It is raining. Be careful. But hurry!"

After Maya left, Prisca tiptoed back into Aquila's room. She started to snuff the lamp and thought better of it. The warm light fought back the shades, which added their gloom to the unremitting drizzle that had continued through the night. She leaned over the bed, holding the lamp to Aquila's face. His temples were sunken, as though the flesh were melting away. His eye sockets were shadowed, hollow rings. She had attempted to shave his beard once, but he had tossed so erratically that she gave up, fearing she might cut him. She smoothed the black, tousled hair away from his forehead. Prisca ached with love for him, in fear that he would die.

She thought of how much like her he was. Was that possible? That some men took the same sudden joy in discovery that she did? Needed as much comfort in despair, as much acclaim in triumph? Could make the same kind of seemingly irrational decision, as to leave a secure berth for an ideal? Could love an impossible man such as Jesus?

And now, if Aquila were to die, she would have lost the center of her love, the core of her life. "O my God," she cried, "how can it be better to serve thee alone?"

Suddenly Aquila's eyes flew open. He stared through her. "Prisca."

She leaned over his bed. "Yes, Aquila, I am here."

His eyes rolled back, his eyelids closed, and he slipped away from her again, down into the regions where he fought the terrible fever.

Prisca cocked her head. Someone was in the shop. Could Maya have found a physician already? Bless her! She hastened through the atrium.

But it was Adah and Philip waiting for her, cloaked in heavy wool on which the water beaded like evil black diamonds. She smiled, summoning strength to hide her disappointment.

"Good morrow," said Philip. "We were on the way home from synagogue and decided to call. I have not seen Aquila there lately."

"Good morrow, Philip. Adah," she said, choking back her weariness. "Come in. How is the baby?"

"Much better," said Adah. Her lashes were stuck together from the rain. She looked years younger, like a new bride. "She is at home with a neighbor girl. It has been a long time since we felt safe leaving her. We are not sure whether it was the tea, the swinging bed, or the prayers—or all three," she finished with a smile.

"Is your husband home?" asked Philip.

Prisca threw him a startled look. It had never occurred to her that their neighbors would naturally assume they were married. "Aquila is very ill. He has a fever that Maya and I know nothing about. I sent her for a physician—"

"On the sabbath?" asked Philip. "He will not come."

"Not come?" Prisca's voice rose.

"For Jews, it is against the Law to work on the sabbath, even a physician."

"I know what the Law says!" she snapped. "Oh, Philip, forgive my bad temper. I am nearly out of my mind with worry. Jesus taught us that the sabbath was made to serve man, not man the sabbath. You have lived here long, perhaps you know what—"

"There is a Rome fever, that people who dwell near the marshlands get. It can be very bad."

Prisca caught her breath. "Can they—can they die from it?"

"Now Prisca," Adah took her hand in a firm grip and put her arm around her, suddenly taking charge in a most gentle way. "You look nearly done to death. Why did you not send your servant for me? Come, I will make you some tea. Philip can build us a nice fire in the brazier."

"We are out of charcoal."

"Then he will fetch some, will you not, husband?"

"No!" Her cheeks burned with humiliation. "I must save our money for the doctor. Aquila has been unable to work, and I—I have been no earthly good in the shop, though he wanted me to learn—"

"Where is Aquila?" asked Philip as they hustled under the protective overhang around the atrium, dodging most of the rain, and stepped into the gathering room. She gestured toward his bedroom. Philip disappeared and reappeared moments later. She caught a glimpse of his face as he rearranged his features in a semblance of a smile. "He is sleeping."

She nodded.

Philip and Adah held a mumbled conversation, then Philip left. She looked questioningly at the petite woman, now moving with sure gestures about a strange house.

"He's gone home to fetch a few things," was all Adah would say.

Philip returned, divested of his sabbath clothes in favor of workaday garb, with his arms full of bundles. He built a new fire in the charcoal brazier, looked at Prisca standing stiff and silent to one side, and spoke in low tones to Adah.

"Philip thinks you should rest. I am going to make some soup. Don't worry. Leave everything to us. We will call you when the doctor arrives."

"But if you keep the Law, it is the same for you. You must not do this on the sabbath," protested Prisca.

"There is little comfort in the Law, Prisca." It was the first time Philip had ever addressed her on any matters not concerned with daily living. His large eyes were liquid. "Sunset had fallen, marking the beginning of sabbath last week, when Aquila finished the bed for Zoe and you kindled a fire to make her the herb drink. Would your Jesus have said that was wrong?"

"No."

"By the gods, if I had had to listen to her one more night—"

Adah smiled. "We were nearly at our wits' end last week, Prisca. It seems a small thing, a baby who will not cease crying. You took us in and shared your supper and prayed with us. Somehow we have grown away from God. We felt close to him here that night. We want to know more about Jesus. We want to find God again."

Impulsively Prisca hugged Adah, forgetting her tiredness and fear. What a beautiful gift Adah had given her! She smiled tremulously at

Philip. Philip looked away in embarrassment and prodded the fire vigorously.

"Philip finds it strange for women to discuss such matters outside the home. It is not you," she added. "Please rest."

"When Maya returns," she promised.

Prisca prowled from Aquila's room to the gathering room, warming her hands at the fire, fetching water for Aquila, moving ceaselessly, lest the fear overtake her again.

It was another hour before Maya returned. Prisca met her at the door. Her wool cloak filled the room with a pungent, wet odor.

"Where is the doctor?" she demanded.

Maya threw her a baleful glance and tugged off the sodden cloak. "Nobody will come." Adah threw the cloak over a line. Maya was soaked through to the skin, her thin, gray hair plastered to her skull. She leaned over the kettle and sniffed the soup, taking her time about it, as if deciding whether to be miffed at the incursion on her position in the household or grateful for the savory aroma and cheery warmth.

Prisca seized her arm. "Did you tell them how ill he is?"

"I told them, mistress. They said it is the sabbath. When I insisted, they threatened to have me arrested. Where are you going?"

"To fetch a physician. Get into dry clothes, Maya. If Jew will not come, another will." Over the protests of Maya and Adah, Prisca stalked out of the room to fetch her cloak.

When she returned, Philip was waiting in his cloak also. "No sense both of us getting wet," he said. "You stay—"

She summoned a firm but gracious smile. "I shall be very glad for your company."

The rain had lessened to a fine mist as they stepped out of the shop onto the wet, granite blocks of the Appian Way. Overhead, a sharp rim of silver scalloped one edge of cloud. To the north, the clouds were breaking up.

"Whom shall you seek?"

"Tribune Marcus Sistus," she told Philip, turning north toward Capitoline Hill.

Philip stopped. "Tribune Sistus! He is a very powerful man. Do you know him?"

Prisca thought of the woman with a sick child who had endured the scorn of Jesus' followers because she needed his help. "I will get help from anyone I can," she announced. "A powerful man can afford the best physicians."

The valleys of Rome were drenched in ground fog. It swirled about their feet as they walked. Ahead the hills were bathed in pearl mist, through which the state buildings rose like remote palaces of the gods, more attached to heaven than earth. Muted voices and street sounds belled from stragglers like themselves, on errands that would not await better weather. They passed the temple of Diana the Huntress, the Roman goddess whom the Greeks knew as Artemis. A wild wish as strong as a stray boar in the streets charged her mind. A prayer dropped to Artemis—

"How easy it is to be strong in one's belief when things go well," Philip said innocently. "We would have made any sacrifice, if it would have helped our daughter."

"Yes," she agreed. *Thank you, Lord.*

Three-quarters of an hour later Prisca and Philip were standing before massive cedar gates set in a dark red stone wall flecked with orange. Alone they would never have found the estate of Marcus Sistus. For a drachma a boy lingering near the Forum had been willing to guide them up this winding street of spacious estates, high on the side of a hill overlooking the Tiber River. Vines tumbled down the tribune's walls in profuse bursts of defiant magenta and glossy green. Water dripped in soothing cadence from dark red tiles overhanging the gates.

"What if this is not the right place?"

"Then I'll find the little beggar and kill him," replied Philip.

Prisca shot him a horrified glance, discovering to her relief he was teasing. She smiled, grateful for the ease in tension, and waited while he pulled the bell cord, summoning a servant to the gate.

Taking in their peasant dress, the servant was ill disposed to admit them.

"Tell your master Prisca of Tyre wishes to see him."

Philip glanced up at her in surprise, but said nothing. The servant disappeared. Long minutes passed. Rain began to descend again. Her leather sandals soaked through, and her feet were growing cold. To bolster her own spirits she smiled encouragement at Philip. Finally the gate reopened.

"Come in, please." They found themselves in a courtyard large enough to contain the whole of the house and shop they had left. The servant led them swiftly down neatly trimmed gravel paths, past formal reflecting pools, rose gardens hedged in boxwood, and graceful Grecian figures sculptured in marble. He left them in a formal receiving room rich with tapestried hangings. "Wait here, please."

Philip and Prisca stopped where he left them, in the center of the room, dripping water on a thick wool carpet, one of several thrown about the inlaid marble floor. Bronze candle sconces were spaced with military precision every few feet along the walls, illuminating fancifully painted doors and busts of bronze and marble that were displayed on waist-high columns of painted hardwood. She recognized some of the works as Grecian and Phoenician. *Spoils of war,* she thought.

"You see a fire anywhere?" asked Philip.

"No, why?"

"The room's drawing heat from somewhere. I've heard about—"

"Prisca! Is it really you?"

Prisca turned. Tribune Marcus Sistus was striding toward them from one of the inner doors. A ruby velvet, fur-trimmed sleeveless robe flapped about his ankles. Under it, he wore a long-sleeved toga such as worn by statesmen. She waited, frozen with panic. What could she expect from him?

He seized her hands with hands as dry and smooth as harness leather. He gazed into her face. Joy mingled with inexpressible emotions in his tanned soldier's face. "What gods have I pleased to deserve this?" At arm's length he continued to behold her, the muscles of his square jaw working.

"But you are all wet, and your hands are frozen!" For the first time he noticed Philip and took in their generally sorry condition. "What are you doing here in Rome? Is there some immediate emergency?"

"The Rome fever, my lord, like they get in the campagna," Philip ventured. "Her husband's as sick as they get."

"This is Philip, our friend."

The tribune fixed Prisca with an unreadable stare. "Your husband! Indeed!" All business now, he summoned servants and ordered fresh clothing and hot wine. He stopped to pierce Prisca's eyes with a demand. "You will not disappear on me, will you?"

She shook her head without thinking. "Please, I need your help now, Tribune Sistus."

Another long stare. Another series of orders issued. "My personal physician shall see him. Do have the wine and put on dry cloaks. There is time," he added gently.

While they waited for the physician, the tribune ordered a huge fire to be built and couches drawn. Meekly Prisca and Philip obeyed when he hustled them before it, grateful for the drying warmth of the fire and the inner warming of the wine. Sistus paced back and forth before them, stopping abruptly to stare at Prisca, shaking his head with a bemused smile, then pacing again.

Suddenly he stopped in front of Prisca. "Have you any family with you?"

"My husband's family dwells in Pontus—"

Impatiently he waved away her answer. "You. Yourself."

She gazed up at him, intimidated by his manner. "No. None."

"What did Thyatira tell you about me?"

"What?" she said, startled.

"Answer!"

"N–Nothing! We fought. I left. That day."

The tribune grunted with an air of satisfaction.

Within an hour they were back at the shop. Tribune Marcus Sistus had provided chairs and runners, so they traveled home in much greater ease than they had left. The physician was a small, upright Roman of indeterminate age, with hair like hoarfrost, thoughtful blue eyes, and a face nearly unlined. His name was Hyrcanus.

Quickly she led him through the shop and the atrium to Aquila's side. They could hear his stentorian breathing before entering the room. The cavities of his eyes were sunken and dark. His faded hands picked at the cover. "Did he waken at all?" she asked Maya, who had followed them into the bedroom.

Maya shook her head. "I think he'll soon breathe his last," she said sadly.

Prisca almost struck her. "Do not ever say that again!"

"Has he lived in Rome long?" Hyrcanus asked.

"No," Philip said.

"We arrived at the beginning of winter," said Prisca. "But he lived here years ago."

"Where, do you know?"

"No, I—in the poorer part of the city, I would imagine. He was quite young then and without family."

"The lowlands," nodded Hyrcanus. "They breed fevers like rats."

"Can you save him?"

"He will probably save himself, since he has lived this long. He has likely had bouts before. The disease progresses this way, the fever coming and going, until finally the patient becomes too weak to fight off the next attack." The doctor spoke matter-of-factly, as if death and life were interchangeable.

Prisca blanched. *Look behind you and remember you will die!* Hyrcanus observed her cynically. "We must all leave sometime." Then he relented. "A small pinch of incense to Asclepius would not be amiss. He is a healing god, and sick men need every prayer."

"Are you all right?" Adah asked Prisca with alarm.

"It's just the cold." Prisca felt a great weariness sweeping over her and shook it off. "Do you need anything, doctor?"

"If he does, I will fetch it, Prisca. Go now and rest."

Prisca nodded, and Maya took her to her room. Fighting sleep, Prisca fell on her knees. Into her mind she bade the comforting presence of Jesus. Through him she prayed. When she finished, she added, "In thy hands we rest, Lord." She was asleep before she drew the cover around her.

Chapter 19

Two mornings later, of a bright spring day, she entered Aquila's room and found him awake and lucid. He had been staring out at the brightness in the atrium. He turned to regard her. A slow smile spread on the wasted, bearded face. With a cry of joy, Prisca ran to his bed.

"My darling! My dearest one! I was so afraid I had lost you. The doctor said he thought you had had the fever before."

Aquila nodded weakly. "What physician?"

"Hyrcanus is his name."

"Not a Jew?"

"A Roman. We could not find a Jew who would come on the sabbath, when you were the worst. Tribune Marcus Sistus sent his personal physician. He will be back later today. He knows so much about fevers."

"Tribune—"

"Marcus Sistus. You know. The one entering the city the day we arrived."

"How did you—?"

"Please, my love. Later." She kissed him tenderly. "Can you eat something this morning?"

He nodded. "A horse."

Slowly Aquila regained his strength. At his insistence, Prisca and Maya moved his bed to a pallet in the shop, where he could direct the work. He attempted some himself, but tired easily.

Chastened by Aquila's death dance with fate, Prisca began to learn his craft, enduring for his sake bruised fingers and aching shoulders. With awkward determination she wrestled with the tough, tanned hides as well as wool goods.

Watching her one morning, with a quiet, amused smile, Aquila said, "It pleases me that your Jesus has a sense of humor."

Prisca glanced over at him, a look of irritation on her perspiring face. She said nothing.

Aquila lay back, his hands under his head. "I remember when my father used to tell me to do something. 'I won't!' I'd say. Of course that was the signal for him to make me do just that."

"Sounds perverse of him."

"With him, yes, often it was. With Jesus, it might be because he loves you so much."

Prisca's hands stilled and fell in her lap.

"To show you a way you can serve him."

"Where's the humor in that?"

"Took me to get sick to make you do it."

A corner of her mouth twitched. "That would be just like him. Using each other to serve God's purpose. You think he wants me to learn how to mend tents?"

"We'll see, Prisca. Right now, I want you to do something for me. Remember Fabianus?"

"Of course." The wiry little horse trainer had been so kind to them when they first came to Rome that she would always be grateful to him.

"In the days of our w-i-i-ld youth, Fabianus and I worked together. We were going to own a string of shops from here to the sea. He's good with the needle. Good with wool, good with leather."

"What happened?"

"Thrown over for a pretty face."

"What?"

Aquila laughed. "He fell in love with horses. Wasn't long after that I went to work for Barnabas and gave up the wild life. Until I met you."

"Aquila, you are impossible this morning! You must be getting better."

"So do me a favor."

She looked at him warily.

"Kiss me."

"I thought so!"

"And then send for Fabianus."

With brief thought for his own schedule, Fabianus agreed to come by daily for an hour or two to dispose of their backlog, until Aquila and Prisca could manage alone.

As most of their tent-making neighbors handled only leather, their repair trade for woolen tents and orders for smaller goods had built up quickly. Many of their customers were nomads from the eastern provinces of the empire, who had never grown used to living in the leather tents favored by traveling Romans.

As Prisca worked in the easy company of Fabianus and Aquila they exchanged tales. She spoke of Jesus. Aquila had spent little time in the company of Barnabas and knew far less about the Christ than Barnabas had taught her. Fabianus, though a Roman and fond of recounting martial exploits, was a willing listener.

Aquila in his turn proved a gifted storyteller and was blessed with a liking for people. By the hour he spun adventures of the sea to her and Fabianus. Philip, when he was free, sometimes dropped in with Adah and the baby, and customers who lingered in the shop grew to look forward to the tales of all three.

Watching his animated face as he talked, loving the bent nose, and the sense of humor that refused to allow him to take his recuperation seriously, Prisca reflected often on how close she had come to losing him, and she blessed God all over again for his life.

One day, when the air was warm and Aquila stronger, he began to think of returning to the synagogue. Philip had been in the shop, hanging about more than usual that morning, and he asked his friend if he might accompany him the next day, which was the sabbath.

"Of course," replied Philip.

Aquila studied the small, swarthy figure. He liked Philip. Unlike many small men, he had none of the ways of the cock, but the natural modesty of a man content with himself. "You're awfully quiet. Little Zoe well?"

"Yes, she is fine."

"Adah?"

Philip looked uncomfortable. Aquila glanced over at Prisca. "Mind the shop while Philip and I take a break?" Prisca nodded with a smile. "Come on." The men left the shop and began to stroll slowly down the Street of Sellers. Aquila waited patiently for his friend to speak of what was troubling him.

They talked of nothing in particular for several minutes. Finally Philip said, "Did you know that Adah was barely fourteen when we married? Just a little mite. Maybe that's why I chose her. Even at that age, most girls were taller than I. Zoe did not come along until four years later. Adah was in dread that she would not be able to become a mother. Having Zoe was like being given a new life."

"She is a good mother."

Philip nodded. "She was gently reared, and I had to—ah—proceed very slowly lest she be frightened by the duties of marriage."

Aquila nodded. "Only natural."

Philip agreed. "But now Prisca has been telling her things."

"Prisca? What things? Woman things?"

Philip laughed uneasily. "This isn't easy for me."

"I know you speak in love," replied Aquila firmly.

"Neither of us is educated like you and your wife. Adah always left that up to me. Oh, she knows the Scriptures that every good Jewess is required to know, about managing the household and teaching the young. But Prisca has given her some sort of idea that that is not enough. Adah feels now that being a good wife means that she should—well—we all know women who, once they marry, become slothful and lazy, especially if their husbands can afford it."

Aquila laughed in agreement. "Some of them seem to think it is expected, as a means of broadcasting that their husband can afford so many servants. Praise the Lord that does not include our women! What exactly has Prisca been telling her?"

"That women do not serve their Lord well if they shirk to use all their abilities."

"You don't mean she wants her to set stone with you? She is hardly strong enough for that!" The thought amused him. He had always considered it ironic that Philip, with his small stature, should have become a stonemason himself. He supposed it had been the trade of his father. "I made no secret that I wanted Prisca to work with me, but only because I wanted her near, and she wanted to draw people to teach."

Philip smiled. "Nothing so simple. I always thought it was my duty to protect Adah from the world. It is a harsh and evil place, Aquila. She should be spared. Now she has begun asking me questions about other lands, other gods, how our God chose us to be his people—," Philip ran a hand through his hair. "Frankly, Aquila, I am afraid that so much learning will render her infertile. Women's mental powers are far short of men's."

Aquila gave a grunt of surprise. "Better not let Prisca hear you say that. She might not agree."

Philip opened his mouth, then shut it. Aquila had an idea what was on his mind and voiced it for him. "True, we have no babes yet, but it is not because Prisca is learned."

"Then it is all right letting her teach Adah these things?"

"Does Adah wish to learn?"

"I fear she does."

"Has it interfered with her household duties?"

"No. . . . She is happier, if anything," Philip admitted hesitantly. "Then you think it is all right."

"Yes, my friend. And I have come to believe that this is what our Lord intends. One of the stories they tell about Jesus concerns two sisters, Mary and Martha. Mary anchored herself at his feet and listened to his teaching. Martha stormed around like a rain squall, because all the work had fallen on her. She complained to the Lord, but he told her Mary had chosen the good portion."

"Truly!" Philip slowed to a stop and looked around. "Upon my word, see how far we have come!" Without another word, he wheeled and headed back to the shop, new spring in his step.

Aquila smiled to himself, realizing how naturally Jesus' example had come to his lips to help him ease his friend's fears. *Was* Jesus God's long-awaited Son? Yes. Suddenly he knew it so deeply and so completely he felt his heart would blast out of his chest. Yes! He must choose a special time to confess it to Prisca.

The following morning, the two men departed for the synagogue. When they returned several hours later, Aquila was wearing a black scowl.

"What happened?" asked Prisca.

"Nothing!" He stalked on through the atrium, where she and Adah and Maya had been playing with Zoe. Close on his heels came Philip. He grimaced at the women.

"What happened?" Adah hissed.

"He was talking about your Jesus of Nazareth. The rabbi threw us out."

Prisca excused herself and went after Aquila. She found him squatting on his haunches in the rear garden, among the early vegetables. "You're right," he said, examining a bunch of earth-clotted leeks, "they are better looking than the peddler's."

"Aquila—"

Disgustedly he arose, slapping the leeks against his hand to dislodge the dirt. "I lost my temper, Prisca. They are so fearful of anything new. They are like my father. A half-point off his course and you're running for ruin."

"What will you do?"

"Keep going."

"Is that wise?"

He laughed. "It's worth it."

"Mistress," said Maya, appearing at the edge of the garden. "A messenger is waiting in the shop. He looks important. Will you come?"

Prisca looked at Aquila. "We will both come," said Aquila. "Thank you, Maya."

162

Adah, Philip, and Maya filed silently into the shop after them. The messenger was wearing imperial livery. He handed Aquila a stiff parchment, sealed with a blob of red wax.

"My master asks me to wait for your reply, if convenient."

Glancing at Prisca, he opened it. "We are invited to dine with Tribune Marcus Sistus at his home, at the end of next month."

Tribune Sistus! Adah's mouth dropped open. Philip met the announcement with raised eyebrows.

Prisca caught Philip's intent stare, as if he were wondering just what was the connection between the powerful tribune and his friend's wife.

Prisca smiled at Aquila with a confidence she did not feel. "What shall we answer?" she asked carelessly, as if it were the most everyday thing in the world to be invited to the palace of a tribune.

Aquila shot her a look meant for her interpretation alone. "Tell the tribune we are honored to accept," he said stiffly to the messenger. He was uncharacteristically quiet the rest of the afternoon.

As soon as their friends had gone and they were alone in the atrium, Aquila dropped his silence. "Now is as good a time as any."

"What?" Prisca said. "I wish you would not always bring me in on the middle of a conversation."

"The tribune, Prisca, the tribune. How was it he happened to send his personal physician to save my life?"

Prisca had been dreading this, fully aware an accounting would be required, from the time she had made the decision to seek his help. "I met him in Tyre."

"At the temple?"

"Yes. He seemed to take an interest in me."

"He seemed to take an interest in you. By all that's holy, Prisca, what are you telling me?"

"Nothing! He seemed to take an interest in me! Nothing more. If only you were not so jealous! I never saw him after that."

"Did he—did you—"

"Ask him yourself!" she retorted.

"By the gods, I will!" Aquila sprang to his feet, swayed dizzily, and lowered himself to the couch again. "But not right now."

Prisca burst out laughing. "You goose. If you could see yourself."

"All wind and no sail," he muttered, grinning in spite of himself.

"Aquila . . . ." She sank on the couch beside him and picked up his hand. It was still too thin. She rubbed the bony knuckles. "Do you still wish to marry me?"

His eyes glowed softly beneath the heavy black brows. "I'll have to think about it."

She played with his fingers, aware of his eyes on her face, and kept silent.

"It was the prayers to God through your Jesus Christ, plus the skill of a Roman doctor, that saved my life."

"Yes."

A slow grin planted itself on his face. "So, the work of Christ is accomplished with the help of pagans. I think you yourself said that once."

"Well—"

"And though your Christ—from what you have told me—held marriage in holy esteem, the leaders of his band decided it would interfere with the quick return of God's kingdom."

"Yes—"

"And—"

"Yes?"

"Prisca no longer considers herself a stone."

"Oh, Aquila!"

"You still can't live without me, no matter what they say!"

"Yes! I mean, no. No, I can't live without you."

"And I win!" Aquila yelped triumphantly. "That man is on my side!"

"Who?"

"Jesus, of course!" He wrapped his arms around her and pulled her into his lap. "We're going to have a wedding, we are." He kissed her resoundingly.

"Aquila," she murmured against his ear.

"Hmm?"

"I win, too. The Christ—Jesus—is the Son of God. You believe this."

"Yes, dearest Prisca."

Prisca twined her arms around his neck. "Oh, I love you so!"

They sat for hours, bundled against the chill spring night, planning their future together and watching the slow progress of the stars through the open door.

"Aquila, will you do something for me?" she nestled deeper in the crook of his arm.

"Anything, my heart."

"Accompany me to an audience with Tribune Marcus Sistus."

Aquila moved to protest.

"It is for myself, as much as you. I must know what he is to me. He said he wished to meet you and that he would keep informed of your progress through Hyrcanus. It was little enough to promise to save you!"

Aquila's hand moved up to stroke the hair away from her temple. "Prisca, whatever he was—or is—to you, I love you and always will. We will meet him the night of the dinner. Married."

Prisca said no more, but in her heart she felt great foreboding.

Chapter 20

A few days later Fabianus drew up in front of the shop in a cart. Prisca watched him spring down. "Good morning!" she called from the door.

"Hallo. The invalid here?"

"Where else?" bellowed Aquila.

"We're going sight-seeing." Fabianus grinned cockily from the doorway. "Prisca needs a break, don't you, love?"

"Where are we going?"

Fabianus laughed. "My, you were hard to persuade. Come on, Aquila, up! Now I've got your business caught up and your wench trained, it's time she saw my Rome."

The air was pleasantly warm and humid, scented with an amalgam of flowers and pungent kelp from offshore beds a few leagues away, mixed with musky street odors of dust-coated animals, dried fish, and freshly baked bread. It was market day. Street sellers were in abundance, and pedestrians crowded their stalls.

"Where first?" called Aquila. He and Prisca sat on a makeshift bench behind Fabianus as he drove the horse cart up the Appian Way, toward the center of Rome.

"The Pantheon. There's a new statue of Diana I want Prisca to see. The sculptor is a friend of mine."

A short while later, the three were inside the temple. A reverent hush lay about them as citizens wandered from room to room, some to plead causes before their patron gods, others to view in silence the mighty works of the human imagination. Dedicated to all the gods, the temple afforded room for all, including emperors who had had themselves declared gods during their reigns.

Their sandals echoed hollowly as they strolled through one hall after another. Prisca paused before a marble base below an empty niche. "Did someone fall out of favor?" she asked Fabianus with a laugh.

"That is for the Unknown God," answered Fabianus seriously.

"The Unknown God?"

"We claim it for the One True God," said Aquila. "God the unseen. . . ." His glance flicked past Prisca's shoulder, and she turned. A tall man in charcoal robes, made taller by a round, high hat, with long full beard, was swooping toward them. His expression was stern. Several others followed, like a phalanx of geese winging after a leader.

"Well if it is not Aquila of Pontus, self-appointed rabbi. Leading tours, too, are you?" His deep voice reverberated through the marble chambers.

"Rabbi bar-Elymas." Aquila's handsome face closed as his hand went casually to the hilt of a small dagger in his girdle.

Rabbi bar-Elymas caught the move and looked at his face with scorn. He next glanced down his nose at Fabianus, dismissed him as obviously Roman, and studied Prisca with a needle gaze. "So you are the one. Most beautiful, they did not lie." To Aquila he said, "I see now, my son, who has led you into this heresy."

"Watch your tongue, rabbi," said Aquila in a low, deadly voice.

"I have heard of this priestess of Artemis, so lovely she makes men forget their own God."

"We preach Jesus as the Messiah, Son of the One God, rabbi," said Prisca quietly.

The Jews stirred. "By whose authority?" said the rabbi sharply.

"Jesus' himself," said Aquila. "Rabbi bar-Elymas, I spoke to you in the temple, and you would not listen." He gestured at the silent walls of gods and goddesses staring from their niches. "Here is not the place to find the Son of the Living God."

"That is a relief," said bar-Elymas, glancing round for approval from his colleagues. Then he leaned in with a menacing expression. "And neither is our holy temple! Let this be a warning to you. If you do not cease this rumor mongering, if you whisper one more word about some obscure prophet with messianic delusions, if you only once more open your mouth anywhere near the synagogue, I shall appeal to the civil authorities to arrest you for disturbance of the peace." The rabbi drew himself to his full, self-impressed height. With a final disdainful glance at them, he swept out, followed by his entourage.

Aquila stared after them, stunned with outrage.

Prisca felt suddenly afraid. "Could he have us arrested? What shall we do?" she whispered.

"Preach as before and trust in our Lord," said Aquila, bristling with anger.

"Whew!" said Fabianus. "Your friends are a stiff-necked bunch!"

"Oh, Aquila, why force a confrontation? Could we not reach as many people if you simply stopped going to synagogue and we invite people home? Surely it is safer to preach in our own house."

"I think Prisca's right, my friend," added Fabianus.

Little by little, they calmed him. He would not agree to stay home from the synagogue, but he did agree to keep silent there. For a time.

Many of their customers had heard of Jesus, the rabbi from Nazareth. Seated side by side, finishing each other's sentences as they worked together, Prisca and Aquila began to develop a pattern in these conversations. Aquila would ask the traveler from whence he had come. If Jewish, he asked what he knew of a rabbi whose disciples called him the Christ.

"The Christ?"

"Yes. The Anointed One, the one prophesied from ancient times, indeed the Son of God."

"People are saying Jesus is this Christ?"

"Yes."

"Hm. A miracle worker, I have heard. . . . A healer, great healer." And the visitor would stroke his beard thoughtfully. "I—ah—also heard some inconceivable tale about this Jesus, that he arose from the dead after being crucified."

"He is the one," Aquila would say. "My fellow worker knew Jesus."

Often the sojourner would glance around for another man. Seeing none, he would finally settle on Prisca a bright, curious glance.

"I met him in Tyre," she would say demurely, working industriously as she talked. Then, with a radiant smile for their customer, she would tell the story with great simplicity, so that her words could not be misunderstood. She would relate all that she had heard and seen, his great love for everyone, Jew or Greek, son or daughter, slave or free. How anyone might approach him, without going through a priest or a priestess. He himself was the intermediary between people like themselves and the one God.

"I can vouch for that," Philip would add, telling how they had been helped through Zoe's illness by the loving attention of their new friends.

The mending was always done before the tale. The customer, if he were abiding near, would beg to return the next day to hear the rest of the story.

As spring warmed into early summer, fewer customers bothered about rents in their tents, but came to have halters and straps and sundry other items mended or fashioned. Content, Aquila and Prisca worked on.

On an especially fine spring day, after Aquila declared he was again fit, he and Prisca were quietly married in the office of a minor city official, with Maya, Fabianus, Philip, and Adah in attendance, and went back home to celebrate.

Decorum prevented Fabianus from shooting all the bows in his quiver until the men were huddled in one end of the garden and enlivened with wine.

"We'll take Fabianus with us when we leave," Adah said, as the women listened to the men's lively guffaws drifting across the atrium. "Otherwise you'll never get rid of him."

Prisca burst into laughter. "Adah, dear, you are so practical."

A hush fell over the house as their guests departed. Prisca carried a lamp into her chamber. Maya had decorated the room with boughs of greenery and fresh spring flowers. Herb-scented linens covered her bed. She set the lamp on a small side table where Maya had placed a salver of sweets, a platter of fruit, a decanter of their best wine. Aquila came into the room noiselessly and touched her elbow.

She turned. His eyes glowed with love. She caught his dear face between her hands. Her body was trembling with new passion. She felt so alive that his touch rippled through her like aftershocks.

"I love you so much, Prisca." His voice was raw with passion. "I love your hair, your body, the way you move, the expression that comes over you when you are trying to explain things you think I don't understand—"

He shut off her protests with a kiss, a long, tender kiss filled with contentment and promise. Together they removed their clothing and beheld one another in the freshness of a love committed to God.

"Oh, Aquila, you are my other half!"

Chapter 21

What you fail to grasp," said Josephus, leaning over his couch to select another delicacy from the low table before his couch, "is that Jews have spent their entire history throwing people out of their land and keeping them out, rather than inviting them in." With immaculate, bony fingers he lifted a plump, brandied strawberry and considered it before popping it between his pale lips.

Marcus Sistus uncoiled his muscular frame and planted both feet on the floor. He fixed the young scholar with a stare. "And that is your explanation why duty in Palestine is every soldier's nightmare?" He glanced around the glittering dining hall, where a dozen of Rome's social elite and as many of her military leaders were reclining on couches and feasting on foods brought to the tables from every corner of the empire. He selected his target.

"Lucius Seneca. You've spent years away from Rome."

Everyone laughed appreciatively. Seneca had just been recalled to Rome from eight years exile on Corsica.

"You agree with our brash historian?"

Seneca was a shrewd-looking man with sharp nose and swept-back gray hair, a man whose ideas were considered so dangerous by his political enemies that it was only by the direct request of their new emperor's wife that he found himself restored to Rome. He seemed to gauge the mood and inclination of his host before answering.

"It would be much easier on the occupying armies if Jews were more like the Corinthians. As you may know, my brother Gallio is proconsul there. Corinth has enjoyed status as a city of a favored province because she has not fought her victors, but embraced them. So, yes, I would agree. Though I find it difficult to understand why a backward nation such as Palestine would resist Roman culture."

"For the sake of argument, my lord Seneca," said Josephus smoothly, "it is not so difficult to understand, when you consider how fervently the Jews of Palestine desire to be left alone. It is hardly surprising that they should chaff under Roman rule, just though it is."

"Pity us, if our roles were reversed," laughed Marcus. "They have never struck me as being overly tolerant." He glanced at Prisca and Aquila, couched on his right, Prisca seated between the two men, his guests of honor at the banquet. He had had difficulty keeping his eyes off her all evening. So, he had noted, had most of his other guests. He could see the questions eating away behind their glances. Who were these obscure peasants? How could someone as lovely as Prisca remain unknown all these years? The tribune's mistress? Or—more delicious—an unholy threesome? Her beauty was breathtaking. The noble carriage, the quiet grace with which she sat, put to shame more bejeweled women at the tables. Marcus leaned toward them.

"You young people have never lived in Palestine. But what do you think of our historian's reasoning?"

Aquila grinned wickedly at Josephus, seated to his right, before answering Marcus. "I think historians are happiest, tribune, when they can plumb the deepest path to an answer. They have not learned that life is best when it is simple."

The tribune studied him. Aquila's eyes held his, challenging. There would be a reckoning before the evening was done, he knew. But he, Marcus, would choose the time.

Aquila was darkly handsome in a robe of wine red wool edged in silver braid and clasped with a silver buckle on one shoulder. His thick, black hair, trimmed by Prisca before they came, curled crisply about his brow and neck. His face relaxed as he reached for his wife's hand. He would have it out with the tribune, he thought, but later, at a time of his, Aquila's, choosing.

Prisca's hair was piled Grecian fashion in a dark, gleaming coronet that set off the classic perfection of her features. "Vanity, you shameless wench," Aquila had teased when she'd pulled one piece of goods after the other off the shelf trying to decide which would look the best draped over her linen shift in lieu of a new robe. Together they had picked a fine wool the color of the Great Sea. It mirrored the clear depths of her eyes. She and Maya had sewed silk braid of the same hue on the wool and fashioned a matching girdle for her shift.

When they had been ready to leave for the banquet, Aquila had taken her hands proudly. "Just remember you belong to me," he'd whispered huskily. Stepping outside to enter the chairs that the tribune had sent to carry them to the banquet, they'd found to their surprise a handful of neighbors and strangers mustered to see them off.

Prisca had turned to Maya with a bewildered look. The old woman had affected innocence. "Well, it does business no harm if they know you have wealthy friends."

Holding his wife's hand, Aquila turned away from her to converse with Josephus.

A smile played on Marcus's lips as he watched them. He said to Prisca, "All this talk started when I asked how you could possibly forsake Artemis for an obscure Jewish sect. You have not answered me. By the gods, the loss to Artemis!"

"Your gods are beautiful playthings, Marcus, just as Artemis is," Prisca said lightly. "No one who values her life dares believe in the gods, nor in their service, pretend that she does not."

Josephus listened to her reply. "Well spoken," he murmured. Prisca had held him to his promise that she might visit his library. Several times, in company of her maid or another friend, she had come to pore over his manuscripts while her husband recuperated. Her searching questions, the depth of her understanding, had astonished him. A pity he was no longer court historian, since the death of Caligula. It had meant a sudden drop in income with which to add to his library, which was the love of his life.

A plump lady opposite Prisca, garbed in pink robe with tiny rosebuds embroidered around the neck and wearing much pink makeup and a lavish layer of blue eyeshadow, regarded her from across the circle of small tables with eyes round with sympathy. "My dear, are you not afraid to criticize the gods? Why just last week our son won the discus throw at the coronation games. He broke the record, did he not, husband? It was entirely due to the large donation I made to the temple of Apollo."

"Too large," said her husband.

"Congratulations on his victory," Prisca smiled at the woman. She glanced around. "Is your son here?"

"No," said his father, "he is in training."

Marcus smiled fondly at Prisca. "I hope I may count on you to enliven many an evening for an old warrior." His smile broadened to include Aquila.

"Thank you, my lord." Prisca's smile embraced the others. "And may I add that serving my Lord Jesus, the Christ, is not serving a Jewish sect. Exactly the opposite. Many of the Jews, especially those with power, are less willing to accept him than you yourselves."

"Those with power never willingly give it up. That is axiomatic, Prisca," said Marcus. "Aside from that, what need have I of another god?"

"What need have you of any other god?"

"And there you have another axiom, my lord," put in Josephus, "any new sect must be intolerant to survive. Ergo, only their god will do."

"Our God sent Jesus to proclaim that he is God for all people," amended Aquila.

"Ergo, ergo!" cried Josephus with delight. "The reason his name is becoming anathema to the Pharisees—the Jews in power, if you will. Can you imagine! This God, this Jehovah, chooses an ancient, insignificant desert tribe and makes a covenant with them. If they will be faithful to him, he will be their God—forever.

"Now comes a prophet—one of many down through the centuries— proclaiming that God is about to send his own messenger to dwell among them as flesh. Do they believe it? It had been foretold for centuries. But actually happening now? And whom does the prophet proclaim? An obscure rabbi from Nazareth! Is any Jew living who has never heard the old saying that nothing good comes out of Nazareth? No! It is too much!" Josephus leaned back on his couch and addressed the ceiling with raised palms. "A Messiah, *their* Messiah, now telling them, Open the gates! Let everyone in the kingdom!"

His eyes glittered in the ascetic face. Lowering his arms, and dropping his voice, he went on. "And the worst horror, which they must deny or else renounce their own history, is the possibility that they have crucified the man who is—truly—their own promised Messiah." He lifted an eyebrow. "The Messiah of every one of us?"

Not a hand moved. Not an eye blinked. Josephus surveyed the others with a small, triumphant smile.

Marcus rubbed his chin thoughtfully. "Do you believe this is true, Flavius?"

"My lord," Flavius Josephus answered, "I do not know. I think it is —possible."

"Hm. Do these Pharisees give you two any trouble, Aquila?"

Aquila glanced at Prisca. "Several of them have accosted us. One day at the Pantheon, of all places. But threats are easily spoken."

"Hear, hear, for the leniency of Rome," said one of the Roman guests, relief in her voice, breaking the spell which had gripped them all.

"Aye!" laughed Aquila, avoiding Prisca's alarmed gaze.

"Lenient, but not entirely without impatience," warned Josephus. "Recall, if you will, a century ago, during the reign of Tiberius. Certain Jews then abiding in Rome professed to preach the greatness of Moses. They persuaded a noble lady of Rome to donate gold for the temple in Jerusalem. Great was her anger when she came upon the men having a marvelous time in town at her expense!"

Laughter erupted around the room. "What happened?" someone asked.

"Oh, when all was said and done, Tiberius solved the affair most effectively. He banished the entire race from Rome."

Prisca studied Josephus thoughtfully. How easily he removed himself from the ranks of his race. "For the sins of four, all the Jews were banished?"

"Emperor Tiberius looked upon it as a family squabble, so to speak. If they could not keep their own house in order, he wanted no more truck with them."

"That was a long time ago," said Aquila comfortably.

"Aquila, have there been incidents you have not told me of?" Prisca asked in an undertone. "At the shop, perhaps, when I was gone?"

Josephus pricked up his ears. Aquila shifted. Marcus chose this moment to reach for his cup and motion to the servants to refill the goblets of his guests.

Josephus sighed with the exaggerated air of a martyr. "Newlyweds are fearsomely tiring, always worrying about each other."

Prisca and Aquila joined in the general laughter. "Only time, hard work, and a houseful of babies will make us sensible again," said Aquila.

Marcus lifted his wine goblet. "May your joy never desert you."

The others lifted their goblets and drank. Prisca's eyes glowed softly at Aquila. "Amen."

"And now, my good friends, a second toast."

Goblets in midair, smiles held in suspension, his friends waited. What new delight had Marcus concocted? An outlandish gift for the newlyweds? What could compare with the Corinthian bronze horse, life size, that he had presented last week to their new emperor, Claudius, on his coronation?

Marcus raised his goblet. "To you, I present a glory greater than any campaign—the daughter of my loins: Prisca!"

The wine goblet slipped from Prisca's fingers. A scarlet stain spread down her white shift. Aquila's arm flew about his wife. His eyes glared with impotent fury. "By all the gods of the underworld, tribune, what manner of jest is this?"

Tribune Marcus Sistus faced them. The expression on his bronze face was a mixture of pride and stubbornness. "It is not a prank, Aquila." He turned back to his guests. "Please! Feel free to amuse yourselves. More wine! Musicians, play! I shall retire with my new family—and attempt to get our own house in order."

Laughter greeted his witty pun. Oh, the streets would bubble with the tribune's latest news! His daughter, a lowly—what was it?—*tentmaker?* And how long would she remain a tentmaker with a wealthy and powerful father? Or remain married to one? Delicious! The bets would fly!

At the tribune's invitation, Prisca submitted to attendants who would help her into a new robe. Marcus Sistus gestured to Aquila. Without waiting to see if he followed, Marcus quit the hall.

Aquila was left with no choice. Angrily he strode after his host, into the fresh, perfumed air of a secluded garden. Laughter, music, and singing drifted after him. His sandals crunched harshly on the fine white gravel path as he dogged the other's steps away from the palace.

Marcus headed for the far edge of the garden, which came to an abrupt end before a low wall of chiseled granite. Beyond it the ground fell away in a steep slope. From this vantage, the last pale rays of sun illuminated a fine panorama of Rome. Spring rains had brought green to the hills. Among the crests and hollows, the palaces and civic buildings gleamed crisply in the waning light.

As Aquila caught up to him he turned, keeping the advantage. "So."

Aquila paused, chafing for an excuse to smash in the handsome, arrogant face.

"Not pleased, are you? I have had you investigated, Aquila."

"By what right?"

The tribune smiled. "Because in Rome I am strong and you are not."

"I warn you, tribune, do not try to take Prisca away from me. I'll fight you."

"Would you? Aquila, that would be such a temptation, more's the pity. I have no intention of trying. I wanted to find out what manner of man my daughter married. Surely a father has that prerogative?"

Aquila uttered an oath. "When were you ever a father?"

They heard women's voices, and both turned.

"Yes, I hear them. Thank you." Prisca approached them, her face composed. From Aquila's red face, she knew they had been arguing. She walked past the tribune and kissed her husband. She nodded at their host.

"You have quite an extensive ladies' wardrobe, tribune. Thank you for the loan of this gown. I shall send it back in the morning."

"Prisca, please—"

"Are you ready to leave, Aquila? I confess I am not used to such late hours. And you must still guard your strength."

"Remember, it was you who sought me out." The tribune fixed Prisca with a remorseless gaze. "Shall I guess what tempted you to accept my invitation, Prisca?"

Color flooded her cheeks. "I would not have my name shadowed with secrets from my husband."

"He was not your husband the night you came."

"Philip thought we were married. To correct him seemed beside the point. I needed your help."

Sistus nodded. "Quite right. Logical. And I gave it. Now I am entitled to knowledge, too."

"Aquila knows who I am and what I was. Until tonight I had no idea you were my father—if you are truly. I came to you when Aquila fell ill because I recognized you on your triumphal entry into Rome last year. It seemed, as you would say, logical that a powerful man could afford the best physician."

"Hyrcanus was satisfactory?"

Prisca relented. Her voice grew tender. "You know he was, my lord. He could not have given better care had Aquila been the emperor's son."

"Ah. Well spoken. I shall be equally frank. I would do this and much more for the happiness of my only child."

The wool throw slipped from Prisca's shoulders, leaving her slim and straight and very vulnerable looking in the borrowed shift. "You are my father."

Aquila saw the open longing in her face. "Why did you tell her now?" he demanded angrily. "Why tell her at all?" His mind was a tumult of emotions. Above all he desired her happiness. But he could not rejoice with her in this. He cursed himself for his weakness. A plague on the man!

Marcus answered him. "It seemed pointless to tell her when she was dedicated to Artemis."

Prisca searched his features, seeking something familiar, finding nothing.

"Thyatira was at liberty to tell you, of course, but she felt the same way."

"Tell me? About you? About you and her? She is my mother, in truth? Not just my priestly mother?" Prisca was stunned. She stared at him, seeing only her past. "Oh, why did she not tell me?" she whispered, so heartrending that Aquila gathered her into his arms. Her mother. Her mother had allowed a man they both detested to steal her virginity. *Why?* Would she ever know?

Suddenly Tribune Sistus seemed tired of the sparring and the revelations. "Prisca, Aquila, come. Sit." He motioned for servants to bring refreshment, then waited for them to retire.

Prisca's eyes were like deep, lost pools mirroring an unknown landscape. Aquila faced him with the wary posture of a prisoner brought to bay, his eyes cynically waiting to be shown how the tribune expected to benefit from this. They sat on a stone bench facing the tribune. The tribune leaned forward, cupping a kneecap with each square hand. "We met in Ephesus. . . ."

It was not an uncommon story. A well-born but poor soldier, constantly on campaign, a priestess, forbidden to marry unless she willed to leave the temple, a baby daughter, less desirable for adoption than a male, kept with the mother at the temple out of love. Thyatira had demanded this right. When Prisca was seven, Thyatira had accepted the post at faraway Tyre, to be closer to Sistus during the years of the Alexandrian campaign.

"Your mother tried to protect you as best she could. I sent her money as my own fortunes increased, and she fulfilled her promise to me that you should be educated as befitting a Roman citizen." Sistus rose and stared out over his city. "We did not see each other for several years. Then, five years ago, when I knew you would have been of marriageable age, I journeyed to Tyre to see you, and if you pleased me, to bring you to Rome."

A sneer curled on Aquila's face. *If he was pleased! As if Prisca were a prize mare!*

"To Rome!" Prisca said.

It was the tribune's turn to smile. "That was why I asked you, the night you came for my help, what Thyatira had said about me. I had forgotten how willful your mother could be. Yes, I would have brought you away with me then. I found you an enchanting maiden, Prisca. But Thyatira begged me to leave you with her one more year. She said you were reaching the point of full commitment to Artemis. You would have followed in her footsteps."

"Never! She knew that!"

"She did not write at the end of the year. Rome was involved in a campaign again; I could not leave my legion. I sent a trusted messenger. Thyatira sent word that you were no longer at the temple, and of your whereabouts she neither knew nor cared." Marcus scoured his eyes with thumb and forefinger. "I have been seeking you for five years—"

Suddenly it dawned upon Aquila what it was that the tribune intended to do. He reared off the bench. "No! That is enough!"

Marcus waved a placating hand at him. "With your permission, Prisca, and Aquila's, I desire now to—"

"Tribune!" A servant hurried quickly through the garden. "I beg your pardon, my lord, but I must speak to you."

"Speak freely."

The servant glanced at Prisca and Aquila. "It is about them," he hissed. "Say it before I cut your tongue out!"

"A riot down on the Appian Way. Some peasants are here, saying the tentmaker's place is destroyed."

Chapter 22

P hilip had brought word. A band of rioters howling through the neighborhood at dusk, seemingly drunk and disorderly and bent on random mischief. A few goats loosed in the streets, a line of wet wash dragged through the dust, a cart overturned. Then for no apparent reason they had converged on the shop of Aquila and Prisca.

Aquila arrived with Philip, Tribune Sistus, and a cadre of mounted soldiers to find the shop reduced to rubble, wool and leather goods knifed to shreds, precious tools hacked out of shape, and the vandals long vanished. The charcoal brazier had been overturned and its ashes strewn. Obscene blotches of paint streaked the walls from shattered pots of dye. As they picked through the shop by the light of torches a soldier uttered an angry oath. He had stepped into a mass of fresh human dung.

Aquila gazed around in shock. All they had worked for—nearly a year's careful work—all their money sunk into this.

"Who could have done this, Aquila?" asked Marcus.

He might not have heard the question. "I don't want Prisca to see this."

One of Marcus's soldier's stuck his head in the door. "Sir, the lady is here."

"She is! Keep her outside," Marcus ordered him.

Aquila flicked a glance at Marcus. Didn't take long for him to start giving Prisca orders. But he held his peace and went out himself. A throng of onlookers moved away from the door. As they helped Prisca dismount from the chair Marcus's runners looked ill at ease, having disobeyed the tribune's orders. Aquila sympathized with the men. Prisca could make very convincing demands.

When she saw him, Prisca let out a small cry and rushed to him. "I could not wait there and do nothing, Aquila! I made them bring me."

He nodded. "It must have been vandals, Prisca. Stay out here. They made a job of it."

Prisca craned to see into the shop. "What did they do? Where is Maya? Is she all right?"

"Maya? She must be with Adah." He threw a look over his shoulder at Philip, who had followed him out.

Philip had made it only to the heavy open door and remained there, ringed by soldiers averaging a head taller than he. Aquila called him. He looked up. "Come here and look at this," Philip said.

The soldiers backed away. Philip hoisted his torch to illuminate the door. A gilded silver arrow impaled a branch of laurel leaves to the door.

Prisca gasped.

"It's only a bunch of leaves," said Aquila. He wrenched out the arrow.

"The sacred asherah of Artemis." She fought down an unreasoning sense of fear. She stared at the arrow in Aquila's hand. "That is Diana's."

"Diana's?"

"The goddess Diana the Huntress." Prisca shivered. "It's a warning—I—I do not know. *Where is Maya?* I must find her!" She broke through the ring of men and dashed into the shop. Scarcely aware of the destruction there, she plunged on through the atrium, calling her servant's name. She was not in the gathering room, or in any of the sleeping rooms.

Shaken, an unnameable fear interfering with her breathing, she returned to the atrium. "M-Maya?" With dread she walked deliberately around the enclosure.

"Bring torches," Aquila commanded.

An unnatural silence fell over the soldiers. Prisca watched the dreadful hunt, unable to do more than follow as Aquila and Philip, joined now by Marcus, raised their torches, gingerly pulling aside the broad, leafy foliage of plants bordering the atrium. At last a grunt of sorrow from Aquila. "Lord, help us. Here she is."

With a dreadful cry Prisca thrust past them and fell on her knees beside Maya. She was heaped in a corner like a forgotten rag doll. The gray hair streamed over her face. A dark blotch matted the top of her skull. "Oh, Maya!" cried Prisca, pulling the lifeless shoulders into her arms. "Maya, Maya!"

Then strong arms gently pried her burden from her grasp and lifted Prisca to her feet. Dimly she was aware of Marcus ordering his men to begin scouring the neighborhood for information, of Aquila leading her into the gathering room, quietly asking Philip to fetch Adah.

Marcus followed them. "Prisca will be safer at my house until we find the men who did this. I've given orders—"

"No! I shall not be driven from my home."

Reluctantly Aquila agreed with him and urged her to go. He explained to Marcus about the arrow and branch on the door. "If this is somebody with a grudge against her, somebody connected with the temple—"

180

"That was years ago!" she cried. "Please, Aquila! Let us see this through together."

Aquila hesitated.

"She is not responsible," Marcus began.

Over Prisca's shoulder, Aquila threw Marcus a scathing look. "All right, Prisca. We shall trust the Lord to keep us." To Marcus he added, "Thank you for your help, tribune."

Prisca collected herself. "Yes. Thank you."

Within minutes, friends were descending upon the shop to begin, unasked, the task of cleanup and repair. Some of the women came to assure Prisca that they would be preparing food for the mourning period. Others brought oils and linens and set about the task of cleansing and anointing Maya's body.

The depth of their friends' compassion showed in gruff promises to lend Aquila scarce tools until new ones could be made by the metal-workers guild or in drachmae pressed on the couple to purchase new supplies, accompanied by a brief clasp to the shoulder. Outside, men of the neighborhood consulted briefly. Then Philip came in to announce that they were setting up a watch to scan strangers in the coming days.

When Marcus saw that his men were not needed, he dismissed them, but something he did not understand held him there, observing, well into the night. Would his friends help so unstintingly, were he faced with a similar tragedy? Prisca and Aquila had been in Rome less than a year. Without wealth or power they had attracted a large and loyal family of friends. How? What was their secret? Finally he left, after extracting a promise from Prisca and Aquila that they would call upon him as a kinsman if they needed further help.

As the days passed they were no nearer to discovering Maya's killer than they had been that night. Maya was buried, Prisca reflecting sadly that the old woman had always feared dying. But Prisca felt relieved, in a way, that the end had come upon her servant so suddenly, with no more than a moment or two of fear, no time at all to ponder the empty void that Maya remained convinced lay beyond.

One day not long afterward, Aquila was sitting in the atrium, taking a break from the shop, when Prisca staggered through, carrying a huge bundle of soiled linens. "You ought to get a new servant," he called to her. "We can afford it."

She dumped the laundry with a small grunt and came to sit with him. "I suppose so. But I miss Maya."

"I'm sure Marcus would be glad to pay for a whole crew of servants. All you'd have to do is ask."

"Aquila, that's unkind!"

"Unkind!" His eyes widened. "Me?"

"You know what I mean."

They sat in irritated silence. Aquila broke it by saying, "You know what he was leading up to that night, don't you?"

"What night?"

"The riot. The shop. When Maya was killed. Throwing that big party. Announcing to one and all that you were his daughter. You have a way of ignoring things you do not want to face."

"I do not! You have a way of jumping me in the middle of a private conversation that's been going on in your head for weeks!" Prisca swept the damp hair off her neck with an impatient flip of hand. "It is hot. . . . What things, Aquila? What was he leading up to?"

"He wants you back. He wants you with him."

"What makes you think so?"

"What does a woman need family for? Only to provide a respectable background and training for marriage. Once you are past the dowry, her family is useless; a wife belongs to her husband's family. Marcus knows this, and he's ignoring it. Just as you are."

"He's my father! The only person in the world that I am related to by blood, save for my—for Thyatira. Marriage does not change that."

"Legally it does."

"Even a tribune cannot take a wife from her husband."

"He could entice her by other means," Aquila said in a very low voice. Prisca looked at him, speechless. "Aquila! You are jealous!"

Aquila rubbed his bent nose and looked down. "Not either."

"My dearest one, do you think I would leave you?"

"He is rich, he has power. He knows the most important people in Rome. Tentmakers and followers of the Christ may inherit the kingdom, but not his kind of kingdom."

"Oh, Aquila! Who would want his kind of kingdom if our Christ were not part of it? It saddens me that you think so little of my love for you and for our Lord that I could not resist such a small temptation."

A slow, guilty grin spread across his face. "Is it small, Prisca?"

"Less than that. It is nothing to me. But he is still my father, and I will honor him."

Aquila nodded. "So be it."

Weeks went by. No other outbreaks disturbed the neighborhood. Gradually former habits replaced fear, and suspicion of strangers relaxed.

As summer built toward its zenith, the hot, dry sirocco swept through Rome, off the deserts south of the Great Sea, leaving the inhabitants gasping for relief. To escape the heat, those who could afford to do so migrated to Corinth or other popular resorts.

The migration of the wealthy affected little the humble houses and shops on the Appian Way. To them, a quiet Rome meant a peaceful Rome. Aquila, watching Prisca, prayed that the languor of summer would subdue the mourning that overtook her now and then. One morning they sat in the atrium, breaking the fast in the fresh, dew-scented air, which would be gone by midmorning. Prisca glanced up, catching Aquila's questioning gaze, and smiled automatically.

"When will you let Maya's spirit rest?"

"What?"

"I've been watching you. I know you, Prisca. You are still grieving for the old lady."

"She wasn't so old."

"If you trust the Christ, you will rejoice that she dwells with the Father."

The gray green cast of her eyes deepened with melancholy. "I could only teach her about the Christ. I could not force her to say 'I believe.' "

Aquila made a small sound of sympathy. "And she didn't."

Prisca shook her head.

"Not your fault. Every person must arrive at her own decision." Calmly Aquila bit into a juicy peach.

"If only I'd had more time—"

"Oh, is that it? You can bring anyone to the faith, if God only gives you enough time."

Prisca cocked her head in self-deprecation. "It is a hard lesson," she said softly.

Aquila wiped his hands and mouth on a towel and tossed it aside. He got up and pulled her gently to her feet. His black eyes were liquid with compassion. "I love you," he said huskily and kissed her.

Prisca's refusal to leave the shop of her husband for the palatial house of her father earned her an unexpected reputation. It embarrassed her, so she tried to make light of it.

"What if I grew accustomed to all that luxury?" she had joked with Aquila as they worked in the shop together. "What if I forgot how to sew a seam the wind could not find?"

Their friends smiled at each other. The onetime priestess, bona fide daughter of a popular Roman tribune, wife and co-worker of a tentmaker, together preachers of a new savior. What a man, this Aquila, that his wife doted upon him so openly, that they seemed so perfectly happy with each other! Well. None could doubt that something, or someone, was blessing this marriage.

And so word spread of a God who so loved the world that he sent his own Son. . . . And soon the shop would not hold all who wished to listen, and Prisca and Aquila began to preach in the atrium as well. Frequently Josephus was among the listeners, prodding thoughtfully at his thin jaw.

Before the heat drove them out of town, a few highborn Romans, friends of the tribune, came, intrigued by sheer novelty. Many left, bored with the idea of a kingdom that promised few material thrills. Incomprehensible to them, turning one's back on Fortuna, goddess of Chance. If any of them had overnight been offered kinship to one of the comfortable fortunes of Rome, well. . . . Safe to say none would have been so stupid as this beautiful young woman, Prisca of Tyre, who rumor had it, had snubbed her father and his fortune. After all, despite the Greeks, physical beauty was the most illusory of gifts, was it not?

Marcus Sistus had suffered many wounds in many campaigns. Sometimes one or another flared up to give him pause. Yet none of these old injuries pained as much as the recent, still bleeding, piercing of his pride. He had fully expected to be asked to help restore the meager fortunes of his daughter.

He'd vowed to intimates that he would help, of course, but not until she came to him. But as the weeks passed and Prisca made no attempt to contact him, he convinced himself that she would, but that her husband kept her from doing so. Therefore as a father it was his duty to visit the shop himself.

Fifteen or twenty others were crowded inside when the tribune arrived, causing a stir among those who recognized him. Prisca flashed a smile at him. He returned it with an impassive nod, deliberately breaking eye contact to give the shop a swift, authoritative glance.

With difficulty he connected the orderly, clean shop with the havoc of that night. The walls were now whitewashed. New bins and racks held their materials and assorted tools. From habit, his eyes went over those present. Few, he noticed, were well dressed. Philip and Adah he recognized from that night. Four others, dark-robed, somber men, he guessed were from the Jewish temple. Not all were Jewish in appearance. Fabianus, sitting next to Aquila, a Roman. The tribune had seen him several times on the Field of Mars. He nodded to him. He admired the tough, fearless horse trainer.

In the midst of their company sat Aquila and Prisca, side by side before a low work table. As they worked they went on with their teaching. Some of the others had also brought handwork to do as they listened.

Folding his bare arms over his chest, Marcus leaned against the door-jamb and listened, too.

Aquila was speaking, his brow knit in earnest concentration. "Suppose a ship is on the rocks, and the only way to rescue the people in the ship is for one of their number to jump overboard with a rope and swim to shore. Then he can tow the others to safety."

Their listeners nodded.

"That is like what Jesus did," said Prisca. "He led the way. He jumped out of the ship of life, into death, but came out the other side with the line that binds us to him intact, so that we can follow him and be saved."

"You mean we won't die if we believe in Jesus?" asked a woman, a placid matron who was cradling a young babe in her lap.

"All of us die, but Jesus rose from the dead," said Prisca. "I knew Jesus. He would not lie. He spoke to me again after he had died and risen. He knows us. He knows that everyone is afraid to die. That makes us slaves to our fear. Jesus doesn't want us to live in fear. By knowing that Jesus has passed through death and come out of it victoriously, we do not have to be afraid any longer." Prisca smiled tenderly at her. "We need only to put our trust in him. When death comes, he will be there to lead us to eternal life on the other side."

Questions tumbled out of the other listeners. Marcus Sistus held back. A stern smile played on his face, hiding his confusion. He felt as if he had stepped into the midst of a family bonded by love of the sort that comes only when its members are not afraid to expose their weaknesses as well as strengths, sorrows as well as triumphs. He had known such love only rarely. On a field of battle, among survivors. But never as all-embracing as this.

His eyes kept returning irresistibly to his daughter's face. It shone with radiant warmth as she spoke of the man Jesus, whom she called the Christ. It was a love almost palpable, reaching out, touching all.

Their eyes met. She smiled. He knew suddenly that she loved him as much as, but no more than, the beggars who had crept in among the listeners after him. He could not help returning her smile.

Someone jostled those behind Marcus in the doorway, and a messenger crowded through, a compact, leather-limbed man with small, bright eyes. He glanced around as if surprised to find such a crowd in a shop. "Prisca of Tyre? Is Prisca of Tyre here? Or one named Aquila, formerly a ship's master?"

Aquila arose, "Here, man. Welcome."

A smile broke over the stranger's weathered features. "You be hard to find. I have letters for you." From a leather pouch he produced two tightly rolled scrolls.

"Thank you. Stay with us and share our meal. It is nearly time. You will find water and a place to rest through that door." Aquila directed him to the atrium.

The scrolls were from Barnabas, one for each of them. Prisca tore hers open with trembling fingers.

"Greetings to Prisca, my fellow worker in Christ," the letter began. "I hope this letter finds you well and happy. Not knowing if Aquila is still with you—though something tells me he is, and I pray that it is so—I have written separate letters to each of you. As I wrote him, the *Lotus* returned in due course, after a profitable and uneventful journey—uneventful save that the master jumped ship! I envy him his good sense." Prisca smiled. How like Barnabas to put generous interpretations upon the actions of his friends.

"After you departed from Cyprus, Mark and I sailed to Jerusalem. You would be pleased to see how that young man has grown in godly ways. We stayed some months with the brethren. A most amazing thing happened. Remember Saul, the man who was so bent on harassing the brethren? Our Lord recognized the tenacious spirit dwelling within his breast and turned him around. Saul became Paul and is fast becoming a leader among those serving the Christ.

"Paul went for a time to Antioch, from whence I have just fetched him back to Jerusalem. Some of the brethren disagree with him, but it is within a spirit that strives to accommodate different views of our Lord and of our mission. You see, my dear Prisca, our friends in Jerusalem have grown also in their understanding of the words of Christ, in the years since they rejected your ministry out of hand.

"From Cyprus, Lydia sends her dearest love and hopes you will return someday. The twins miss you and remember your lessons. They continue to grow in grace and beauty. From Jerusalem, your friends, particularly Andrew, send love and blessings. Our new apostle, Paul, also sends greetings. I have told him about you, and he is anxious to meet you. We will be traveling much in the years just ahead, and it may be within God's plan that one day we shall greet one another with a kiss. Your brother in Christ, Barnabas."

Prisca lowered the letter to her lap and closed her eyes in a transport of joy. How near he made her feel to him, to all of them serving the Christ! She looked around with a start. The shop was empty. Through the doorway, she could see their friends mingling in the atrium.

Springing lightly to her feet, she followed. The women had gone ahead and were laying out food on low tables in the dappled shade of an olive tree, plain but substantial fare, consisting of loaves of barley and wheat bread, smoked fish, grapes and figs, and bowls containing small chunks of cold marinated lamb and vegetables in spiced olive oil. Some of the guests had brought contributions of their own in baskets or jars. No one seemed to notice if some had brought nothing to share.

Aquila caught her eye. "What did Barnabas have to say?"

"News of the brethren, mostly. Here," she offered him the scroll.

"Not now." He gestured at their guests. "Hungry herd. He says he owes me more money."

"Who?"

"Barnabas. For my half of the *Lotus* and cargo." Aquila grinned. "He calls it 'not an immodest sum, but enough to keep a wife if she be prudent.' " His black eyes teased her, and they both broke into laughter.

After Aquila's blessing, Marcus was urged to tear off bread and dip it in the pot, along with everyone else. Aquila watched him, but Marcus seemed perfectly at ease sharing the common pot.

Finally the day was done, and Aquila closed up shop. Marcus was still there. Aquila said, "Let's go out to the atrium, it's cooler."

The men settled on benches. Aquila threw his father-in-law a challenging glance. "Well?"

Tribune Sistus raised his sun-bleached eyebrows. "Well, what?"

"What do you think of your daughter?"

"Prisca is a remarkable young woman."

Aquila nodded.

"She is also a patrician, well educated, wealthy if she chooses—"

"And married to a Jewish tentmaker."

Marcus Sistus regarded him with hooded gaze. "An honorable craft."

The tribune's carefully phrased words irritated Aquila. "Yes, it is." He glanced uncomfortably toward their house. Where was she, anyway? When the shop had nearly emptied of customers, toward the end of the afternoon, Prisca had excused herself to prepare their evening meal.

"What are you afraid of, Aquila?" said the tribune softly.

"Here you are!" sang Prisca, entering from the gathering room, bearing a tray with a tall, gracefully made pottery pitcher and three clay goblets. She had changed into a pale pink gauze shift, voluminously layered to trap any hint of breeze. Her feet were bare. She gazed impishly at her husband as she served him. "It's just barley water with mint. Poor man's drink, but best in this heat."

Aquila scowled. Did she have to mention "poor man's drink"?

The tribune was smiling at his daughter. "I'd never heard of this Jesus before you came. Interesting fellow."

"Interesting? Well," she said after a pause, "that's a start."

"Through our young friend Flavius Josephus, of course, we know something of Jewish history. But I don't recall him mentioning Jesus."

"Jesus is new to him, too, father."

"We always knew a Messiah was coming. But never when. And never by name," Aquila said shortly, as if begrudging Marcus a share in anything. He caught Prisca's eye. A slight frown troubled her forehead.

"You are really committed to this—to preaching about your new Messiah?"

"Yes," answered Prisca and Aquila in unison.

A brief smile touched the tribune's face. "It is good to see people care about something. . . . Believe in something. As for me, I ceased believing in anything but my own strength long ago."

"And does it make you happy, father?"

This time his eyes drank in her beauty unashamedly. "It has, yes. But having you here—well, it's enough to make one believe anything is possible."

Aquila's face looked thunderous.

Marcus laughed and added carelessly, "Wives, daughters—women have the power to make men very happy. Right, Aquila?" He rose easily. "I must leave, my children. Thank you for a most instructive day."

"I hope you will visit often, father."

"Do you? Then I shall! Good night."

Marcus returned home in a state of dissatisfaction. How could his daughter be happy in such mean circumstances? But she was, and that was the disturbing factor in all this.

From what he could discern, their ministry extolled peace. Loving one another. Depending on one another. Seeing that which was good in everyone and calling it by the name of God. He felt a brief moment's compassion for Aquila. Poor wretch, uneducated, powerless. How long could he hope to keep his wife? Still, there was this supposed Christ in their midst. How strong? How strong?

He spent an hour going over reports from his network of spies, whom he had planted throughout the city, after the assault on Aquila's shop, to discover a motive for the sacking. He no longer believed it was the work of vandals, desirous of nothing more than an evening's fun at the expense of some Jews. And could anyone seriously believe the gods were at fault, angered because a former daughter of Artemis forsook one god for another? They above any human understood the nature of fickleness.

Marcus was growing impatient with the lack of progress in the affair. Or perhaps it was just that with no new military campaigns in the wind, he was impatient for action of any kind. He went to bed in an ill temper.

Late the following morning he ordered his chair and paid a visit to the temple of Diana, near the Pantheon. He was ushered into the chambers of the high priestess. Within moments, a rustle of curtain announced her arrival.

"Marcus Sistus, what a pleasant surprise, my lord," said a low, provocative voice.

Marcus wheeled on the balls of his feet to face her, a half smile playing over his features, and appreciated the beauty of the woman before him. Of indeterminate age, she presented a striking figure, with red hair, clear skin, and twilight blue eyes. The lavender silk layers of her gown, each layer a deeper color, were exquisitely draped to honor her long neck and milky bosom and bathe in mystery her full, supple figure. He inclined his head in salute.

"Phoebe, you are so beautiful it is a wonder the gods leave you among us mortals."

Her eyes shimmered with delight and some curiosity. Silently she ordered refreshment, motioned him to a silk tapestried couch, and pulled a cushioned stool near for herself.

Marcus felt suddenly awkward. He had not realized the complexities of the situation. "I have a daughter," he began.

She smiled, making it easy for him. "Yes. I have seen her, Marcus. She is very lovely."

"Her mother is equally so. Or so I remember."

"Where is she?"

"In Tyre. At the temple of Artemis."

"Ah. Not a wealthy temple, I hear. Have you visited her recently?"

"Not for over five years. Prisca was herself a priestess then."

Phoebe nodded.

His sunburned face crinkled in amusement. "You know the truth of the matter. Why toy with me?"

"Not all. I know she does not serve Artemis any longer. And I did hear tell of some sort of mystical experience she had while she was still a priestess. She believes that the Son of the God of the Jews is someone she knew, doesn't she? She came to Rome and married a man of the same belief."

He threw a chagrined glance at her over the rim of his silver goblet. "Your people keep you better informed than mine do."

Phoebe laughed good-naturedly. "We all talk on it. It is passing strange that a god would want to save people from themselves. What if they do not want to be saved? What if they are—," she bestowed on her guest a slow, sensuous grin, "just too busy?"

She came to sit beside him and placed her soft hand on his inner thigh. "Marcus, you've no idea what delicious speculation your name brings! Your exploits are endless. And now a beautiful, penniless mystic, your daughter! I suppose she wants you to declare her your heir?"

Marcus did not join in her throaty laughter. How did Phoebe know he himself was mulling over just such an idea—except that he was afraid what she might do with such a fortune?

Her expression altered. "I am sorry, my dear friend. What is it you desire of me?"

Briefly, Marcus recounted the events of the night that Maya died. "The death of her maid I see as unplanned. But it does serve to point up that whoever killed her wanted their identities kept secret."

"And a silver arrow was used to fix a branch of laurel to the door. I heard about that."

"Yes."

"To make it seem the gods were angry at her and demanded her return to the fold. Or that vengeful priestesses were involved."

"Does that seem likely to you?"

"Given the beauty of your daughter, they would more likely rejoice to have her gone. Unless it was her mother's doing. If she saw her daughter growing in power, that might be threatening. Did they part with love?"

"I do not know. But Tyre is weeks—months away." But who knew if Thyatira was still there? Thyatira bent on revenge against a willful daughter? Marcus considered it, thinking of her. It was not hard to see where Prisca got her determination, with the two of them for parents.

"I haven't seen much of Prisca since she came to Rome. Frankly, I am a little in awe of her, Phoebe. She seems so self-assured. She would make a great field commander. But she does not seem to know that she is in danger."

He made a restless, throwaway gesture. "I doubt if she'd trust me with anything about her mother. You think her mother might have engineered this?"

"Families can be the worst."

"Verily."

Phoebe rose. Marcus caught an elusive scent of perfume in the lavender silk as she drifted by him. "Gossip flows easily among the temples. I will see if anything more can be learned. For now," smiling, she turned and slipped onto his lap, "let us take this pleasant afternoon for our own pleasure."

As his arms went about her, she dipped her head to meet his raised lips.

Chapter 23

ucius Seneca was a frequent visitor at the court of Claudius, being tutor to the royal son. He had promised the tribune to keep an ear open for some mention of that piddling Jewish riot affair, but certainly had no intention of putting himself in debt for favors. If some knowledge came his way, fine. He would pass it along with honor. No one had a right to expect more. Marcus might be a friend, but he was still only a tribune. A soldier. Honored at court and well thought of by the rank and file, but quite lacking in apprehension of the finer things of life.

Seneca, on the other hand, though he might lack the physical beauty of his friend, was renowned for his dramas and knew himself a fine poet, a revelation he was about to share with the world. On this morning he hastened through the marble halls of the Forum in high humor. He had just completed what he believed his best poem. He was eager for the judgment of another man of letters before debarking for Corinth, where he planned to visit his brother, Gallio, the proconsul, and enter his poem in one of that city's omnipresent contests.

Spying a tall, narrow-shouldered figure before him, he called out: "Flavius! Good morrow, my friend! Dame Fortuna has led me to just the man I need."

Flavius Josephus turned and smiled at the energetic dramatist, taking in the shrewd, narrow eyes, the carefully swept back gray hair. A vain man, he knew—a dangerous trait—but Josephus, too, was in a mood to be amiable. Emperor Claudius had just appointed him to recontinue his task as court historian, which had been temporarily suspended with the unfortunate murder of Caligula.

"Good morrow, Lucius. What keeps you in the city with this heat?"

"Unimportant business, nearly complete," said Seneca, dismissing it. He favored Josephus with an engaging smile. "Sir, I've always thought it a pity you were born neither Roman nor Greek. You've my admiration as the most learned man at court."

Flavius lifted an eyebrow and braced for the inevitable favor. "Thank you, my lord, but of course that is not true. The soul of a historian is a pedestrian one, while that of the philosopher soars."

"Why—thank you!" Seneca was touched by the graceful words. "Might I ask if you have time to read a few small stanzas I've scribbled off? It is nothing, of course, but as I am planning a trip to Corinth—"

"Of course, the competition! My lord, a splendid idea. I shall be honored to read your work."

The two started down the high, fluted corridor at a stately pace. "Nasty business, that with Tribune Sistus's daughter," Seneca remarked.

"The sacking, you mean?" said Josephus. If Lucius Seneca were plotting to discredit him by getting him to utter remarks about the girl herself, he would be disappointed. Josephus had survived emperors by always perceiving the proper loyalties.

"Yes. Never caught the scoundrels, I hear."

"Nor likely to," murmured Josephus.

"Pity. Marcus is genuinely fond of her. She is quite a lovely creature. I understand she refused to move into her father's home." Seneca laughed. "Rather shortsighted in one so bright, is it not?"

"Her first loyalty is to her husband, and that man Jesus, if he be a man."

"Yes. Interesting. We should get together some time and discuss it, my dear fellow," said Seneca. "Well, I have an appointment to keep. Here is my poem," carelessly thrusting a slim packet at Josephus, "when you have time."

"Certainly, sir. Thank you for the trust." Flavius Josephus bowed as Seneca swept on. The smile died on his face. Ah! Poets were a ticklish lot. If he praised the poem and it did not do well in the competitions, Seneca would be humiliated and think him a fool. If he appraised it honestly and found it lacking—and it went on to garner a prize—he would appear equally foolish. He sighed. Better to take one's chances among strangers than to so burden one's friends.

The historian paced on more slowly, disturbed by another matter that Seneca's casual remarks had brought to mind. Marcus Sistus had recently done him an enormous favor, though without mentioning it to him. Months ago he had sent over to his house a handsome silver urn encrusted with topazes, with a simple note of thanks for sharing his library with Prisca. But the favor that now he was in a position to return was the word Tribune Sistus placed in the ear of the emperor, on the advantage of continuing royal patronage to a poor Jewish scholar as court historian.

Flavius doubted that Prisca knew of either generous act. The information he had gleaned, pieced from bits and pieces that had trickled in, disturbed his conscience. His brethren of the Jewish community had often accused him of being a sycophant of the Romans in power. If they caught word of what he now knew, he would be hounded out of Rome. Still . . . yes. The tribune's generosity had earned him the right to know.

Quickening his pace, Flavius Josephus left the cool halls of the Forum and emerged into the bright sunshine. At the top of the steps he paused momentarily to admire the work in progress on the Colosseum. Objectively he watched the lines of sweating slaves as they struggled with the roped granite boulders, could imagine the hot sirocco drying their sweat before it had a chance to cool them, cracking lips, and scorching shoulders. Pity the Colosseum would not be finished in his lifetime. What games, what pageants would be seen there!

More slowly, he descended the steps to his waiting chair. If he told Marcus what he knew about the riot and the servant woman's death, he could not control the consequences. Was that wise? Marcus wished only to protect his daughter. Perhaps he might serve the tribune and himself better by a more direct approach. He ordered his bearers to take him down the Appian Way.

Waves of heat shimmered from the baking pavement. When he arrived, the shop of the tentmaker was devoid of customers. The drone of flies heightened his sense of oppression as he stepped into the confining semi-darkness.

"Times like this I wish I was back on the sea," said Aquila by way of greeting. He mopped his sweating brow and smiled at Prisca. "Any sensible person has found a bit of shade and hidden in it."

"Let's move into the atrium," Prisca suggested. A sheen of moisture covered her upper lip. She pushed back damp tendrils of hair clinging to her neck below her ears. "How have you been, Flavius?"

The air seemed immediately cooler under the lacy shade of a tree bearing huge clusters of lavender blossoms. Josephus settled back with a sigh of contentment. "I do not know what it is, but here with you both, I have such a feeling of well-being." He laughed awkwardly. "It is like being with my family, who loves me no matter what my failings. Hah! And that from a man who deals in facts."

Prisca smiled with pleasure. "Then you are feeling the presence of the Christ among us. He dwells here. He brings God close."

"You mean others have said this?"

"More and more," answered Aquila. "Even that stone among men, Tribune Sistus."

Prisca flashed him an outraged look. Josephus did not notice.

"Strange," mused Josephus, gazing dreamily into the trees. For a moment he was tempted to withhold his information. Why disturb such rare peace with matters beyond mending? Then he noticed the curiosity that both Aquila and Prisca were attending upon him. He sighed.

"I have just quit the Forum. Rome is buzzing about you two."

"It is? Why?"

"Curiosity, mostly. Especially since the attack. And of course, some of your followers are servants in the emperor's palace. Word spreads about Jesus."

Prisca and Aquila exchanged wary glances. "So?" said Aquila.

"Did you know that Tribune Sistus has had spies out for months, seeking the men who killed your maid and destroyed the shop?"

"He said nothing about it."

Suddenly Josephus blurted, "I know who wrecked your shop."

"*What?*" demanded Aquila. "Who?"

"How did you find out, if he could not?" chimed Prisca.

Flavius fed them a melancholy smile. "A historian's lot is to reflect. He is always present, therefore never present. Some of those who took part boasted of it in my hearing. With righteous fervor, I might add."

"*Righteous?*" Prisca exclaimed.

"Flavius, please. No more riddles."

"Very well, Aquila. The raid was ordered by Rabbi Ezra bar-Elymas."

Prisca stared at him in openmouthed shock. The Jews, of all people! Why not itinerant tradespeople, jealous of their business? Why not hot-headed Roman youths full of misguided patriotism? Blood of her husband! The people of the Covenant!

"Are you certain?" Aquila's voice shook.

"It's true. It's true. Apparently bar-Elymas was fed up with some in the congregation who wanted to restudy the old prophecies." Flavius fixed him with a pointed stare. "I believe that included you?"

Aquila looked bewildered. "But all we asked was that he appoint a committee of elders to examine Jesus' claim that he was the Son."

"That could have been the start. You and the others presented rather a good argument, I thought. Dismiss the claim without dealing with the issues, and one only fuels the rumors. Examine it rationally, and one dispels for all time the man's claim, if he is an impostor."

"But he isn't!" said Prisca.

"*If,* Prisca, *if,*" said Aquila impatiently. "How could one argue with that?"

"Ah. But they did, obviously." Josephus turned to Prisca. "Though I sincerely doubt anyone intended for your maid to get killed."

"Have you told Tribune—my father?"

"No, my lady. Your father has done me several kindnesses. Had he asked for my help, I would have gladly rendered it."

"Then you are going to tell him."

"No, Prisca," Josephus said reluctantly. "I did consider it. But if he knew, he would be forced to act."

"Only to report the matter to the civil authorities."

Flavius smiled. "Perhaps I know the tribune better than you do. He is not a man to call in civil authorities to redress a wrong to his own family. This could be dangerous for him."

"Dangerous? How?"

"To his position at court."

"He would not let that stop him!"

"Precisely."

"Then why did you not give their names over, Josephus?" asked Aquila.

Josephus's voice went up a notch. "I, my lord? I am Jew. I am Roman. A foot in both worlds. To continue writing my history of the Jews, I cannot afford to antagonize those upon whose libraries I depend, nor the Romans, whose might gives me liberty to travel unmolested anywhere in the world."

"The matter does not concern you, Flavius. Now that you have told us, there is no need for you to become further involved," Prisca said soothingly.

"Then we must report it ourselves," decided Aquila. "Flavius, will you give testimony?"

Flavius looked uncomfortable. "If I may counsel you, as one who has lived in Rome for years, to report the matter at all is inadvisable."

"*Why?*"

"Knowledge is power. Use it wisely. Or in this case strongly. As a sword over the heads of the guilty."

Aquila shook his head angrily. "You are not making sense."

"The courts would look upon this as a religious squabble among the Jews. Let it out of the family, and you invite unknowable consequences."

"You are saying forget it? By Poseidon, no!" roared Aquila. "Those men murdered a helpless old woman. It might be Prisca next time!"

"Aquila, please, let us consider Flavius's advice."

Aquila sprang to his feet and looked down at her. "Don't worry, Prisca. I am a Jew. I know how to keep it in the family."

"What are you going to do?" cried Prisca in alarm.

"Meet with the brethren," he called over his shoulder. She looked helplessly after him as his footsteps receded and the shop door slammed behind him.

"Oh, Flavius. I've seen that look in Aquila's eyes before. Didn't you guess what would happen?"

Josephus was on his feet, staring after Aquila with something like awe. "I thought telling Aquila was the least dangerous course. After all, he does have the discipline of love to guide him."

Prisca cried in despair, "He is still young in the faith! A violent course is still his first impulse. Please, you must do something."

His jaw worked. "I don't know what I can do, Prisca. The Roman authorities must be kept out of it. What do you think he might do?"

"I think he will force a confrontation."

Chapter 24

Aquila returned home late that night.

She was waiting for him, nervously pacing in the gathering room. "What happened?"

"You should not have waited up. Go to bed."

She followed him into the bedroom.

Aquila threw open a chest and dug out a much stained leather vest and a long dagger she had never seen before.

"Couldn't we at least talk about it?"

"You could talk all night and not change my mind," he said. Finally he met her eyes. "You think this would be the end of it if we did nothing? The Pharisees are bound to learn that we know what they did. Where is our strength then? Where is the power of our Lord if we let them get away with it?"

"It is not on the battlefield!"

"This is men's work, Prisca."

"*Men's work?* What is it going to solve? You taking matters into your own hands, perhaps getting killed. Is that what you think our Lord demands? Another sacrifice to the gods? And shall you offer incense to Mars first?"

In two strides Aquila was across the room and struck her with his palm.

Prisca cried out in pain and shock. Her hand flew to her cheek. Tears burned her eyes.

Aquila stopped. His face whitened. "See what you made me do!"

She stared at him. Silently she picked up her cloak and started out of the room. Aquila seized her arm. "Prisca. . . . You don't understand!"

"I'm going to Maya's room. Please let me pass."

The morning of the sabbath dawned sluggishly. A low mass of clouds hovered over the north horizon, presaging winter. Sleeplessly Prisca stared out at it. She had been up most of the night, curled in her cloak in the atrium, praying for guidance.

She heard someone in the shop. Philip emerged and was halfway through the atrium before he saw her. He stopped in embarrassment. "Oh, I did not know you were here. I mean, that you were up."

"Good morrow, Philip." The clothing of the small, dark man looked bulky. Prisca heard a movement behind her.

"Thought I heard you, Philip. Ready?"

"Yes." Philip's hand went in an unconscious movement to his waistband. He glanced nervously at Prisca.

Prisca struggled to her feet, feeling the weight of sadness pressing on her. In a low, passionate voice she said, "Philip, Aquila! I beg you in the name of our dear Lord—"

Aquila stared at her from behind a bloodless mask. "This is the Lord's work, Prisca." His face was pale. He threw one side of his red cloak back over his broad shoulder and looped the other over his arm. His forearms were protected by leather gauntlets. A wide girdle of tough hide replaced the narrow one that he usually wore to synagogue. Under his tunic, she knew, was the leather vest.

Prisca watched the two men. "May our Lord watch over you." Aquila made a move toward her, and she turned her back.

"Come, Philip," said Aquila shortly. "The others will be waiting."

The men left. "Sweet Jesus!" she whispered to herself. "This is not the right way, I know it. Why do men think only to fight?" If only Josephus had kept what he'd learned to himself. She fought down her anger at him. The man was a gossip. How lustily his eyes had shone yesterday, fueled by possession of his delicious secret. She almost convinced herself she had seen it in his face when he walked in.

Aquila's and Philip's footsteps receded through the shop, and she heard the door close behind them. The descending silence plucked at her with seeping fingers of dread. She had never felt so alone in her life. Slowly she lifted her cupped palms and began to pray.

Aquila and Philip, now joined by a dozen others, walked without speaking up the Appian Way toward the Jewish temple. Ahead, they could see people converging on the synagogue from several directions. To spare them from worrying, Aquila had given orders that none of the men's families were to attend worship that day.

The headiness of excitement blunted the coolness of morning. Aquila could feel the blood churning. He wondered if his companions felt the same righteous anger aching to be released. As they made their way up the steps he noted with satisfaction that the rest of the brethren, a smattering of Romans, Greeks, Ethiopians, and others, were casually positioning themselves in groups of two or three in the square outside the temple, ready to rush in with support should the confrontation erupt into violence.

For it had been decided last night that Aquila must accuse Rabbi Ezra bar-Elymas before everyone.

If they could force him to admit his part, or at least sow strong suspicion among his hearers, bar-Elymas would think twice before instigating another attack against them. And, he hoped, it would cause the rabbi's supporters to press for further examination of the whole issue. "Jesus will be with us," Aquila had promised them. "It is his name we are justifying."

"Are you sure this is what Jesus would have us do?" one of the newer converts had said uncertainly.

"Certainly," Aquila had asserted with more assurance than he felt. "We will be showing all Jews what evil can be done by a few men who misuse the power of God's love."

Philip had looked uncomfortable at that but said nothing.

Aquila thought about this as he reached the top of the steps and strode across the portico. He nodded to several men lounging about the women's court with their families, the only area into which their wives and daughters and mothers were admitted.

Is it you? he wondered as he smiled this way and that, occasionally stopping to exchange brief greetings. *Were you the one who killed a weak, old servant?* As they moved slowly among the Jews, Philip touched his arm. Ahead of them was Rabbi Ezra bar-Elymas, holding court among a coterie of worshipers.

At first bar-Elymas nodded politely. Then his face blanched. He stopped in mid-sentence, reading the expression on the two men's faces. Seeing this, a sudden hush fell over his listeners and like shock waves rippled outward.

Aquila guessed at once that before him stood the nucleus of the rioters. Philip and other brethren moved in to flank him.

"Rabbi Ezra bar-Elymas," he said in a hard-edged voice, "I accuse you of the murder of a Tyrian woman of venerable years. I accuse you of maliciously destroying my shop and all the goods therein. I accuse you of planting a pagan symbol upon my door in order to cast suspicion away from yourself. I accuse you upon this sabbath of breaking our holy Law."

The entire forecourt fell silent. The rabbi's jaw worked up and down spasmodically. He pulled his robes about himself and threw his head back. "How dare you befoul this holy day with such drunken talk? Begone!"

"It is you who will be gone, bar-Elymas, you and the others who are guilty."

The rabbi's men arced out around him. Aquila's men shifted, challenging any sudden moves. The Jews and the new followers of Jesus glared at each other with hot, wary eyes.

Aquila stared across the impasse he had created, seeing former friends among enemies. Seeing anger erode into fright as they realized God was the holy prize. Realizing this fight could not be won here. Wondering what he had wrought, in the split second remaining before bar-Elymas screamed at him, "Heretic! Teacher of a false prophet!"

"Murderer! Hypocrite!" flung Aquila.

"*Hypocrite?* You, Aquila of Pontus, who lived with a priestess of Artemis before she seduced you into marriage, you call me a hypocrite?" Bar-Elymas blazed a scornful look at Aquila's followers. "You call yourselves men, yet you allow his woman to teach you heresy! Women, whom God eternal created as inferior beings, unclean creatures—"

Aquila leaped for bar-Elymas's throat. Instantly the courtyard was in an uproar. Loud cracks as knuckles met jaw. A flurry of missed blows and flailing arms. Suddenly a high, shrill scream from a woman onlooker as a knife leaped in the air and the next moment blood gushed down a spotless tunic. More and more men rushed in. Bar-Elymas's men came to his defense and tore Aquila away. The fight spilled out of the women's court to the portico and down the steps.

The waiting brethren charged into the fray. Within minutes, Roman guards on horseback were clattering down upon them from every direction. Aquila had his dagger ready and was fighting back toward the rabbi. Smears of blood stained his tunic, from a gash on his cheek. Suddenly he saw the shining point of a lance a handspan away, aimed at his midsection.

All around him, men were being forced back against the walls or to their knees, Jews and brethren alike.

The Roman guard held out his hand for Aquila's dagger. The fight was over.

When they told her, it was all Prisca could do to keep from screaming. Aquila had been arrested, Philip, too. And a dozen others. When they left her, she prostrated herself on the floor and prayed for the safe deliverance of the brethren.

The next morning, at first light, Fabianus presented himself at the shop. "Good morrow, Prisca."

"Come in. Have you heard?"

He nodded. "I expected to find the shop locked up. Why have you not gone to your father?"

Prisca glanced aside. She had not wanted Marcus to find out. She knew what his view would be: Aquila the hot-headed radical. "It is none of his affair."

The horse trainer grunted, offering no opinion on her decision. "Well, as long as I am here, does Aquila have any work that has to be gotten out in a hurry?"

She smiled. "You know he does. Have you eaten?"

At the shake of his head, she went to fetch bread and fruit. When she returned, Fabianus was sitting cross-legged in Aquila's usual place, with piles of work laid out neatly before him. While he ate, she told him what she knew.

Fabianus worked steadily. Prisca picked up needle and wool a dozen times, only to put it down again, to pace restlessly around the shop. All morning their friends from the Street of Sellers dropped in, anxious to know the latest.

"I have not seen Adah this morning," remarked Fabianus. "Nor any of her friends."

"I expect my Jewish friends are angry with Aquila for dragging their husbands into this."

"It has been coming," said Fabianus. "The attack on your shop, this rabbi goading Aquila at every chance."

"Bar-Elymas has never acknowledged Jesus as Messiah. I think he wanted to keep their struggle a private contest of wills."

"Divide and conquer."

"What do you think will happen now, Fabianus?"

"It depends if the court sees it as a private quarrel or a civil riot."

Prisca looked up as five women barged through the door from the street. Tiny Adah was nearly lost among them.

"Good morrow—"

"A pox on that, Prisca!" said one. "Why did your husband force Benjamin to join him in this?"

"My Aram has never done anything so foolish in his life!"

"Scandal! I shall never be able to hold my head up."

". . . Explaining to my children that their father is in jail!"

Prisca scrambled to her feet. Fabianus rose silently to stand at her side.

"I am glad you have come. Sit down and let us discuss what is to be done."

"What's done is already done!" shrieked the first woman.

Adah broke away from the others and squeezed Prisca's hand. "I tried to keep them from bothering you. I told them, whatever happens, our

Lord Jesus will see us through it. They are just frightened, Prisca," she added apologetically.

"What if they put our husbands in prison?"

"Or in the galleys?"

"Please!" Prisca begged. "My friends, first let us pray for strength and still hearts, so that we may know we are in the hands of the Lord."

Adah promptly lifted her arms and tilted her face upward, eyes closed. "O gracious Lord," she began. Fabianus and Prisca lowered their heads. One by one the others reluctantly followed suit. Adah's prayer was swift and to the point. When she had finished, the women were calmer and willing to sit.

"Has this changed things?" Prisca asked quietly. "Do we still believe in the Christ? You are no longer babes in the faith, needing to suckle milk at the breast, but are ready for meat. Those who have tasted the good things of God, how can they back away?"

"How can we know if what we do is pleasing to God?" asked one of the wives. "My Benjamin probably thought he was pleasing God by defying the rabbi."

"He probably did," agreed Prisca. "And maybe he was. I do know that without faith it is impossible to please God. For whoever would draw near to God must believe that he exists and that he rewards those who seek him."

"Then do you think our husbands were right to do this?"

"That is beside the point. It is done. I am thankful no one was seriously injured. At the least our men have forced the congregation to face the claim of Christ."

"Now it is up to us to support them," added Adah.

Prisca threw her friend a look of gratitude, her heart filling with pride. How Adah had bloomed in strength and understanding!

"Please excuse us. . . ."

Everyone turned. Three strangers were poised uncertainly in the doorway. "We come in peace. We seek the dwelling place of Prisca of Tyre, a teacher of the Christ."

Fabianus rose. "This is the shop of Aquila the tentmaker. The lady you seek is his wife, Prisca, and I am their friend, Fabianus. Come in."

The strangers broke into smiles and accepted the invitation. Their robes were travel stained and their sandaled feet grimy with dust. "We bring you greetings from your fellow Christians at Antioch, in the region of Syria."

A whirl of excitement ran through the crowded shop. Questions tumbled from all directions at once.

"Shouldn't we invite them into the atrium, Prisca, and wash their feet?" one of the women asked.

Prisca nodded. "By all means."

A few moments later they were all seated in the atrium, eager to hear the incredible news. Christians—*Christians they were called!*—in a land hundreds of miles away. Barnabas had mentioned Antioch. Was it the same city? Prisca ached that Aquila and the others were not here.

Refreshed and sipping a cool drink, the man who appeared to be the leader of the travelers spoke. "Yes, we call ourselves Christians. Two men came to us over a year ago. Paul of Tarsus first and then one named Barnabas. Together they taught us about the Christ. Then some months ago, we heard there was famine in Judea, and Paul and Barnabas feared for our brethren in that land. They took up a collection for our sister church in Jerusalem and departed from us."

"Paul said it was important," said the second traveler, "for the churches to help each other, so that we would know we are never alone."

"He also said before they left that we of Antioch should carry the good news, too, wherever our journeying took us," said the first traveler. "Barnabas knew we were to come to Rome shortly and asked to be remembered to Prisca, his sister in the faith, and to one Aquila, should we meet him also."

"You could not have arrived at a better time," exclaimed Prisca. "The faith of some is being sorely tried." She began to tell them how it was in Rome. . . .

". . . For Joseph ben Cain, murderer, death by stoning. For the rabbi known as bar-Elymas, three years at hard labor. For. . . ."

The commissioner's voice droned on. Prisca sat with Fabianus, her back straight, staring with dry eyes at the tribunal. Next to her perched Adah, drawn up to her full diminutive height, arrayed with the other wives and families of men involved in the riot. One by one the men were brought back before the tribunal to receive sentence.

"For Aquila of Pontus . . . ," Prisca's stomach knotted with fear. Her fists slowly clenched, the fingernails biting into her palms. "And for all other Jews now residing in Rome, the Emperor Claudius, most divine god among the pantheon of gods, who in his mercy had excluded your race from the worship of the caesars, does declare that you be banished from Rome, together with all your families, goods, and possessions. All properties must be sold, all goods not transportable assigned to other Romans, and you shall not again set foot in this noble land that did freely welcome you and grant you freedom of worship and all other freedoms. In the abuse of such tolerance, after sunset a week from tomorrow, fair Rome is yours no longer."

"That is not fair!" screeched bar-Elymas. He struggled with his guard. "We have been good Roman citizens. We have obeyed your civil laws, paid our taxes. Why should our people be banished because of an outlaw Jew?" Wildly his eyes fastened on Aquila. "For your heresy, may your seed wither and the demons of the deep claim your soul! Wherever you go, men of the Covenant will follow. Wherever you and that witch-wife preach, they will hound you unto death."

Tiredly Aquila gathered his strength. With a bitter smile he said, "I forgive you, bar-Elymas. May the peace of Jesus the Christ be yours."

Bar-Elymas's face purpled with rage.

The high tribune of the justice court rose. He stared down at bar-Elymas and at Aquila. "You would do well to study Roman history, Jews, before you meet again. The secret of her greatness is in her tolerance toward all. Good times have made you unmindful of this. See where it has gotten you." Majestically he strode from the Forum courtroom, followed by the lesser justices.

Prisca closed her eyes. What would happen to their new friends in the faith? Were they strong enough to continue without their leadership? She thought back to the dark period after Jesus' death. How impossible it had been for her then to ever consider going back to the worship of Artemis. Were her new friends strong enough yet to forsake former ways? The new joy, the deepened friendships among their tiny group of believers in the Christ, oh, how precious it was! What would become of them? She felt an arm go around her shoulders.

"Don't worry about Aquila, Prisca," said Fabianus. "He'll be all right. A man like him can always find a way to turn a coin."

"It's not that, Fabianus. We'll be all right, I know we will. It's—it's all those who have been coming to the shop, who have been learning the faith. Their lives are so precious to us. What will happen to all of you?"

Tribune Marcus Sistus, sitting among his friends, flashed a look from Aquila and the other defendants across the gallery of onlookers to Prisca. Her head had gone up, and she was sitting straight and proud again, one hand to the incredible perfection of her throat as she spoke with the horse trainer.

Mingled with pride at her bearing, Marcus felt the unfamiliar ache of a parent for the suffering of a child. He struggled to suppress the uncomfortable feeling. Finally he looked over his shoulder and beckoned one of his servants.

"Send a message to my daughter." He spoke in a voice that could not be overheard. "You know where—"

"Yes, Tribune Sistus."

"I do not wish it delivered until tomorrow. Bid her and her husband to join me for dinner tomorrow night. I will send chairs at seven. Tell them it will be just the three of us. And do not take no for an answer."

"Yes, tribune."

When the man left, Marcus turned his restless gaze elsewhere. Several aisles away he spied Flavius Josephus. A slight smile twisted the tribune's lips as he realized that the historian must have deliberately distanced himself from the others of his race. Little good it would do him. The tribune rose and left the Forum.

Behind bright, watchful eyes, Flavius Josephus's fertile brain was hatching and discarding a succession of schemes. How could he protect his newly won position? For the emperor would not make an exception for him. At least not for a year or two. Busily his mind touched down on fronts of the Roman Empire. Alexandria, Egypt, possibly, now that summer was ended. A good class of Romans lived there permanently. Corinth? Educated, but too frivolous for his tastes. Judea? He sighed. The Jews were far from ready to be counted among civilized nations. Too intractable. Too . . . by the gods, how he wished he had never opened his mouth about the Jews who had destroyed the shop!

Spectators began to get up and shift around now, laughing and jostling one another in high fettle. It had been a good show, a good entertainment. In a way it was too bad the Jews were leaving. Fine craftsmen. Dependable. Painfully honest. Most of them. Peculiar about the gods . . . unsettling the way they clung so tenaciously to their past. No feeling for progress! They would be missed, both good and bad.

Aquila remained on the warm marble bench after the others had risen dispiritedly to join their families. He hung his head between his hands. All he and Prisca had labored for. The fledgling community of believers they had grown to love. What would become of it now? Surely they had lost more than he had gained by his rash, vainglorious actions. What a fine example he had set. Would he never learn? Living and dying by the sword was expected of men like bar-Elymas. But for the followers of the Christ? And for trying to teach him this, he had struck his wife.

O Christ! Forgive! Forgive. He saw before his downcast eyes Prisca's sandaled toes peeping out the edge of her gown. He looked up. "I've lost so much for us!"

She sat beside him and took his hand. "It was well for both of us that you were in jail. I was so angry I would not have been able to speak to you." She gazed quietly at his dejected face. With her forefinger she traced the healing scab on his cheek.

"What shall we do?" they said in unison. Their eyes met, full of sadness, full of love. "Let us go home." They rose of one accord and left the courthouse. They walked the first mile in silence.

Suddenly both began speaking at once. Prisca smiled. "You first."

"I was thinking that it is about time you visited your friends on Cyprus. I know you miss Lydia and the twins," he said earnestly. "You talk about them so often."

"And what of you, my love? That is so like you, putting my welfare first."

"I just want to see you safe," Aquila said stubbornly.

She reached for his hand. "I think when the Lord wants people to change direction, temptations always remain as false reasons why one should do what one should not."

"There you go again."

"All I mean is, you are my other half. Without you I would be worthless."

He smiled down at her and squeezed her hand. "You have a better idea?"

"Perhaps." Her voice grew animated. "After you were arrested, some travelers came to the shop, seeking the *Christians.*"

"The *Christians?*"

"Yes. They were followers of Christ, too. They are from the city of Antioch in Syria. The brethren there call themselves Christians now. They told us they passed through the city of Corinth some weeks ago and met a learned Greek by the name of Chloe. She is also preaching Jesus as the risen Messiah. She sent us greetings."

Aquila was stunned. "She knew of us?"

"Yes. And even the names of some of our brethren."

"And followers, too, in Antioch!" he marveled.

"Yes! I wish you could have met them. They were full of stories."

"It is wonderful, it is a miracle!"

"Chloe begged that we come and visit the brethren in Corinth. It seems that followers who actually knew Jesus are in great demand. I think this is what our Lord would have us do."

Aquila pursed his lips. "What about that little weasel, what's-his-name?"

Prisca laughed. "What can he do, if our Lord wants us in Corinth?"

Tribune Sistus advanced across the marble floor to greet Prisca and Aquila the following evening. Aware of hostility in the eyes of his son-in-law, Marcus awarded him an impartial nod and turned to Prisca. His eyes softened. He was relieved to note that their ill turn in fortunes did not seem to be affecting her health. She looked beautiful and serene.

"Thank you for coming. Shall we sit in the garden?"

Once again he led the way, giving them no choice but to follow. As soon as they were seated, Marcus came to the point of the visit. "An unhappy affair," he said quietly. "I am glad for you, Aquila, that matters did not turn out worse."

"Thank you," was the brusque reply.

Marcus ignored it and went smoothly on. "I assume you both realize your dilemma. I have given it considerable thought and may have a solution. Not without its drawbacks, but then, what is life but compromise." He had taken a seat beside Prisca and now reached for her hand.

After a moment's hesitation, she gave it. He smiled at her. "I had hoped you would call on me in your difficulty."

"We have been through that, father," she said gently. "What is your suggestion?"

"I own two merchant vessels in a consortium with other men. I propose hiring Aquila as master of one. When the ship is in port, he could live just outside Rome, where you could join him. Claudius's edict extends to the oceans, it is true, but I believe we could manage it. I would be happy to provide such a residence."

Aquila stared moodily at the graying warrior. "And Prisca?"

Sistus hesitated slightly before saying, "Prisca would reside with me as your wife, my daughter, and mistress of my house, lacking nothing, in utter safety and freedom. You have my word."

Aquila hardly dared look at Prisca, dreading what he would see there. Was that eager shine of anticipation he knew so well already lighting her eyes? He made himself say, "That is very generous, Marcus." He turned to his wife. "You would be safe here. I'm sure Marcus would not object to your preaching. You could continue to lead the Roman faithful."

Prisca gazed at Aquila, her eyes unreadable. Then she turned to Marcus. "It is hard to find you, and then lose you, my father. But I am joined to my husband. If he is banished, then so am I. We will seek a new home and new peoples ready to receive the Son."

Aquila's eyes misted over. He looked away.

It was not lost on the tribune. Prisca's answer did not surprise him. She was, after all, his daughter. An ironic smile flitted across his face. He rose. "Very well, then, we shall say no more about it. Shall we dine, my children?"

With good appetites they ate the excellent cold supper of roasted game hens stuffed with fruit and nuts, marinated mutton and vegetables, and several kinds of bread and cake, washed down with a variety of chilled wines. Aquila, content to lay their rivalry aside, elaborated on their plans to sail to Corinth.

Marcus listened with half an ear. Regardless of Prisca's decision, he had been prepared to settle an allowance upon her. But years of experience dealing with men in diverse passions and circumstances had taught him not to ignore signals such as Aquila had exhibited by his behavior.

Prisca's love for her husband was deep and unswerving, any fool could see that. Yet Marcus hazarded a guess that Aquila felt keenly that he was the cause of their losing their home and friends. It did not help a proud man to have a powerful father-in-law who could provide all that Aquila could not, at the snap of two fingers.

When they had finished eating, Marcus invited them to see his caged birds from Ethiopia. He directed a servant to escort Prisca to the glen that housed them, then laid a restraining hand on Aquila's arm.

"A moment, please."

At once the old wariness resurfaced. "Yes, tribune?"

"This is a matter that could have waited, had you remained in Rome. As Prisca's father, it is my duty to provide her with a dowry. I am proud of my daughter and have no wish to deny her her birthright. I would be honored if you will permit her to bring to your household a dowry of twenty thousand drachmae."

"That's not nec—"

"I think it is! She comes from a temple. She has no heritage unless it is acknowledged by others. By me. By what right would you deny her this?"

Aquila shoved his fingers through his black hair. "I am sorry, tribune. Of course it is your right to give your daughter a dowry. I am unfortunately possessed of a quick temper."

And a jealous disposition, Marcus added to himself. "Thank you, Aquila. How would you like the dowry delivered?"

"Will you keep it in safekeeping for her? Prisca will write to you from Corinth."

Marcus took his arm and clasped his hand in a rigorous shake. "Then it is settled. Let us join Prisca.

Aquila hesitated. Finally he blew a sigh out his lips. "Tribune . . . in all good conscience, I should tell you how matters stand between Prisca and her—and Thyatira."

"Sit down, Aquila."

Aquila shook his head impatiently. "Listen. Remember when you first told us about Thyatira? How shocked Prisca was to learn Thyatira was her earthly mother? Prisca never meant to stay in the temple. Thyatira tried to force her to stay by using her as a harlot. Once. Only once. It was a deliberate travesty. The man openly disavowed Artemis. Both Prisca and her mother knew this. She despoiled her own daughter to render her worthless for an honorable marriage."

Marcus's face remained impassive. "A maneuver that failed, obviously."

Aquila waved away the words, meant to compliment.

"If I seem to overprotect her, it is because, whether she knows it or not, she needs that assurance of security." Aquila permitted a smile. "Without it, she could not serve our Lord half so well."

So that's why the young fool cursed himself so roundly for causing their banishment, thought Marcus. He smiled. "Thank you for telling me—my son. Shall we go now?" As Aquila preceded him down the path to the aviary, Marcus sobered. The gods have a way of repaying vengeance in kind. Thyatira, above all, should know that.

When he had seen Prisca and Aquila off a short while later, Marcus summoned his solicitor.

"Write this," he said. "Upon my death, my entire estate, together with all lands, chattel, ships, and goods, shall be given to my daughter, called Prisca of Tyre, who is presently the wife of Aquila the tentmaker."

And that, Marcus thought with satisfaction, after the scribe left to restate his wishes in legal form, *will solve everything. For then Aquila the tentmaker can scarce be jealous of Sistus the tribune.* He laughed.

The shop was full of well-wishers as Aquila and Prisca prepared to leave Rome, one week later. Philip and Adah, carrying Zoe, now a happy, wiggly eighteen-month-old, were among the travelers gathered to share a final blessing. Adah's face shone with excitement.

Prisca could not help comparing anew this self-assured young matron with the shy, worried woman who came to the shop that night so long ago.

"I confess that when I heard we must leave Rome, I was frightened out of my wits," said Adah. "But Philip said, 'Now, Adah, we've grown enough in the faith that our Lord is ready to use us. He must mean for us to leave Rome.' " Adah captured Philip's hand and pulled it around her waist.

"When I went to sleep last night, I was given the vision that Philip and I started a new family of believers in our home in Alexandria and that the Lord blessed this greatly."

Philip grinned. "Adah used to be so quiet I worried she wasn't well. Now she's ready to take on the world. We both are, I guess." He glanced at Aquila expectantly. "Well? Aren't you going to say something?"

"Don't expect it to be easy. Remember that we came to Rome expecting to teach in peace. Preaching the faith of Jesus has become risky. Something about it excites men's fears."

"But see what joy it has brought to many," Prisca reminded him.

"Aye." Aquila clapped Philip upon the shoulders, giving that lopsided smile with a touch of wistfulness that Prisca loved. "Just be aware of the dangers. Once you commit yourselves, our Lord expects you to stay the course."

"Whether it be Rome or Alexandria or Corinth," said Prisca. "I was not strong enough to do his work in Corinth before—"

"Before she married me," prompted Aquila.

"You think you jest," said Prisca. "In truth, if Aquila had not been patient with me, we could not go yet. Together we can face anything." Her eyes met Fabianus's. "Our only concern is for those of you we leave behind."

"We will still meet. We will find another place. Those of us who are left." Fabianus's face was lean and sharp boned. Not a spare ounce of fat found home anywhere on his lean horse trainer's body. He grinned, exposing a wide mouthful of teeth, like a skull shrieking in merriment. "Truth be told, I know just the place."

"Where?"

"The catacombs, south of here."

Prisca shuddered involuntarily. "Those are burial chambers."

Fabianus shrugged. "Some in there, yes. Most of the caves are just passages and empty chambers. Dry, secure, secluded. People living in some of them. The Jews'll be gone, the Romans won't care. It is ideal."

Silence suddenly fell over them. Into the void Prisca said softly to Philip and Adah and to Fabianus, "Remember your leaders as you begin to lead.

Barnabas taught me the things of God. You must also remember what is taught by Aquila and me. Remember that Jesus Christ is the same yesterday and today and forever."

"We will, Prisca," Philip promised. He smiled down confidently at his wife. "We'll be all right."

"We'll write to you through Fabianus," Adah said, "until we are settled."

The brethren lapsed again into silence, the sadness of departure hovering over them. Aquila cleared his throat. "Well, my dear friends. The Lord Jesus has brought us together, and now he is sending us apart. We have no lasting city, but we seek the city that is to come. Do not neglect to do good and to share what you have, for such sacrifices are pleasing to God. Philip and Adah, may he bless your new gathering in Alexandria. Fabianus, old friend, may he bless and guide you as you keep our Roman brothers and sisters."

Aquila spread wide his arms. Prisca, Adah, Philip, Fabianus, and a dozen others crowded together, feeling the love of Jesus and the strength of God flowing through them, in and among, outward and inward, currents of faith and strength so strong that in their midst rose a wild cry of joy. They broke into song, tears streaming down their faces, joy on every countenance.

"Maranatha!"

Chapter 25

The coaster sped into the crescent-shaped harbor at Corinth. The dock was deserted as if the ferocious winds and rains driving the boat down the Macedonian coast had sheared the land of human and beast.

Bundled in cloaks of earth-brown cilician wool, Prisca and Aquila struggled down the sodden wood ramp. The journey from Rome down the Appian way and across the heel of the Roman peninsula had taken weeks. Setting sail from the east coast of Italy, they crossed the Sea of Adria at its narrowest point, touching port on the coast of Macedonia at Apollonia. From there the ship clung to the coast as storms blew them southward into Achaia and finally into safe harbor at Corinth.

Angry winds whipped Prisca's cloak against her body as she waited for Aquila to find a driver willing to take their possessions into town. In addition to being wet and cold, she felt sick to her stomach. The ground, after her weeks on ship, felt unstable underfoot.

At last Aquila returned. As he and the driver lashed their bundles and boxes to the pack beasts she examined her husband's face anxiously. It wasn't rain. Aquila's face was sweating.

"Dearest. . . ."

Aquila glanced at her over his shoulder.

Her heart sank. The glitter in his eye brought memory of only one thing: fever.

They started into Corinth. The streets were nearly empty, a far cry from the noisy jubilation of their last visit. "The Corinthians are not fond of wind and wet," Aquila commented. A few minutes later their eyes were drawn upward, to Acro-Corinthus, looming above them on the right.

"That is where I shall go, Aquila."

"There?"

"I feel exactly as I did the first time we came to Corinth, only more strongly than ever. I feel as if I know my sisters. And the cores of their lives are as empty as mine used to be. Worse, no one ever told them how precious their lives are. What a rare and unique person each of them is. I shall begin there and gradually coax those who hear down off that mountain and into our shop!"

"That means we'll need a large place." Aquila smiled.

Prisca scarcely heard him. Her thoughts had turned to Thyatira. Her love for her mother was a distant memory of love for an idea of motherhood that had never really existed between them. The vengefulness of the high priestess also resurfaced.

"We'll need to be careful," said Aquila, as if reading her thoughts. "The head priestess will not take it kindly once she knows what we are up to."

"Thanks to my father's dowry, we have the money for a larger shop."

"Yes," he grumped.

Prisca studied him thoughtfully. Was it the fever making him ill-tempered, or was it that he had not come to terms with himself about the tribune, despite her prayers? She had also hoped, vainly, to convince her father that God existed, a singular God, and that her Master, Jesus, was his Son. If only she had had more time. Not true, Prisca. As Aquila had reminded her, time alone would never bring people to Jesus. Finally she said, "Our Lord uses even pagans, remember? Shall we not bless him for this?"

"Sistus expected you to stay in Rome."

"I do not think so. We all have hopes that are never filled." She rubbed against him, after a quick glance at the driver plodding ahead of them. "I expect he was jealous of you. Such a handsome, virile young man."

Aquila allowed her to tease him out of his black mood. "Prisca. Let's find an inn. Do you realize we have not been alone since we left Rome? The Lord has more than one use for virile, handsome young men. And women."

"What about Chloe? We should let her know we have arrived."

"She can wait."

After finding a public house, Aquila sent the driver with a message for Chloe, requesting an audience the following day. Prisca persuaded the innkeeper's wife to heat them a meal.

After they had eaten in their room, Prisca rummaged through the wicker chest containing their clothing. "Whew! Everything smells like mold. If it was summertime, I swear I'd run naked through the streets!"

Aquila's lip curved in a smile. "That's the trouble with you hot-blooded people. Prisca the enchantress. From priestess to preacher to enchantress. Come here, wench." He was lying on a raised pallet, sweating more profusely now.

She came to sit beside him. "It's the fever again, isn't it?"

He nodded. He ran his hand up her arm. His touch felt clammy and cold. "Do me a favor. Make love to me."

"While you still have the strength?" she giggled halfheartedly.

214

"If I am going out of my head, I want to have something besides nightmares to dream about."

"Oh, Aquila, be serious! We do not even know of a doctor here!"

"I am serious. I want to make love." His hand moved over her, his fingers seeking out her curves in familiar caress. "Look, my love, I've had these attacks for years. They always go away. Even Hyrcanus didn't have anything to cure it."

She slipped to her knees beside the pallet. "Dearest, let us pray to our Lord to cure you, now! Once and for all time. He sent us here to do his work. He needs you strong for that."

"If that is his purpose," agreed Aquila.

"Then let us ask him, together, if that is his purpose, to cure you!"

Aquila turned on his side and gazed deeply into her eyes. "Are you willing to trust him that far?"

"How far? To ask him to make you well again?"

"What if the answer is no?"

"Then at least we asked. And we will do as well as we can anyway."

Aquila slipped off the pallet and knelt beside her. They clasped hands and prayed as Jesus had taught, claiming his promise to grant what they asked. ". . . In Jesus' name, amen."

They looked at each other. Prisca swept back the damp locks of black hair clinging to his forehead. He took her face in his hands and kissed her. "Oh, my love. . . ."

Prisca arose at dawn the next morning, awakened by the clucking of fowl right under the window. She glanced at Aquila. He was still asleep. She crossed to the window, a small opening in the thick walls that overlooked a yard roughly enclosed by saplings. Small, fat, gray and black fowl strutted about the yard. A servant girl was at work building a fire in a mound-shaped oven. On the top of the oven, a stick platform held three loaves of bread, placed to catch the first warm rays of the sun. The sky was clear.

She smiled, filling her lungs with the crisp, scented air, catching, she imagined, a whiff of the yeast leavening the three loaves. She recalled Jesus' words one day when she had asked him what the kingdom was like. Jesus had smiled, cocked his head to one side and said, "The kingdom of God is like leaven which a woman took and hid in three measures of meal, till it was all leavened."

She whispered her morning prayers and turned back to the room. Aquila was sitting on the edge of their bed, watching her. His eyes were clear and bright. She crossed to him and felt his brow. It was cool and dry.

"Aquila!" she cried. "Are you well?"

He rose and took her in his arms. "Praise the Lord, I think I am." His lips compressed, and unbidden tears filled his eyes.

Modesty and soft-spoken decorum forgotten, Prisca let out a whoop of joy, threw her arms around Aquila, and danced him around the room.

"Hush!" laughed Aquila. "The innkeeper will think we started the day with wine! A prayer of thanks first and then celebration!"

Later in the morning a young, blond man of brawny build appeared at their door. He was bearing a bowl of fruit in his thick fingers. Comically for one so husky, he shifted nervously from one foot to the other and finally stammered, "My mistress is the good matron Chloe. She says welcome to Corinth. She hopes you will honor her with your presence this afternoon . . . ," he took a deep breath and stared at them with earnest blue eyes, "if you are rested enough from the boat." He glanced hopefully from one to the other. "Did I do it right?" he blurted.

"Just fine, son," said Aquila. He gave the young man a coin.

"Please, sir, my mistress would not want me to accept a gift for doing my duty."

"Then tell her the coin was not for doing your duty, but because we are happy to be in Corinth and to accept her invitation."

The man frowned. Slowly a smile spread across his face. "Would that be right?"

"Yes. Tell her."

Carefully the young man pocketed his coin, smiled again, and stepped to the door.

"What is your name?" asked Prisca.

"Seth. Bye."

"I already like Chloe," said Prisca as they watched him leave.

An hour later as they approached Chloe's estate Prisca was consumed by curiosity. Who was this woman, and how had she heard of the Christ? Seth answered Aquila's knock so quickly that they sensed he had been waiting on the other side for their arrival.

"Good day, Seth."

"Hello," said Seth. "Mistress Chloe says come in, please. She says you wait in here." Seth pointed out a small chamber where three lounging couches and several cushioned stools were placed with studied artlessness. About the borders of the room, a collection of small bronze figures rested on shelves or narrow tables. Prisca was startled to see an exquisitely wrought statue of Artemis as the Corn Goddess.

"Not you," Seth told Prisca as she started in with Aquila. "You can come to Chloe now." Gently he pushed Aquila back toward the small chamber and pointed Prisca down a spacious hall. She raised an eyebrow at Aquila. He nodded.

"Show me where she is, Seth."

Seth led her into a large, secluded room. "She's here, mistress," Seth called and quickly disappeared. A woman wrapped in an immense white apron was standing with her back to her, vigorously scrubbing her hands over a shallow tin bowl.

"Good! Welcome, Prisca of Tyre." Chloe turned. She was a tall, patrician looking woman of perhaps thirty years, with thick, corn colored hair cut at an even length just below the ears. A slight curl gave her head a halo effect. Her brow was wide, above fine, clear, intelligent blue eyes.

"Well, Prisca," she declared with a broad smile. "I have been hearing of you and your husband for months. Every time one of our flock returns from Rome. What brings you to Corinth?"

The hands she was briskly drying paused as Prisca told her of the banishment. It was the first the news had carried. "Then all Christians had to leave?"

"No, only Jewish Christians. A Roman brother by name of Fabianus will go on with our work." Prisca glanced curiously around the well-lighted room. A large table in the center was draped with linens. At either end was a lampstand. Several wooden benches lined the walls and a small table upon which rested a variety of metal instruments and small pottery and ivory flasks. One end of the room was screened off by a drapery.

As Prisca watched, the drape parted and a young girl, no more than fifteen, came shyly forward, wearing only a loose, knee-length shift.

"Up on the table, dear," said Chloe. "That's right. Now lie back. Put your legs up. Are you comfortable, Julia? Good. I will not hurt you, dear. Relax."

Chloe seemed to forget Prisca was there. Prisca felt acutely embarrassed at her own presence. She moved back toward the door as Chloe examined the young girl's private parts with complete lack of self-consciousness, talking to Julia in a low, reassuring voice while she probed. When she finished, she pulled the girl's shift down and helped her sit up. "All right, child, into your clothes."

Chloe retreated to the wash table and poured fresh water into the bowl. When she had finished, she returned to Prisca. "I am a midwife and healer. Fathers send their daughters to me for assurance that they are virgins. Some prospective fathers-in-law demand proof before they will accept a girl into their family."

Prisca was shocked. "Is Corinth as bad as all that?"

"In a city where men play year-round, I suppose it is to be expected." She laughed. "A pity the parents of daughters cannot demand the same thing of their new sons."

Prisca's eyes widened. Chloe acted and spoke unlike any woman she had ever met.

The girl reappeared, modestly but expensively garbed, with a veil of fine silk covering her hair. She gave Prisca a shy smile and took a document that Chloe had signed.

"I wish you a long and happy marriage," said Chloe, "and many children."

"Thank you. You are coming, are you not?" Chloe nodded. Julia bobbed her head and slipped out the door as if she could not wait to escape.

Chloe chuckled, understanding Julia's relief. "Shall we join your husband?"

When they rejoined Aquila, Chloe greeted him with a hearty embrace. She was as tall as he. Unused to women who touched his person, much less threw arms about his middle, he could only clear his throat uncomfortably. It was all Prisca could do to keep from laughing. Yes, Chloe would take some getting used to. Their Lord did indeed choose strange brethren!

"You'll stay here, of course," Chloe was saying.

"Thank you," Aquila managed to get out, "but we could not think of—"

"Nonsense! You've been feeding brethren in Rome, have you not? And a few freeloaders, I'll warrant. That is the price for following a Lord who insists we use our talents. Well, I praise him for a talent people are willing to pay for. I try to use it for the Lord's work. Any objections?"

"Only until we find a place, then," Aquila said hurriedly, put off by such directness.

She was a widow, Chloe told them as she poured them a refreshing, hot herb drink and offered a tray of small cakes and sweetmeats. While her husband was alive she had developed her skills as a midwife and caring for the sick and had practiced with a physician. Her husband had left her well off, but her gifts were in such demand that she had continued to improve her lot.

"Ministering to the sick is the perfect instrument for carrying the good news," she told them.

"Almost as good as tent making," declared Aquila. Then Prisca had to tell their hostess how the Lord had tricked her into learning a useful trade when Aquila became ill.

"She learned so well, that the Lord healed me."

"Healed you?" Chloe's voice altered. "That is more than I have been able to do. Are you speaking truly or in jest?"

"As surely as we sit here, Chloe, our Lord healed Aquila of Rome fever."

"I have seen many cases of Rome fever! There is no cure. You have been healed of Rome fever! A miracle! Barnabas told us about—"

"Barnabas? Barnabas of Cyprus?" Prisca broke in.

"Yes, you know him?"

"I—Yes, we do! Is he still here?"

"Not now." With single-mindedness worthy of a fox stalking its dinner, Chloe continued her tale. "Last year, Barnabas and Paul were in Lystra, in Galatia. They were preaching the gospel, and one of the men listening had been crippled from birth. Paul saw that he had the faith to make him well, so he told the man to stand up. The man did, and he was healed."

Chloe looked at them triumphantly. Then she laughed. "Let me tell you what happened next! The crowds were so shocked, the only way they could believe what he had done was to believe that he and Barnabas were gods come down to earth. So they called Barnabas Zeus and Paul, because he did the most talking, Hermes. The priest of the temple of Zeus in the city wanted to offer sacrifices to them.

"They had a dreadful time denying they were gods and at the same time convincing people that none of their stone idols were gods either." She looked curiously at Prisca. "You worshiped Artemis at one time, did you not? Barnabas said that Jesus himself called you to follow him. He said that you knew him in the flesh."

"Yes," Aquila answered. "He called her by name to follow him."

Chloe nodded impatiently. "And now he has brought you both to us." Full of nervous energy, she bounced to her feet.

"A moment, Chloe," said Aquila. "While I was waiting for you and Prisca, I was noticing your artwork." He gestured at the numerous works of bronze and marble.

Prisca walked over and picked up the statue that had caught her eye previously. "This Corn Goddess depicts Artemis."

"Yes it does," said Chloe airily. "Beautiful, isn't it?"

"Aren't you afraid that some of the brethren will misunderstand a statue of Artemis in your house? Might this not tempt them to see the Christ as no more than another Greek god? As you said, even Barnabas and Paul did not escape this comparison."

"These are works of art, Prisca! No more than that." An awkward pause. "Corinth is not Rome, you know. People feel very strongly about —well, to bring the Lord into their lives, it has been necessary to become part of those lives ourselves. It is easy for me, of course, for I was a Corinthian long before I was a Christian."

Prisca threw Aquila a puzzled glance. He lifted his shoulders in an eloquent "wait and see" gesture.

"Perhaps the best way is to let you see for yourselves. Yes! You shall be my guests at Julia's wedding celebration. Meantime, Aquila, we shall choose the proper place for your shop." She paused, tapping her teeth with a manicured forefinger. "There is only one right place, you know."

"Where is that?"

"Why, next to the temple of Apollo, of course."

That night, their possessions retrieved from the public house and the goods for the shop stored snugly away until Aquila found the right shop, Aquila stared moodily out the window of their new quarters in Chloe's house.

"What is the matter, my love?" asked Prisca, coming up behind him.

Aquila shook his head. "I'm not sure coming to Corinth was such a good idea after all. I don't feel right here."

"Oh, Aquila, you're too cautious! We are exactly where we should be. Didn't we both decide the Lord could use us in Corinth?"

The next morning, Chloe, Prisca, and Aquila set off for the square of the temple of Apollo, Seth and two slaves in attendance.

"Oh, Seth is not a slave," said Chloe, in answer to a question from Prisca. "He is a hired servant."

Seth, hearing the proud tone of his mistress's voice, smiled with self-conscious pleasure.

"No one knows where he grew up. He was begging near my house one day—it was directly after Barnabas was telling us about a time Jesus' men tried to keep some children from him. At any rate, it was after his story that I found Seth. It struck me that here was a child of the kingdom, no matter that his body was that of a man."

Daunted for days by the ill-tempered rain squall, Corinthians were out again in full show. For a moment, Prisca was haunted by memory of the dreadful encounter with Limaeus, right in the square where they were walking. She was tempted to ask Chloe if she had heard of the man, but quelled the idea. One does not disturb sleeping harpies.

"Will Barnabas be back?" Aquila was asking.

"Oh, yes," promised Chloe, "I am sure of it."

Suddenly the temple came into view. Its beauty washed away all her ill thoughts. She thrilled anew to the fluted marble columns, through which she glimpsed Apollo eternally strumming his lyre. She glanced uncertainly at Chloe, striding confidently along. *A tentmaker's shop, here?*

Chloe led her entourage into a narrow street behind the temple. Here throbbed the true heart of Corinthian life. Sellers were hawking pottery, milled and whole grains, spices, fresh vegetables, preserved and dried fruits. There were sellers of amulets and aphrodisiacs, woven goods, dyes, perfumes, and jewelry.

"It is very like the Street of Sellers, off the Appian Way," said Aquila. "How many other tentmakers are here?"

"What does it matter?" said Prisca tartly. "You are better than any of them."

"Spoken like a true disciple of Christ."

She smiled shamefacedly. "Well, it is a good place, with all these people to talk to."

Aquila grinned. "That is better. Wait for me while I take a look around." Off he plunged into the milling crowd.

The women sauntered by a meat shop, where a butcher was hacking away at freshly killed lambs. "Good morrow, Chloe!" called a well-dressed matron. In her wake were Julia and several attendants.

"Good morrow! Preparing for the wedding?"

The matron laughed. "Yes, indeed. Some things one must do for oneself."

For their virgin child, only the best of meats, thought Prisca with a smile, *not to be left to an indifferent servant.*

"Isn't it fortunate that feast days for Apollo and Artemis came so close together? The meat supply is marvelous! I would love to talk, but . . . ," the matron gestured helplessly.

"Yes," laughed Chloe. "A lot to do."

"What does a feast day have to do with the wedding?" asked Prisca after they had gone.

Chloe seemed amused. "Don't you know? Meat is so scarce that no one buys it before it is used for sacrifice. Nowadays, of course, it is big business. None of the priests burn the edible portions anymore. They give the gods the entrails. They eat the choice cuts and sell the rest to the people."

Prisca was revolted. "Don't they know animal sacrifices are useless?"

Chloe laid a hand on her arm. "The brethren do," she said in a gently chiding tone. "What is to be gained if we hold ourselves aloof from other Corinthians? Is that not what the Jews of the patriarchy do? They feel no need to share God with outsiders. Did not Jesus himself eat with tax gatherers?"

"You mean you yourself eat meat that was sacrificed to pagan gods?"

"Prisca, you sound like a child. Meat is meat."

Prisca stared at her. For the first time, she began to wonder if Aquila might be right. Coming to Corinth had seemed to her the perfect choice. Corinthian society was doubtless in need of change. But who would change first—the Corinthians or Prisca and Aquila?

Chapter 26

The day of the wedding arrived. Aquila hung back, reluctant to spend even part of the day away from his shop, now that they had found a good location between a meat market and a seller of oils and spices. "It is the perfect place," he proclaimed, when haggling over the price had ended.

"Indeed," Chloe agreed. "Meat for the body, perfume for the senses, and Christ for the soul."

Prisca had looked askance at her, struggling with a part of her sensibilities that worried about Chloe's apparent lack of reverence for the Lord's business. It was not, after all, a mere matter of gloss on life. It had to be the essence of life. Was it essence for Chloe?

Julia Mikoinos, daughter of a wealthy Corinthian shipper, had been married in a private family ceremony. The day-long feast following was to be celebrated in the temple of Aphrodite. Using a combination of reason and threats, Prisca finally persuaded Aquila they must attend. And since learning of the tribune's dowry, she had even spent money to have new garments made.

Now as they joined other wedding guests at the foot of Acro-Corinthus, she caressed her husband with a critical, loving eye. Nor was she the only one observing him. Young maidens chaperoned by their families cast bold, bright-eyed glances in his direction, excited, perhaps, by the presence of a handsome stranger in their midst. The fine maroon cloak with its silver shoulder clasps set off his dark good looks. The bent nose, the slight scar above one black brow, lent a rakish air to the straight, well-muscled body.

Aquila glanced down at her as they started up the wide limestone steps inset in the hillside, perhaps feeling her eyes upon him. He smiled. "I am the envy of every man here," he whispered. "You are beautiful."

His words caused a blush of pleasure. She had striven to look well. She had brushed her chestnut hair until it sparked with life, then bound it loosely under a veil of pale, translucent silk. Tendrils of curl escaped around her ears and under the soft jaw line. In her ears were fiery emeralds, a gift from Marcus when they had left Rome. He had insisted, and Aquila had not the heart to refuse the extravagant gift. The emeralds matched the brightness of her eyes when she was happy. She had chosen

223

a pale cream silk for her gown, clasped with a gold girdle. Her matching cloak was an ingenious weave of silk and wool, rich of sheen yet warm on this blustery spring day.

The rocky hillside burst with green. Unexpected pockets of tiny white and purple-blue flowers peeped from hidden glades. Hundreds of other guests, chattering and laughing and calling to friends, climbed the steep steps around them, two or three abreast.

As they reached the top Prisca paused to catch her breath. The steps gave way to granite walks, laid in geometric patterns of gray mosaic, leading to the temple. Their eyes were drawn first to the magnificent rosy marble of Aphrodite's earthly dwelling place, then farther upward, along the stately columns, to friezes below the roofline, which depicted ancient battles. Between the columns dwelt breathtakingly beautiful statues of all the Olympian gods, frozen in stone, looking as real as Lot's wife. For the wedding celebration, swags of greenery as thick as a man's trunk had been draped between the columns.

"Oh, Aquila," she laughed breathlessly, "I am so glad we did not miss this!" They moved forward into a reception line, greeted their hosts, presented them with a gift for Julia, and were escorted into the great hall. A scattering of hundreds of bright cushions of crimson and gold and lavender and peacock lent an illusion of warmth to the marble floor. Silken draperies added enclosed spaces to the illusion.

A fresh breeze swept through the hall, carrying the scent of sea and fragrant blossoms and beckoning the eye toward faraway shores. The day had been made to celebrate happiness. The waters of the sea that divided the world reflected the benign blue of the sky. Pillars of clouds over the southern half of the world carried one's imagination to the blessed land of Ethiopia, where the gods of legend delighted to sup with mortals.

Prisca heard a tinkle of silvery laughter amid the flow of conversations and music. "That sounds like Chloe." Eagerly she searched the throng of guests. To her surprise, she discovered Chloe nestled in a man's lap.

She was laughing at some remark he had made. Her arm lay around his neck, several slim strands of beaten silver about her wrist. In her free hand she held a wine goblet. A companion band of silver twined across her forehead and around her shining blond head. A ruby cream ripened her lips, and her eyes were limned with kohl. Her silken robe was dyed in a manner Prisca had never seen, all colors of the sea, so that it resembled waves and foam in constant rhythmic movement. When she rose off his lap, it was apparent that Chloe wore little else. Her full, firm breasts stood out against the soft fabric. Altogether she appeared more like a devotee

224

of Artemis than of the Christ.

Prisca was not entirely successful in veiling her shock. An amused frown crossed Chloe's face as she caught her guest's expression. Then she smiled and grasped her hand. "Prisca, dear, come and meet a good friend.

"This is Paris. He and I have been close since childhood. Paris, Prisca from Rome. Where is Aquila?"

Prisca looked around. "Here a moment ago."

Paris climbed to his feet and gave her a friendly nod. His eyes were a piercing blue, his hair black brushed with silver. His handsome, heavy face wore a good-natured expression, not entirely free from guile.

At that moment trumpets announced the serving of the wedding feast. Servants appeared to usher the guests to low couches facing banquet tables that linked up like prongs of Poseidon's trident to the table where the bridal party ranged in places of honor.

Aquila had reached her side. Together with Chloe and Paris, they found places at a side table. "I met some old friends from Pontus here!" said Aquila, after introductions. His eyes followed the progress of his new-found mates to a place at another table almost directly opposite them. "They have heard of the Christ. I am going to look them up again when we are settled in."

"Isn't it exciting?" said Prisca. "So many people here, more than we could meet in a month of sabbaths!"

Lines of servants in thigh-length red tunics embellished with gold braid marched in, bearing platters of steaming food. Each was passed ceremoniously before the bridal couple for approval before disappearing down the long side tables. The first platters bore roast pork, garnished with loops of sausage, flanked with more sausages and mouth-watering giblets done to a turn.

Aquila glanced covertly across the table. His Jewish friends were reacting with consternation. They waved away the platter with obvious regret. Well, they should have expected that Jewish dietary laws would be ignored at a Corinthian wedding.

Prisca watched Chloe help herself to a generous portion of meat. Their eyes met, Chloe's challengingly. Suddenly Prisca felt famished. Jesus had not forbidden eating meat used in sacrifices. Indeed, the old testament prophets had encouraged men to feed their families with the remains of sacrificial meat, before Jesus had come and removed the need for such sacrifice. And as Chloe had said, meat was meat. Prisca put a tiny piece on her plate. Aquila passed.

"What's the matter?" she whispered. "Jesus said it is not the food we put in our bodies that is sinful. All food that nourishes is equally good."

"I know. But my Jewish friends might be offended if they saw me eat meat they consider unclean."

Prisca studied her husband. She considered the tempting grease coating her fingers and the succulent bit she had chosen from the platter.

"You are not Jewish," Aquila hissed.

"Right," she said promptly and popped the morsel in her mouth. The least she could do was not to let him know it was utterly delicious. With a straight face, she examined with him the next platter: pickled beets. They both had some. Then whole-wheat bread made without bleach. The main course was roasted bear meat.

Aquila grinned and helped himself to a lavish amount. His friends across the way did the same, then toasted each other in silent agreement on the excellence of the meat. "If bears eat men, why shouldn't men eat bears?" Aquila whispered to Prisca. Then came a cold fruit tart served with a mixture of Spanish wine and hot honey. Then a snail apiece, some tripe hash, liver in pastry boats, and eggs topped with pastry, and turnips and mustard, and beans boiled in the pod, chick-peas and lupins, no end of filberts, and an apple apiece. The final course consisted of soft cheese steeped in fresh wine.

Two hours after they had sat down, Aquila leaned back and groaned. "That is more than I ate all last summer," he complained appreciatively. "Weddings are indeed one of God's good gifts to men."

Chloe leaned across Prisca to tell Aquila, "Paris is almost one of the brethren."

Prisca laughed. "How can one be almost one of the brethren?"

Paris, on Chloe's other side, leaned in to answer. "I was baptized by John." He whispered something else in Chloe's ear.

Chloe screamed in outraged delight. Unwillingly, Prisca overheard. She colored and glanced at Aquila. Paris's crude remark had not reached his ears. "Do not be shocked, Prisca. The man is not as terrible as he seems. We have had the same argument for years."

"What is that?"

"Are you familiar with John the Baptist?"

"The one who prepared the way for the Lord," Prisca answered. Aquila was now listening, too.

"And lived on honey and locusts in the wilderness," prompted Paris. "That would make anybody crazy. John said that life in the flesh is as nothing compared to what is coming in the spirit. Therefore, love affairs are of no moment." He began nibbling on Chloe's ear.

"Please!" she said. "Didn't you have enough to eat? Further, Paris, do not distract me." Chloe lifted her wineglass unsteadily. "I wish to make a point. If the body is nothing, we should be strong enough to deny it entirely, as John did."

"Should. Should," said Paris. "I'll be scared the day you say *will*."

Prisca felt a drumming in her ears. This was *Chloe*? The teacher, the healer, expounder of the Christ? She fought down a desire to flee. What was going on here in Corinth? Both were gazing at her with expectant smiles.

"Where does that leave love?"

Chloe looked genuinely surprised. "Why—everywhere. Christ told us to love our neighbors as ourselves."

"As the Father loves us! As a father, as a mother! Not as a—as a—," she could not say it. She rose from the couch. "What would Jesus say?" Her voice rose. Several others were now looking at them. She felt overwhelmed with shame. "Aquila. . . ."

Now Aquila was on his feet, too. "This is not the place," he whispered in Prisca's ear, his fingers digging into the flesh of her elbow. "Let us pay our respects to our hosts." He awarded Chloe and Paris a set smile and escorted Prisca from the table.

An hour later, back in his work clothes, Aquila paced back and forth in the house he and Prisca had moved into just days before the wedding. The smells, noise, dust, and confusion of a central marketplace had boded ill for peaceful teaching and reflection, so with the aid of Marcus's dowry, Aquila had agreed that they could afford this house, which sat on a quiet hillside street of Corinth. His brow was furrowed in thought. Finally he faced his wife.

"Prisca, you must not associate with that woman any longer. How could Barnabas approve of her? He must not know what she is doing."

"We do not know for sure what she is doing—"

"By the gods, she is sleeping with the man!" Aquila expostulated. "Anyone could see that! I am writing to Barnabas."

Quietly Prisca clenched her fists to her temples.

Aquila ranted on. "How could anyone partake of a celebration at Aphrodite's temple and then be surprised when humans behave like their gods? A widow behaving like an adulterous woman. A man uttering crudities that pass for humor. Where is the love in *that*? Where is the chastity? The modesty?"

"Perhaps she *is* sleeping with Paris," conceded Prisca. "That is not our problem to judge. She is no longer married, nor, I gather, is Paris. Jesus would have held them equally guilty. What worries me more, husband, is how Chloe could so badly misconstrue the words of Jesus that she would think it all right to behave like a Corinthian."

Aquila scowled. All over the world, behaving like a Corinthian meant indulging in licentious behavior. The Lord had sent them into the fire.

"She is right in one thing," said Prisca calmly.

"Which is?"

"The people she knows certainly need the words of the Christ to direct their lives." Her eyes met her husband's. "I do not think we should drop Chloe."

"It is dangerous, Prisca. Just being up there on Acro-Corinthus, it will look like we approve her behavior."

Prisca sighed and picked dispiritedly at a hangnail. "What would the Christ have us do?"

Aquila stopped his pacing and dropped down beside her. He covered her hands with his. "First, we will pray for his guidance. Then we will work in our shop, just as we did in Rome. There we will stand the watch. He will not keep us in the dark."

Prisca nodded slowly, though not completely satisfied. "Our Lord chose me from the arms of Artemis. He must have seen those years of training as useful to him—"

"You still want to meet the priests and priestesses of Acro-Corinthus." She nodded.

Aquila smiled ruefully. "If that is so strongly fixed, we must assume the Lord planted it. It is settled, then."

She caressed his face. He drew her into his arms and a waiting kiss. "I love you so," he murmured.

She nestled into his shoulder. "And I you. Aquila—"

"Hm?"

"That pork was delicious—Ow!"

Prisca waited in Chloe's garden while Seth went to fetch her. More than a week had passed since the wedding. For another week, an idea that had lodged in her brain had been growing into a conviction: Chloe must be told how she and Aquila felt. It had not been easy to convince Aquila to let her come alone.

The early summer day was alive with birds swooping by with bits of stick and straw, bees and hummingbirds droning briskly among the new blossoms. She rubbed her fingers together, aware of their clamminess, wishing her stomach did not feel like birds were fluttering there, too.

"Prisca." Chloe's tall form, clad in its large white work apron, moved gracefully toward her. The sun struck gold in her short, wavy hair. "Beautiful day, isn't it?" Her voice was cool, guarded.

"Yes. I hope I have not come at an inconvenient time."

Chloe shrugged and waited.

"May we sit?"

Chloe indicated a bench and remained poised at one end of it.

Prisca sat and gave her a tremulous smile. "Chloe, you will not like my words, but please, for the sake of him who loves us, hear me."

Chloe composed her hands in her lap and tilted her head. "Well?"

"The Lord has blessed those near you. Your gifts as a physician, your compassion in accepting a man like Seth into your household—"

"You did not come here to tell me that."

Prisca caught her lip, then headed on a different tack. "At the wedding feast, Aquila would not eat the pork for fear of offending some Jewish friends."

"I noticed you had no difficulty with it."

Prisca laughed. "It was delicious, wasn't it? If I had been with a friend who objected to eating pork, I might have done as Aquila did. Persons new in the faith look to those more experienced. Not that those men were in the faith yet."

"What are you getting at?"

"You are in a position of great visibility here in Corinth. You have wealth, professional skill, freedom, and power to do as you wish. That you are a Christian is a great blessing to the community. Other Corinthians see the Christ in you."

Chloe was frowning now, striving to understand. "The Christ in me."

"Yes. How else does our Lord win his flock, except through believers? We teach one another. We open ourselves for others to see by our actions the Christ working in us. New Christians are like babes, able to digest only milk. These we nourish, gently. Mature Christians can move within a broad diversity of life and not be tempted.

"Many in Corinth are new or at the brink of faith. They look to you. They see you ministering and caring." Prisca paused, and then blurted, "But they also see you in all ways loving a man to whom you are not wed."

"So that's it!" Chloe flushed angrily. "That is no one's affair but mine."

"And Christ's," said Prisca gently. "Do you best serve him by denying sanctity to your love? Perhaps this is why you have not been able to heal as Paul heals."

Chloe arose and headed with angry, determined strides back toward the house, then stopped short.

Paris was coming toward them. "Good morning, girls! Seth said I'd find you out here." Paris's heavy features creased in a grin. It retreated into wariness when he saw Chloe's face. "What is the matter?"

"Prisca came to inform me how I should conduct my business."

With deliberate authority he placed an arm around her waist. His eyes challenged Prisca. "By what right?"

Prisca quaked before the menace in his voice. "Not my own," she stuttered. "The Lord whom we all serve."

"You do-gooder whore! What do you know? When I lost my wife, Chloe was the only person who understood. How can you know what we mean to each other? Jesus said to love one another, didn't he? Tell me what is wrong with our love!"

"Something must be," said Chloe with a touch of venom. "Prisca says it is. I must be strong like her."

Prisca reeled from the hate behind their words. "That is not what I said, dear Chloe," she managed, trying to block out the menace of Paris. "We must be strong in the Lord. I am not strong."

"Oh, but you are! Strong enough to tell me what I should do."

"Only to ask you—to beg you—to look at yourself through the eyes of a new believer! Of a girl taken to Acro-Corinthus to lose her maidenhood in the name of some goddess before she was old enough to know what it meant. If you tell her Christ makes all things new—that her body is the temple of her spirit, and it is precious to God—what will she believe when it is common knowledge that you give your body to your own pleasure without the holiness of marriage?"

"As if you haven't done just that," said Paris.

"Wh-what?"

"Lain before Artemis, with a man I happen to know. Would you like to know what he said about you?"

Prisca was shaking now. "I—I made no secret—"

Paris smiled with vicious pleasure. "That is all right. In the name of John the Baptist, I forgive you. John taught the secret knowledge. The celebration of the body will always be an earthly pleasure and could not matter more to our attainment of heaven than if we were earthworms."

Prisca felt nauseated, wanting to rid herself of this living nightmare. "John was a burning and shining lamp. Those who knew him rejoiced awhile in his light. But he did not seek glory in his own name. He proclaimed the coming of Christ, whose shoes he said he was not fit to tie."

She swallowed and forced herself to look at their faces. "I'm sorry I handled this so badly. Please forgive me." She turned to leave. Neither offered to show her out.

As she disappeared Paris muttered an oath. "If she had no man of her own, I'd swear she was unnatural. Wooing you away from me. Making noises like a Cassandra."

Chloe stared after her. "No, not Cassandra. She did not prophesy doom. Only remind me of my loyalties." She glanced at Paris. "Do you really know a man who lay with her?"

Paris answered her with a grim smile. "His name is Limaeus. He knew the Christ, too. Now he's in the silver market. By Aphrodite, that woman makes my flesh crawl. There is such a thing as being too pious, you know. Barnabas never said anything about—"

"Oh, for heaven's sake, Paris, Barnabas didn't know!"

"I wonder what he would do if he knew she was trying to drive a wedge in the fellowship."

"What are you planning to do?"

Ignoring her question, he said, "If she wants to play rough, I'll just have to teach her her place."

Chloe looked at him with dawning distaste.

Prisca could not wait to get home and cleanse herself and head for refuge in Aquila's comforting arms. Instead she found Aquila waiting for her, brimming with news.

"A maidservant belonging to the temple of Aphrodite called. The high priestess wants us to call."

"Both of us? Oh, Aquila! Do you think they have heard about the Christ?"

"Wouldn't that be something? I told her we would come this afternoon."

She removed her cloak and shook out her hair. "First I must wash."

"How did the woman talk go with Chloe?" he called after her.

"Not well. But that is unimportant."

For the second time that month Prisca and Aquila mounted the stone steps. Someone had seen them coming, for immediately they reached the temple, a young maid hurried forth.

"Are you Aquila and Prisca? Welcome. Please follow me."

The maid led them to a massive oak door. While the girl struggled with the door, Prisca saw a notice chiseled in stone beside the entrance. She touched Aquila's elbow. Together they read, "Men and women presenting themselves to the temple should abstain from intercourse with their spouses one day, from others two days, and have completed their rites of purification." Her eyebrows lifted.

The maid led them down a passage. Small rooms opened off to the left and right. Ill at ease, Prisca groped in the semigloom for her husband's hand. It was too much like the temple she had grown up in, though many times larger and wealthier.

Their destination was a large chamber at the end of the hall. They entered to find it expensively draped and well furnished with couches and small mahogany tables inlaid with ivory and gold. Two women were in the room: a small, gray-haired woman with papery cheeks was bent over a writing podium; the other, wearing a cloak of evening blue, stood with her back to the room, framed by a long, narrow window overlooking the city. She had thick, curly, dark hair. Neither was veiled. "Excuse me, mother," said the maid. "Aquila and Prisca are here."

The lady at the desk looked up. The younger one at the window turned. Her eyes were very large, very deep blue, fringed with heavy lashes. "Prisca!"

"Daphne!"

With glad cries the women flew into each other's arms. Aquila remained just inside the door. He cast a dumbfounded look at the elder woman. The younger women were both laughing and talking at once. Unceremoniously Prisca reached for his sleeve and tugged him over.

"Aquila, this is my heart-friend, Daphne, from Tyre. Daphne, my husband, Aquila."

Daphne managed to pull herself together with some portion of dignity and introduce them to the mother-priestess, who had pushed slowly to her feet. She acknowledged them with a bare nod. Her hooded eyes were a flat, observant gray.

The mother-priestess summoned a slave to serve refreshments, they sat, and Prisca and Aquila heard Daphne's story. She had fallen in love with a handsome Greek and left the temple. After their marriage, he had brought her to Corinth, home of his family. She had sworn never to mention her service to Artemis, for his parents did not believe in the gods. They had a son. He was now four and victim to a troubling illness. He had been purged and leeched within an inch of his life and still showed no signs of recovery. His frantic parents had even made incense offerings to Aesculapius, but his fever came every afternoon, blooming in his cheeks, bringing rare beauty to his face even while his flesh slowly wasted.

"I did not tell my husband I was coming here. He would be angry, but he would understand," said Daphne. "Of course his father would never forgive either of us if my secret came out." Motherhood had imparted a radiant maturity to Daphne. Her quicksilver laugh and sense of fun still simmered below the surface, but the dreamer that Prisca remembered seemed left at the temple in Tyre.

The high priestess spoke. "Daphne came here, knowing that every temple has a few sisters who are also healers. Unfortunately we have no one with the gifts she needs. That is why I sent for you."

"Never dreaming that her Prisca was my Prisca," amended Daphne. "All we had heard was that she is a healer."

Prisca traded surprised glances with Aquila.

"Are you not she?" said Daphne with less certainty.

"Are you sure you didn't mean Chloe, the midwife?" suggested Prisca.

"We are priests of the Christ," said Aquila.

"Priests!" exclaimed the elder.

Daphne shook her head. "The Christ?"

"The man called Jesus, who died and rose again and who lives in our hearts and is the Son of God," Aquila explained patiently.

"Isn't that the name of the storyteller you knew in Tyre, Prisca? And caused Thyatira such agitation? The one you left the service to follow?"

"Yes, oh, yes, Daphne! I've so much to tell you about Jesus!"

"Can—can it wait?" she said apologetically. "*Are* you a healer? I must know."

"Jesus is the healer. I lend my poor skills, what I know of herbs—what you know, too—in his name."

"In his name she has healed some who were sick, Daphne," affirmed Aquila.

Daphne smiled prettily at him, looking more like the old Daphne every moment, Prisca thought. "May she look at Jason?"

Aquila grinned. "I doubt that I'd be able to keep her away. Our Lord would tend the sick and hungry first, then show them the kingdom."

"We shall come straightaway and see your son. And you must come to our house, too," said Prisca. "Then we can chatter to our hearts' content. Do you realize—why, we have almost ten years to catch up on! And you look exactly as you did in Tyre!"

Daphne smiled at her wonderingly. Who would have thought. . . . Impulsively she decided, *I must write to Thyatira. She will be so thankful to learn that Prisca is all right.* Everyone knew Prisca had been her favorite and how she had grieved after she left.

Prisca threw an impassioned glance at Aquila before turning to the mother-priestess. "And I hope you will also visit our house, you and any of the sisters."

"No. Thank you." Her eyes rested on Aquila. Her meaning was clear. Priestesses had no part in the lives of ordinary citizens away from the temple.

"We will welcome you," Aquila said firmly. "Prisca has been praying for the opportunity to meet you and your—er—those who dwell here."

The priestess straightened her back. "It is foolish to expect priestesses who serve on Acro-Corinthus to anger the gods by giving ear to a foreign god. However, I will grant a concession. Many of the older sisters are ready to leave the temple. They are more a liability than an asset, you understand. If you could lure them away of their own volition, I should not be angry."

The coldness of her words made Prisca shudder. This could have been her own fate, to be unthinkingly tossed aside when no longer young and attractive.

"We will welcome any and all with open arms," she said.

Chapter 27

But they ought to wear veils, at least!" said the gray-haired wife of Anonymius the fisherman, drawing Prisca into the garden of Prisca's house, away from the room where in a few minutes she would be teaching. The woman folded her arms across her spare bosom with finality. "Every proper woman wears a veil in public. Those three who just came in are never veiled."

Aquila had drawn Anonymius into conversation one day as he was peddling his morning catch in the marketplace. He soon succeeded in whetting the interest of the poor fisher in the Man who turned men such as he into fishers of men. It was not long until Anonymius's wife followed him to the tentmaker's shop, full of curiosity. In delight, Prisca had befriended her and invited her to their home.

It had taken the fisherman's wife four weeks to gather the courage to say privately to Prisca what had been on her mind since the day the three women of her own age came down from the temple of Aphrodite to hear Prisca preach about the Christ.

"Not everyone wears a veil," Prisca responded mildly. "Jewish women brought up in the tradition of their faith have worn them before strangers, but Corinthian women often don't."

"Corinthian women!" snorted Anonymius's wife. "They cut their hair, too!"

"Do you really think our Lord cares if a woman cuts her hair or wears a veil?"

"But Prisca," her forehead puckered in distress, "everyone knows that women who do not wear veils are prostitutes!"

"By Jewish custom. Shall we accuse them, too?"

"Well . . . I suppose our Lord has more important things on his mind. After all," the fisherman's wife paused and rubbed a finger against her flat, sunburned cheek, "they do not have to go on being—what they were. We all came from somewhere."

Prisca gazed with dawning respect at the spare woman. "What a blessing you are to me! I love you!" She hugged her impulsively.

"Why, Prisca!" Anonymius's wife blustered with pleasure.

They returned to the waiting women, entering the room arm in arm. Prisca saw with joy that Anonymius's wife sought out one of the newcomers, sat uneasily beside her, and awarded her an awkward smile.

Nor was it lost on Daphne, who looked radiantly happy. She caught Prisca's eye as Prisca found a seat. "Jason sends you all a kiss. Shall I tell you his latest adventure?"

Smiles raced around the circle, lighting one face after another as they prepared to share another mote about the child they had all prayed back to health.

The robust shrieks of laughter emanating from the room where the women were gathered invaded the room adjoining, where Aquila was teaching the men. Aquila glanced at the door, then gave a deprecatory smile at the men seated on the floor around him.

"Them women ought to know to keep silent before the Lord. It an't respectful," said Anonymius, cosseting his broken front teeth with his tongue.

"Our Lord loves the sound of laughter," defended another. "If he didn't, he wouldn't've always wanted children around."

"From the likes of *them?*" Anonymius shot back. "Never did like the idea of them sitting together with my wife. Aquila, you *sure* she an't learning bad things?"

"Not with my wife teaching. Are we not all equal before the Lord, slave and free, man and woman, rich and poor?" Aquila laid a reassuring hand on Anonymius's shoulder. "Remember, Jesus went to Samaria and met the woman at the well, who had had five husbands. He knew that she had never married any of them, yet he chose her to carry his message to the town."

That night, Anonymius climbed into bed beside his wife. He did not think she was asleep. He put an arm around her and was rewarded when she snuggled closer. "What you women doing in there?"

"Prisca teaches us about the Christ. About how he wants us to live our lives."

"What else?"

"Well, we talk about our families, and we—"

"What about them prostitutes, they talk about what they do?"

His wife moved uncomfortably, torn between an entrenched loyalty and a gently budding one. "They talk about themselves, too. About their families, about what they are afraid of. You know, husband, I—I think —that we are not so different."

236

"That is sacrilege!"

"These women have renounced their old ways," she replied firmly.

"Yah, well, a leopard don't change its spots."

Anonymius was only voicing what many of them had thought for weeks. First Prisca and Aquila had healed a Corinthian boy of a wasting disease. For some unexplained reason, after that time the priestesses of Acro-Corinthus had been coming, by ones and twos, in ever-increasing numbers, to the airy house on the hillside, to learn about the Christ who loved them and considered them worthy humans.

At first Prisca and Aquila taught the gathering together. Then it became apparent that those who had known the Christ and followed his teachings for years were ready for the more mature responsibilities of their faith, while newcomers needed more time and loving patience.

"Most of the newer Christians are women from the hill," said Prisca one evening when she and Aquila were talking it over. "They feel comfortable with me. Perhaps I should take them apart for a while, to teach while you lead those deeper in the faith."

This left few women among the mature Christians, so the fellowship decided it was easiest to merely separate the men and women for teaching purposes.

"How is it working, do you think?" asked Aquila after they had used the new arrangement for several months.

"Better than I expected. Do you know, Aquila, some of those women are so shrewd! They grasp immediately what Jesus means to their lives. They see how far short of glory they were under the old gods. And you should hear the questions they ask!" Prisca got up to refill their teacups. Her eyes sparkled with merriment. "Anonymius's wife never opened her mouth when we taught wives and husbands together. Now she is like a different person. Still his wife, but somehow there is more to her now."

"They feel free to speak their minds," observed Aquila.

"Have you noticed that, too?"

He chuckled ruefully. "I'm hearing it from their husbands! Some are not sure they like their wives so bold."

"Have not the men changed, too?"

"Not so much. Unless it is that now and again an oath creeps in. And there are always a few who love to slip in a coarse joke. But some of your women must be ready to move up to the advanced group."

Prisca slipped her hand in his. "They do not want to. Among men they feel that their opinions and questions are considered worthless. They feel inferior. Among themselves, no one laughs when one voices a new idea. We cry together, laugh together—"

"Mm, that reminds me. Could you go about that a little more quietly?"

"Praising the Lord is serious business!"

"But also a reverent business. And modest. Jesus told people to go off by themselves to pray, not do it where everyone could watch."

She smiled and leaned her head on his shoulder. "We will try, Aquila."

"While I think of it, did you read the letter from Fabianus?"

A frown crossed Prisca's face. "Yes—"

"What did you think?"

"It sounds like they are foundering a bit."

"Some of the Roman brethren seem to want a priesthood like other religions have."

"Romans would feel comfortable with that. They are accustomed to hierarchies. Did he tell them that Christ is now our High Priest?"

Aquila laughed. "I doubt if he would ever think of that. After all, he is a horse trainer, not a man of the temple. We should write to him, Prisca. We should give him guidance, lest he despair."

She nodded.

Aquila set aside his cup of steeped herbs and closed his eyes, thinking. "If the old covenant had been faultless, there would have been no need of a new covenant. Jews would understand that, but Romans would not."

"No, but they understand laws and covenants very well."

"We could tell them that God made a covenant with his people when they came out of Egypt and set Moses to administer it. But that still left God separated from man."

"That would make perfect sense to them," she said, thinking of her father. "Marcus and his friends admire the Greek philosopher Plutarch. Plutarch said that it is blasphemous to involve God in the affairs of this world."

Aquila struggled to sort his thoughts in such a way that they made sense spoken. "My father always taught us that God is holy. But holy in a sense of being different from humans. Separated. Same thing bar-Elymas preached. They'd have gotten along fine."

"The idea of God as a loving father *is* hard to imagine," Prisca said. They exchanged smiles. "New with our Christ."

"In the old times God wrote his laws on tablets."

"Through Christ he writes them in the hearts and minds of men."

"In the old times God used an intermediary, one who was allowed into the inner court of the temple."

"But now no one needs an intermediary. All shall know him, from the least to the greatest."

"Can we make Fabianus understand, Prisca? Can you write it so he can make the brethren understand?"

"We can try." Prisca rose to her feet and stretched. "Aquila?"

"Mm?"

"I miss Chloe. I wish she'd call."

"You would."

"I'm going to pray about it before I go to bed," she informed him.

The next day was warm and humid. Decidedly not the kind of day poets eulogize when they describe the glorious Corinthian summer. Prisca and Aquila had moved their work out in front of the shop to catch the breezes, protected by a linen overhang from the intense heat of late summer, while able to enjoy the goings and comings of their neighbors.

Prisca was thinking of Chloe when she looked up and saw Seth lingering nearby. She called to the husky blond while he was still several yards away.

Seth's face lighted in a slow smile. "Hello." He ambled over to them and squatted on his haunches. For several minutes he watched them work. Finally he said, "Can I do that?"

"This?" Aquila held up the awl and woolen strips he was piecing together.

"Uh huh."

"Would you like to learn?" asked Prisca.

"Uh huh."

"Then you shall." Prisca rose and rummaged through some supplies, returning with the largest awl she could find and a scrap of cloth. She threaded the awl with a bit of twisted wool and gave it to him.

"Like this," said Aquila, slowly and elaborately going through the motions of whipstitching.

Seth stuck his tongue out and copied. His face lighted like a lamp when his thick fingers tugged on the awl and he found the thread following it through the material.

Prisca smiled at them. How good Aquila was. How natural he found it to serve the least of Christ's children! Aquila glanced up at her. "Hey, get to work!"

"Get to work," Seth repeated in delight.

"Seth!" Chloe's voice singsonged from across the street. "I have been searching for you for an hour!"

Prisca scrambled to her feet and called, "Chloe! Come and have a cup of wine with us."

Chloe hesitated. Then she said a few words to the serving girl attending her and launched out, with firm, long-legged strides, across the street. Her black cloak only partly covered the short, bright hair.

"See what I made, mistress?" cried Seth, displaying his stitchery.

"Why, I did not know you could sew," she smiled. Her smile grew slightly remote as it touched Aquila and Prisca.

Ignoring her cool manner, Prisca smiled warmly. "I will fetch wine," she said.

"I'll help," offered Chloe.

The women went into a small room at the rear of the shop, where Prisca kept a few foodstuffs against the days they worked late. Beyond the room was a tiny open enclosure, barely large enough for a bench.

"May I speak to you a moment?" Chloe stepped outside and sat on the bench.

"Of course." Prisca followed and sat beside her.

Chloe looked down at her capable hands, strong fingers plucking at her robe. "Paris and I are no longer sleeping together. I know the Christ, and I love him. I knew before you came that afternoon that what I was doing was displeasing to God, yet I did not change." She threw a swift glance at Prisca, her blue eyes troubled. "Do you think he will forgive me?"

A few minutes later, seated cross-legged in the front of the shop, Aquila heard a double peal of laughter, and then the women reappeared, bearing four cups of wine and some seedcakes. His eyes sought his wife's. Prisca's eyes glowed with happiness. Seth's eyes followed the progress of the cakes. Carefully he helped himself when the plate was offered. The man and women around him seemed to be having an awfully good time. He grinned. "Get to work!"

When Chloe and Seth left a few minutes later, Prisca told Aquila what had happened and that the Christian brethren of Corinth were meeting at Chloe's house the following night. "She wants us to come."

Aquila said immediately, "Good! Let us ask some of those from the street here to go with us."

Prisca nodded. "It will be good for them."

Later that afternoon, Prisca sat hunched over a small stool, her knees supporting a plank upon which she had spread a piece of parchment. On the floor of the shop beside her were an inkwell and several scattered pieces of parchment that were covered with drying ink in her fine Greek hand. She and Aquila had struggled for hours to order their thoughts in the letter to Fabianus, which she had just finished.

Aquila rested a soft, speculative glance on his wife. "I wonder if Philip and Adah are having a hard time in Alexandria, too. I miss them. You should write to them, too, Prisca. Tell them—remind them of the psalmist's song, 'What is man that thou art mindful of him, or the son of man, that thou carest for him? Thou didst make him for a little while lower than the angels, thou hast crowned him with glory and honor, putting everything in subjection under his feet.' "

"Even Jesus for a little while was made lower than the angels," Prisca added wistfully. Dipping the stylus in the thick ink, she labored over her notes for several minutes. "This is such a mess. I want to tell Adah about the Corinthian women, too. Most of the women we've met are babes in spirit, having been denied learning. But you know they are a gay and happy lot, Aquila, a delight to teach."

"You really love Corinth, don't you?"

"I feel at home here."

"It's still not our 'lasting city,' " Aquila reminded her.

Prisca paused in her note taking, thinking of Seth and Chloe and Paris. What perfect examples of imperfect humans! Chloe was as generous and hospitable as Christ could desire, yet. . . . She wrote a few more lines, then added, "Let marriage be held in honor among all, and let the marriage bed be undefiled; for God will judge the immoral and adulterous."

With a sigh she laid the letter aside and gazed out the door. "There is so much to tell them. I am never sure if I am making myself clear. Aquila, when you finish, will you help me?"

Aquila, absorbed in his work, merely nodded. Then he heard his wife utter a strangled cry and glanced up in swift alarm. Prisca was on her feet, her hands uncharacteristically clutching the bosom of her robe. Her face had gone white. He scrambled up and rushed to her. "What is it? Are you ill?"

"I don't believe it. Not here! She couldn't be!" Her voice shrilled with the sharp edge of panic.

"*Who?*"

Prisca pointed toward the street. "Thyatira!"

Chapter 28

At that moment, Thyatira, high priestess of Artemis, was alighting from a chair in the street. Her regal gaze swung around the busy market, and she fixed her eye on Prisca watching transfixed from a doorway. Recognition was instantaneous. She motioned to her retinue. The four chair bearers, locally hired lads from the look of them, clustered in a self-conscious knot to await her commands. The female attendant, clad in the familiar sage green robe worn by those serving the temple in Tyre, started to follow her mistress to the shop and was waved back.

Even in the sophisticated environs of Corinth, passersby stopped to gawk at this splendid incarnation of an Amazon. Thyatira was garbed in a scarlet cloak over a linen robe. The hems of her garments were embroidered with sheaves of gold knots resembling ears of corn. As if she were descending from Olympus, Thyatira swept across the street. Stopping an arm's length from the silent couple, she extended her jeweled hand for Prisca to kiss.

Prisca had to make a conscious effort to stop herself from obliging. "Thyatira." Her voice trembled. "Welcome. My husband, this is Thyatira, high priestess of Artemis."

"And your mother, too," said Aquila in a perfectly reasonable voice. "Welcome," he said positively. "Please come in."

Thyatira was not prepared to be quite that welcomed. It pleased her to note that she had badly shaken her daughter, an effect she had gone to great pains to achieve. Prisca off balance would be easier to convince that she must return to Tyre and accept her destiny. Thyatira quickly effaced a scowl at Aquila's nonthreatening reception and decided to make the best of it.

"Thank you." She awarded him a gracious smile and allowed herself to be shown inside.

Prisca scooped up the sheaf of pages she had been writing to their friends and cleared a bench for her mother to sit upon.

Thyatira's raven hair was streaked with gray. It was fashionably bound into a high cone held by three narrow bands of cloth of gold. The strong planes of her face retained a martial beauty, artfully enhanced by makeup. Prisca glanced at her mother's fingers. Pale, unscuffed predators, carrion with rings.

"So you have learned that I am your mother. Or did you reason it in Tyre?"

Aquila came to sit with Prisca. She felt his comforting arm circle her midriff. He answered Thyatira, "Prisca learned from Tribune Marcus Sistus."

"From—" The priestess could not bring herself to say it.

"From my father," Prisca said quietly. No longer did the desire rage in her to ask her mother why she had concealed their flesh of one flesh. Perhaps if she had known, Prisca would have been unable to summon the strength to leave the temple to follow Jesus. Now it did not matter.

Thyatira's face drained of color, leaving only the unnatural smudges of red on her cheekbones. "Where did you meet him?" she demanded. "Or did you two conspire when he was in Tyre?"

"We met in Rome," said Aquila. How coldhearted she seemed! How could this woman be the mother of his Prisca?

"He made me—," Prisca began. Aquila pinched her vigorously through the back of her robe.

"Yes?"

"Aware who you were. He thought I knew."

Aquila felt a wave of relief. If this woman knew Sistus had settled a dowry on Prisca, she could conceivably spend her life deviling them. He could not guess what lay behind those calculating eyes or what she purposed. She was so far from his conception of *mother* that he was without anchor to cast judgment. Whenever Prisca had mentioned her, which had become almost nonexistent with the passing years, she always referred to her as *beautiful.* Aquila studied the predatory face. By the goodness of Christ, he could see no beauty in the long eyes, the determined, sparring lines encasing her wide mouth.

Suddenly he realized that Prisca was inviting her to stay with them. Prisca rose, and he hastily with her.

"I am taking Thyatira to the house, so she can rest," she said. "I know she must be tired."

Aquila managed to hide his alarm. *My God,* he cried silently, *protect my wife from this creature!* "Of course. I'll be up later."

As they left the shop, Prisca noted the white-knuckled grip Thyatira had on each side of her cloak. "Would you prefer to stay at a public house?" she asked courteously.

"I did not travel all the way to Corinth to stay at a public inn," Thyatira replied crisply.

Prisca threw a side glance at her mother. Playing the great lady was wearing on her. *She is finding this even more difficult than I,* Prisca realized with surprise.

When they reached the house, Thyatira dismissed the chair and set her attendant to unpacking and shaking out her clothing.

An hour later, mother and daughter sat with goblets of pomegranate juice in the garden. Thyatira had grown progressively uncommunicative and now seemed to be struggling to continue the picture of determination and strength that was so much a part of her.

"Why did you come, Thyatira?" Prisca asked softly.

Thyatira lifted her chin. "The coincidence of two omens. My visions have been so troubling. Urgent and repeated visions of danger."

"Danger to whom, my mother?"

"To Artemis . . . to you . . . to me. It is unclear."

Prisca did not trust herself to lay a hand of comfort upon her mother. "And the other omen?"

"Daphne sent for me. Which made me certain the visions involved you."

"*Daphne!*" Prisca bolted upright.

"Well," Thyatira modified grudgingly, "she wrote and told me you were here. I—wanted to see you. She told me you still served that Jesus of yours." Thyatira stared intently at Prisca. "I had to make one last effort to save you. I would be less than a mother, less than your mother-priestess, if I shirked."

"You cannot be serious! Thousands of miles, enduring great discomfort and great expense, to tell me this? You are not my mother-priestess, Thyatira. I will never return to the temple! That part of my life is dead. Didn't Daphne tell you this?"

"Prisca, my child, listen to me!" Desperation entered Thyatira's voice. "I understand something you do not. There is much superstition abroad concerning women. Men have always feared women because of our monthly flow. They fear it because none can explain it. Our bodies are inextricably tied to the cycles of nature, ebb and flow, the moon and its cycles, and even the cycle of the seasons. This draws us close to Mother Earth. Women have wisely seen how this fecundity is the basis for all life and celebrated it by worshiping the divine goddess.

"Because they can in no way, by magic or otherwise, duplicate or imitate this cycle, men call it impure and women with the flow impure vessels. It is part of the lore of nations. To convince themselves of women's ritual impurity, they have even written her inferior status into their laws. They have said that because of this mysterious flow, women have secret powers and accuse them of using their powers to bewitch men and cause men to do evil where they would not."

Thyatira leaned back and closed her eyes. Exhaustion crept into her voice. "Tell me this is not so."

Prisca felt a deep sadness as she recognized the truth of her mother's words. "This has always been so. Not only for you, Thyatira, but for the women of my husband's people also, to be called thus impure."

"Drawing apart from this world, serving the goddess, has saved many women from madness."

Prisca nodded. "But for this, they must sacrifice all hope of a loving family. Here in Corinthian temples, when their bodies are no longer desirable, they are cast out."

Thyatira smiled, her eyes still closed. "Some have said it was not a bad exchange. In the temple we have status, position, more freedom than—," the eyes flew open, "you."

Prisca thought carefully before she answered. "I have pondered this for years, Thyatira. It is true that nations hold women in slight regard. Everywhere in the world this is true, except for one man, and that man is Jesus.

"He is the only one who has seen women fully as worthy of his love as men. He openly and without shame included women among his best friends. He had compassion for a woman whose flow had become a hemorrhage that was killing her, and he healed her. He even broke the Jewish sabbath law of rest to heal a crippled woman."

"Your Jesus could actually do that?"

"Does it still. But greater, Thyatira. Before Jesus came, Jews had to sacrifice animal parts—burnt offerings—to supplicate their Jehovah. As vestal priestesses of Artemis—and priests of Apollo and the others—we had to make our bodies the sacrificial vessels. The Greeks—," she smiled slightly, "well, they seem to sacrifice anything that is convenient.

"Then Jesus came. And he made the perfect sacrifice. So perfect that none of us ever have to do so again."

Thyatira's head lifted. "What was that?"

"Himself. God asked of his Son the perfect sacrifice. That he let himself be crucified for the sins of all of us. When he died he showed us what God wanted. The only thing he wants."

"Crucifixion?" Thyatira said in a scathing tone.

Prisca smiled gently. "Total obedience. Even as he was perfectly obedient."

"Total obedience! To whom?"

"To God."

"See where it got him!"

"It was not the end, Thyatira. Jesus was resurrected from death, just as in the eternal cycle of earth spring follows winter. Perhaps that is why women follow him. Through him each of us will be reborn in eternal life."

"And what must one do to attain this eternal life?" said Thyatira cautiously.

"Only follow his commandments."

"Which commandments?" she demanded.

"To love God. To love one another. To be perfect in love."

"That's all?"

"Oh, yes. Not that any of us can ever achieve it. But we try."

Thyatira stared at her in disbelief. "And for that you left the most beautiful life in the world."

"It was no longer the most beautiful life in the world after I met Jesus. He heals the human spirit."

"And where does that leave our beloved goddess?"

Prisca had no answer.

Suddenly Thyatira flung herself out of her chair and clapped her hands smartly together, summoning her attendant.

"What are you doing?"

"Leaving, Prisca. Leaving you to your precious Master." Biting the words off in sarcasm. "When you recover your senses you can find me at Acro-Corinthus."

"Thyatira—no!"

"Yes, mistress?" The attendant cringed in the doorway of the atrium.

"Pack my things. Summon the bearers. We are leaving immediately."

"Yes, mistress."

Prisca watched the girl dart silently inside. Thyatira's clever eyes were upon her, as if gauging the effect of her words.

"Unnatural mother!" she cried. "To punish me for not following your own ambitions!"

"Punishing you, Prisca? What an odd thing to say."

"I want only to bring you to the Father. To love God as I love him. Why will you not let me?"

"Stupid child. Every mother has a sacred duty to lead her children into the way of life. For your own good, my daughter." Thyatira hesitated, as if unwilling to utter her thoughts. Finally, she said in a soft tone, "If you cannot live in the spirit of the goddess, it is better to perish."

Prisca felt sick to her stomach, as if her mother had dealt her a sharp blow. "I—I must go back to the shop for a while. Aquila needs help. Please, stay till I return. Let us not leave it like this."

Thyatira turned her back.

When she heard Prisca leave the house, Thyatira stalked back into the gathering room, her face full of fury.

"Are you finished packing yet, you lazy girl?" she called.

"Not quite, mistress! I am hurrying!"

Thyatira strode around the room, muttering imprecations. Suddenly she drew to a halt before a writing desk. She lifted the lid of a large box. Writings in Greek. They looked like her daughter's hand. She picked up the top sheet. *The old ways shall pass away,* she read. Her lip curled as she scanned the words below. *Every priest stands daily at his service, offering repeatedly the same sacrifices, which can never take away sins. But Christ has for all time made a single sacrifice for sins. If we sin deliberately, after receiving knowledge of the truth, comes a fearful prospect of judgment.*

A tremor of fear fluttered at her, like the scarcely felt wings of a butterfly. Angrily she brushed it aside. "I am nature," she began to chant, "the universal Mother, mistress of all elements, primordial child of time, sovereign of all—"

"We are ready, mistress," came the attendant's timid voice.

Thyatira glanced at her. Without a word, she replaced the sheets of parchment with extreme care, closed the lid, and walked out into the afternoon.

In spite of the heat of the day, Crispus, ruler of the Corinthian Jewish synagogue, hurried across the Outer Court of the temple, thinking not about the heat or the letter carried in his hand for Sosthenes, the chief rabbi, but about his wife. She was due to deliver any day. It was their first child. He wished he were permitted to be with her. She was badly frightened and trying to keep it from him. Crispus's square, good-humored face creased with worry. His hair was reddish and curled close to his head. Wouldn't it be something if their son was born with red hair!

The worried lines had relaxed a little by the time he reached Sosthenes' office. Sosthenes was seated behind his desk. He examined the seal on the letter with a smile.

"It is from the Rome synagogue, from Rabbi bar-Elymas." He broke the seal. As he unrolled the parchment and began to read, his face paled. "No! it is from his followers in Alexandria! Emperor Claudius has expelled the Jews from Rome, and bar-Elymas is in prison!"

"In prison! What happened?"

"Some trouble with those revolutionaries who call themselves Christians."

"We have some of those in Corinth. They don't seem very revolutionary."

Suddenly Sosthenes sprang to his feet. "By all that is holy!"

"What is it?"

"The leaders were coming to Corinth. They have probably been here for months. And probably already organizing mischief. We must stop them, Crispus! It says they go by the names of Aquila and Prisca. Tentmakers. How is that for an innocent cover?"

"Yes. . . . Still. . . . What was it bar-Elymas did exactly?"

Sosthenes scanned the contents again. "The letter does not say. Strange. But we must make certain that nothing of the sort happens here. You say there are already Christians in Corinth. Who is their leader?"

"A widow by the name of Chloe."

"A woman!" he said with scornful disbelief. "A Jewess?"

"Her husband was. She is a midwife, I believe."

"Witch, more like." Sosthenes rerolled the letter and tapped one end thoughtfully against his chin. "Perhaps we can root out the whole evil at once. Send a letter to Alexandria, thanking them for their information. I am wondering how the proconsul of Achaia will take the coming of known troublemakers to his peaceful province."

"You would place it before Gallio, rabbi?" said Crispus.

Sosthenes glanced at Crispus, sensing some hesitation. "Well?"

Crispus thumbed his jaw. "Gallio is wont to think that anyone who brings a civil matter before the court is himself the troublemaker."

"True. Have you a better plan?"

"The exiles have been here for some time already. Why not wait and see if any trouble actually develops before stirring the dogs?"

"Well, I suppose that might be the better part. Yes," Sosthenes said with finality. "We will watch them until they begin barking, Crispus."

"Then I believe I will call it a day."

"What is that? Oh, your wife. Yes, go home."

"Would you like some wine before I leave?"

"No. Thank you."

Had they not seen Chloe drunk with too much wine, uninhibitedly enjoying herself at the wedding feast, none could ever have persuaded Prisca and Aquila that the lovely, dignified matron seated with twenty or thirty men and women in her home that evening was the same person. To their surprise, Paris was there, too, and the parents of Julia, the bride. Nearly all were well dressed, aristocratic in bearing, and spoke beautifully enunciated Greek.

The half dozen Corinthians with Prisca and Aquila were not well dressed. It was evident from the poorly managed haircuts, the broken teeth, and poor skin textures, that proper care and health had been considered luxuries in their lives.

Decorously they were ushered into the room and found places along a wall. After their first bright, interested glances, Chloe's guests moved with alacrity to give them plenty of room to sit. Thick sheepskin rugs covered the floor, with numerous cushions, making it easy to find comfortable positions. Prisca noticed a few lips wrinkling in distaste as the newcomers settled in.

Chloe, watching the behavior of her friends, frowned. "My friends," she said evenly, "tonight we have a teacher who actually knew the Christ. Prisca and her husband, Aquila, started a community in Rome, and now they have come to be with us." Her eyes took on a soft glow, and she smiled at Prisca.

"First, though, I have a surprise for Prisca and Aquila and for you. We have had a message. Paul is coming. Paul of Tarsus. He will visit us on his way to Spain. He sends word that his ambition is to preach the gospel not where Christ has already been named, lest he build on another man's foundation, but as it is written."

A tremor of fear shot through Prisca. She glanced at Aquila, but he was engaged in talk with one of their friends. Recalling the animosity of the disciples, she wondered what Paul would make of their ministry. Corinth was enough to try the most gentle of minds! And then there was Thyatira. Suddenly Prisca felt physically ill.

"Is Barnabas with him?" she said hopefully.

"No. Paul hints at some sort of disagreement. Barnabas and Mark left for Cyprus. He is now with a new disciple. Shall we begin, Prisca?"

A sense of foreboding settled over her as she rose and began to speak.

At midnight only a single guttering candle lighted the beautifully appointed room where the guests had listened enchanted while Prisca and Aquila told their stories. Chloe sat alone, gazing into the candle flame. She heard a noise and turned. "Are you still here? I thought everyone had gone."

Paris's heavy bulk moved into the candlelight. The silver in his black hair gleamed softly. "I thought you might want company."

"No, I don't want company. Did you notice how they acted?"

"Prisca and Aquila? Or that ragbag of followers they've collected?" His voice was ripe with scorn.

"No. My friends. Our friends. When she was leaving, Hazel actually said to me that if that rabble was going to heaven, she wasn't sure she wanted to go after all."

Paris laughed.

"It is not funny," said Chloe. She rose, feeling weary. Paris moved in swiftly and took her in his arms. Chloe struggled. Paris laughed, his voice swelling with knowledge of his power over her.

"You are not strong enough to fight me, Chloe. You love it."

"Lucas! Barsabas! Jonah!"

Angrily Paris released her. His face twisted into an ugly mask as they heard feet running along a corridor outside the room.

"Yes, mistress?"

"Please show Paris out."

"You fool! Aquila and Prisca may have you hooked, but not me! We'll see who wins." He turned a glance on Chloe's servants, which stopped them where they were, then stalked out.

"Good morrow, Anonymius! Fine day the Lord has made." Standing amiably beside Anonymius, Paris gazed out over the harbor, then peered into the bucket beside the fisherman. "Looks like a good catch."

Anonymius stood up, wiping the blood and slime on his hands on his apron. The wooden bucket beside his squat stool was filled with large catfish, which he was cleaning. "Good day to you, sir! Yah, good catch." He shuffled from one leg to the other. "Er, sure enjoyed that meeting last night at Mistress Chloe's."

Paris smiled broadly. "Yes indeed. I couldn't help noticing how much you know about our Lord."

Anonymius thrust out his chest and glanced about, hoping his fishing companions were taking note of him talking with such a fine lord. "Well, we been meeting four—five months now over to the tentmaker's. Knows a lot, Aquila does."

"Really? How about his wife?"

"Prisca? Oh she teaches the women. You know—they like to feel part of what's going on. So he lets her give them some diddly-doo."

"You think that is a good idea?"

The lord Paris asking his opinion! Well, times *were* different! Anonymius cleared his throat. "Didn't at first. Wife, of course, she thinks it's fine—"

"But you don't."

"They make so much noise. Not respectful, I'm thinking. And them from the temple—"

"The synagogue," Paris supplied quickly.

"Oh, no, sir, lots of us from there. Ones I's talking about be the women from Acro-Corinthus. Wife says they are all right, but just between us men, I an't so sure. No veils, faces painted like whores, loudmouthed, too. Not so bad as they was at first, but. . . . No, sir, don't look so good to me. Prisca, she don't seem to mind. Like I say, I an't so sure. Hard for us men to keep our minds on the Lord's business, I can tell you."

"Yes, I can see how it would be." Paris chatted about inconsequential matters a few moments longer, thanked him for his time, then bade good-bye.

"Yes, sir, er, Paris. Good-bye, Paris!"

Grinning broadly, Paris hastened away from the harbor and headed back toward town. Aphrodite was no fool, he acknowledged. Perhaps a goddess, but just like any woman. Out to defend her territory. Last night when he had left the house of Chloe, he had gone to Acro-Corinthus to release his frustrations in the bed of a temple virgin and to leave a generous donation with the high priestess. Already this morning his sacrifice was showering him with blessings.

Paris glanced at the sun. He was a man who firmly believed in riding the wave of Fortuna as long as she was smiling. If he hurried, he might catch one of the rabbis at the Jewish temple to set in motion another part of his plan. When he was through with Prisca and Aquila, they would wish they had never set foot in Corinth.

As he entered the market street behind the temple of Apollo, he spied a familiar figure richly dressed in black, despite the promise of another sweltering day. He called to him. "Limaeus!"

Limaeus halted and turned. The years had not been kind to Limaeus. His hair had thinned to long, dull wisps of brown, barely sufficient to cover his small skull. His robe was expensive, but on closer examination was matted with accumulated dirt and rubbed to frayed exhaustion along the edges of the neck. Limaeus squinted suspiciously as Paris approached, exuding strength and confidence.

"How's the silver market these days?"

"All right," Limaeus said guardedly. He wondered if Paris had discovered he had been coating lead with silver and selling it to people who were only passing through. *No,* he judged with the shrewdness of one who has lived marginally by his wits all his life, *the man's got his own scheme going.* "Just fine, in fact." His usage of Greek was abominable.

"Good! Say, Limaeus. . . ." Paris took him by the elbow and walked him out of earshot. "Remember that priestess in Tyre you told me about once? Heh?" he jostled him in comradely fashion.

"So what?"

"Prisca, wasn't that her name? You know she's here in Corinth?"

"How do you know? You never met her."

"You, ah, remember that man called Jesus?"

A light entered Limaeus's eyes, then faded. "Why?"

"Well, she's here, she's preaching Jesus is the Son of God. What do you think of that? Leaving her goddess for him. Just like she's too good for the likes of you and me."

If the linking of his name with Paris's struck him as odd, Limaeus did not reveal it. "What's that to me?"

"Well!" Paris scrambled for words that would meld this little man's failures in life into lust for revenge. "You wanted her to stay with you, you said. If she'd stayed with you like you told her to, you'd be a different man today!"

"What's wrong with me now?" Limaeus demanded.

"Nothing! I only meant—ah—well, you know how Jesus' crowd feels about amulets and things. Seems to me that cuts right into your silver market. And now she's here," he repeated. Paris shook his head in commiseration. "One man to another, it hardly seems fair."

Limaeus frowned, his ferret eyes studying Paris's bland face. "Why you come to me now?"

"No reason. Just happened to see you." Paris glanced about. "And we are on the street where her husband, Aquila, has his shop. Ever meet him? He's a tentmaker. Good-looking devil." These words, Paris noted with a pleased sigh, sent Limaeus's eyes darting up and down the street. "Well,

I must be going. I certainly do wish you a prosperous year." Paris nodded farewell.

Limaeus seized the amulet he wore on a chain around his neck, one of the few he possessed of genuine silver, and rubbed it thoughtfully. *I'd've been a different man today. By the gods, I would've.* Did Prisca ever think of him, he wondered. Maybe he ought to find out.

Leaving Limaeus standing in the street, scratching his verminous scalp, Paris hid a smile and strode rapidly away. He was certain that the seed, once planted, would grow as vigorously as unwanted weeds in a rose garden. Let Prisca explain Limaeus to her fawning Christian followers!

Now to settle accounts with Aquila, he had something quite different planned. By the gods, it would be some time before either of them interfered with his life again! He turned his steps to the synagogue.

Reaching the synagogue a quarter of an hour later, Paris gave the servant a brief message and paced impatiently in the Outer Court while he watched him disappear.

The servant hurried to Sosthenes' office. "Begging your pardon, rabbi—"

"Well, what is it now?"

"A man is here who desires to speak with you. He has the strangest tale, something about a plot against the temple."

"My word!" declared Sosthenes. "Send him in."

Chapter 29

L ucius Seneca was a poet and little addicted to physical exertion. Nevertheless he enjoyed coming to the Circus and hobnobbing with the foolish fellows who spent their energies in pseudocombat for want of something better to do.

Thus it was on this late summer day that, sitting on a circular stone bench facing the dusty arena, Seneca's lips curled in a mocking smile (lest anyone observing think he truly enjoyed the spectacle and was not gathering material for new philosophies) as two men fought not eight feet away.

Stripped to the waist, heavy muscles rippling and glistening with sweat and dirt, the two men fought with short swords and wooden bucklers covered with scarred leather. They wasted no energy on talk: An hour of hard combat had reduced their speech to heavy grunts of exertion.

The older combatant was breathing heavily. If he did not overpower his man soon, the youngster would outlast him. A vision of the accompanying humiliation lent new strength to his shrieking limbs. He looked into the eyes of his opponent. A dirt-gritted smile bared the teeth of the younger fighter, as if he smelled victory. His sandals ground into the dirt, and he recklessly lunged forward.

Marcus Sistus feinted and brought the flat of the blade down across the youthful shoulders as he lunged past. At the same instant he tripped him and jammed a foot on his nape. "Hah!" he roared, reeling away, lightheaded with euphoria and exhaustion. A round of laughter and catcalls greeted the shamefaced young warrior. Marcus wrenched him to his feet and clapped him on the shoulder.

Lucius Seneca admired openly the prowess and strength of his friend. In a handsome gesture he got up off the bench to give him his own capelet to wipe his sweating flesh.

"Watching you fight is like appreciating a fine poem," he observed. "One can see the mind at work behind the execution."

"Thank you," Marcus panted. "Didn't know you were back." He started for the baths, and Lucius followed. "You had a poem in the Corinthian competitions, didn't you?"

"Ah, yes." Lucius hesitated. "Regrettably the judges were friends not of my brother Gallio but that hack Filio."

Marcus smothered a smile. "Too bad." Reaching the baths, he stripped and plunged into the cold water.

Lucius perched companionably near the edge.

"Did you see my daughter in Corinth?"

"I did not know she was there!"

"You must have left before the exile." Briefly Marcus told Lucius what had happened.

"I am sorry, my friend. I know that you cherish your daughter. That is interesting, though, because I did hear her name."

Marcus hoisted himself up on the lip of the pool. "In what manner?"

"A strange tale. I always visit Acro-Corinthus while in Corinth. Naturally. This time I met a most fascinating creature. I tell you, Marcus, my next epic poem shall be devoted to her. Ode to Artemis. And Thyatira shall speak the chorus!"

Thyatira! Marcus was seized with a terrible foreboding. "You ramble, Lucius."

Lucius eyed his friend with surprise. "I heard it said, when telling others about this remarkable woman, that she is the mother of your Prisca."

"What did *she* say?"

"Oh, Thyatira never mentioned her. She is deep in the mysteries of the goddess. One of the few, I heard, who still induces visions with the aid of a certain snake. Strange, strange tales she spins. The woman ought to be a poet herself. I told her this and it pleased her. She—"

"Prisca, Lucius!"

"Nothing more, Marcus. Do not get upset. Prisca's name is pure. I only guessed it must have been your daughter because the rumor concerned a beautiful young woman of that name who had left a temple to follow the new Jewish sect that she and Aquila spoke of at your house."

Thyatira in Corinth. Practicing her arts in the Stygian shadow of Acro-Corinthus. His hands shook as he groped for his garments.

"Marcus! Where are you going?"

While Tribune Marcus Sistus was wearing out relays of horses to reach the Adriatic coast, across the sea Rabbi Sosthenes was reading a brief communication from a member of the high council of Jerusalem.

"Have you heard of a man named Paul, Crispus?" he asked. "He says by way of introduction that his father is a Pharisee from Tarsus."

"No, I do not think so."

"He seems to be quite a traveler. He is passing through Corinth on his way to Spain and informs us he will speak at the temple on the sabbath while he is here."

"Good! Our men will be delighted."

"Humph," said Sosthenes. "You mean they tire of listening to me."

"Not at all," said Crispus. Nothing could dent his sunny humor these days. His blessed wife had delivered a healthy son, a red-haired son, last week. "I meant only that fresh speakers always bring new worshipers to the temple. If he is good, perhaps we can persuade him to tarry with us a few weeks."

Slowly, summer's heat relented. The hot, yellow skies cooled to ivory and then to an exhausted blue. The coolness of morning began to extend a little longer and creep back a little sooner in the evening.

Now that winter was approaching, Aquila and Prisca went to the shop earlier in the mornings. With people reminded again of the need for warm and hole-free tents, they had no shortage of work.

Aquila loved to watch Prisca work. This morning she was humming to herself as she stitched, her thoughts obviously engaged on a pleasant subject. Her cheeks bloomed with health, although she seemed a little thinner than she had been a few years ago. Her forearms, he noticed, had developed long, smooth muscles from working with the heavy materials. Her neck was finely corded, too, a pale pillar supporting the shining mass of chestnut hair swept back behind her ears. Her bare head still rode with as proud a carriage as the first day he had seen her, on the windswept shore of Cyprus.

"When are the women coming?" he asked as she looked up.

"They are gathering at Chloe's after the noon rest. But I have plenty of time to help you this morning."

Aquila waggled his black eyebrows and scratched his bent nose. "And time for a little romp under the mizzen, my pretty wench?"

Prisca laughed. "Please, sir, I happen to be a married woman!"

They were both laughing as a man entered the shop. He was a small, ordinary-looking individual with a large head and prominent eyes that bulged slightly.

"Good morning!" he said in a surprisingly hearty voice.

Aquila's eyes swept him with a practiced glance. His garment was expertly mended, of an unremarkable brown wool, but his sandals were another matter. The leather sole at the side of the ball of his foot looked as thin as parchment. The straps were stretched and grainy. A traveler. "Have a seat. Looks like you've been on the road a piece this morning."

The stranger nodded. "I wanted to reach Corinth before the heat of the day." As if he had done so a hundred times before, he pulled over a bale of canvas and settled on it with a sigh of relief.

"Are you thirsty?" Aquila continued.

"Never—but again much of the time," he threw out. Then he smiled. His eyes were blue, bleached pale like the sky. "Yes, if you have any water."

Prisca threw him a puzzled glance. It would not be good manners to question him before heeding his thirst. But surely he had meant to be questioned. She rose. "My husband and I enjoy barley water with mint. It is very refreshing when you are tired. Let me fetch some for you."

When she left, the stranger looked around the shop curiously. "You've a good variety of awls and tooling pieces." He leaned over to feel the hand of a length of wool. "Cilician, isn't it? Used to work with it myself."

"Did you! Not in Rome, by chance? We had a shop there before coming to Achaia."

"No. I have not yet been to Rome. Did you prosper?"

Aquila grinned. "With the exception of one bad time, when rioters destroyed the shop. But with the help of our Lord and our good friends we managed to stay in business."

"Your Lord?"

Aquila laid down his work and smiled warmly. "Jesus, the Christ. Have you not heard of him?"

The man's face lighted up. "I serve him, too, friend, wherever I go. Right now I am looking for work so that I will have the means to continue."

"What do you do?"

"I am a tentmaker by trade." The stranger's eyes held Aquila's boldly.

"Well." Aquila glanced toward the back of the shop. "You are welcome to abide and work with us. Business is not good yet, but it should improve as winter comes."

Prisca returned with the draught of barley water. "I had not any made," she apologized. "The flavors are not well steeped, I'm afraid."

"Thank you." He drank from the cup and pronounced it delicious.

"Prisca, this man needs work and a place to stay. He is a tentmaker and a follower of our Lord."

"You are! Then you must stay with us." Prisca dropped to her knees with a glad smile. "Tell us where you are from. We have occasionally had travelers from other churches that serve our Lord Christ."

"I am Paul of Tarsus."

"Paul!" Prisca rocked back on her heels. "Paul! We heard you were coming!"

Against her will, a cold knot of fear began to congeal in Prisca's already queasy stomach. The vision that had impelled Thyatira to Corinth had been frighteningly prescient. She forced herself to remain calm and concentrate on their visitor.

Paul smiled, a wide grin splitting his homely face. "Then you are Aquila and Prisca, and I have found those I have come to visit."

"We have heard of you over the years," said Aquila. "From Antioch, from Cyprus, from Jerusalem, like a wind, whirling and touching down at will."

"We heard that you performed miraculous healings," Prisca added.

"Through the power of our Lord, who found me and healed me."

"What happened, Paul? How was it that you were claimed?" asked Aquila. "I recall that Barnabas wrote that one day you were persecuting the brethren in Jerusalem, and the next you were seized yourself with the vision."

Paul's face lighted with relish. It seemed obvious that he never tired of recounting this tale. "I call myself Christ's apostle," he began, "even though I did not know Jesus while he was a man on earth. I did, as you say, persecute his followers. It happened about three years after the crucifixion of our beloved Lord. I was traveling to Damascus at the time. Suddenly a voice calling itself Jesus told me that he was the one whom I had been persecuting. He blinded me with a vision for three days. When I regained my sight, I knew that Jesus was the Son of God."

Prisca began to relax. If Jesus called Paul, surely there was nothing to fear. Perhaps, as Barnabas had said of the disciples, Paul, too, possessed a deeper understanding of Christ since the days when the disciples had rejected her ministry.

As if to affirm this, Paul was saying, "When I was traveling through Macedonia last year, I stopped to preach in the city of Philippi. A wealthy businesswoman gave me hospitality. Her name was Lydia. Though she was not Jewish, so great was her belief that not only was she baptized, but all her household. She became the first Christian in Philippi and in all that land. Eventually I established a church in her house. Thus our Lord instructed me that I should carry the good news to the Gentiles, who were left out at the beginning."

He glanced expectantly at his listeners. "Now pray tell me how you came to know our Lord."

"My wife brought me to Christ," said Aquila.

"It was Barnabas," protested Prisca.

"He wasn't as comely. I had no desire to follow him to the ends of the earth." He gave Paul a grin of cameraderie. "I knew when I met Prisca that wherever she took it in her head—"

"Wherever the Lord led me—"

". . . To go, I'd be bound to follow."

"To keep me out of trouble."

"And our blessed Lord keeps us both."

Paul laughed. "Amen!"

That evening, Aquila summoned the brethren to hear Paul. Rather than recount more of his adventures, Paul spoke to them of the faith that had carried them from before the days of Moses to the new covenant with Christ.

"A legend tells of a time when Abraham was a youth," Paul began. "He lived in a cave. One day he came out and looked across the face of the desert. The sun rose in all its glory, and Abraham said, 'Surely the sun is god, the creator!' And so he knelt down and worshiped the sun. But when evening came, the sun sank in the west, and Abraham said, 'No! The author of creation cannot set!' The moon rose in the east, and the stars came out. Then Abraham said, 'The moon must be god and the stars his host!' So he knelt down and adored the moon. But when night passed, the moon sank and the sun rose again and Abraham said, 'Truly these heavenly bodies are no gods, for they follow a law. I will worship him who imposed the law upon them.' "

A sigh arose from Paul's listeners, as ones who had received drink after a thirsty day.

Paul spoke, and they listened, far into the night. At last Paul said with a hoarse chuckle, "My brothers and sisters, your ears will fall off if I do not give them a rest. I leave you with this: If faith can see every step of the way, it is not really faith. It is sometimes necessary for the Christian to take the way to which the voice of God is calling him, without knowing what the consequences will be. Like Abraham he has to go out not knowing where he is going."

The following morning Paul insisted on accompanying Aquila to the shop. Prisca was glad for the respite. It was unlike her to be ill, but the humid days, unexpected excitement attending Paul's visit, and lack of sleep combined to entice her to give in when Aquila suggested she remain home to rest before the women arrived for her daily teaching.

By early afternoon she possessed her normal good spirits again. Chloe, Daphne, several other women, and two young men appeared simultaneously at her door. The young men were nephew and son to Anonymius.

"I confess it is out of curiosity that the boys came," laughed Anonymius's wife. "But as you say, Prisca, how we got here is unimportant to our Lord."

Daphne agreed. "Everyone was talking this morning about Paul. Even my husband is sorely tempted to come and hear him. I think he's looking for an excuse to come anyway, to thank everyone for praying for our son Jason's good health." With a toss of her thick, black curls, she added, "But he is still afraid of what his family might think."

"Would he feel more comfortable in Aquila's group?"

"No, not yet."

An hour later, the group was absorbed in discussion of Jesus' behavior at the wedding at Cana.

"He provided wine because his mother wanted him to," decided Anonymius's wife.

"I think it was because he knew it would have embarrassed his host to run out," suggested Chloe.

"Wasn't his responsibility, though."

"Perhaps not, but I've an idea that convention didn't bother him that much."

"I think he did it to demonstrate his power," said one of the young men.

"But what has turning water into wine to do with the kingdom of God?" said Daphne.

"After all, he *was* a guest at the wedding feast," Prisca reminded them.

"But he had more important things on his mind."

"What more important? He loved people. He loved to see them happy. He wanted them to come to the Father out of love and joy, not misery. . . . Once he even asked me to go swimming," Prisca blurted.

An outbreak of disbelieving laughter met her words.

Embarrassed at her own confession, Prisca joined in the laughter. Catching a movement at the doorway to her left, she glanced over her shoulder.

There, with an expression of outrage on his face, was Paul. He seemed rooted just inside the door. His gaze swept every person in the room.

Prisca glanced around also, trying to see with his eyes, noting how his gaze dwelled on uncovered heads, cropped hair, and the few painted faces among the women. Few of those present, save Chloe and Daphne, had met Paul last night.

To those who had not, he said, "I am Paul the apostle. I heard you laughing, and no one answered my knock."

Prisca scrambled to her feet. With a superhuman effort she controlled her anger at his unbelievable breach of manners. "This is Paul of Tarsus."

"Paul the apostle of Christ," he repeated.

Prisca stared at him, trying to fathom the reason for his anger. He met her gaze with a stubborn set of face. His manner so intimidated them that, after introductions were complete, a wall of uncomfortable silence entombed the worshipers.

"You are welcome to join us," offered Chloe, sitting cross-legged on the floor again.

Prisca remained on her feet with Paul. His prominent eyes seemed flat, as if he were cutting himself off from what was going on about him. He looked wordlessly at the two young men.

The men looked at each other and smiled helplessly at Prisca and Chloe. *By the holy ground Jesus walked on, he is acting like Mark!* thought Prisca. She trembled and drew a deep breath, but before she could speak, Daphne was on her feet. Her face was pale. "Is it that you have just heard that some of us are from the temples, Paul?"

A sister who had only recently forsaken Acro-Corinthus rose to put her arm around Daphne. "I am Jewish, Paul of Tarsus. Begot by my father to a temple maid. Does it shock you that I should be here?"

Paul stared at them, aghast.

Prisca thought quickly. Above all, she knew, men and women who served the Lord must not let their differences separate them from his love. She spread her hands out as if trying to calm the storm, wishing that Aquila were with her. "Paul, is it that you think Anonymius's boys ought not to be taught by women? Surely our Lord Christ came to change that."

"With all of this," Paul's arm swept the room, "you also claim authority to put women over men!"

"Beside men," she said firmly.

The meeting came to a harrowing end. Chloe and Daphne did not want to leave Prisca alone with her unpredictable guest. She refused to listen. Reluctantly her friends followed the others out. Prisca closed the door and faced her guest.

"Please sit down, Paul." Without apology, Prisca related her own story, seeing herself as a vessel through whom their Lord was reclaiming many women. She told him about Thyatira, too, whose continued presence in Corinth aggravated Prisca's ability to concentrate wholly on the Lord's work.

Paul, for all his learning, was not a man to discount portents either. He commented, with a wry, cautious smile, that one could choose his friends, but not his relatives.

Until Aquila's return in late afternoon, she and Paul maintained a wary politeness.

Aquila came in wearing an easy grin and glanced from one to the other. He kissed Prisca. Then with all deliberation he kissed Paul. "So ought Christians to greet one another," he said mildly. "Let us sit in the garden."

"I have a jug of pomegranate juice cooling in the cistern, if anyone is interested," Prisca announced. When she carried it into the garden, she said, "Paul has raised the question of women's authority to teach."

Paul seemed to have completed the change back into the agreeable man who had presented himself at the shop that morning. "Jesus said authority was to be used in service to others, and power was to be used for leadership in ministering to needs. All of for which women are untrained."

"Untrained but not unable." Aquila leaned forward. "Women are well suited to minister to human needs, Paul. It took the coming of Christ to give them the authority to use their training. Many women in our church had no feelings of usefulness before coming into the Lord's service. Now, some of them find great happiness in serving the church."

"Doing what?"

"Baptizing females," said Prisca. "Teaching Scripture to children, visiting the sick, preparing the bodies of the dead, conducting physical examinations."

Paul sat back and seemed to think about this. "All right. I find nothing wrong with that. If it makes the women happy."

"It does some of them." Prisca smiled. "As you say, Jesus has use for us all, in different ways."

"And you believe Jesus wants you to preach."

Both Aquila and Prisca nodded.

"On what do you base your authority to speak for the Christ?" he demanded of Prisca.

"Our Lord himself, as with the other disciples. As Barnabas may have told you." Again it seemed to Prisca that Paul could not have traveled long in the company of Barnabas and not know that.

"It is customary for women to keep silent in church," Paul ventured.

"But Paul, their joy overflows!"

"I'll admit a neighboring room filled with laughing temple maidens can cause sober men to be undone," Aquila added with a laugh. "But we cannot expect them to worship in the manner of Jewish men."

"Then they should become used to it! Dissension divides the church. If their noise upsets men who are used to more decorum," Paul repeated doggedly, "let them keep silent."

"If you deny what Jesus meant women to be, you deny his authority. Without Jesus, who is left to speak for us? No, Paul. Let the men rather grow more joyful, like my Aquila," said Prisca.

" 'Silence confers grace upon a woman,' " retorted Paul.

"So said Sophocles," returned Prisca. "A Greek, not a Jew. Not Jesus."

Paul said in a gentler tone, "You must know that it is forbidden for a well-bred Jew even to speak to a woman on the street. 'One must not ask a service from a woman, or salute her,' " he quoted.

"Treat her, in other words, as if she did not exist!" Prisca said angrily. "Jesus approached the woman at the well in Samaria, a fallen woman, and not only did he salute her, he asked a service of her."

Paul's voice took on a metallic edge. "The Jewish Talmud lists among the plagues of the world 'the talkative and the inquisitive widow and the virgin who wastes her time in prayers.' In another place it likens the teaching of women to 'casting pearls before swine.' "

"That's enough, Paul," said Aquila. "Those are some of the very traditions Jesus came to turn upside down. If it were not so, why did he heal the crippled woman who touched his garment, and she not even Jewish? That was clearly against the old laws. Why do you make Prisca and Chloe's work harder?"

"Chloe began this church!" added Prisca.

Paul threw up his hands in frustration. "I do not know what to make of you two. We both know that Corinth is exceedingly immoral, even to the rest of the world."

Prisca and Aquila glanced at each other. "Yes," they agreed.

"It has been my practice to agree wherever possible with local customs. But in this city of such licentiousness, it is understandable that worshiping side by side with noisy women would upset the elders, therefore it should be stopped.

"Our church of Jesus Christ is like a delicate flower. We must protect it at all cost from destruction by stronger elements. Nothing, absolutely nothing, must be done that would bring upon it the faintest suspicion of immodesty."

"Such as preaching the gospel to harlots?"

"Of course that is not what I meant!" Paul said, a plaintive note creeping in his voice. "But must they look like harlots and sound like harlots?"

"And how did you look when you witnessed the stoning of Stephen in

Jerusalem? Would one have taken you for a beloved of the Lord? Did not our Lord lift you and reshape you, as he did me and Aquila and Chloe and Barnabas and all the others who serve him? And as I pray he will lift my mother and father? Who among us were saints?"

Paul fixed his eyes upon her. His breathing was heavy, as a lion in the midst of battle will pause to regroup his faculties. "I am unused to arguing with women. It demeans a man."

Prisca relented with a sympathetic laugh. "To argue is not demeaning, my brother. To deny that women have the ability to think and speak for themselves is demeaning."

As passions cooled the three sat up until past midnight discussing less-heated concerns, Paul relating the administrative affairs of their fledgling church, Prisca and Aquila learning with astonishment of the existence of churches in a dozen communities like theirs.

Learning what had befallen them in Rome, Paul said, "I shall carry the good news back to Rome before I am done." He threw Aquila a swift, challenging glance. "Perhaps you shall, too."

"Wherever our Lord sends us," Aquila replied stoutly.

Prisca breathed a sigh of relief as they bade Paul good-night in his chamber. Perhaps, with much prayer and meditation on all their parts, Jesus could mold them to a unified usefulness. If there was such a thing.

"What are you smiling about?" asked Aquila as they undressed for bed.

"Our blessed Lord. How much easier it would be if he would come back now and tell us all exactly what he wants."

Chapter 30

The following sabbath, Prisca rose before dawn, as she had done for years, using the still, new hours for reflection and prayer. Her rest had been disturbed, filled with visions of Thyatira. For weeks, reports had filtered to her that her mother, by constant fasting and supplication, had achieved almost constant portents of the future. Prisca could not rid her mind of the image of a chill morning, of a green snake striking warm flesh. . . .

An involuntary shiver rippled through her, and she got up to awaken her husband. Leaving Aquila to call their guest, she prepared breakfast. Paul had announced his intention yesterday to speak at the synagogue this morning.

Aquila drew her aside after breakfast. "Are you all right?" Gently, with the ball of his thumb, he brushed at the dark shadows under her eyes. "You were tossing much of the night."

"I am fine, my love."

His black eyes softened with love. He kissed her. "Tell Paul I am waiting on the street."

"I shall."

Aquila stepped into the morning air and drew a deep breath, savoring the flavor of the new sabbath. He glanced up and down the street. Suddenly he caught sight of a figure that seemed vaguely familiar. He took a few steps down the road, but it had vanished. A moment later Paul joined him.

"Is it far to the temple?"

"Farther coming back," replied Aquila.

Paul threw him a puzzled glance.

"Uphill."

Paul laughed. "Is something the matter?"

"No. I just thought I saw someone I knew. . . ."

The men moved down the hill at a swift pace, enjoying the vigor of the fresh fall morning. Aquila paused when they reached a low promontory overlooking Corinth. Acro-Corinthus rose opposite them. "You can see the temple from here. See the temple of Apollo? Now look to your right, a little farther—"

265

"Down the road of the fig trees? Yes, I see it. Aquila. . . ."

"Yes?"

"I could not sleep last night. I arose, intending to put my thoughts to paper and so free my mind for sleep. I found your writing box and did not think you would begrudge a little paper."

"Of course not!"

"I discovered your writings therein. Seeing that they pertained to the Christ, I took it upon myself to read them."

Aquila flashed him a look of annoyance. "Surely you should have asked first!" They started forward again.

Paul merely shrugged. "I am always about the Lord's business. This seemed the Lord's business. What you wrote was extremely lucid and reasoned. I confess I am a little amazed, my friend. I had not thought you that well read."

Aquila smiled at Paul's directness. " 'The Lord's business' led you to read Prisca's efforts."

"*Prisca!*"

"She was brought up with a classical education and spent four years with Barnabas and Mark, studying Jewish history. She has labored months over it. We both have."

Paul took a moment to absorb this. "Yes. I see a lot of the generous outlook of our friend Barnabas in what she writes. And Mark's insistence on the letter of the Law. There is in addition a thoughtfulness to what she writes, a maturity—a womanliness, perhaps."

"Perhaps her womanliness enables her to see Jesus with a different eye."

"This is all most interesting! For whom are the writings intended?"

"Our brethren in Rome and Alexandria. We feel keenly that they must not suffer a lack of leadership while they become strong themselves."

Paul nodded with short, decisive thrusts of the head. "Good. Her letter should go to all the Hebrews. It will encourage them."

Aquila stopped and studied his companion's face. He shook his head. "You are an extraordinary man, Paul. Prisca will be thankful for your praise." Suddenly he stopped short. *Limaeus.* His face paled.

"What is it?"

"Go ahead, Paul, I'll catch you later!" Turning about, Aquila dashed up the hill the way they had come.

Limaeus watched Aquila leave with the stranger. For weeks he had been shadowing Prisca, here and at the shop of her husband. His thoughts were in turmoil. The first full glimpse he had had of her was at the marketplace, chatting with some women at the fruit seller's stall. She'd looked him full in the face and yet not seen him. He had always loved watching people who did not know they were being watched, hoping they might reveal some secret part of themselves—something that would betray what made them who they were.

By the gods, she was beautiful! Like a fully ripened fruit. Her eyes. There was some difference, of course. Gone was that wistfulness. Gone that dreamy grace bending a supple young body of a priestess celebrating the dawn with Artemis. Gone were the ill-concealed flashes of fear and hurt. Gone the innocence before she understood that he was to have her. He, Limaeus. Did her husband know that Limaeus had first possessed his wife?

But as Limaeus had eyed her at the fruit seller's, he tried to summon images of that night and could not. The deep green eyes glowing with profound happiness were those of a total stranger. No part of her came to fill his mind with warm, exhilarating sweetness.

Wasn't that how it had been, he asked himself, standing here in a deserted street on a sabbath morning. Warm and sweet? He scratched his unshaven face. So many years ago. So many other women since then. Not one who had wanted him to stay, who had been grateful for a man who would bring in a bit of silver now and then, in exchange for a warm bed and warm meals. Bah! A pox on them all!

Churning up a righteous anger to bury the fear that lay always within him, Limaeus darted a final glance down the street. The two men had disappeared down the hill. Not another soul around. Swiftly he scuttled across, leaned an ear against the door, and suddenly, finding the door unlatched, let himself in.

He found himself in a spacious though modestly furnished room, made airy by a large opening on his left, leading to a roofed porch. The air was fragrant with the yeast of rising bread dough, the scent reaching his nostrils as he spied half a dozen long, shaped loaves, set on a palmetto leaf in a patch of sunlight. He heard a woman's voice humming, becoming louder. Instinctively he looked around for a place to hide.

Suddenly there was a gasp and a clatter of crockery.

"Limaeus!"

Prisca stood in a doorway opposite him. At her feet were shards of a bowl, fruits still rolling away.

Limaeus shot a frantic look back at the door through which he had come. "Pr-Prisca."

She stayed in the doorway, her hands gripping either side of the frame at hip level.

Limaeus tried a swagger that carried him into the center of the room. His knees wobbled.

Prisca advanced gingerly. "Are you ill?"

Her voice was controlled. There was no trace of fear in it. Instead, unbelievably, it was tinged with concern. Tears sprang to his eyes. Furiously he wiped them on his sleeve. "I di'n' mean to come in. I don't know what made me. I'll leave."

"Wait!" she said imperiously.

Limaeus ground to a frightened halt in his pursuit of escape.

In a gentler tone she said, "Come back. Tell me why you came."

Limaeus fixed his gaze on the garden. "I wanted to see what you was like."

"Why?"

Limaeus shrugged. Who knew how far that power of hers could reach. Oh, yes, his ears had not been idle while he'd watched. Tucking his hands under his arms, he remained stolidly backed up to the wall near the door. The length of the room yawned between them, like an unfathomable chasm.

He could not stand the way she was looking at him. What could she be thinking?

He still reminded her of a ferret. Used to the dark alleys of life. Afraid to reach for the sunshine of God's love. Afraid or unable?

"Limaeus, do you remember when you first told me to come and hear Jesus?"

He nodded.

"Then you know now that he rose from the dead."

"Know you believe it."

"I am a different person because of him. Not a priestess, but a disciple. Not alone any more. Never alone. He is with me always, filling me with happiness."

For the first time, Limaeus ventured to meet her eyes. "You got to be sore as a whip at me."

Slowly Prisca shook her head. "I used to fear—"

"You was afraid of me?" he asked quickly.

"No. Of myself. I could not see how God could love someone whose body was used so falsely. Someone whose anger was as great and deep and destructive as mine."

"*You?*"

"Yes. Why do you sound so surprised?"

"You." A sneer curled under the ratty moustache. "You always looked like you owned the world. Like you could've done anything. That's why I wanted to—I never believed that—well, you was the only thing I was ever close to that I said to myself, *Look here, Limaeus, you and her.* That feeling di'n' ever leave me, Prisca."

The little man's eyes were hollows of emptiness. She sensed a lifetime of defeat in his words. All the scheming, the greed, the lust had left him with nothing. She found herself pitying him.

"Christ can change your life, too, Limaeus."

"Mine?" The fear surfaced once more.

"You would not ever be lonely or friendless again."

His body swayed slightly as if torn between desire to believe her words and the cruel realities of his life. A smile twisted a cynical path across his face. That'd be the end of the silver market. No amulets for the Christians!

Seeing the look, Prisca quickly said, "Do not decide now. Come back at eventide on the last night of the week. Meet some of the Christian men. Men just like yourself."

Limaeus sucked in his breath. "You give a man a turn, Prisca."

Prisca remained exactly where she was. "You will never be afraid again."

"I dunno. There's lots I got to do."

"Do this, Limaeus. For your own sake. And for me."

"For you?"

"Yes. Will you come?"

He mumbled something unintelligible. His feet seemed to be made of lead. Finally he broke free and ducked out as quickly as he could.

Sunlight seemed to swell inside the quiet room. Prisca closed her eyes, and as the minutes passed she bathed in the suffusion of God's love.

"Prisca!" Aquila rushed through the door, his chest heaving. "Limaeus was hiding around here this morning! Was he here?"

"Yes. And I would swear the Lord sent him. Oh, Aquila, wouldn't it be wonderful if he found peace with our Lord? He is such a pathetic little man. What is the matter?"

His face bore a comical mixture of relief and indignation. "I missed the synagogue this morning, do you know that? I wanted to hear Paul preach. And you seem to have managed quite nicely without me."

Prisca erupted with laughter. She went to him and slid her arms around his middle. "Do you realize, my husband, how long it has been since we were alone?" Slowly her hand crept up and caressed his chest, his neck, his ear. In a low, soft voice, she said, "I think this morning was all a glorious conspiracy so we could spend an hour making love."

Aquila grinned, his face dropping years as his body responded to her loving touch. "Praise the Lord for unexpected blessings." Slowly his lips bent to hers, and his arms tightened around her body.

Murmuring a brief prayer for Aquila and the unknown crisis that had caused him to turn back, Paul continued on. Within minutes he reached the synagogue. Placing concern for his new friend in the back of his mind, he emptied his thoughts and prayed to receive the words he was to speak. Thus prepared and at peace, he entered the Men's Court.

Giving his name to the clerk, he awaited his turn. As he was motioned to the floor of the Inner Court a change seemed to come over him. The rather knobbly body straightened. The large head seemed leonine rather than ill proportioned. In his eyes, flat and hooded at times, a fire seemed to kindle as if the message he brought so stoked his imagination that it burned in his soul.

Sosthenes, Crispus, and Paris were standing near the back of the Inner Court as Paul entered. For weeks passing into months the three had taken a similar post every sabbath while the faithful entered the temple.

Sosthenes was out of patience with Paris; he had promised to deliver a rebel and had given them nothing. The man Aquila seldom came to the temple and had yet to speak. One could not arrest a man without some provocation, even if he had caused rioting and exile in Rome and his wife was the daughter of a pagan. Sosthenes scowled meaningfully at Paris. "Another wasted morning, Paris."

"He will be here this morning, I heard him say it."

"Who is the man who just began to speak?" demanded Sosthenes.

"That is Paul of Tarsus, the one who wrote to us," said Crispus. "A very interesting man. He—"

"Do you see Aquila anywhere?" Sosthenes asked.

"Not yet," said Paris. "But when he speaks, you may be sure that what he utters will be seditious. He has been preaching Jesus as the Christ. I have heard him myself, calling Jesus not only our Messiah, but the Son of God."

Crispus cast an ironic glance at Paris. "You mean you attend the meetings of the Christians."

Paris glared at him. "One cannot spy without spying."

Sosthenes folded his arms and gave his attention to Paul. Until Aquila showed his face, he might as well hear what the newcomer had to say.

"All things are lawful, but not all things are helpful," he heard Paul tell the congregation. "The God who made the world and all things in it does not live in temples made by man. . . ." Sosthenes leaned forward. Was he hearing correctly? He glanced at those around him. The man's voice was not loud, but it seemed to have spun a web around those closest to him. He edged closer.

"Whatever you do, do all to the glory of God. Give no offense to Jews or to Greeks or to the church of God, just as I try to please all men in everything I do, not seeking my own advantage, but that of many, that they may be saved. Be imitators of me, as I am of Christ."

With a bellow of rage, Sosthenes leaped forward. "Of Christ? Who are you? You do not speak for the Jews. Seize him!"

The guards of the temple, who had been alerted to seize Aquila, looked at Sosthenes in confusion, then rushed to obey.

Many of the hearers were Christians. The moment Paul began to preach, they knew that here was the man they had been alerted to by Christians in other cities. Startled by the swift descent of guards, the Christians tried too late to rescue Paul. "Get to Chloe's house!" someone shouted. "I will find Aquila!"

Meanwhile, Sosthenes raced at the heels of the guards, hustling Paul from the Men's Court. "Hurry!" he cried to Paris and Crispus. A great uproar filled the temple behind them.

"Paul! Paul! That man was Paul, the apostle of the Christ!"

"Where?"

"They took him!"

Listening to the uproar, Sosthenes cried gleefully, "By all that is holy, Paris, I think we snared a bigger fish than we went after!"

Paul paced back and forth in the small, windowless room where the guards had imprisoned him. Someone was certain to tell Aquila what had happened. Unless . . . unwillingly Paul faced the possibility that Aquila's pretext of having to return home was a ruse so that he would be alone when captured. At once he dismissed it, counting himself a better reader of men than that. And he had already decided to approach Aquila about traveling to Ephesus with him in a few months. Prisca would not like it, of course, but she would understand. The Lord's work must come before family life.

He heard voices outside the door, and then a tall, muscular man with red hair entered.

"I am Crispus," said the man.

271

"Welcome," Paul responded gravely, not seeing the humor of a prisoner welcoming his captor to his cell.

Three days later, Aquila was still unable to locate Paul. At first Sosthenes had denied any knowledge of him, claiming Corinthian pagans had spirited him off. The following day Aquila returned with several Jews who had witnessed Paul's detention. Sosthenes stared at them coldly, then responded that Paul was guilty of seditious statements and would be tried accordingly.

Shortly after Aquila and his party left Sosthenes' office for the last time, Crispus appeared at the door. "You will not be able to hold the man much longer, Sosthenes," he advised.

"I shall! You read the letter from Alexandria." He thrust out his jaw. "Same sort of disruption."

"And the Roman authorities refused to act."

"I know Gallio. I have supped with him. He'll try him next court day. Two days. Did you get those reports written that I asked for?"

"I will attend it right away, Sosthenes." Crispus withdrew. Well, at least he knew Sosthenes' plans. For some reason, Crispus could not sit back and let this go on. He would just have to get in touch with Aquila himself. Then he would go back, he promised himself, and hear more about the one they claimed was the Messiah, from the fascinating man who was their prisoner.

"Gallio, the proconsul! We know him!" cried Prisca when Aquila reported what Crispus had relayed to him at the shop. "He is the brother of Seneca, the poet. We have met both of them at my father's house in Rome. Oh, I can see the Lord's hand in this!"

Aquila thumbed his chin. "Gallio. Not the ill-tempered one who slung his goblet at the servant because the wine was too warm?"

"The same. I almost feel sorry for Sosthenes!"

"I do not see quite the fair wind you do," said Aquila. "But at least I shall be able to see Paul."

"I shall make up a packet of food. Poor man!"

That afternoon Aquila followed Crispus down a long, musty corridor in a rat maze within the bowels of the synagogue. "Are you sure this is where they are holding him?" he asked Crispus.

"Sh-h! Keep your voice down." Crispus stopped. A key turned. "In here."

Aquila slipped inside. By the light of a single candle he saw Paul. He compressed his lips to keep from crying out in outrage. Paul's face was bruised and haggard. His hair was stringy, as if he had attempted to comb it with his fingers. Wordlessly the two men embraced and Crispus withdrew.

Aquila pushed the packet of roasted meat,. a loaf of bread, and two apples into his hands. Paul blessed it and tore into it hungrily while Aquila spoke. "Crispus just told us where they were keeping you. Also that Sosthenes intends to try you before Gallio on a charge of civil disobedience."

Paul looked up. "In all things I do the Lord's will. Any trials suffered on earth are but a mosquito bite compared to the glories of our heavenly city."

"Do not be so eager to suffer, Paul. We feel confident Sosthenes lacks the power to hold you. Prisca is acquainted with Gallio, and her father is a powerful man in Rome. Tools our Lord can use to free you."

Paul smiled briefly, his cheeks bulging with food. He nodded briskly. "So be it. I have had several fruitful conversations with my jailer. I hope I am here long enough to win his conversion."

In spite of himself, Aquila erupted with laughter.

That night the Lord visited Paul in the room where he was being held, and said, "Do not be afraid, but speak and do not be silent; for I am with you, and no man shall attack you to harm you; for I have many people in this city."

Paul slept, contented.

The day before Paul's trial dawned gray and overcast. A horseman clattered boldly up the wide limestone steps leading to the temples on Acro-Corinthus, south of the city. A gardener came rushing forward as he crested the hill.

"Please, sir, horses are to be left below."

"The horse is to be left here," countered Marcus Sistus. "If he is not ready for me when I leave, I shall have you beaten."

"Yes, lord. I am sorry, lord. I will see to him. Fine animal, your worship." The gardener tugged his forelock and grasped the stallion's reins at arm's length, clearly frightened of the beast.

Seeing this, a smile touched the tribune's face. He took the reins and looped them over the arms of a statue. "Just see that he is not spooked."

"Thank you, your worship," the relieved gardener said. He started to walk away.

"Wait. I want to see a priestess of Artemis. Her name is Thyatira. Find her."

"But—"

Marcus glowered at him, and he scurried away.

Minutes later Marcus was ushered into a modest cell. Soft gray light entered through two long slits in one wall, shrouding the vacant cell in gloom. A pallet was draped incongruously with an expensive coverlet embroidered in gold and blue silken threads in an intricate pattern of peacocks. It looked vaguely familiar to him. On a table beside the bed rested two rolled scrolls, an oil lamp, a small brazier with a dish of incense ready to be lighted, and a covered basket. He heard a slight rustling noise, as if something scraped against straw. The sound made prickles dance up the hairs on his nape.

While he waited, Marcus thought of the bustling shop he had just left. He had sent a prayer to all gods known and unknown at the sight of his dear Prisca, hale and happy beside her husband. Both had welcomed him effusively. He had learned that their friend and fellow disciple of Christ was to be tried before Gallio the next day on a civil charge. He offered to intercede with Gallio on their behalf.

"Is this why you came, Marcus?" Prisca asked him pointedly. "Does mighty Rome care for the fate of a poor disciple?"

He smiled, noting for the first time that she looked paler than he had first supposed. "No, my daughter."

"Then—"

"Very well. I learned Thyatira was also in Corinth. I intend to hasten her return to Tyre."

Prisca was thoughtful. "Good," she said at last.

And that single word, loaded with relief, had ended his indecision. He had been right. Something was afoot. Plenty of time to see Gallio. He would seek out Thyatira without delay.

"I will see you at the trial," he had promised them.

"Marcus," said a throaty voice behind him. He turned and was shocked. Thyatira was as gaunt as any holy man sequestered in a cave. "Thyatira!"

"How did you find me?" Her words were slow, her voice remote.

"I heard you were in Corinth." He could not get over the change in her. Her vitality seemed to be missing. He noticed she was favoring her left arm, cradling it in her right. "Are you ill?"

She shook her head with an odd, jerking motion. "Why are you—in Corinth?"

He thought quickly. "To see my—our—daughter. A friend of theirs is being tried in civil court at noon tomorrow."

She nodded listlessly and sat on the pallet. As she did not offer him a chair—there was none—he settled on his haunches, facing her, pitying her in spite of himself.

"And you are going?"

"Yes. I would not miss it," he added with relish. "By thunder this new religion Prisca's got hold of intrigues me. It turns lives upside down! And she is something, isn't she?"

Thyatira turned her face away from him. "There was a time when Artemis fascinated you."

"No. Not Artemis. You. That was a long time ago." He got to his feet. "You ought to go home, Thyatira," he said in a gentle tone. "Go back to Tyre. Do you need money?"

"Shall you see Prisca?" she asked suddenly.

"Certainly. Not before the trial. She and Aquila are probably enmeshed in their friend's behalf."

"And you will rise to defend her," mocked Thyatira.

"Prisca is not on trial."

"Isn't she?" Thyatira murmured, so low that he was not certain he heard her.

"Thyatira?"

"I said . . . never mind. You think I should leave Corinth. Leave my daughter."

"Yes. As soon as you are well enough to travel." He got to his feet.

Her lusterless eyes traveled up to his face. "I am well enough. Very well, Marcus. Is that all you desire?"

"My desires are my own. Good-bye, Thyatira."

After Marcus left, Thyatira sat unmoving for a long time. Finally she roused herself to call a sister. "I wish you to take a message to my daughter in the city. Deliver it to the shop I tell you, but not until the morrow. Is that clear? Tell her that her mother begs her to see her at home. At high noon. Tell her . . . that I am leaving Corinth forever."

The day of the trial began even colder than the day before. At noon the sun still had not appeared. Aquila wrapped his cloak snugly about him as he mounted the steps of the tribunal. He was irrationally irritated at Prisca. That mother of hers. If he thought it possible, he would have counted it deliberate on her part to insist on meeting Prisca just when he and Paul needed her.

"Aquila!"

He turned. The tribune was leaping steps three at a time. "Is Prisca already inside?"

Aquila scowled. "That woman—her mother—sent a message to the shop this morning. She insisted Prisca meet her at our house at noon. Said she was leaving for good. Prisca said she had no choice but to go. I hope the trial is delayed until she gets here. I sent her home by chair. Bearers will bring her here as soon as Thyatira gets her business off her chest."

Marcus Sistus blanched and swore an oath. "Where is your house?"

Quickly Aquila spewed directions. "But what is it? What is wrong, tribune?"

"I'll handle it!" he flung over his shoulder. "I'll have Prisca here safely within the hour."

Thyatira was already inside when Prisca arrived home, breathless. She stared at her mother in shock. "Thyatira! You are not well."

"Can we go into the garden?" Thyatira asked, with a last, satisfied glance around the gathering room.

Prisca hesitated. Her mother really did look ill. Feeling guilty at her own impatience, she drew her mother into the garden. "Is it urgent? This is a most inopportune time. Our brother Paul is being tried before Gallio at this moment. I must go as quickly as possible. Why do you not lie and rest here until I return? Have something to eat. Then we can talk all you wish."

"Paul!" Thyatira spat. Her voice was surprisingly strong. "Prisca, do you not see what that man is doing? He is determined to undermine you. Before he is through, he will drive the goddess out of men's hearts. Leave him where he is! And thank sweet Artemis for putting him there."

"What is it you want of me, mother?"

"Come back to Tyre! Where you belong."

Prisca gaped at her. "I told you—how could you think I would ever come back? You did everything you could to drive me away!"

"Everything I did I did for you!"

"Mother!"

"Because you are to be the next high priestess, you fool!"

"No!" she screamed.

"And I say yes! My visions bear me out. Bedding you with that—that creature was the only way I knew to make you stay, to bind you to the goddess forever."

Prisca's voice trembled with anger. "You failed, mother!" As suddenly as it came, the anger vanished, and she was filled with sorrow for her mother. "Give up Artemis. Stay here with me. Let me teach you about the Christ. He will fill you with such love—"

"I will never forsake my goddess!" Thyatira said passionately. "I would let Poseidon carry me to the underworld before I would forsake Artemis."

Tears streaming down her face, Prisca wrapped her arms around Thyatira and placed fingers over her mouth. "No, mother. No more. There is a better way. Jesus has shown us a better way."

Thyatira pulled Prisca's fingers away from her lips. "I will never, never leave my goddess." Her eyes glittered fearlessly. "Beware, Prisca. Women will never regain their power if they lose faith in the goddess. This is what my visions tell me." She pulled away.

"Then I must leave you."

"Very well. Before you go—"

"What is it, mother?" Prisca waited.

"Would you bring me some writing materials? There are certain matters I must take care of before I leave."

The request struck Prisca as odd, but she returned to the gathering room to fetch her writing box. As she stepped inside the door, a huge hand clamped gently over her mouth, and she found herself staring into her father's grim face.

He placed a finger to his lips. "Aquila needs you now. I will see to Thyatira's needs."

"My writing box," she whispered.

He nodded. "Go."

He waited until he saw the bearers help her into the chair and depart at a run. Then he picked up the writing box. As he lifted it he felt a weight shift within the box. Staring at the box, his mouth hardened. He carried it to the garden.

Without looking up Thyatira said, "Thank you, dear. Open it please."

"You open it, Thyatira. It is not just a ceremonial snake this time, is it?"

Thyatira looked up, and a scream froze in her throat.

Chapter 31

P risca slipped onto the bench beside Aquila. She threw him a tremulous smile, encompassing Chloe on his other side, Anonymius and his wife, Daphne and her husband, and the rest of the brethren.

Aquila found her hand and squeezed it. "Where is Marcus?"

"With Thyatira." She would have said more, but at that moment Paul was led onto the floor of the tribunal. He appeared to be perfectly at ease, ignoring the unkempt appearance he must have known he presented to the court. His ease brought a corresponding relaxing of tension to the bodies of his friends. Prisca let out a sigh and turned her glance elsewhere.

The Corinthian court was smaller than its Roman counterpart, but similar in detail. She could easily pick out the scribes' table, where the hearing was recorded in laborious detail. She picked out the austere form of Gallio, proconsul of Achaia, flanked by four other men in white robes, seated before a table on a knee-high dais. Occupying a bench near the dais, Sosthenes, Crispus, and other temple elders waited rigidly, as if declaring awareness of their own righteousness.

Paul was led before the dais.

"Who is this man?" intoned a clerk.

An end man on the dais leaned forward. "You are to answer."

"I am Paul of Tarsus, Roman citizen."

The heads on the dais leaned together.

The clerk spoke again. "With what is this man charged?"

Sosthenes, Crispus, and two other men rose and advanced into the white marbled arena. Sosthenes spoke. "This man is persuading men to worship God contrary to the law."

Gallio sighed. "If it were a matter of wrongdoing or vicious crime, I should have reason to bear with you, O Jews; but since it is a matter of questions about words and names and your own law, see to it yourselves; I refuse to be a judge of these things." Gallio started to rise.

"Wait!" commanded Sosthenes. "You may regret it if you do not hear me out!"

Gallio grimaced and resumed his seat. "Well? The court will hear you."

"This man is a member of the revolutionary Christians, no friend of honest Jews! In Rome itself, my lord Gallio, these same men caused such civil turmoil that all honest Jews were banished with them! In fact—," Sosthenes turned and drew himself up. He pointed at Aquila. "The leader of those revolutionaries sits right here in your courtroom!"

Gallio frowned in their direction. "Ah. Aquila. And Prisca." He turned back to Sosthenes. "They are not accused in this court."

Suddenly Aquila climbed to his feet. He appeared slightly unsure of himself, as if undecided what made him put himself forward.

"Yes, Aquila, what is it?"

"My lord Gallio, Sosthenes calls us revolutionaries because in the life of the Jew there are only the Pharisees and the orthodox who keep the Law. The rest of the Jews are thought of contemptuously as the People of the Land, who never fully kept the details of ceremonial law. I count myself among these. They—we—are outside the pale, lumped with the dregs of human life. It is forbidden for orthodox Jews to fellowship with us, even to journey with us. As far as possible they are taught to avoid trade or business dealings with us."

Paul nodded vigorous approval.

Aquila faltered. "Well, I—I just wanted you to understand that."

In a swift motion Prisca rose. "May I speak, too, lord Gallio?"

Gallio hesitated. "I see no reason—"

"Let her speak," someone murmured.

"Come forward."

The radiant maturity of her beauty stirred the watchers. Prisca smiled at Gallio. "I bring you greetings from my father, my lord," she said in a low voice.

Gallio nodded. "Does what you are about to say have bearing upon this, Prisca?"

"Yes, my lord." She threw Paul an encouraging smile. "I am not Jewish. But I am married to a Jew, Aquila of Pontus. I have discovered that the God of the Jews has always been set apart by them as a holy being, entirely separated from the human race. This is the upsetting factor, the reason Paul was brought here and the reason Rabbi bar-Elymas persecuted Aquila in Rome."

Paul watched her with an intense frown of concentration.

"Aquila worshiped the God of his fathers until manhood, but without ever identifying with him. Jesus, the Son of the Father of us all, came to share our human experience. To be one with us. To bring us hope of life eternal."

279

"Your lordship!" said Sosthenes sharply. "It is common sense that when earth once drinks the blood of a man, there is death once and for all, and there is no resurrection."

Prisca turned to Sosthenes. "You Jews have your separated God. The Greeks believe it is blasphemous to involve God at all in the affairs of this world. And the gods and goddesses of Acro-Corinthus are mere playthings of human imagination." She turned back to Gallio and opened her arms in a plea for understanding. "I can only say what I know: Into this fearful world Christ brought a godliness that deliberately underwent all human experience in order to be a human emissary to God and an emissary of the house of God to men and women."

Her graceful speech brought a murmur of approval from the galleries.

Gallio stirred. "I know you are learned, my dear Prisca. My brother Lucius and our friend Josephus assure me of it. But it appears you are using my court as a forum for religious instruction rather than a vehicle of law."

Her face broke into a sunny smile. "Behold, I am done, my lord. Thank you."

Paul gazed at her in astonishment, aware for the first time of her power as a leader in her own right. He could hardly credit the revealing way Jesus had touched her life.

Gallio scowled at Paul. "Have *you* anything to add?"

Paul said, "I can attest that the real proof of becoming Christian is that it changes the lives of men and women." He looked at the retreating form of Prisca. "And goes on changing us." He glanced again at Gallio, then at his adversaries and those crowding the tribunal galleries. "Yes, my lord, since you graciously provide the forum, I do desire to speak. I would urge you all to be perfect in love, even as Christ is perfect.

"If I speak in the tongues of men and of angels, but have not love, I am a noisy gong or a clanging cymbal. And if I have prophetic powers, and understand all mysteries and all knowledge, and if I have all faith, so as to remove mountains, but have not love, I am nothing. If I give away all I have, and if I deliver my body to be burned, but have not love, I gain nothing. . . .

"Love bears all things, believes all things, hopes all things, endures all things. Love never ends; as for prophecies, they will pass away; as for tongues, they will cease; as for knowledge, it will pass away. For our knowledge is imperfect and our prophecy is imperfect; but when the perfect comes, the imperfect will pass away. . . . Now I know in part. Then

I shall understand fully, even as I have been fully understood. So faith, hope, love abide, these three; but the greatest of these is love."

Spring in Corinth brought a rash of joyous celebrations of renewal and rededication. Every temple was festooned with ferns and bright flowers and garlands of ivy. Prisca was not sorry to see it, though Paul rankled at the legion of gods and goddesses who dwelled in Corinth. It seemed to him a cross peculiarly fashioned for himself alone.

His trial had been speedily disposed of. Gallio was as ill inclined to waste time arbitrating a Jewish dispute as had been the legate in Rome. And for bothering him at all, he had Sosthenes tossed bodily to the mob of men whom Aquila, during Paul's days of confinement, had convinced of the injustice. It was weeks before Sosthenes could walk unaided.

Having been set free, Paul shook off the trappings of the synagogue in disgust. Crispus defected with him and invited Paul to abide with him for as long as he abided in Corinth. Paul baptized him and his entire household and then declared that he would thereafter concentrate entirely upon bringing the good news to gentiles instead of the chosen race. Putting deeds to words, he reaped the whirlwind at every chance.

Winter for Prisca had meant quietly serving her church, shoring up the first shaky steps of faith of their increasing flock, earnestly praying to drop the feathers of ego with which she had once adorned her pride at being called to serve the One Lord. Winter had been a time, too, that she grieved for Thyatira. The day Prisca left her to go to Paul's trial had been the day of Thyatira's death. Apparently she had changed her mind about leaving Corinth and returned to Acro-Corinthus. Here she had somehow received a fatal bite, whether from a ceremonial snake or a poisonous viper that bit her while she was resting was never known. The snake was never found.

Tribune Marcus Sistus had returned to their house late that night. To the three of them he explained what must have happened. Paul and Aquila tried to comfort father and daughter. Marcus, with a wry lift of his head, refused to listen.

"Do you read Marcus Aurelius, Paul? 'When a man dies and his spark goes back to be lost in God, all that is left is dust, ashes, bone and stench.' And a good thing."

The tribune's words chilled Prisca's heart. They remained with her all night. Marcus was impatient to be back in Rome and insisted on leaving at dawn. She went outside with him, alone. "I shall never cease praying for you, my father." Tears welled in her eyes. "I love you. I do not want to lose you as I lost Thyatira."

Marcus felt a lump rise in his throat. "You will not lose me. We will be good friends in the years to come, you and Aquila and I."

"Friends in Christ, too?"

Marcus stared in the distance. "Perhaps. . . . I confess I am intrigued. I will give it thought." He held out his arms. They embraced, and he was gone.

On a gusty May afternoon, Paul, Aquila, and Prisca strolled along the shore near the harbor. The men lagged behind. Prisca disliked walking slowly and moved ahead to be by herself. She had a new and exciting secret to think about. In the distance the fishing boats were coming in from the day's work.

"How precious is freedom," Paul observed when Prisca was out of earshot. "It fills my soul to see men laboring happily for what is good." He turned to Aquila with a smile. "Your Prisca is a blessing to us."

"Yes, she is."

"Capable of running the shop, too?"

Aquila grinned, thinking of Rome. "Aye. She had to learn in a hurry, when I was ill with fever."

Paul nodded. "I have since listened to her and to Chloe. They are both women of great good sense and devotion."

Aquila glanced at him in amazement. "I never thought I would hear you say that. When you first came—"

"One must expect surprises, in the service of our Lord. I continue to grow in understanding," he added simply.

"Paul, why haven't you ever married?"

Paul grinned. "Truth to tell, my stomach does sometimes repay me for so many ill-cooked meals."

"Well then, what a blessing it would be to have well-cooked meals, not to mention a woman who loved you."

"And subject her to the life I must lead?"

"If she loved you, would she not count it the best of life's blessings to share it?"

"God and mammon—"

"What?"

"It would divert time from my purpose," Paul said hastily. "Time is so short! And I confess I do not want the responsibility of a wife."

Aquila snorted. "Responsibility. Burdens shared are burdens halved."

"Or burdens doubled." A subtle change came over his face. "Aquila—"

"Mm?"

"I want you to come with me to Ephesus. I've heard reports of a man preaching there—a good man, but misguided—who needs the strength of a man like you to set him straight."

"Well, it would mean closing the shop. The Lord has plenty for us to do right here."

"I thought you said Prisca could handle it."

Aquila stopped walking. "You mean without Prisca?"

"It is an arduous journey. Women should not be subject to. . . ." Paul's voice dwindled to a stop.

Aquila smiled a brief, wintry smile. "You have my permission to tell Prisca your wishes."

"Go to Ephesus without me?" she said, when they had caught up to her. "Aquila, how could you think such a thing!" Prisca's eyes flashed green fire.

"And Paul—well, for goodness' sake!" she sputtered. "Shall only men's versions of Christ and his kingdom be carried to the world? Shall not women hear his welcome words and be freed from laws made by mere mortals?"

"You do not understand, my sister," said Paul. "Time is so short! We must move with all haste to spread his message before his return. It has not been done. How shall we dare answer Jesus, if he comes and we have failed?"

"If time is so short, how can you turn away half of the laborers from the harvest?" she retorted. "Jesus changed my life when he made me understand that the glory of women was in doing the will of God, just as it is for men."

"This church has both Jew and Greek, slave and free, male and female," Paul pointed out. "All are equal in the sight of Jesus."

"But not yet in the sight of Paul!"

Unexpectedly Paul broke into laughter. He sat down on the edge of the dock and wiped his eyes. "Ah, Prisca! I have no wish to quench anyone's gifts. A man has received from God whatever gifts he may possess, not for his own sake, but for the sake of the church, not for his own glory, but for the greater glory of God."

"And for women, too, Paul?"

"Yes, I meant women, too. When a man—"

"And a woman!"

"And a woman, can say, 'To God be the glory,' only then will they use their gifts aright."

He turned and looked at them, a bemused expression on his face.

Prisca, her arm linked through Aquila's, smiled back.

"My dearest friends, you who have saved my life more than once, our Lord needs us in Ephesus. Will you both come with me? There we will build another strong church!"

A radiant smile spread over Prisca's face. She hugged Aquila with surprising strength, and he gazed at her with a question in his black eyes. "There will be a new Christian with us in Ephesus," she said softly.

Author's Notes

Historically it has been the opinion of many biblical scholars that Paul wrote the book of Hebrews, but its authorship has been a matter of conjecture for centuries. In *The Daily Bible Study Series: The Letter to the Hebrews,* the renowned William Barclay writes: "The title in the earliest days was simply, *To the Hebrews.* No author's name was ever given."

The author of *Halley's Bible Handbook* mentions Paul as the traditionally held author of the epistle, while also citing several other possible authors suggested by various scholars. William Barclay says, "The style is quite different from that of Paul." Tertullian thought Barnabas wrote it: Barnabas was a native of Cyprus; the people of Cyprus were famous for the excellence of the Greek they spoke, and Hebrews is written in the best Greek in the New Testament. Martin Luther was sure Apollos was the author: Apollos, according to the New Testament reference to him, was a Jew, born in Alexandria, an eloquent man.

Barclay suggests another possibility when he states that the most romantic of all conjectures is that Prisca and Aquila wrote it between them. Prisca and Aquila were teachers (Acts 18:26). Their house in Rome was a church in itself (Romans 16:3–5). He believes that possibly the letter begins with no greeting and the writer's name has vanished because the main author was a woman, and women were not allowed to teach. This view is also advanced in Ruth Hoppin's book, *Priscilla, Author of the Epistle to the Hebrews; and Other Essays.*

Part of the continuing fascination of the Bible for Christians who study it occurs because of the gaps in our knowledge. We seek continually to read between the lines, to imagine what times were really like in Jesus' day. No one knows unequivocally who wrote Hebrews. Each scholar can only advance his or her research and offer informed conjecture. As a fiction writer, I have the additional blessing of being able to select facts and gaps and weave them into a story that, it is to be hoped, the reader will read and think, "Yes, it might have happened that way. . . ."

There is no biblical evidence that Jesus fed thousands of people on a hillside outside Tyre, as I wrote in chapter three. According to Mark 7:31, "Then he returned from the region of Tyre, and went through Sidon to the Sea of Galilee, through the region of the Decapolis." Somewhere in the desert cities of the Decapolis, before returning to the western shore of Galilee, they fed four thousand men, plus women and children (Matthew 15:29–38, Mark 8:1–9). Earlier in his ministry, all four gospels report the feeding of the five thousand. However, this swing through Tyre and Sidon was part of his last Galilean ministry, coming during the final months of his life, when incredible numbers of people followed him wherever he went. It was probably not uncommon that wherever Jesus went, he fed his hearers not only spiritual bread, but nourishment for their bodies, too.

Flavius Josephus, the Jewish scholar who became chronicler of the Roman emperors, was not born until 37 A.D. Therefore he would have been only an adolescent at the time Prisca and Aquila lived in Rome, rather than a recognized historian as depicted in chapter seventeen.